PRAISE FOR *RIDGERUNNER*

NATIONAL BESTSELLER
WINNER, WRITERS' TRUST FICTION PRIZE
FINALIST, SCOTIABANK GILLER PRIZE
A *GLOBE AND MAIL* TOP 100 BOOK OF THE YEAR
A CBC BEST BOOK OF THE YEAR
AN APPLE BEST BOOK OF THE YEAR
A KOBO BEST BOOK OF THE YEAR

"The kind of book that forges the possible from the impossible, despite age and borders. It's a hearty, brave novel that challenges us to live life on our own terms."—*Chicago Review of Books*

"Part literary Western, part historical mystery, it's a vivid story that grabs you by the eyeballs on page one."—*Globe and Mail*

"*Ridgerunner* is truly magnificent. It hearkens back to when novels were generous and ambitious, big-shouldered and big-hearted. Gil Adamson writes worlds utterly unto their own." —Robert Olmstead, award-winning author of *Coal Black Horse* and *Savage Country*

"Ferocious, entirely authentic, funny, and tragic, *Ridgerunner* is a wild adventure spun in exalted prose: the book I've been wanting to read for years."—Marina Endicott, award-winning author of *Good to a Fault* and *The Difference*

"A beautiful and moving novel about the durability of family ties, *Ridgerunner* is a brilliant literary achievement, and in Jack Boulton, Adamson has created one of the most vividly rendered children you will ever encounter in fiction. I loved every page of it." —Michael Redhill, Scotiabank Giller Prize–winning author of *Bellevue Square*

RIDGERUNNER

ALSO BY THE AUTHOR

FICTION

The Outlander

Help Me, Jacques Cousteau

POETRY

Ashland

Primitive

RIDGERUNNER

Gil Adamson

ANANSI

First published in Canada in 2020 and the USA in 2021 in hardcover
by House of Anansi Press Inc.
www.houseofanansi.com

This edition published in Canada in 2021 and the USA in 2022
by House of Anansi Press Inc.

25 24 23 22 21   1 2 3 4 5

Library and Archives Canada Cataloguing in Publication

Title: Ridgerunner / Gil Adamson.
Names: Adamson, Gil, author.
Description: Previously published: Toronto: Anansi, 2020.
Identifiers: Canadiana 20210218487 | ISBN 9781487009038 (softcover)
Classification: LCC PS8551.D3256 R53 2021 | DDC C813/.54—dc23

Book design: Alysia Shewchuk

*House of Anansi Press respectfully acknowledges that the land on which we operate is the
Traditional Territory of many Nations, including the Anishinabeg, the Wendat, and the
Haudenosaunee. It is also the Treaty Lands of the Mississaugas of the Credit.*

 Canada Council   Conseil des Arts
for the Arts   du Canada

 ONTARIO ARTS COUNCIL
CONSEIL DES ARTS DE L'ONTARIO
an Ontario government agency
un organisme du gouvernement de l'Ontario

With the participation of the Government of Canada
Avec la participation du gouvernement du Canada |  Canadä

*We acknowledge for their financial support of our publishing program the Canada
Council for the Arts, the Ontario Arts Council, and the Government of Canada.*

Printed and bound in Canada

I lost my way. Water in water fell

— JAMES WRIGHT, "THE ASSIGNATION"

RIDGERUNNER

Part One
Without a Map

✦ One

WILLIAM MORELAND KEPT moving south. If the moon was
bright he walked all night, wading through dry prairie grass.
He was alone and carried his meagre belongings on his back.
It was November and snow clung to the hollows and shadows,
but that snow was old, dry, delicate as meringue. He had come
down the leeward side of the Rockies and had descended into
the rolling grassland that runs from Alberta all the way into
Montana. Having left the only real home he had ever known,
he was heading for the border.

Cold as the days were, the sun was intense. Every noon he
boiled in his coat and every night he lay shivering on the frigid
ground and whined like a dog. After four days and nights, his
feet were very bad. He suspected they were bloody by now
but he couldn't bring himself to pull off the boots and look.

This was open country. To the east, long grass and low
trees all the way to the horizon, but to the west, the land
bled into the cloud-like silhouette of the mountains. Days
ago he had lost sight of the ranges he called home, and now
he paced alongside peaks he remembered only dimly, from
long ago, when he was a younger man, a line of only half-
familiar shapes, the faces of past acquaintances. He'd stolen
everything he could from a ranger's station outside Banff,

including a knapsack, a hatchet, matches, and a blanketcoat with ROCKY MTNS PARK stencilled across the shoulder blades and STN 153 on the chest. He'd found nothing useful for hunting. No gun, not even a knife.

The jerky he'd been eating began to fume right through the canvas of his knapsack and sicken him as he walked. Holding the bag to his belly he clawed through it, dropping behind him the last strips of meat. Then the reeking square of oilcloth in which they had been wrapped fluttered down to settle on a tuft of grass like a tiny umbrella. He took out the hatchet and considered dropping it as well, to get rid of the weight, but couldn't open his hand. The hatchet had great utility, so he slid it back into his bag. He was god-almighty thirsty and dreamed as he walked, dreamed of a river, of drinking gallons of water from that cold river.

One afternoon he came upon a gully packed with young trees, which turned out to be mostly dry, but he dug down and sipped at a muddy pool. Then he rolled onto his side under the cover of shrubs and slept hard. When he rose a few hours later it was getting on to dark and he was stiff and trembling.

That night he found himself on the road he had been looking for. He followed it until he was standing, as planned, outside the little guard hut at the Sweetgrass border-crossing between Alberta and Montana. He stood by the lightless window and swayed on numb legs. A bright coin of a moon overhead and no wind at all. The world was utterly still, so quiet he could hear his own ears humming. William Moreland stood like an idiot before the hut and waited for the guard. He stared about with hollow eyes and slowly came to the conclusion that he should probably do something.

Beyond the hut was a small gabled house and an unoccupied corral. There was a motorcar up on blocks by the kitchen door, but no lights to be seen anywhere. Moreland tried to call out with his dry throat but all that came out was a thin hiss; his first attempt to speak in more than a week. The applicant to cross over simply waited there, as he should, trying to either speak to authority or call for service, but could make no sound at all, while the guard slumbered somewhere out of sight.

A barn owl melted out of the dark and alighted on a gable of the house. They gazed unblinking at each other until the owl tilted off and moved without sound to the west.

The absurdity of the situation was not lost on Moreland: this was after all the border between two countries. But all around him was a sea of grass and rolling land and wind and animals and dust and seeds that flowed this way and that across the imagined line. A decade and a half earlier he would not have stopped, nor intended to stop, nor have approached the crossing station at all. He would not have given it the slightest thought, he would have gone his own quiet, solitary way, neither wild nor domesticated, just alone. But now he had been so long among people he'd forgotten that part of himself. So it came to him very slowly that the natural world, having long ago defined its own precincts and notions of order, was simply waiting for him to become unstuck.

He cupped his face and pressed it to the thin glass. In the darkness of the hut he saw a wooden counter and a high stool. He wandered around to the rear and pulled open the door. Inside, he found a shelf under the counter on which stood a few romance books, a clean plate and a fork, long-dead bees and bits of bee, and below that, bolted to the floor, a small metal box. On top lay a heavy padlock, twisted open, and the key was stuck in it. He gathered the padlock into his fist and opened the box.

Moreland stood for a long time looking down at the revolver. An army model, Colt single action. There were a few spare rounds in the box, some of which didn't match the gun but seemed to have been put there for tidy housekeeping. He considered taking the pistol, but in the end, he shut the lid of the box, put the padlock back on top, shut the door to the hut, and left everything as it had been. He went back out into the night, moving south, always south, wading through a vasting nothingness of grass. An ocean of grass.

TWO DAYS LATER, Moreland found himself looking down at the twin ribbons of steel at his feet, the exact rail line he'd been aiming for. He stepped between them and followed the tracks. All that day and into the next he neither saw nor heard a single train; saw no people in the distance, no roads, nothing but hawks and grouse and other birds he could not name.

He woke that night thinking his son was with him — "Jack, quit squirming" — only to find himself alone and on the ground, an infant rabbit exploring his coat sleeve. He lay still and let it crawl onto his chest and chew his buttons, wander his lapels, taste the salt in the hollow of his throat. His hand came up to stroke the tiny animal but it dashed away. After a moment that same hand settled over his eyes to shut out the stars, and he gave in and wept.

He could not stop seeing her, his beautiful wife, dead in the bed, curled in on herself like a sleeping child. He could not stop seeing her that way, so he saw nothing else.

• • •

THE DAYS GOT progressively warmer and Moreland was as light and dry as firewood, unable to reflect on anything beyond the surety of where these vacant tracks would lead him. Drawn almost by gravity to his goal, he was thoughtless, relentless, stiff and awkward. And the day he walked into the mining town of St. Croy, Montana, and opened the door onto a diner full of people, he looked like some ghastly being out of mythology. Burned by the sun and looking half his natural weight, he was the colour of the mud he'd slept in. His stolen uniform was dingled with burrs, and his hair was worse. His gait was uneven. Everything hurt. He floated into a booth, already drunk on the damp fragrance of cooking, hitched up his pants, and settled daintily on the banquette seat. The sticks of his shins showed above his boots.

The terrified waitress stood with a hand to her throat. Moreland attempted a friendly smile but it backfired entirely for it was more like a rictus, and she clip-clopped into the kitchen and harried out a tall Black man, who stood by the kitchen door wiping his hands on a tea towel and scowling at Moreland. This was the owner. He walked up to Moreland's booth, laid down a printed cardboard menu, and waited for an order, which involved watching the filthiest finger ever allowed by God as it trembled and pointed at items on the menu: Cheerwine cherry soda, roast ham dinner, mashed potatoes, carrots, and then back at the soda. He particularly wanted the soda. With a palsied hand Moreland thumbed three coins out onto the table.

The man swept the foreign money into his palm like crumbs, poked through it with disinterest, and gave it back.

He said in a low voice, "How you doing otherwise?"

Moreland recognized the generosity. His eyes welled, and he worked his dry throat. "Scared her. Sorry."

The cook seemed amused. "Well, she's like that. Scared of everything. And you look . . . dug up."

"I'm sorry."

"It's no bother. Man's got a right to eat." He hooked his thumbs in the waistband of his apron and assessed his customer. "Been out long?"

Moreland's eyes slid around the room as he tried to fathom the days and weeks.

"What's your name?"

Perhaps fatigue, or hunger, or the sense he was not quite himself anymore caused William Moreland to make a mistake: he said his real name.

The cook gestured at the oversize ranger's uniform with its white lettering. "Not from up there in Canada, are you? Not originally, I mean."

Moreland seemed to properly notice his coat for the first time, the grand spectacle of it, and he withered into his collar. He shook his head on a very stiff neck and managed, "Idaho."

"Yeah, I knew it," said the man with satisfaction. "You don't have their accent." And he took his long legs back into the kitchen.

The discreet stares of other diners, the murmuring. The quiet hiss of the soda machine and the clink of dishes. So many pies in the pie safe. A line of sugar bowls, and a pile of folded white napkins. Slowly, the smell of frying ham suffused the room. Moreland closed his mouth and swallowed dryly.

A woman somewhere behind him was talking too loudly. "Look at that," she said. "It's going to happen to us, too, you wait and see. Our country bankrupt, our best boys dead, or ruined like him. Don't shush me. What is that damn war to us?"

William Moreland sat in excruciated patience and waited for his meal. He put his hands between his knees to stop them shaking. He was not a soldier come back from war, not a park ranger, not any sort of a good man. In fact, to his own astonishment, he had firm plans to become even worse.

✦ *Two*

TWO STRAIGHT LINES of identical miners' houses faced each other across the rail line, their shadows angled in the moonlight. Moreland perched atop a hill to the south of all mining interest in St. Croy and marvelled at his old place of employ, how much it had changed in almost three decades. Last time he'd been here he was in his twenties. Here was the same old headframe looming to the north, built right into the mountain. In the valley he saw the same field where westbound trains turned in a wide arc and headed back east. But now there was a new metal slide below the minehead, held off the ground by sturdy trestles. His old bunkhouse was gone. All the bunkhouses were gone, replaced by dozens of evenly spaced homes, each with a pitched roof, glazed windows, and its own discrete outhouse. Some even showed signs of children being present.

Where had it been, his bunkhouse? He recognized the mine entrance he used to walk into each evening, the rail line exactly where it had always been, but everything else seemed skewed by change — jumbled together, smaller, in the wrong place.

He moved laterally around the west margin of the mine and up the north slope so he was behind the headframe. There he clambered down the rocks til he found a low overhang that allowed him to lie comfortably on his belly and gaze down at the toplander's deck, or this mine's version of it, and beside that a kind of boxy office built for the bosses and accountants. This wooden building was cantilevered out over the slope so they could see most of the yard, the rail line, the tipple, the coke ovens, everything. Years ago, this was where they kept the money, and as far as he could tell, the building was unchanged from days past. How often he'd gazed up at it on his way into the mine entrance and seen figures up there moving through lamplight. Now he was looking down on it. The office was dark and showed no signs of movement. He rested his chin on the cold rock and waited.

After many minutes he dangled his knapsack by one arm over the deck and let it go. The bag dropped eight feet and the hatchet within clobbered the floorboards with such a shocking bang that Moreland crabwalked backwards into the foliage and cowered there, watching for movement in the lightless office, scanning the empty mine grounds and roadway.

Three minutes on, there were still no sounds of footsteps, no curious faces in the distant windows of the miners' houses, but still he could not move, could not begin. He closed his eyes and listened to the wind sighing through the scrub at his ears. Mary's voice saying, *Get up, you've come this far.* And finally, he slithered belly-down off his perch, dropped quietly to the deck, toed his knapsack into the shadows, and from there he spooked past a bank of windows until he found the oak door of the mine bosses' office. Shocked to find nothing but slack on the handle, he pushed the door inward with two fingers and stepped into the lightless room. Then Moreland simply stared.

The safe was new, like so many other things in St. Croy. No real point locking your office door when you had hardware this good. The matte black box stood as high as his chest, and it had a thick brass handle and painted filigree around the combination dial. It stood rather daintily on kitten-heels and had been positioned in the middle of a large, square metal plate that the owners had brought in to distribute its massive weight over the floorboards, lest those kitten-heels punch through the old wood. He approached the safe and saw a blur of scratches and dings around the entire circumference of the door where drunken miners had tried in vain to use their tools to pry it open.

He shouldered his knapsack and allowed himself a deep, sob-like sigh. He hoped they still kept the dynamite where they used to.

IN THE END, he knew it wouldn't work, but tried anyway. Because Mary would want him to. When the last night shift was still hours from coming topside and the day shift slumbered in their houses, he took four half-charge sticks of Aetna extra-dynamite, with a combined weight strength of eighty percent, and tucked them under the brass handle like cigars in a man's breast pocket. Then he lit the foot-long fuses, ran halfway down the external wooden staircase, and curled up in a foetal ball.

No novice at destruction, Moreland had used blasting sticks while on logging crews, on road work, and in mines, including this one at St. Croy. He'd been so prudent with the stuff, so nimble and clever, that eventually blasting became his only job. He was sure-footed and he was shrewd, and most of all William Moreland was fast. So it was also his task to dispose of old, unstable explosives, walking into the mouth of this very entrance as men bellowed, "Here he comes!" Entering the evacuated mine alone, lantern tied to his hip and swinging, holding those bombs in his gloved hands, a hoarfrost of crystalized explosive that had leaked through the paper sheaths and now clung there like flakes of salt. He'd make his careful way to the edge of an exhausted and abandoned shaft, open his gloved hands like a devil in an opera, and release those sticks into the dark, where they fell for two breaths and landed unseen atop all the other garbage down there, the broken carts, winches and wheels and pick handles, the rotted rope and clothing, tin cans, the skeletons of expired pit ponies. Sometimes he heard a distant whump and felt a body blow in the constricted air of the shaft. Sometimes he didn't. He always slid the gloves off, too, and let them flutter into the hole. William Moreland, young and cocky back then, striding back up the lonely stope with his lantern held high and a grin on his bloodless face, following a pinhole of daylight.

So the particularities of wood and stone and pebbled earth, of explosion and implosion, impact and scatter, were as familiar to him as his own hands. But this safe was solid steel. He knew what would happen, and it did. The blast knocked the safe onto its back, reduced every window in the place to flying daggers, and removed half the office floor. The roar was horrific. In the silence afterward, everything in the room began a leisurely slide into the jagged hole and, piece by piece, office equipment fell out into the world.

The metal plate on which the safe had been standing whanged off a trestle and cartwheeled downhill to embed itself a foot deep in the wall of a coke oven. The safe missed the trestle, landed thunderously, and tobogganed down the rocky slope, screeching the whole way until it finally came to a stop. Of course, the safe door remained firmly locked. Wisps of smoke issued from the door seams because something inside was smouldering. Finally, there followed from that ruined office a flutter of paper and a tinkling rain of glass. One wicker desk chair with two legs bounced off the safe and spun merrily out into the road. And by the time the first curious miner wandered to his front door, Moreland had vanished.

It was the weirdest and most festive thing to happen in St. Croy since the previous year, when the kindly and senile priest had lost his marbles during a sermon and begun to repeat pornographic details told to him in his confessional. This failed burglary was almost as electrifying. It also happened just in time for a rousing editorial in the local monthly mining news, a full-page vociferation in support of better lives for miners and their families, taking the general view that until the hoggish and swindling mine owners paid a fair wage they deserved everything they got.

Of course everyone remembered the Canadian park ranger in the diner, even if they hadn't been there themselves. He was the sole topic of conversation for weeks. With suitable melodrama the waitress recounted his striking entrance and his tragical look. She assured anyone who asked that he had smiled at her knowingly, like a modern Robin Hood, and that he was handsome. The cook spelled out his name to reporters and insisted the man was not from Canada but from Idaho. From there it wasn't difficult to link the bomber to a man known to police for a string of burglaries from long ago — so long ago people wondered if it could even be the same man.

. . .

SIX NIGHTS LATER, in the pretty little town of Helmingham, Montana, at four-thirteen a.m., there was a concussive bang and the front door of the bank blew out into the street. It lay there in six pieces like a broken dish. The bank was just off the main street, on its own cul-de-sac, and the fairy cloud of dust and particles within the building was still sighing out of the breach when the first few people gathered round it to gawk. Within seconds excited guests streamed out of the small but posh hotel, tenants descended the stairs from their apartments on the upper floors of the stores on the main street, cross-country travellers galloped out of the hostel. It was a variegated throng of people, stunned out of their slumber, some still drunk, some with dentures not in, hair in a mess, clutching housecoat collars to their throats, bare bony ankles and ratty house slippers. They all made their way round the corner and down into the cul-de-sac to the bank's front door. Late to the party, the single on-duty policeman elbowed his way to the violated bank, which stood in a sea of spectators.

Moreland stood on tiptoes at the periphery of the crowd, inspecting his work, looking like any other filthy itinerant guest at the travellers' hostel, as curious as the rest of them. A man next to him offered him a plug of tobacco and they stood there chewing. They took little notice of each other but stood shoulder to shoulder, arms crossed, watching the mess like a couple of farmers looking over a field. He was a railway worker, he said, awaiting his next week-long shift, and he opined that this kind of event didn't happen ever, not in Helmingham, it was just the quietest place. After a moment, he glanced to his right and realized his companion was gone, people were heading back to their beds, and he too yawned and left the spectacle behind.

By morning it would be confirmed that no money was missing from the vault. Apart from the door there was no other damage to the building, and the charge seemed to have been set simply in order to make a noise, to use the mostly empty, high-ceilinged bank as an enormous drum. No one had bothered to guard the hotel lobby or manager's office, from which was stolen more than nine hundred dollars, the manager's gold spectacles and gold pocket watch, and every last coin from the front desk.

HOW TO KNOW YOUR exact age when you were born and raised in the woods? William Moreland knew this to be 1917, therefore he was approximately forty-nine years old. As early as age sixteen he had worked in mines and logging outfits all through the Rockies. He'd done road work and dug fire-breaks, but sooner or later every job would begin to worry or vex him, proximity to other men became increasingly arduous, so that in the end, he often just dropped his gear and walked away. He'd met his wife, Mary Boulton, in 1903, when he would have been about thirty-five. He'd been living rough, entirely alone for thirteen years, and as he'd once told Mary, "I only wanted to live like a coyote, just go along from day to day." Notions of his own age, or even of the exact year, had been of little interest to him. But after he'd found her, everything had changed so violently that he felt as if all those years he'd been facing the wrong way, and now some unseen hand had swung him round to face forward, into her intense brightness. Intimate life with a woman like her, and later when he became a father and held a baby in his two hands, instilled in him a sharp interest in the notion of time. The child was eight weeks old, four months old, and then he was one. Mary holding out a little doll made of cloth and saying happy birthday, Jack reaching for it, their faces only a few inches apart. Birthdays became very much more important. And his own age began to worry him; getting old seemed a problem only insomuch as his death would have meaning, at least to someone else. If not for Mary, he might already have expired like a coyote, and not a single person on the earth would have known or cared.

But, in truth, he had not lived exactly like a coyote. Even a woodsman likes his comforts. Given the exigencies of human life, not least the powerful need to eat, for ammunition and matches, something to sleep under, Moreland had been well known, at least in a localized sense, for a long campaign of burglaries of empty ranger's stations all over Montana and Idaho. It was a good solution, for they were well stocked and very often empty. By the time he was in his twenties, he had made a woodsman's career of equipping himself with everything he needed by stealing it from the U.S. Forest Service. He ate their food supplies, collected candles and gun rations, bathed in their tin bathtubs, and always tidied up after himself. Once, he had entered a station to find rangers asleep upstairs, so he had relieved one man of his good boots, and left his own broken ones in trade. Nothing of much value was ever taken, rather it was his persistence that had drawn the Forest Service's fury down on him. On the few occasions they spotted him, rangers chased him through the trees only to see his footprints disappear. He was quiet and quick, travelling always on foot, and no one knew who he was. Attempts to catch him proved so fruitless and exhausting that he was eventually given a nickname: the Ridgerunner.

This notoriety had also resulted in an arrest warrant that took so many months to serve, it was an embarrassment to the Forest Service. Two trackers hired by the director finally caught up with the elusive thief, and they found him almost by accident, Moreland being so quiet, his fire so deliberately small they nearly walked right by him at no more than three hundred feet. If he hadn't been so tired and worn out that winter, he might have heard them coming. As it was, they took him first to the nearest ranger's station and handcuffed him to a cot, and the next day, they walked him into Orofino and the Clearwater County Jail, where he was fingerprinted. During the one-day trial, the members of the jury had found the Ridgerunner a charming young man, even funny. His startling commitment to independence had made some of them wistful; and anyway, they'd all been bored and finally annoyed by the prosecutor's endless enumeration of costs. He was acquitted on the grounds of insufficient evidence and a total lack of damage done to any building, except perhaps broken padlocks, and on that day in 1898, the Ridgerunner had walked down the steps of the courthouse a free man. He owned nothing but the clothes on his back; the rest had been confiscated. He made immediately for the mountains, moving in a straight line toward the Clearwater Ranger Station where, for the twenty-eighth time in his young life, he broke a padlock, stocked up on everything, and disappeared. From there he had headed north all the long way into Canada, and had not been seen in the northern states since.

Almost twenty years later, he was back. Only now it was money he wanted, and he was using dynamite to get it.

→ *Three*

EIGHTEEN DAYS LATER and forty miles from St. Croy,
William Moreland jolted awake on the hard ground and
pawed at blankets that weren't there. He didn't understand
why he wasn't in bed, couldn't remember where his family
was. After a moment he stopped thrashing, stopped reaching for them. Everything around him was blowing and wild.

The night was unseasonably warm and the gusts were
powerful, vast weather systems changing places overhead.
He collected his scattered things, packed them carefully into
the knapsack, and sat cross-legged facing the wind as if to
shield the bag at his back. So far he had managed to steal
more than eleven thousand dollars in cash, which lay rolled
up inside everything else he owned, in order to keep the bills
dry, unstained, pressed flat. This money was for the boy. For
Jack Boulton and no one else.

Every few nights he woke to the sound of his son screaming. Those long legs kicking weakly as doctors pulled him
from Moreland's arms and hurried him into a back room. He
had tried to follow his son but a nurse had barred the door
and refused him entry.

"We might allow a mother," she said in a tone that
suggested even that was unlikely, "but fathers are of no

practical use around children, and they have a habit of fainting. Go home."

He stood frozen in the echoing hall as the terrified boy cried out for him. Those howls had gone up Moreland's spine like a virus and reordered his dreams.

He remembered the trip home only in flashes: the realization the horse was already exhausted and if he pushed it past a gentle trot it might collapse under him and he'd be running; the miles crawling by as he whispered encouragement to himself and to Mary; the single drop of rain on the crown of his hat, like the tap of a finger, and the immediate knowledge that came with it — she was already gone.

Now, weeks later and hundreds of miles away, every few nights Moreland woke again to his boy screaming. He didn't know how to stop it, didn't know if there was a way for a man to speak to that part of his mind and counsel patience, to reassure it. By now he knew his son's life had been saved. Jack had defied the doctor's terrifying prognosis and someday soon would be living under the protection of a good woman — of all things, a nun. That woman knew everything a doctor did, and she was fierce. It was the one scant consolation left to Moreland: he still had a son, and his son had a protector.

Moreland shuffled down and lay his head back against the knapsack and watched his lapel flap wildly in the wind and aspen leaves scatter across his coat. He closed his eyes.

Jack at sixteen months, sitting at the table on his mother's knee, trying with furious concentration to use a spoon on his own.

Jack at seven, winging stones at the outhouse wall and giggling until Moreland, from within the box, bellowed, "Cut it out!"

Jack at ten, standing at his mother's shoulder, the two of them so similar, grinning like crazy at Moreland as she said, "How did it happen? He's almost as tall as I am." The kid as pleased as if he'd pulled off a great trick.

Jack at twelve, pale and ghastly and unmoving in a hospital bed, wisps of his long, dark hair falling from his scalp.

Moreland would sit like a wooden statue by his son's bed until someone came to push him away and then he would wander into the hallway and sit on a bench. That first hour, a doctor came and spoke to him but he heard almost nothing the man said.

A young red-headed nurse bent down and spoke gently to Moreland and her words seemed to pass right through him. *You have a nice young chap there, and he's tough.* Her warm hand on his frigid one.

People moved round him, gossiped quietly, but he listened only for the boy's voice. A nun he'd never met came and spoke to him, or rather at him, and during these talks he mostly stared at the floor with burning eyes, a man buried under the rubble of his own life.

"I know who you are," she said, "and I dare say you know who I am." He had looked at the habit, dully, and nodded. Mary, saddling the horse, saying happily, "She always pays me too much, but I learned as a young girl not to argue with one of the sisters."

The nun hovered over Jack, fed him medicine, wrangled and fought with the doctors. She sat next to Moreland in that hallway, her thin waist wrapped in a crisp white apron sewn by Mary Boulton's own hand. Moreland stared at those small stitches running the seam.

Sometimes she sat with him for a long time, saying

nothing; they just waited in common terror. Other times she had a lot to say. She talked of herself and of the boy. Once, she held Moreland's hand and intoned things about faith and heaven until that same young nurse with flaming red hair hurried into the hall and hissed, "You must *stop* this talk of eternal bliss unless you want to call my patients to it." This was the only time he would ever see the nun chastened.

Sometimes her only desire seemed to be to rip him down and flay him for his utter failure as a man. Everything she said was like an echo of his own thoughts, the words so repetitive and droning he thought it was his own inner voice.

"You left them regularly, didn't you? And not for work but simply because you wished to ramble about and be selfish. I know it is true, she told me as much. Why she put up with you I cannot understand."

Other times, she spoke gently to him, calmly, as if to reason with a cretin. She said, "Tell me what your plans could possibly be now. What will you do without a wife? Scrabble along, just as you always have? Well, you can't. She is gone and everything will be twice as hard. You can't take a job and leave him to fend for himself, alone in whatever hovel you have chosen to live. And when you are home, what exactly can you offer him? Without a woman how can that boy thrive at all? Away from his peers, away from school and the company of good, decent people. And what about you? The way you have chosen deliberately to waste your life is indecent. May I point out the horror of that good boy turning out like you? A hermit. A weird solitary, impoverished in means and aged beyond his years. Do you want that for him?"

"No."

"What? Did you speak?"

"I don't . . . want that for him."

"Good." she said. "You are starting to see your way. The boy comes first."

"Yes."

"So give him to me."

He had looked at her with dawning awareness: a plan. She was telling him to form a plan to better his son's chances in life — because she assumed there was a life to be had. She was giving him, Moreland, time to do something about it. Time to work. She was going to help.

Even in the smoking ruin of his mind he had seen a hard, bright penny of good omen in her optimism, and his heart leapt up, too, hard and bright.

"You know what to do," she had said. "It is staring you in the face."

"Yes," he had said. "I know exactly what to do."

A FORTNIGHT LATER, when the boy was no longer deathly ill, but was recovering, and the nun was still hovering over him, almost jealously, ready to take him home and care for him, Moreland had returned once more to the empty family cabin. He'd put the Morgan away into the corral, walked up to his own front door, but could go no further. She was not there, he knew as much, but still he stood in the wind and the dark, his mind frozen, dumbstruck. But eventually, like a bear breaking in, he pushed through and stood in the awful silence of the room, unable to look at the empty bed. Over that long night he worked diligently and did not weep. He made not a sound, because no one cries for the dead, they cry for themselves, and Moreland did not pity himself. Far from it.

By morning he'd gathered up anything a boy would want or need to live easy and free in town, including the saddle, saddle blanket, tack and a fishing rod, and the boy's buck knife, and then he'd ridden the horse into town, ridden it right up to the nun's house before dawn, where he'd laid it all out on her porch. And then he'd waited in silence, holding the horse, until she emerged, handbag over her elbow, ready to go to the hospital. She'd looked at the man, looked at the gear, and said, "What is all this?"

He explained. All of it was to be kept by her for his son's benefit. He thanked her for her counsel. He'd made her promise Jack would live with a fair degree of autonomy, the kind of freedom the boy was used to, and that any young person deserves. Of course, William Moreland hadn't told her his actual plans. Instead he'd said, "I'm going to find some money." Which was true enough; he just didn't bother saying how.

She'd nodded with a vaguely unbelieving look in her eye and said, "Off you go, then. He's mine to care for."

"You'll be good to him? He isn't used to town, and some of these kids are worse than snakes."

"No one will interfere with him, I won't allow it. He will have a good life with me. That I can promise."

"A few months is all it'll take. Then I'll be back, and you can let him go."

All she'd said was, "I will do right by *him* and no one else."

He'd believed her.

He left the Morgan hitched outside her old disused stable, the kid's belongings still lying on the clean, swept boards of her wide front porch, and then William Moreland headed out of Banff on foot, making for the nearest warden's cabin.

His last sight of her was her bell-like shape in her black habit as she stood looking down at the pile of rustic goods at her feet. It was the first time he'd taken any notice of her fine brick house — she must be from money. Hard to tell with any nun where they come from, whether she be an uneducated farm girl or a refined woman, one of those folks people call "the quality." And yet there was the precise way she spoke, and a superiority in her he'd seen only in flashes, and only when she was angry at him. A nun, an apothecary, and she was wealthy. There was no safer place for Jack than with her.

Moreland yanked up the collar of his sweater and breathed against his own chest. He felt the pounding of his heart subside. He crossed his arms over the thick warden's coat, slid his hands into his armpits, and listened to the wind.

Four

ONCE CLEAR OF ST. CROY Moreland exchanged his warden's coat for something less memorable and stole a fine pair of leather boots with thick wool socks, thanks to which his feet recovered marvellously.

In Whitefish, Montana, known in his youth as Stumptown thanks to rampant logging, he spooked around the residential streets and back lots, where foxes and cats shot past him and cantered up alleys, busy with their own predations. Still weak and shaking from that long first walk, he slipped into the shadows between houses and rested, peered into lighted windows. One night he paused to listen to a baby crying weakly in its crib, and it seemed to him that he was the only one listening. He heard honest talk between men and women. He heard bosses described in unflattering terms. Once, a woman's voice had blasted out from a kitchen, loud and alcoholic, saying, "She can *have* him if she cares so much," and there followed a laugh so derisive Moreland scrambled along the dirt path between houses to escape it.

He slipped into empty kitchens in broad daylight and sipped milk from bottles while people murmured in other rooms. He stole pies and ate them whole leaving the pie plates and nothing else but crumbs.

Looking for news of the war in a blind hope that it had somehow ended without his knowing, Moreland had picked up a discarded newspaper and instead found his own name in it. And his nickname. They had reported only two of his eight burglaries and those only because he had used dynamite. The article opined that "Moreland is a depraved and callous individual who is doing the enemy's job for them." At the bottom of the article was a hand-drawn likeness of the Ridgerunner, done in pencil, a face described by witnesses in the St. Croy diner and recreated by an artist. It looked nothing whatever like him. There was something gallant in those features that were absent in his own: a jutting chin you might see on a prizefighter; the eyes were keen, icy pale, and as he saw it, a little lopsided. With delight Moreland looked at that drawing for a long time. It was a portrait of a man who did not exist. The Ridgerunner could have stood next to that drawing in a post office all day without the slightest danger of recognition. He tore the article out, folded it neatly, and put it in his breast pocket. In a few weeks, when he got home, he would show it to Jack.

In one house he found an elderly and undersize Henry rifle, a model common to the Civil War but usually still serviceable. He and the gun were not unalike in vintage, and he'd never handled one, so he took it. In exchange he placed on the kitchen table a gigantic sculling trophy made of solid silver. He'd left the trophy to be rid of its weight and awkward shape, and because selling it posed a problem, and also because leaving it made him feel like Robin Hood.

In another backyard, at the end of a long, wintering garden full of tidy tomato stakes, he slipped into a large shed and scrounged among carpentry tools, bottles of straightened nails, rusty hinges, broken chairs, and discarded toys. There was some excellent rope, a basket full of good potatoes, a bowl of sour apples no bigger than golf balls, and six cans of green beans. He took it all. At the back of the shed was a windowless anteroom, a kind of rough cupboard, from the ceiling of which hung a charnel line of severed ham legs. Moreland had never seen prosciutto before. He leaned in and inspected them. The meat looked like carrion, horribly frosted with grey-green matter. Every leg looked too far gone to eat — or worse, given the lack of maggots, poisoned, bait for coyotes perhaps. He pondered this horror for many minutes, then backed away scandalized by the waste, and left the feast where it hung.

This was how he lived, stealing his own supplies; this was how he travelled, on foot, hefting the weight of his spoils, periodically well fed, sore in every joint of his body, exultant. Moreland had formed a two-step plan and for better or worse, he was following it. First, start in St. Croy and work north accumulating as much money as he could carry the only way he knew how, by stealing it; walk everything back into Canada and leave it with his son; check on the boy, but tell the boy only what he needed to know. Second step: head back out and work the Canadian side, starting with the Crowsnest Pass. He had a final sum in his head, an amount of money that could not possibly fail to put the boy in a different class, afford him a better life, an education, a way to start his own business if that's what Jack wanted. The Ridgerunner would leave nothing to chance, he would settle his son's future prospects once and for all. But he knew it wouldn't do to wait until he had collected it all; it was foolish to wander around with a great excess of loot on his back. If he was caught, that would be it for Jack. So, in the way of all superstitious men, he decided to bargain with fate, bamboozle it. He chose two attainable steps over one great leap.

And so, in the final days of November, by the time he was done burgling Eureka, Montana, and had trotted out of town in the dark, heading north toward the border, he was carrying what would be the boy's Christmas present: more than fourteen thousand dollars.

→ *Five*

NOW, OF A SUNDAY EVENING before dinner, Jack Boulton was standing behind the enormous house off the main street, with his back to a tree, weeping into his hands. Weeping for his mother, raging at his father, mourning his old life until he was raw with it. The feeling came on so quickly he had no choice but to rush out the kitchen door and into the pines.

Within a minute she noticed his absence, her *yoo-hoo* so shrill it scared the breath out of him. Stuttering to a stop, the boy gazed through the lattice of his fingers at the dead grass bending into the river, caught and swimming there. The snow, the water, the hands pressed to his face, everything glowing red as the sun burned and sank below the ranges.

The boy dropped his hands and gazed up at those peaks. Imagining his father out there, free. Jack raked back his hair, blew his nose sideways into a snowdrift, and tramped up the steps again. Back into this new life, in the nun's house, in these ridiculous starched trousers.

All he wanted to do was go home, but there was nothing left to go home to.

THE GREAT HOUSE was far too large for two people. Several bedrooms, the sunroom, and the drawing room were never used, their doors closed, curtains drawn, and even in summer the air in those rooms was chilly and damp. Afternoon sun fell through stained glass in the front hall and threw a sundial of coloured light on the Persian runner. Mornings he watched the needle of light crawl until it was time for school. He was still a little sick, still weak, still vomiting up his breakfast some days.

The nun too had a plan, to resurrect the child from the ashes of his sad former life, to save him through good works. She was frantic in her labour, hopeful, determined. Jack was a patient kid, and he mostly liked her, so he submitted to the dismal diet of politeness and decency, teatime, bedtime, school time, prayers. He tolerated his starched new clothes, the unaccustomed bunching of underwear between his legs.

He was walking within a month, running errands in two, and was by now almost fully recovered, all thanks to her. She did her best to keep news of his father, William Moreland, now widely thought to be a thief and murderer, a mad bomber, from him. But he heard things anyway, mostly from the taunts of other children, and this was how he found out his father had both a past he'd never been told about and a nickname he'd never heard.

The nun only ever spoke of the present, of herself and him together, and never of his past, for she believed that if children could be trained to remember they could also be trained to forget. She hoped to make this boy's past, that cabin, those parents, all the shadows laid across his life admit their final defeat and vanish from his mind. Neighbours, teachers, visitors to the house were all instructed never to mention the parents, so they didn't, they simply stared.

He was tall for twelve, slender, long of limb. His dark hair fell almost to his shoulders. The nun couldn't bring herself to barber it. After all, there were men in town with hair that long and some of them were respectable. His face was still as smooth and hairless as a girl's. He was beautiful and unaware of that fact. He had no idea why people stared at him, why schoolgirls went all squirmy when he tried to address them, why grown men seemed irritable and fond almost at the same time. He thought this was just the way people were. He was awash in his own life.

Raised by two hermits in the woods, much was new to him. The ill will of other children shocked him. And girls, they were everywhere, all over town, a profusion of women and girls thanks to the war. Lipstick; he had never before encountered such a thing. The way women's hats neither shaded their eyes nor kept them warm, nor, most times, even stayed put on their heads. The way they fussed over a fur stole, the way they snuggled into it and pretended they were warm. Jack knew exactly how to stay warm, and a little scrap of fox wouldn't cut the mustard.

But the boy delighted in town life. Despite the war, Banff attracted tourists from still-neutral countries all over the world: Swiss explorers and mountaineers with their skis and gear, American photographers and landscape painters, an entrepreneur from the Argentine whose left ear had been shot off during the invasion of Patagonia. They paraded the main street in their motorcars, women daring to wear trousers, men sporting spats and fine hats. He saw a drunken Hollywood actor ejected from the hotel bar at noon, brushing off his mink coat and doffing his hat to no one in particular. Plumbing, electric lighting, garbage collection, baby carriages, false teeth, cufflinks, the black armbands of mourning, perfume, wedding rings. Cliques of local girls scampered along the boardwalk laughing. The Chinese spoke to one another, the Italians, Norwegians, the Dutch. Most residents in town still travelled on horseback, thanks to the shocking cost of a car, but also because a car required a smooth graded road, and those were pretty rare. Numbers on houses. Mail delivery. The fire department's new vehicle, a slick thing everyone called the buzz wagon. The great circus of town managed most days to distract Jack Boulton from the truth of things: that he considered himself to be orphaned.

The nun was only fifty-eight but to the boy she seemed prehistoric. She fussed fondly with his shirtcollar, forelock, cuffs. A knobby thumb poking his lumbar when she caught him slouching. He was never allowed to sip coffee, though he used to at home.

"My mother lets me," he told her.

She looked at him for a long time, and they both registered the present tense. Finally, she said, "That was wrong of her."

Nor could he touch a cigarette, even though all the boys at school smoked. The tough ones even walked into class still smoking and ground their butts out on the floor under their desks.

He was suddenly exposed to mirrors. His father only ever owned a shaving mirror the size of a bar of soap, but this house was rotten with them. A convex one in the front hall framed in gold leaf; louvered mirrors over every chest of drawers, a setup that she called a "vanity"; mirrors inside cupboard doors, for what purpose he couldn't fathom — why should the closet look at itself?

The hallway outside her bedroom was lined with two enormous mirrors, one covering each wall.

"It's something you see in old houses," she said. "Hopelessly out of date. But look at this." She stood between those mirrors, her body solid and real, and in those two mirrors there were hundreds more of her to the left, and to the right, a perfect repetition of the same woman, each succeeding copy slightly smaller and darker, all the way down into the murky infinite.

"You try it," she said.

So he took her place and lifted an arm. Numberless boys lifted their arms in a chorus line. He hopped and an infinitude of boys hopped with him. But after the first burst of fascination with his own face and body and eyes and hair and mouth, he wearied of mirrors, began to mistrust the trick of them. Rooms seemed to distort, the corners to sink into darkness. Even the old lady didn't look like herself in a mirror, so how could he?

She was once Emelia Cload, a great family surname, and there were Cload banks all over the country to prove it. But her name in religion was Sister Beatrice, pronounced in the Italian way, she insisted: "*Bay-a-tree-chay.*" No one in town could say it properly, and some thought it a Nakoda name. Mostly they just called her ma'am. Late of the Anglican Order of Saint Mara, she had taken a more or less permanent leave of absence from the abbey, at first to nurse a sick and dying father, and now to live a secular life with the boy, a family life. She often wore the veil, and on those rare days when she suffered one of her nervous moments, she would revert to the full habit, for comfort.

She always rose early because the nuns did in her previous life. She was kindly with the boy but strict and relentless. The war in Europe showed no signs of ending, so she encouraged her neighbours to follow her frugal example: ration your candles, ration butter and soap. Neighbours just smiled and went about their business as they saw fit.

In her bedroom each morning she curried his hair with her late father's hairbrushes, wielded simultaneously with vigour, one at each side of his head, as had been the method in past days. She purchased a toothbrush and a peppermint-flavoured tooth powder that made his gums bleed. A boar's-hair brush under his fingernails and toenails during bath time four mornings a week. Neighbours suggested in a roundabout way that no one needed to bathe that often, and after all, the boy was twelve, he looked almost grown and stood taller than the nun. But she insisted it was a mother's responsibility to keep her child clean. Crabbed fingers working in the milky bathwater. The joy on her face. Her veil hung on a bathroom hook. These mornings were agonizing for the boy and he stared slant-eyed at the wall and tried to breathe normally.

She had even scrubbed away his real name, just as hers had been erased when she joined the Order. Where he had once been Jack Boulton he was now Charles D'Arcy Euphastus Cload, de facto scion of the great family, and she called him Charlie when she was being fond. He saw no harm in such foolishness; she could call him whatever she liked, he still knew who he was. But he refused to tell her his birthdate, pretended in fact that he could not remember it, so she had chosen her own birthday in July and inscribed that date on the fly-leaf of her Bible, just below her own birth record. Mary Boulton had done the same thing years ago in a different Bible. With her thin finger, the nun tapped his new name and said, "Now the recording angel can find you."

He'd leaned in and stared at his new identity. "Who was Euphastus?"

"My great-great grandfather. It's a beautiful name, isn't it?"

He did not think so, but seeing her exultant face he said no more.

Passing a café in which the local jobless sat drinking coffee, he saw faces turn to watch him pass, and the waitress shook her head. He was already well known in town, a sad tale still in the telling. But the nun gathered his hand into hers and said, "Don't you listen to one word they say. Not about anything. Most people are terribly ignorant. Your father didn't rob anyone or blow up anything. He left you with me because he knew what was best for you." It was the one time she admitted to William Moreland's continued existence on the earth, and in that admission was a lie, something she told him out of kindness, a desire to reach through the boy's cloud of melancholy to soothe him.

But a small town is a living engine run on talk, innumerable bees grumbling in their paper cells. Jack heard it everywhere he went. Gossip, opinionation, conjecture, speculation, debate.

In the grocery store, a customer's voice came through the canned goods and price tags to him: "It makes me sad to think of that woman dying, but there, that's what you get when you live rough like she did. It's much safer to live in town. People will help you if you are in trouble. Most of them will, anyway. She sewed this dress for me, oh ages ago, and I still wear it. Too bad she's dead or I'd order another one."

Jack stood in the aisle trembling, and he saw nothing but the floorboards.

In the pharmacy, as the nun roamed the shelves with a handwritten list in her fingers, two other women bent together by the counter and whispered.

"I don't envy clever women."

"Oh goodness, I do."

"But so few of them are happy."

"That's true enough."

"If Emelia were a man she might have been a doctor. But what else was open to her? Just to marry some man to take over the bank. She tried twice, and look how that turned out. Both sickly, and they died young. Poor judgement on her part."

The nun was in full habit, the long dark skirts and white apron assiduously starched. They watched her intense scrutiny of a particular bottle of liquid.

In the optometrist's store, where the nun purchased a magnifying glass, the owner said, "Takes after his mother, doesn't he?"

To shut him up she said, "May I pay you now?"

But the man had warmed to his subject. "She came in here once and got her sight tested. Considerable lack of trust, I'd say, because she kept standing between me and him, like I was going to eat him. That boy wasn't scared of anything. But her? The whole time I'm testing her sight she kept looking at me, checking where I was, watching where I went. She spooked me." He handed over a bill and a few coins and said pensively, "The only calm one in the room was that kid."

And in the sunny schoolyard, two young teachers standing together with arms crossed, watching the children, their eyes full on Jack Boulton, talking as if he couldn't hear them, one saying, "She's the last woman in town who should have taken on the burden of a child. I think she hasn't got the stuffing for it. And why would she willingly do it at her age?"

Try as she might the nun could not stop the town from talking.

It was unbearable to him that he must keep going back to that schoolhouse. Every day he felt the weight of his infamy there. He'd had little experience of other children until he was thrown among them. In vain he'd tried to fade into the background, to let someone else be the target, but he was as alluring to them as a sideshow exhibit. The girls gusted around him, chattering as if he weren't there, but later they had spats over him. The boys assured him he was of no account, but they thought of nothing else — wherever Jack went they would congregate nearby and punch at the air, rooster each other up. Even the small children invented rhymes for him, and they scrawled words on fences so that he might ponder them on his walk home. Kindergartners flitted behind him as he sprinted down alleyways and they pecked the stupid song into his back.

Sing, sang, sung
Your daddy's on the run.
Sung, sang, sing,
Your daddy's going to swing.

The jokes he had tolerated, the pantomimes of his father being beaten with clubs or hanging by his neck, with no reaction from the teachers except mild chiding. And then one day, as he knew it must, the subject had strayed to his mother.

Three older boys had gathered round him, all false jovial and loud, slapping his shoulder as if, surely, he too could see the humour in her death. He'd lunged at the nearest face, ridden it to the ground, and punched it until he saw blood.

Somewhere far away, girls were shrieking, teachers shouting his name, and then he'd felt hands pulling him away, lifting him by the shirtcollar, the wrist, the hair. For a moment he got loose and swung his fists at any teacher who came near, until the women just stood there, with fallen hair buns and dusty skirts.

Finally three men in khaki uniforms rushed in from the roadway to help restrain the skinny lunatic, bear-hug him, grip his ankles and hold him as he bucked and twisted, hold him until finally he went limp and dangled in their arms, gazing down at his tormentor, who now lay red and howling in the schoolyard dust, a broken incisor trembling on his spattered chin. The men dragged Jack to the back of the schoolhouse and set him standing on legs still shaking. They stood between him and the other children, a windbreak of male authority, and they pretended to scold. But these men had seen worse violence and there was no heat in the reprimand.

One of them tousled Jack's hair with bonhomie and laughed boozily into his face, "You're pretty tough for a string bean."

Of course, the strapping he got was titanic. The young teacher who administered it appeared to be in shock, for she took up a wooden yardstick and beat him in a kind of luxurious trance.

Afterward, he had sat wincing on the bench outside the schoolhouse door. His filthy face was streaked with tears and no one would go near him, not even the girls. He watched scarves of dust whirl and chase each other down the empty street. In little horrified hiccups, his mind kept returning to that red face. He saw himself working on it, like a man hammering a nail into a board. He was frightened of himself.

He inspected his bleeding knuckles, picked at sand and slivers embedded in his forearms and elbows. He had no recollection of the other boy managing a single punch, but clearly, he must have. One cheekbone throbbed horribly, and his upper lip was numb. He brought his trembling fingers up and touched a swelling above the hairline. Now, as the energy drained sickeningly out of Jack, he remembered that someone had got hold of his fists, so he'd tried to use his own head as a battering ram.

When he looked up, *she* was standing stone-faced at the gate, in full nun's regalia, with her skirts rippling in the wind. His heart leapt and, for a moment, he considered running. Faces appeared at the schoolhouse windows to watch the scene, but the nun settled on them a gaze so cold and reptilian they all soon fluttered away.

Jack rose and limped to her. She said not a word, simply opened the gate until he joined her, and then she carefully drew it closed with a *click*. Her face was set and sober and her eyes were shining. She seemed to be holding something in, nursing some wild emotion as they walked along the wooden sidewalk, past the hotel, past the café. It briefly occurred to the boy that, once they arrived home, she might kill him. Because at that moment, as he read her profile, that outcome seemed possible. But to his bewilderment, the second she had closed the front door and they were alone together in the hallway she had covered her mouth with her hands and dissolved into giggles.

"Oh, you wonderful boy."

He gaped at her.

"You showed that little rat. He deserved everything you gave him."

"No," said Jack. "He didn't."

"Don't be sorry. Not for one second. They are a despicable family, every last one of them." She did a strange little dance of girlish glee on the Persian runner and then fixed him with a smile. "I've always wanted to do that to his mother."

The boy was weak-kneed already, but this sucked the life out of him. He collapsed heavily on a hall chair, his head thumping.

Her delight faded as she looked down into his baffled face. "Well," she said. "It's over and you won't do it again." Then she went to make him a nice bowl of hot chocolate.

Clearly, he saw it now. She behaved one way outside the house, in public, and another way inside it. This worried him because he had never learned how to navigate falseness. His mother was never anything but her own raw self, incapable of deceit or performance. Jack saw integrity in that.

If he was not at school or doing chores, he was with the nun. The only fires he ever set were in the kitchen stove, an enamelled, canary-yellow, many-chambered hulk installed near the door and attached to the wall by an umbilicus of bent pipe. It would not hold heat unless coddled, and it was the boy's expressed opinion that it had been designed by a moron.

He yearned to disappear and lie in the grass and look up at clouds, or wander the riverbanks, swim, fish, hunt. But even his suggestion that he might only wade to his knees in the river filled her with terror that the current would sweep him away and drown him. She spent far too much time fussing about things that might kill him. Horses, dogs, dangling tree limbs, rusty nails, the kitchen cleaver, bridges, all motorcars. There was a single electric switch in the house, a black button set into the plaster wall by the stairwell; she alone was allowed to operate it, and did so wincingly, wielding an old rubber galosh against the bolt of electricity she assured him could come at any second.

He was astonished at her shriek after he carried a baby garter snake into the house for her to inspect. A tiny, helpless thing the size of a pencil. He hurried it back outside lest she harm it. Jack came to understand his benefactor was utterly ignorant on the subject of animals. She considered all wildlife to be potentially lethal, even frogs.

To his mind they ate too little and with unnecessary regularity, and everything was tasteless. His solution was to pilfer constantly from the cold box and cupboards, and when she confronted him, he defended himself gamely and accused her of being stingy. They woke painfully early every morning, and she marched him off to bed at an hour normally reserved for infants. Every evening he lay under the blankets, squirming with frustration, a wash of daylight still visible in the evening sky. As a result, he barely slept anymore, but lay awake all night, and walked around hollow-eyed all day. Eventually this numbing process bewitched him into a state of acute awareness of time passing, the predictable stages of the day creeping forward.

In the high cupboards of the kitchen she kept a hoard of herbs and tinctures and metal tools, glass flasks, a cast iron clamp, and a wee burner that ran on alcohol, for she had been an apothecary at the abbey, a kind of nurse and druggist, chemist, occasional midwife. On such subjects she knew nearly everything. She read constantly and made notes in her nurse's shorthand. He hovered over the paper and asked why *po* meant "by mouth." In this way he was introduced to the various modern uses of Latin: *per os*. If he cut himself she

applied a greenish poultice that stung but worked like magic
and allowed no scar. Once a week she dosed him with a health
and vitamin concoction of her own making that tasted like
chalk and left a queer buzzing in his throat. When he'd been
sick and alone in the hospital, she'd come every day with a
special soup, the most extraordinary colour of blue. His fever
subsided and he came back to himself, began to sit up and eat
bread. With blue tongue and blue lips he began to talk to her,
to his fellow inmates in the ward, to anyone who passed his
bed. In fact he recovered so well the doctors grew suspicious.

"Jealous," she said, "because a woman did their job for
them."

For the first time in his life he had his own room, his own
bed. The chest of drawers held no clothes but his. She had
purchased for him what he considered to be twice the number
of shirts and trousers and socks anyone needs; to him it just
seemed like more laundry. This bedroom, she told him, was
all his, and as if to prove it, she never set foot inside the room
but instead hovered respectfully on the threshold. It was not
privacy, exactly, but it was as close to it as she would allow
in this house and he appreciated it. Still, that woman had
opinions about everything, and so, from her threshold, she
encouraged him to kneel and say his prayers. Which he did,
woodenly following her simple script: *God bless my teachers
and my friends and* . . . He had no friends.

One night he had turned from his bed and said, "I want
to say it in my head."

After a long moment of thought she assented, and in that
silence he closed his eyes and spoke to his dead mother, whispering across an unknown distance to her listening ear.

Thereafter his prayers lasted much longer and the nun

seemed pleased with him. He'd never seen her pray, but he assumed she must do it in the privacy of her room. She no longer had much truck with the Anglican church in town, now that she had a child to raise. Still, they sat together on Sundays on those smooth pews and he guessed her opinion of the week's sermon by the hardness of her expression.

It was rare that she would consider paying for a newspaper; instead she just pumped shopkeepers, neighbours, and women at the schoolhouse for news of recent events.

When she took Jack out to do their shopping, and on those frequent occasions when the subject of women's suffrage came up, she had robust arguments with any man foolish enough to even shake his head on the subject. Some women were even against their own right to vote, some men were for it, but mostly it divided the sexes. The pharmacist had a subscription to a weekly newspaper and so a crowd would gather of a Thursday evening in his store, and he would put his elbows on the cash desk and read out the best sections in a halting voice. From dour editorials on the dangers of unrestricted suffrage, to lampooning cartoons of old maids let loose on the political stage, to rabid opinion in the letters section, the pharmacist laid it all out before the crowd in his store — "When a man comes home at night, he doesn't want a hyena in petticoats yapping politics at him. He wants a sweet, docile creature to bring him his slippers" — which unleashed a roaring fusillade of derision from the women and applause from the men.

Over breakfast one weekend, she told the boy, "Life will be better when we have a say in things. If you leave everything to men, *this* is what happens," and she swept her hand toward the kitchen window, beyond which lay the whole terrible world, the war without end, the death. "Someday," she said, "you and I will vote together." And the boy nodded his head vaguely.

Before school she always read him a Bible story and then leaned back in her housecoat, hands laced across her belly, and offered personal interpretations of it.

Take the case of poor Lazarus of Bethany. Four days dead, raised by Christ as a show of strength, a final shocking statement of divine intent: life after death. In burial garments, he lurched from his cave and passed among the living; he sat at the dinner table beside the other guests, a frightful miracle.

She chuckled and repeated the line, *By this time he stinketh.*

On this subject, the boy wished to know more. Could Lazarus eat the food? Was he aware of himself or was he a shell, a dumb thing animated? Did it hurt Lazarus to wake to the same world he'd just left, to walk again on those ruined feet? And surely he did not live forever or he would be somewhere in the world now and people would know of him. Miracle achieved, his purpose was served. What happened to Lazarus?

He asked the nun directly, and she said, "It's a story, it is what it is, and you are meant to learn from it."

Jack found these mornings tolerable because she always chose subjects that would hold his attention, stories that were thrilling or creepifying. They both particularly enjoyed the Book of Daniel with its dreams and visions and lions. He yawned and stirred his soupy cream of wheat and asked her to explain the beast with iron teeth. He made the mistake of asking what a eunuch was.

After dinner every night they would lean together over the dictionary, a massive book that had its own pedestal and was always left open. They flipped randomly through pages and he was introduced to words, many of which she was surprised to find he already knew.

"Diaphanous?" she said.

"It means sort of wispy."

"Good. How about . . . recumbent?"

He stoked the kitchen stove, stirred the porridge, swept floors, cut vegetables, wrung out the towels, carried the ashcan to the garden. Given his former life in the cabin, he had no aversion to work and was efficient in his chores. Some days she stood in the kitchen and watched him surreptitiously as he bore down on the washboard with the wide heel of his hand. Those long, muscled forearms.

She'd been stunned to discover that her new child knew how to sew, at least a little. It was like having a girl and a boy combined in one person. To see him there, sitting back in a chair with his legs crossed at the knee, needle and thread in hand, letting down the hem of his own pants, one might mistake the boy for someone wholesome and refined.

This impression was destroyed any time he opened his mouth. She corrected his speech with such numbing frequency and such total lack of result the neighbours began to speculate on who was the teacher and who the student. They wagered on which of them would give up first. He was an obedient child except on the point of language.

Call everyone ma'am and sir.

Say shan't not won't.

We do *not* refer to it as the crapper.

She objected to *Jesus Christ, good god, good lord*. Even *jeez* was not allowed. She instructed him to say instead *goodness* or *my land*. None of it stuck. He spoke exactly as he pleased, and he swore like a sailor. Eventually she gave up correcting him, at least in private. She almost found it funny at times, as long as they were alone and no one could overhear his filth.

When he shrieked, "Spider! Size of a goddamn cat!" the old lady did not censure him but instead hastened into his room wielding a house slipper and smacked the creature flat as a penny.

When he said of a boy at school, "What a ass that Jim Macready is," she said, "What *an* ass he is. And so is his mother."

One night, when he heard the hair-raising lamentations of a wandering bloodhound and shook her awake, saying, "What in the flying shit is that!?" she said, half-asleep, "It's just Jasper, got loose again. Go back to bed."

On this one point of language, he was inveterate. She lost the battle, just as his mother had years ago. Mary would say, "Jack! Where did you hear that ugly word?" Then they would both look at Moreland.

Of all of Sister Beatrice's hundred little rules the worst was that he was never allowed near horses. She herself was terrified of them and was sure a horse would ultimately break the child's neck. But the interdiction carried a certain cruelty, too, because the boy had been around horses all his life. He was like a baker forbidden to enter his own kitchen lest he burn his fool hands. At first Jack obeyed her, but soon it was common in the late afternoon to see him standing at the fence around the outfitter's yard speaking quietly to his own horse, a small six-year-old Morgan with a pretty face. On school days they would stand together like sleepwalkers, two young things insensible of the barrier between them, the Morgan's grassy breath on his face, the boy's hands stroking the soft muzzle. Strictly speaking, this animal no longer belonged to Jack, having been donated by the old lady to Wilson's Outfitters, along with most of his other things. After all, a kid owns nothing, not legally in any case.

Thom Wilson had always shown a pragmatic interest in Jack. As Moreland's son he came with good credentials; in fact, he was one of the only kids in town who had any practical skills at all. The outfitter called him "wasted bloody goods in the company of old biddies," as he often said to the nun, cigar protruding from his mouth. Well known in town and beyond as an acid-tongued curmudgeon, never to be crossed lest you wanted even more abuse, his rudeness seemed truly to shock her. At first she had tried to argue the point with Wilson, stammering a little, tried to convince him how much better the boy's life was now, with predictably awful results.

Unless Wilson was on a trek, leading tourists or surveyors or painters out into the more remote regions of the park, treks that required horses and gear and hundreds of pounds of food and ammunition, trips that could last weeks, he was always in town, usually walking the main street, always hungover. As a result, unfriendly interactions between them were many, and over time Sister Beatrice and Wilson became ferocious with one another. Each squabble seemed to spur them deeper into mutual disrespect. Sometimes they made for each other like fighting cocks, hurrying across the street with one object in mind: to have the last word. The boy had no experience with this kind of loathing, and he watched in distress as they fought over him.

"I was raised by nuns like you," Wilson said one day, "and I have the scars to prove it. You're hypocrites, the lot of you."

"Insolent, ignorant idiot!" she spat back. "Brain of a

caveman." And she stormed her way down the street with the boy's wrist in her hand.

It was during one such spat that Jack learned his father had left a pile of his own belongings with the nun, and that she'd got rid of everything without consulting him.

"Dumped them at my door like so much trash," said Wilson, "just to make sure the kid can't use them. It's mean of you."

"He has no use for a wretched saddle."

"No, you saw to that. Thanks to you he has nothing to ride, except your broomstick."

And they were off again.

In her house, Jack's life was circumscribed by rules. After two almost reasonable debates between them, she finally persuaded him not to pull his mattress onto the floor and look out the window at the stars, or to climb onto the porch roof, dangle his legs over the edge, and watch night animals go about their rounds. Nor was he allowed to sit on the back stoop in the late afternoons with a book on his knees and read, as had been his habit in his previous life. More than anything else, this interdiction against reading bewildered him. There was a library on the second floor filled with her late father's books and papers but the boy had been forbidden to touch any of them. The room might as well have been a museum. Of course, he read them anyway, in secret and at night.

Jack suspected that she hadn't loved her father, or that he'd disliked her, or perhaps both were true. Still, she behaved as if the room itself carried contagion, an ugliness she hoped to shield him from. She was also a heavy sleeper and snored ferociously, so Jack knew when to tiptoe into the library, his bare feet enjoying the luxurious carpet as he considered the rows and rows of spines.

One wall was lined with identical tomes on corporate law, their leather covers the exact shade of uncooked liver. Nothing much to identify one volume from another except a strange system of lettering that stopped at LXII. There were banking journals in hardcover, leaflets and pamphlets stacked horizontally, dictionaries in various languages, a biblical concordance but no Bible. The only Bible in the house rested on his benefactor's bedside table. Her father, it appeared, had been a secular man. A man who did indeed care about money.

Jack found a shelf full of books that were clearly hers: an enormous anatomy book, a Martindale pharmacopoeia, a medical textbook with a well-thumbed and dog-eared section on toxicity, three small books on needles and dosages. There was a thick black notebook full of her beautiful handwriting — he flipped the pages quickly, saw a flicker of Latin and repeated nursing code: *po, Tr, tr, digitalis, q4h, q8h, elix, HCN, aconitum*. The boy imagined this was what a book full of coded war transmissions might look like. He plunked it back on the shelf and poked disinterestedly at commercial pamphlets on patented herbals and nervines.

Still, he was impressed by the number of common flowers and weeds that could kill a man, blind him, stop his heart. Or simply produce a rash and give him the shits. Thanks to the anatomy book, he discovered that he had two bones in his forearm, not one. He held his arm up to the moonlight and swivelled his fist, testing the theory. Deer also have two such bones, but elk have only one. Jack Boulton pondered the purpose of two designs for the same thing. He himself had helped butcher both types of animal, held those severed limbs in his hands without giving the least thought to such a question.

At first the anatomy book charmed him. The knob of humerus in the shoulder, the armature of muscle across the abdomen, the scraggly bones in the human foot, it all captivated him — until he encountered a frightful etching of a skinless, bisected human head, its whorls of sinus and picket fence of molars. Thereafter, he avoided the medical shelf entirely.

Closer to the old man's desk he found the real books, titles any sane person would want to read. A small cabinet held a set of nearly thirty outrageously exciting volumes by a William Le Queux, most of which admittedly proved the nun's point. Those novels were full of military invasions, secret societies, explosive devices, German spies, and sex — lots of sex. Frustratingly, the pornographic scenes were so cloaked in euphemism he was forced to guess at what exactly was going on: *Gunnison manifested himself before the girl, to her obvious shock and delight.* Jack struggled to divine the meaning of *manifested*. Some books had been read so many times by the departed father it was obvious where the good parts were. *The Temptress* flopped open naturally to the most salacious pages, so this was the volume the boy snuck away with him to the privy.

At the schoolhouse, Jack had seen other boys furtively sharing dime westerns and illustrated detective magazines. One had an implausible painting on its cover showing Jesse James in full gallop rescuing a woman from a sniper. This booty was hoarded and used as currency among the older boys, but no one ever offered them to Jack Boulton, he'd had to look over shoulders to see them. The younger children were routinely pushed away, palm to the face. Still he yearned to read those magazines, but nothing was ever handed to him for his perusal. He himself was like foreign currency in that schoolyard, without value or purpose.

Some time ago, when life was still normal, his father had taken him aside and, with a burning face, bumbled through a qualified endorsement of self-abuse. It was perfectly natural, he said, and until the boy was married it was a pretty good solution. But he had also promised shame and dishonour if the kid didn't keep it stealthy. Moreland had said, "For god's sake, don't let your mother see you. Women don't know anything about it."

Moreland had been so patently miserable during this conversation that the boy had simply nodded meekly and kept his questions to himself.

Jack reached down *The Perfumed Garden of Cheikh Nefzaoui, a Manual of Arab Erotology* by R. G. Burton, but the title's beautiful calligraphy made him suspect that perhaps this was a lady's book, and then he fixed on the repellent word *Manual* and shoved it back on the shelf unread. Instead he moved on to more promising titles like *The Tiger Hunters*, *Kidnapping in the Pacific*, *The Coral Island*, and *The Dog Crusoe*.

On the south wall was *The Twelve Caesars*, which turned out to be a gossipy catalogue of Roman political intrigue, weird omens, innuendo, filthy tricks, war, murder, and lunacy. *When the people cheered the team he opposed, Caligula cried in fury, "Oh, that all of Rome had a single neck to break!"* This wall held hundreds of books organized into a gorgeous hash of subjects. A history of English architecture, twin volumes on mathematics as applied to the motion of the stars, a shelf entirely devoted to whaling, a little volume of highly violent

Viking sagas, tales of the Scottish clan wars, a complete
compendium of Greek myths, "chats" on Japanese prints, a
book on Egyptian mummies.

Best of all was the natural encyclopedia filled with
gorgeous colour plates, entitled *Brehm's Life of Animals*, which
enumerated all the creatures of the known world. It was a
great, heavy book, and the boy adored it. The cover illustration
was an etching: the face and chest and paws of an enormous
reclining African lion, imperial and sober, whose expression
was one of intense, benign focus on the reader. Some nights
the boy took down this book simply to gaze into those eyes.
The lion's body was surrounded by garlands made of snakes,
leaves and vines, snails and strange fish and butterflies. A
squirming fecundity of life surrounded that calm animal.
Every few pages there was an illustration of such depthless
beauty that the boy wondered if this volume might be the
only one of its kind in the world, an irreplaceable treasure.

He was familiar with the spines of each of these books,
had sat cross-legged in the library's window-well and read
their pages under the moon. The existence of the Vikings
was welcome news, and he wondered why no one had ever
told him about such people. But having never seen a desert,
Jack found the notion of Egyptian mummies implausible. No
dead body lasted a thousand years. In this climate, the only
one he'd ever known, four hundred pounds of dead elk was
nothing more than a ribcage in one year, gone in two. He
gazed at the photos of desiccated faces and grinning teeth
and decided it was just a sideshow gambit. One night he read
Treasure Island all the way through, unable to stop, almost to
the point of being caught by Sister Beatrice as she rose in the
morning. He read *The Coral Island* with rigid attention, riveted

by the idea of a cannibal princess, the brilliant triumvirate of capable boys, the weird animals they ate. He committed to memory the hero's method of piloting a two-masted pirate ship all on his own — that seemed plausible to Jack, possibly even useful someday. *Alone! in the midst of the wide Pacific.* Three castaway boys thrown together by adversity, as mutually protective and inseparable as brothers.

Jack Boulton had always wanted a brother. He'd asked his mother for one, and argued his point earnestly, the way a man might suggest to his family that they build a shed. She'd said, "Would a sister do?" After a moment he'd nodded yes in a way that meant no, it would not do at all.

A brother. Just one. He'd even imagined that boy's face, pictured his confident gait as he walked, divined the sound of his laugh. Sometimes, as he fell asleep, Jack believed that other boy was really out there somewhere in the world, and the two of them were communing, as if everything was possible and nothing of consequence stood between them.

Some books were beautiful to him just for the way they sounded in his head. He would wander the architecture of a certain sentence and consider things for a long time. Later, he might try to recite passages by heart and whisper to himself as he worked in the kitchen: *Blind Pew struck at them left and right and they cursed the miscreant and tried to wrest the stick from his grasp.* The boy thinking: *miscreant.*

Many nights, however, the insomniac did nothing. He had even given up kneeling at his window and scanning the snow for his father's footprints. Instead he sat upright in his bed as the shadows of leaves trembled on the bedroom wall, gazed down his long legs to his bony feet and wished himself somewhere else.

→ *Six*

MORELAND CROSSED INTO Canada on the rolling treed plain west of Roosville. For several days he seemed only to climb, struggling through plains scrub, then meandering up a rock-strewn river valley until he found level ground, the margins of what looked to be a failing logging town named Elko, and to his relief, the railroad track he'd been hoping to see. He trotted to the line and followed it northward.

Snow when it came was almost welcome. Moreland knew very well how to thrive in it, and snow often meant softer weather. The sky went white and the air with it, the golden sun at midday was lost in haze. He made good progress in the light hours but when dark came it was total, so he dug a hole in the snow and made his bed in the hollow, curled up on pine boughs like a wintering squirrel, just as he had done so often as a child.

He'd taught Jack exactly how to do this in case someday necessity forced him to sleep outside for a night. They'd curled up together just outside the cabin, and the boy had called it a snow fort. That night Mary had come out to check on them a dozen times, peering into their little white cave.

Moreland remembered her smooth cheeks half-lit by lantern light.

• • •

SNOW FELL GENTLY for days, a week. In the hollows it was over his head. He'd stolen some good snowshoes strung with babiche, and he stood floating over those hollows, giddy and weightless, a man walking on water. When they weren't in use the shoes were strapped toe-down to his pack, so as he went, he resembled a moth.

Mostly he followed the rail lines because they were deforested on both sides, and because the tracks were level and cleared by the trains themselves, the engines so heavy they blew through anything short of an avalanche. Some days he would hear a train in the distance and he'd jog quickly off the tracks; a minute later a train would roar past, great white rooster tails rolling up its sides, the world thick with snow thereafter, the horn bawling, and Moreland ghostly and staggering and inhaling snow.

Two days beyond Elko, he heard a light twang along the rails and turned to see two maintenance men on a little railway handcar approaching in the white distance. He stepped aside and watched them come. One by one they let go of the lever they were pumping and the vehicle slowed as they neared him, the lever see-sawing on its own. It looked like they might speak to him, but they just sailed by with raised mittens. The sight of an unemployed man walking the line was not unusual, and not at all welcome. And in any case, they had little to offer any traveller.

The next day at noon Moreland saw in the distance another handcar, this one unattended on a siding, a small, black, tilted thing. He worked his way toward and was almost beside the vehicle before he spotted a slim figure perched high up a telegraph pole, balanced perfectly like a trapeze artist, elbow over a crossbeam, one boot braced on a wire. Every pole behind Moreland was cleared of snow while every pole ahead supported a heavy cap four feet deep. The man wore logging spurs to help him walk up the poles, and he brandished a stick twice as long as his own body for breaking up snow caps. He said, "You sure can move on those things. I never got the habit."

Moreland goggled up at the telegraph man, stupid with fatigue. "Are you knocking the snow off?"

"Yes and no." The man grinned. "I'm communing with the dead."

"You're what?"

"Well, I got telegraphs coming through. People needing to talk." The man scraped his cleats on one of the cold black wires.

"That so?"

"Yessir. And I got transcontinental telephone calls. I have the dispatcher, okay? Up at Corbin. He's listening in on every damn thing . . . and now I'm wondering what time it is. I think it's lunchtime."

Moreland nodded but he wasn't following much of this. This man's mind was like a grasshopper, it moved abruptly in unexpected directions.

"Hendrik's the important part. He's the operator, and he has to talk to the trains, in the right order, okay? Or else they butt heads."

Moreland became aware of himself standing between the rails, and despite the unearthly quiet, through which no train could ever travel without his hearing it long in advance, he trotted off the tracks out of harm's way. He stood by the tilted handcar and looked up. In closing the distance, he now saw clearly that the maintenance man was quite young. He looked British or Scandinavian, something blond and prone to blushing, and he was at most seventeen. He was burned by the sun and excessively bearded. Moreland removed his pack and settled it with a sigh on the floor of the handcar, rolled his shoulders. He said, "How often do trains come through?"

The boy seemed to ignore him. He plunged his stick through the snowcap and let it balance there.

"So," he said, "if a wire breaks under this weight of snow, and it *would* break somewhere around here, all communication stops. They'd keep sending their Morse code, checking their watches, just like they do every day. They might suspect something was wrong, but they'd get no signal from down the line, no warning. That would be my fault. Are you hungry?"

"Not at all."

"I am."

Snow fell softly and built up everywhere, on the trees, the handcar, the boy's toque, the shoulders of Moreland's coat.

The kid said, "Hendrik has been drinking again, is all. People worry. So I keep a watch down here."

"Where are the dead in all of this?"

The boy looked down on Moreland like he might be dim. "They're talking all the time."

"Are they."

"Never stop. And it's all bad news. That's how it is now. Are you from round here?"

"Yes and no."

The kid grinned, "That's funny. I guess you're only ever exactly where you are. For instance, I'm up here. And you are down there. My brother is in France, dead as a doornail."

Moreland's face fell.

The boy pawed at the snow stick and watched it wobble. "We didn't like each other very much. But blood is blood."

"Son," Moreland said, "where is your mother?"

The kid shook his head in that gentle way that meant she too was gone. He said, "That message about Colin went right under my foot that day. I think about it sometimes."

They listened to the air around them, the quiet of falling snow. White forest, white sky, the white snowshoe tracks slowly fading from sight. Moreland didn't believe the weight of a snowcap on a telegraph pole was any worse threat to communications than the maintenance man's own boot. He said, "Can you hear anything, any sound on those wires?"

"Sometimes I think I do. Just a hiss, or maybe it's more of a little grinding sound."

Moreland looked up the long, graceful arc of the tracks and the black trees of the telegraph poles. "Well," he said, "I'll push on now."

"Where the hell to?" The boy swung a leather mitten north. "Up there's the middle of nowhere. It's a long way to any kind of town."

Moreland said, "I know." He drew two cans of green beans from his knapsack and lay them on the seat of the handcar. He shouldered his load again and cinched up the leather waistband, then he see-sawed from foot to foot on his snowshoes, working the cording.

"What's your name?"

"Sven."

"Do they pay you much for this?"

"They don't pay anybody much for anything."

"How many more poles today?"

"Eighteen."

"Then what?"

The boy laughed. "Start again at the beginning."

Seven

FOR TWO MONTHS Moreland had been zigzagging from mine to logging camp to small town. In each he would pilfer anything that seemed practical or expensive. He was working hard on his plan, making his way steadily north, heading for his son. Though he had made his way down to St. Croy across the open lowlands, he was forced now to keep instead to mountain passes and canyons and hollows. In years past he'd wandered and hunted in this area and he knew it well enough, remembered the terrain — for after all, a town may spring up and grow where none was before, a road may be diverted, bridges rot and fall into the river. But a mountain will always look the same, and the canyon at its foot will not move; the land is as unchanging as the stars, and just as useful for navigation.

Before every one of his burglaries, he'd scouted and camped first, watched from a distance until he knew the feel of the place, knew when people rose and went to bed, when the work shifts started and ended, where the money was kept.

Now his knapsack was so loaded with spoils the leather straps cut into his shoulders. The money was paper and light as air; he could keep that and drop the rest if he needed to. He rested when he could in any sheltered place. He ate his stolen food. Sometimes he even had chocolate. He knew the approximate date and figured the day of the week more or less accurately, and from this he tallied how many days were left before he could see his son.

One cloudless night in late December he began to taste coal dust on his lips. The Ridgerunner lay his knapsack down and clambered up a ridge where he could scan the valley, and finally, he located the railway line that cut through the trees. There it was: a balloon loop, end of the line, a kind of teardrop shape in the tracks where southbound trains would turn like snakes coiling in on themselves, reverse direction, and run north again.

This was the southernmost tip of the CPR's line, just outside Corbin, where they took on coal before heading north. His assessment of the day of the week must also have been correct because the train was there, exactly where it should be at this hour, motionless and glowing. The engine was almost facing him, therefore he was north of it, and close enough to see the black spew of the tipple pouring coal into the hoppers, the figures of men walking the tracks with lanterns held low, checking the wheels and journal boxes, and in all that light and distant noise he saw coal dust curling into the air, sheets of it running along the ground like black snow blown on the wind.

Moreland danced a little jig of his own making. Without a map except the one in his head he had found Coal Mountain, a deposit so massive and remote it was worth the cost of a spur line and was known to miners as "the big show." Here was his ride north. He ran downhill to his belongings, heaved them up and ran jangling down the valley, right between the rails, until he was forced to stop and gasp for air. He unbuttoned his fly and peed into the gravel, gazing up as he did at the suffusion of stars overhead. Those unnamed peaks stood like gunwales on either side of him, and he was an ant crawling up the keel.

In ten minutes he had worked himself half a mile north and was concealed on the blind side of a bend in the tracks, right where the forest swung out in a kind of elbow and would screen him from the engineer's sight until the last moment. Still crawling on its way out of Corbin, the train would groan past him and he would swing up and ride a hopper car all the way up the rise to McGillivray Loop, where the tracks forked. There the engineer would slow and stop so the switchman could shift the track for the western line toward Michel and Sparwood, and in those few minutes, with the train motionless and the men occupied, Moreland would jump off.

Now he hummed a song to Mary and the boy, just as he used to do, as if they were there with him. He slid the knapsack to the ground. He took out a small apple and rubbed it on his lapel.

Moreland knelt and put his ear to the track, listening for sound along the line. The metal was cold and inert. He pressed his hands to the gravel between the ties and felt the ground for vibration, but . . . nothing.

His breath was the only sound, and in that darkness it seemed too loud. Was he the only one breathing? He stood and listened hard. For days he had felt as if something was pacing along just behind him, some shy creature following his scent.

William Moreland had spent more than three-quarters of his life like this: outside, alone, listening to the world, carrying his life on his back, riding his own uncommon instincts, in bad weather, in bad light, in sickness and in health. This was where it had brought him.

Mary had said, *The horse can't take three. Come back for me.* She'd said, *I'll be fine.*

STRANGE HOW QUIETLY it came, whispering along the line. A leisured drumming in the distance. He pressed a boot heel against the track and felt the train coming.

At first, it didn't even look like light, just the trees impending out of the darkness of their own accord, a palisade that looked miles long; then each branch resolved, hackles rising, until the engine's headlamp floated around the foot of the mountain and its long body followed. It seemed to labour forward, chuffing and radiant, blowing light through the trees, light that ran in lines and streaks, and now it was coming straight on. Everything was quaking in its own shadow. Moreland left the tracks and skidded down the slope, scrambled his knapsack onto his back, cinched it up tight, and braced himself behind a tree.

It was foolish to look into that blinding light, but he did anyway. The engine had three headlamps, not one, and immediately he could see how fast it was moving and how modern it was compared to the trains he used to ride. The rails were purring against the ties, then the plates began to rattle and small runnels of stones to cascade down to him where he hid.

Too soon he forced himself into a run, moving laterally up the slope, disastrously sluggish, wading in the loose gravel. He was washed in light and his shadow shrank to nothing under his pounding boots. Over his shoulder he winced into the glare, tried to aim for the third car, maybe the fourth — was there a handle, a ladder?

The horn erupted, and it was colossal. He couldn't help but flinch, couldn't correct the failure in his angle as he ran. And then the heavy engine sucked past him. His shadow and those of the trees and the entire world swung violently backward, strafing south, and now he could see clearly the cars that ran ahead of him, chattering along beside him in identical repetition, not a handhold or a ladder on any of them. And anyway, it was moving too fast, roaring past him, gaining speed.

William Moreland skidded to a stop, wheeling his arms and sobbing, the ground drumming softly through his boots, and the rail dipping and rising with each passing wheel. The acrid stink of oil and coal and something else burning blew over him and stung his eyes, and finally there came an end to it, a trailing last car he could not have caught if he'd tried a dozen times. He stood and watched his son draw farther away while the horn raked the distances, speaking only to him.

As it had arrived, so it departed, shrinking to a soft rattle until there was nothing but a glow, a hiss along the rails, then not even that. William Moreland sank to his haunches and put a shaking hand over his eyes. He slid onto his side and curled into a ball. The only light in the world seemed to be inside his head, an image burned there: the engineer in his high cab, mouth open in a bellow of disbelief, looking right at him.

It was a long time before Moreland uncurled slowly like a worm, stripped himself of his burden, and stood. He squared his shoulders and spat. The next train wouldn't come for days. From his bag he took out another apple and bit into it, he puckered and winced until it was nothing but core, then, in impotent rage, he whipped it overhand against the nearest tree, where it burst and the bits fell lightly to the snow. William Moreland hefted his bag and resumed walking.

HE PASSED THE NEXT day in smouldering self-reproach, pacing up the line in his snowshoes at a slow trot, making up time. Grinding inside himself, pushing his old body as hard as he could, the way a monk flagellates his flesh. The expiation that comes with pain. As a younger man he would have had that train; there was a time he could outrun anything.

Toward dusk his tracks crossed many others heading southwest; he counted maybe eight wolves, passed by here not long ago. He unpacked the old repeater rifle and swung it along as he ran. At least it would make one hell of a noise. Aware of himself running like a prey animal, he stopped in dread to turn back, scan the open rail line for scattered movement, but he saw nothing, and after a moment the gun ceased to tremble in his fist.

The moon came out full, so he kept going, no longer jogging but striding now, and soon he had made the switch that split the tracks, exactly where he had intended to jump off the train in the first place. Taking the right of the fork he cut northeast and, finally, he made the McGillivray Loop itself, and there he entered the echoing, snowless hollow of a railway tunnel. This was what they called an avalanche shed, and it was a shortcut, a gently curved tunnel that had been blasted through the foot of the mountain. Trains can't handle steep grades, so sometimes the company would decide to cut right through rock to maintain a mostly level course.

Here he paced along until he was unable to see either entrance or exit, he was hidden from sight, and he bent double and breathed out. The sound of a man sighing echoed along the flat walls, and when he *hoo-hoo*'d, the tunnel seemed to *hoo* along with him in syncopating rhythm. The roof above was sloped, the better to guide snow and rockslides over the tracks and away downhill, and here the tracks were clean, the gravel dry. How long since he had been able to bed down in anything man-made? He sat with his back against a timber support and rested in that quiet, aware of the constant suck of air through the tunnel, aware of his own boots lying alongside innumerable bootprints of other men, likely track walkers or hunters. He'd seen a few hoofed tracks, and just inside the mouth, the vaguest old trace of cougar paws, signs that the cat had paced and peered, unwilling to venture inside more than a few yards, spooked by the confinement.

Thus motionless and sunk in thought Moreland spent the night under a roof of sorts, during which he slept not at all. He did not shut his eyes. He barely blinked.

⇥ *Eight*

AT FIRST LIGHT he rose stiffly and looked toward the bright mouth of the avalanche shed. No train, no men walking the lines. He took up his things and passed under the ribs of the tunnel one by one, and out the mouth, a man leaving the belly of a whale. The sun was burning cold and blue, and Moreland stood there blinking at it. He went to the nearest tree and scratched his back against it like a bear, then strapped on his snowshoes and went on again.

The next afternoon he spread out his tarp and sat on it with legs akimbo, repairing his worn gear with meticulous attention. Then he drew things from the depths of his bag and held them up Yorick-like and interrogated their actual worth: to him, to the boy, to anyone sensible. Most items failed the test. Of course he would keep the wad of mixed bills the size of a loaf of bread. Mostly American but some British, French, and even a smattering of what looked like Chinese. There were a few tools and an admirable knife. But twenty rolls of small coins? Three heavy gold pocket watches? Two pairs of gilt spectacles, now glassless and bent? What could he ever do with them? The strangest object was the delicate ivory Chinese dragon, made of dozens of carved sections, its body the length of a rolling pin. He'd lifted it from the window of a grand house in Kalispell that had a poor idea of locks. It was fantastically beautiful, and it looked alive — the only reason he had taken it. Thinking of Mary with her dark hair falling down her back, legs curved around the baby as he lay on the bed, dangling bright things over his face; and the boy, tiny, earnest, wordless, toothless, grasping at them. So Moreland had compromised a back door of that grand house, tracked snow over its Persian carpets, and liberated the dragon.

Now, seated on his oilcloth in the snow, hoping to get to Blairmore before dark, he held the slithering ivory thing before him. Its jaws and spine and legs, even its talons were moveable, carefully articulated, detailed, perfect. A dazzling piece of art, surely worth a mint, but utterly unsaleable outside a big city, and without purpose or interest to a boy about to turn thirteen.

Moreland left the tracks littered with coins and spectacles and watches. Come spring someone would get a nice surprise. The dragon he hung from an aspen tree like a lost hat, and looked at it. Its whiskered old face and gaping mouth. It had come all the way from China only to end up here. Sooner or later a train engineer might wonder what species of thing hung there, and after the third or fourth week of wondering, might slow down to look. Moreland watched the wind shiver its scales for a moment, and then turned away, back to his tarp.

The old Henry rifle lay at his feet, and now he withdrew from the bottom of his bag a scabbard, a kind of sheath made to hold and protect a rifle. This one was originally made for another gun, and it was the ugliest such thing he'd ever seen. That was why he'd chosen it: ugliness was camouflage. First, the scabbard was made of felt in a horrid shade of shrimp pink. The kind of felt they made sports pennants from. It had a long, ridiculous doe-hide fringe that hung along the barrel, and the name PEARL had been calligraphed on the fabric in cracked white paint. It was the kind of thing a lady shooter might win at a fair, her name or monogram painted on it as part of the prize. It was also the kind of thing said lady shooter would immediately put away somewhere she didn't have to look at it, which was why Moreland had found it in a basement in Whitefish. Second, the gun was an ancient lever-action repeater, a model last popular when Lincoln was president. At some point during its overlong life someone had shortened the barrel, probably to reduce its weight, which would also decrease its accuracy, rendering it almost totally without appeal to any hunter.

With great care, William Moreland slit a seam along the pink scabbard, and clawed out the wool stuffing. In its place he forced in the fourteen thousand one hundred eighty-one dollars in paper bills in their varying denominations and varying national currencies; he didn't care how they compared, it was all money for the boy. Then using the point of his knife as an awl he made holes along the slit, teased threads from his coat through each pair of holes, and tied knots. The result was as appalling as a civil war suture.

He held it up, looked at it.

He walked away and looked at it from a distance. The word *Pearl* glared like icing on the pink felt. Yes, it was the least appealing gun he'd ever seen, repellent to thieves.

If he was lucky he would see Jack before Christmas. He would bring the boy the biggest present he'd ever been given.

He'd tell Jack to keep it hidden, keep it safe, and then he'd head back out to get more cash.

The old saying was: never keep all your eggs in one basket. Well, he wouldn't. Having burgled the hell out of Idaho and Montana, he figured he had enough for one trip. He'd drop off the fourteen thousand dollars, turn right around and start again empty-handed, work his way through the Crowsnest Pass until he had exhausted those mining towns, and when he returned again to Banff, perhaps by March, perhaps with an equal amount of money, Jack Boulton would finally have what neither of his parents had ever had: the power to choose the direction he wished his life to go.

Moreland knew what the nun would think of all that. By now she must have an idea of it. If only he hadn't admitted his own name, in a state of exhaustion, to a stranger. The fact of it still stunned him.

BY NOW HE WAS deep into the mountains. Each night he walked away from camp, threw a rope over a tree limb and hauled his goods into the air, away from himself and away from bears. Years ago in British Columbia he'd known a man who had tied his food to the main tent pole, so that when the black bear came — as anyone could have told him it would — the first thing it did was trample the breath out of him, then it dragged food, tent, and man along the ground for ten yards, trying to make off with it, while the man screeched like a rat in a cloth bag. Moreland did not carry a tent, for he didn't want the weight. Instead, each night he rolled himself in a tarp so his head was covered and he waited for sleep to overtake him. But hours would pass and his thoughts would not stop, so most nights, unable to tolerate even the confinement of a thin sheet of oilcloth, he thrashed himself out of his bed and stood panting.

A hand pressed to the breast of his coat, he imagined his son's head laid there, his fingers on that soft hair.

Nine

CHRISTMAS CREPT INTO town bringing red ornaments. Fancy bows and streamers appeared randomly, store by store, some dangling from streetlamps or horse hitches, all of them frozen and stiff as tin. A teen on horseback came down the snowy main street dragging a forty-foot conifer by its severed trunk and made for the government building across the river, leaving behind him a long scuff in the snow spangled with pine cones. Officialdom was celebrating. Jack watched the tree go across the bridge, flanked by local dogs.

On Christmas morning the nun snuck downstairs with a gift in her hand, planning to place it on the table beside his bowl and spoon, where he would find it when he rose, only to discover him standing at the stove, already cooking their breakfast. So stunned was she that she simply handed over the present to him without a word and sat on her chair, watching him open the wrapping paper.

It was a hardbound book with an image on the cover stamped in foil of a cross-legged boy in short pants reading a book, presumably this exact book. On the spine were the words *A Child's History of the World*.

"Happy Christmas, Charles," she said and there was uncertainty in her voice.

"Thank you," he said, laying the book on the counter. "I like it very much."

In fact, he'd already read the book and found it dull. She had taken it out of her father's library, wrapped it, and given it to him as if it were new. But Jack Boulton didn't mind; it was sensible of her, and given her feelings about that room, it showed surprising generosity. He was grateful it wasn't yet another shirt.

"This is for you," he said, and placed something small on the table next to her bowl.

She took it up and held it in her palm. It was a carved bird, made of pinewood. "Did *you* make this?"

"Yup."

"Oh, it's beautiful."

He leaned over her shoulder, trying to see the thing as she was seeing it, assessing his own handiwork. To avoid the problem of delicate legs and feet he had fashioned the figure as if the bird were nesting, wings folded across its back, body settled over its feet; and he'd made sure its head was turned to the side, so she could place it on a shelf and it would seem to be always looking at her.

"It's the prettiest thing I've ever seen," she lied.

She ran a finger along the Y line of the crossed wings, and over the innumerable nicks he'd scored in the wood to suggest the overlay of chest feathers.

"It's supposed to be a Cooper's hawk," he said, "but I guess maybe it just looks like any old bird."

She swallowed, and her eyes were welling.

Jack saw the turmoil in her and turned back to the stove, which was already beginning to lose heat, smoke, and otherwise delay breakfast.

She looked at the bird for a long time, and then said, "But where did you get the knife?"

Immediately, Jack regretted the gift, for he knew he must now either lie and say he'd removed his own knife from its hiding place in her father's library, a place he was forbidden to go, or tell her what had really happened. With deep resignation he said, "Wilson let me borrow his."

He saw her eyes narrow and her mouth draw into a line. "I see," she said.

He waited for more, but there was nothing. After a long moment, she forced out, "Thank you. It's beautiful." She set the carving on the table and looked at it, and Jack, ladling eggs onto plates, watched her. He figured she'd forgive him by afternoon, but it took until evening.

THE NEXT THURSDAY the nun had him bundled up in wool, and as usual when doing the shopping, her small hand gripped his sleeve, the better for him to right her should she slide on ice. It was the kind of weather that made Jack pull off his sweater gingerly to avoid the snap of static electricity all over his body — no way to stop his hair from standing up on his skull like a fright wig. After days of gentle snow the mercury had withered in the glass and now it was a bright and windless afternoon. That was the day Jack Boulton got his first sight of the prisoners.

Together he and the nun stepped out of the pharmacist's, where she had stocked up on supplies, just in time to see a long flatbed sleigh passing down the snowy main street like some bleak Christmas float cut loose from a parade. Eight guards flanked the spectacle, bayonets affixed, and two local men led the horses, enormous black animals that jerked their heads and blew in apprehension at the motorcars, their chains chiming in the frozen air. Riding the flatbed with legs a-dangle was the work gang, two dozen men in their wool caps, dark coats, and unfashionable moustaches, looking for all the world like depressed elves, murmuring together, watching the low buildings float by. They went past the Anglican minister's house. Past the church with its nativity scene, the grocer's windowpanes opaque with steam and lacings of frost. They floated right past Jack Boulton's unblinking eyes.

"Oh no," he murmured, for he felt sure he was about to see his father sitting among those men.

"Austrians," she said. "Prisoners of war out on a work detail. Not a word of English between them."

Nearby, a gaggle of truant children took up a sobered, thoughtful pose, studying the enemy up close. The sleigh floated down the avenue, proceeding under taut ropes strung across the roadway from which hung stiff and frozen Union Jacks. A few of the prisoners turned their weathered faces up to gaze at those flags, staring into the glitter of falling snow, their breath stitching out into the air. The horses *ching-ching*ed slowly past the café, where free citizens sat on swivel stools and enjoyed hot breakfasts. On the street unfriendly faces watched them pass. Intrigued tourists followed them along the boardwalk. The local jobless glowered.

The boy, too, paced the sleigh, past the hotel, past the first cross street, the nun bobbling along as he dragged her with him. They went as far as the second cross street, and here the drovers urged the great horses into a left turn onto a path heading to the river, the sleigh groaning a wide arc, the skids strafing fans in the snow. The show was over.

But Jack yearned to follow them, to see where they were

going, and he swung on the nun and begged her until she conceded and allowed herself to be drawn toward the river. Here there was nothing left of town but a couple of cabins with empty front porches, shutters closed against the cold; dogs trotting away down the empty river road, frightened by the great sleigh and all the men. The river cut a serpentine path along the valley, and it was smooth and level, frozen to two and a half feet this time of year, looking much like a grand thoroughfare through town.

A guard bellowed and the prisoners hopped down and limped on numb feet out of harm's way, where they huddled together. Jack knew his father was not among them, but he could not stop searching their faces and postures for something familiar, some sign of William Moreland. The horses were led carefully round into a backwards motion til they faced away from the river, then the drovers pushed at the animals' chests so they stepped backwards, backwards, and the sleigh slid gently out onto the river and rested there on the ice. They all waited and listened. There came no hiss, no sound of cracking ice, just crows in the trees, their calls echoing. And Jack, with his short lifetime's knowledge of animals and rivers and cold, knew why they were doing this: if the sleigh broke through the ice, the animals would be safe on dry land, the drovers ready to undo the leads or cut the traces if necessary. Better to let the sled sink into the river than lose the horses. For there are always carpenters and cartwrights with enough skill to construct a new wagon. And prisoners, if they have the skill, will do it for free. But who among them could resurrect a horse?

Within minutes the prisoners were spread out on the river with augers and saws. Dark shapes hunching over their jagged tools. They drilled holes, slid the long ice saws into those holes, and working in twos, pressed bellies to the handles and worked, looking less like men cutting ice than men mowing a lawn.

"What are they doing?" Jack said.

"Well," she considered, "some years the town hires an engineer and the men erect an ice maze. Some people call it an ice palace. Just a pretty thing they build in the middle of town, a last hurrah for winter." She watched for a moment, then said, "I suppose they're using prisoners now."

The sing of wet metal, the river's current bubbling in the many boreholes, the slam of the ice hooks into each block of ice, just before it dropped with a *gloop* and bobbed there in its ragged hole. Men seized the ice hooks and hauled, then dragged their blocks one-handed to the waiting sleigh, working together to lever them onto the flatbed. One man moved too fast and dropped his block so it cracked into three pieces. A guard peeved at him in English. Jack began to shiver and his teeth to chatter, the long day beginning to wear on him and his melancholy taking over again, so the nun hauled him away from the river and back home.

Three days later the nun was proved right. The ice maze was finished, a remarkable bit of engineering and a frankly beautiful thing, with its little parapets and faux windows. Jack absolutely refused to go in there and be trapped with other screaming boys. Instead he watched dark shapes move inside the translucent walls. There it remained for a couple of weeks, dripping in the noon sun, freezing again at night; and as evening fell and the lanterns were lit inside the maze, human shapes leapt out so clear and distinct you could almost see faces. It wasn't much of a maze really, just a hallway bent into an S shape, off which ran a few dead ends. Still, when the Queen of Winter Carnival — a local figure skater with fabulous legs — entered the thing and did not exit for a long time, her call for help carried easily over the roofless walls and a buffalo stampede of men rushed in to rescue her.

The prisoners never got to enjoy their maze, except during the short time they were erecting it, following instruction bellowed out by a government engineer, and they were carted back out of town to their internment camp, back to work elsewhere, back out into the cold wilderness.

Lying sleepless that evening in his bed, Jack Boulton pondered the lives of these inmates. Surely they must suffer tormenting dreams of freedom, of their lost families, memories of a time when they could go about as they pleased, as dignified men. Such were his sour thoughts as the last of the sun faded away on the window sash and the long howl of a train sounded in the valley.

→ *Ten*

IN WANING DAYLIGHT a train rolled slowly into the town of Banff. The stationmaster strode out and stood on the platform, glanced at his watch, dropped it in a pocket, and lifted a mitten as the train came on. Wednesday was on schedule.

It rolled with slow caution across the vacant road into town and fetched up by the picturesque little station in a protracted screech of brakes and a besmirching cloud of oil and coal smoke. The engineer drew back his heavy door, unfolded his stiff body from the heated cab, and made for the stationhouse, empty lunchbox swinging in hand, an arthritic hitch to his gait.

On the treeward side of the train a boxcar door drew open and out of that narrow slit flew a packsack. Then the Ridgerunner's boots, his frozen legs, torso, and finally his head and rubbery arms slid to the ground like a birthing deer. He flailed there for a moment, then struggled into an almost human stance, hugged his bag, and hurried into the trees, where he sat on the nearest fallen pine and looked back at the frigid box he had ridden in. It had been like a meat locker in there with the door closed, worse with it open to the wind as the engine reached twenty-five miles an hour and choking black smoke sucked in through the opening. Now the engine idled and dozed by the station, its fourteen cars standing like a blind between him and the two men on the platform.

He assessed his physical condition — this was the first sight his son would have of him. By now he would look primordial, frightful, there was no question. He was sunburned, windburned, excessively bearded, had stinging red eyes, and was filthy in every respect. The boy had seen plenty, but this was too much. An even worse notion was that the good nun might catch sight of him. He did not know what her reaction might be. It was possible she would scream and wake the neighbourhood. For that matter the kid might scream.

So he started his ablutions. With handfuls of snow he shampooed his hair and beard and neck and chest and armpits and hands. In seconds he was dripping, bloodless with cold, soaked to the waistband. Ice ornaments dangled from his beard. He dragged his pack deeper into the trees to find fresh snow, plunged his face and hands into it and scrubbed as if to erase the last few months of his life, to bring himself back to something familiar, all through the simple application of pain. But he made the mistake of trying to stand upright too fast. For a moment he simply stood there, then his hearing went hollow, the blood left his head the way water sucks hard down a drain, and the entire world snapped off. The Ridgerunner dropped first to his knees and then to his bare chest, and lay with his cheek pressed to a bag full of money.

Eleven

COMING HOME SICK from school again, having thrown up during morning prayer, Jack was trudging up the front steps when he spotted bootprints in the snowy soil of the flowerbed. They seemed normal footprints, except for the man's unaccountable need to stand in a dead flowerbed exactly where a person might look up at a bedroom window. And then Jack saw one clear bootprint impressed on the snow — it had something inscribed on the heel, some mark. He back-walked down the steps and bent low over the trampled ground, reading the sign as a hunter might read tracks by a river. The man was smallish, with a long step to him, toes straight on. And he had tapped nails into his boot heels, the little nailheads forming letters: an *M* for the left foot, a *B* for the right. It was something his father had always done, to keep on the good side of luck.

Mary Boulton.

For a long, stunned moment Jack stood looking down at the proof. His father had been standing right there. And recently — the marks were fresh.

He was up in a second, running wildly about the property, touching marks on the ground, scrambling on, following his father's blurred trail, searching everywhere: in the stables, the garage, even the back porch by the kitchen where, brazenly, the man had paced and peered through gauzy window curtains the previous night. No question, William Moreland had been right here. But now he could not be found.

The rest of that afternoon she kept asking the boy what was wrong, did he not feel well? Jack Boulton stared with red eyes into the wood grain of the dinner table. She took his cold hand in hers but he would not speak. She dosed him with a tonic that made his head swim but did nothing to stop the hammering of his heart. He felt sure he was going to die, because it was already too late — his father had come to take him home, and he'd missed the moment, and now the man might be gone forever.

Long after dark the boy was curled into himself, pressing the heels of his hands to his eyes, when he heard a soughing sound as of some large animal moving through foliage. He jerked upright but saw nothing, just the familiar shadows of tree branches on his bedroom wall. Then a shadowform slid huge and elongate along the flowery wallpaper. The kid slid off his bed and hurried through that banded moonlight to the door of his bedroom, where he listened for her snores, then gently shut the door. There was no sound for a long time, but a dark shadow was moving at the left margin of the glass, exactly where a man might stand to look down on the child's now-empty bed. Then a body swung round to the right side of the window and a ghastly face appeared at the glass, a face so wild the boy's breath turned to stone in his lungs. Long tresses of hair, beard and moustache flowing together, a pair of burning eyes as of some Viking revenant sprung from a grave. It raised a filth-blackened finger to where its lips should be, and winked. Then William Moreland, so much smaller than his own shadow, nimbled his way through the boy's bedroom window.

Jack was wrapped around him before he was fully inside the room. The feel of that damp coat on the boy's cheek, the strong arms around him, the familiar pong of wet wool, the press of the man's rough hand at his temple.

"Now, come on," Moreland whispered, "there's no need to blubber."

The kid pushed away and glared up at Moreland, his face flaming. He hissed, "You *left* me."

"You knew I was coming back."

"I knew no such goddamn thing!"

"She told you our agreement, didn't she?"

"What agreement?"

"Oh," Moreland said, considering that information for a long moment. "Then I guess you would be a little hot about it." He eased the boy away and slid the knapsack from his shoulders, careful that the rifle settled silently onto the floorboards. "Well, she promised to hold on to you until I came back. But maybe she figured that deal was dead, once she caught wind of what I've been up to."

"*You* . . ." the boy began, but his voice shredded with anger, and he swallowed. "I want to go home. Right now."

"Lookee," Moreland said as diversion, and he drew the rifle and scabbard from his bag, holding it up on display like the rich Christmas present it was. "Happy Christmas." There was an idiot grin on his face, the same grin he had worn so often imagining this moment, handing Pearl over like it wasn't the ugliest thing either of them had ever seen. The boy did not reach for it; in fact, his hands flew behind his waist as if to avoid touching something putrid. His angry eyes crawled slowly from the pink felt and cracked paint, up his father's dark wool coat, and looked directly into Moreland's own. The gaze was distressingly like Mary's.

"What is *that*?"

Moreland slid the little rifle out and lay it on the bed, barrel pointing at the wall, and he pushed the scabbard toward his son. "Touch it," he said, and crinkled the paper stuffing.

The boy didn't look at it — just waited for his father to make any of this explicable to him.

"That's money," said Moreland. "A lot of it."

Finally, Jack reached out and pinched the scabbard. It was an inch thick on both sides. He scrunched the thing, the way one might work up suds in a washcloth.

"Fourteen thousand dollars," Moreland grinned.

"Four?"

"No, listen: fourteen. I'm aiming for twice that."

"Oh no," Jack said and there was a thundering in his ears.

"I figured I'd better split up the work, you know, in case I got caught."

Caught. Trapped. The boy remembered those cowed, unhappy men riding the prison sleigh along the main street, a spectacle for the tourists, and felt again the fear of spotting his own father among those faces.

Now Moreland was saying, "That woman ripped into me. One night in the hospital. Told me what's what. And she was right."

Indeed William Moreland did not care about money; he cared about his son's prospects, which were bleak. No mother, a feckless and aged father. Jack could look forward to a life of poverty in the woods. It was no legacy to leave a child.

"I blew the door off a bank in Helmingham, Montana.

No damage, just a bunch of flying dirt and a big bang. There's no point trying for banks, son, they lock it up too good. But I needed a distraction and dynamite makes one hell of a noise. Everyone went to look at the bank, which I knew they would, so I just slipped into the hotel office and shook out the cash drawer. Then I went back out to the street and kind of wandered along with the crowd."

"Why would you *do* it at all?" Jack meant the entire purpose of his father's absence, but Moreland heard only the specific.

"Because people were about. What if I was out of practice? What if the roof was too old to take it? But it was fine, just a noise and a ruined door. So off I went, holding all the hotel's money. Couple weeks later I got into two other hotels, quality ones. And after that there was a big mining outfit I never worked for, but men talk, so I knew the lay of the place, and I got the payroll. It doesn't hurt the men much, the company will still owe them, and no manager wants to admit he got robbed. That might give the men ideas. On Thanksgiving I got a little cash from a whorehou— tavern beside the rail lines. Just a hideous kind of outfit. I grabbed the cashbox and legged it for the trees." He smiled at the memory, for this kind of escapade was much to his liking.

"Did they come after you?"

"Sure they did."

"Oh god." Jack put his face in his hands.

"Now, come on, don't cry. Drunk men can't run for shit."

"How many people did you kill?"

Moreland's smile fizzled. "What?"

The boy sucked in an enormous sob. "They say you left no survivors."

Moreland held his son's thin shoulders. "Who told you that?"

"People."

"I said who."

"Kids at school."

"Son, I don't know much, but I can lay a proper charge. And I don't hurt people, you know that."

The boy seemed to deflate, to sigh into himself. "I know."

Moreland began to chuckle. "But I don't mind taking their money. No, I do not."

"What if they catch you?"

"Good luck to them."

"But what if they do?"

The man sobered for a moment. It was clearly not the first time he'd considered the question. "I'd go up shit creek and never come back. And you'd stay here." They looked at each other then, the father thin and soaked and ragged, the boy livid from crying. They fathomed the devastation of such an outcome.

Moreland patted the scabbard fondly. "I guess you can't keep this here, not around her," he said. "I'll leave it with Wilson. I'll tell him it's your favourite gun."

"Don't you dare."

"That's a little funny, actually."

"No, it's not."

Moreland slid the rifle back into the scabbard and said, "It'll be safe with Thom Wilson, but son, this is yours. The money is for you, no one else. And there's more coming. Swear on your mother's name never to tell anyone that you know what I did with this money. Go on, now."

Jack sighed out, "I swear it."

"On your mother's name."

The boy shook his head violently, for to him it was intolerable to bring her into this mess.

"It's not safe to confide, either. You cannot trust people. Not anyone."

By this point the boy was pushing Pearl away, choking with sobs and nearly hysterical, and his father had a hard time hushing him. The man's palm came down soothing and smoothing the boy's cheeks until Jack was calm enough to wheeze out, "I don't want any goddamn money. I want to go home."

"We will," he'd said. "I promise. I'll be back by your birthday."

The boy's eyes drifted away.

Moreland faltered. He held the kid's rigid shoulders and rocked him back and forth, a slow shake as if to wake him. "Jack, I have to do this. So you'd best wish me luck."

And then, as he always did, William Moreland disappeared. There was no preamble, no final hug, for Moreland had learned in years past that to force the kid to let go of him was worse for both of them. He ducked out the window silent and swift, dropped from the roof, flashed across the lawn into the trees, and was gone.

FOR JACK BOULTON it was like waking repeatedly, each time unsure of where he was. He became aware of the nun calling from the kitchen, her voice increasingly shrill. Became aware of her standing at his bedroom door. She had questions, and he tried to conjure answers, but there were none. He sat like an exhausted runner, legs splayed and elbows on his knees, staring into the patterned rug at his bare feet.

I blew the door out. Dynamite. The scrawlings of cruel children on fences. A stick man hanging from the crossbar.

Finally, his guardian broke her own rules and entered his bedroom, the soft bell shape of her skirts swinging back and forth over that pattern on the rug. She put her cool palm on his cheek, alarmed by the heat coming off him. Then the sound of her clip-clopping downstairs to boil some tea with lemon, meanwhile tears dripped off the end of Jack's nose.

When she arrived again at the threshold of his bedroom he lifted his despairing face to her, the eyes enormous, and whispered, "He won't stop."

She froze, in total confusion, put down the tea, and fled away to find the brandy.

Jack stared at a single, still-wet bootprint on the rug, proof of the fugitive's entry into the house. Slowly, he rubbed it out with his own bare foot.

Twelve

THE NEXT WEEK she took him to Leeton's studio for a family photograph. To cheer him up, she said. Which it most certainly did not.

She was dressed in secular clothes, reclining in a wicker chaise, he at her side. The place smelled of chemicals. Behind them stood a painted backdrop showing a European seashore, complete with bathing tents. None of this was to Jack Boulton's liking, so he shut up and wouldn't speak to the photographer. He was instructed to rest his hand on her shoulder, and after a glaring moment he did.

While she was settling up the bill he scrutinized the standing backdrop. It wobbled badly if anyone even shifted from foot to foot on that stage, and when Jack peered behind this painting he saw other backdrops leaning against the wall: a snowy landscape with a vacant skating rink, a drawing room with velvet curtains, a child's nursery with a single striped ball discarded on the floor. Hidden behind these images stood other, unknown alternatives, surely just as lonely and devoid of people.

The finished portrait when it arrived was a wishful sort of scene. Mother and son, somewhat ruined by the intensity of his gaze. But of course, she adored the thing and mounted it, in the front hall no less. He refused to walk past his own unhappy face, so henceforth he always walked to the back door of the house and entered through the kitchen.

"Charles," she laughed. "Come in the front door. You're not a charwoman, you're the man of the house."

"No," he said. "There is no man of the house."

HE BECAME QUIET and pensive; a sober, sobering presence in her house. He sat up late most nights and tended the fire in the kitchen grate, staring into its dance of light.

Clearly, he was not sleeping, so she gave him teas and tinctures, but he often refused them in such a flat and definite way that she didn't dare argue with him. Sometimes, midway through the school morning, he would stand up, weave his way between the desks, and leave the building, whereupon the truant would walk along the main street to Wilson's Outfitters, where he was put to work for the afternoon. The big Australian might say, "Where ya been, sprout? That rope's been waiting since yesterday," and the kid would gather up coils left out after a trek, shoulder them out into the bright, cold yard, unravel and untangle them, and hang them in loops and bights along the fence to dry, for wet rope doesn't last long. He would muck out stalls, organize the stock shelves including his own former belongings, anything Wilson asked of him. Then he'd wander home to her, by which point she had always heard the news of his truancy and was incensed. But on that subject he would brook no argument from her whatsoever.

"I cannot believe you would abandon your lessons to run off to that horrible man. And for what exactly? What could you possibly learn from that —"

"Don't worry yourself about Thom Wilson," he said, stirring a pot of carrot soup. "He's all right. And anyway, he pays me."

"Oh child," she said, in misery. "Why do you leave school?"

"I don't learn anything there. And that teacher spells everything wrong. She's only seventeen."

DULL WORK SEEMED to bring Jack out of it, so she poured it on. Now he was doing her laundry, too, and the sheets, the kitchen linens, everything. He attended to household chores well and even suggested to her that they find the source of the moths in the drawing room. It turned out to be a red wool blanket moist with insect-life, which together they burned in the backyard.

One morning as she was brushing his hair, he reached back, took the hairbrushes from her hands, and lay them firmly on the dresser, saying he would do it himself from now on. The next morning he said he would bathe himself and closed the bathroom door on her. She stood alone in the hallway, open-mouthed, proud of him, bereft.

Something in him was changing, evolving. She failed to see the enormity of it, and he was glad of that, for her sake and for his own. Standing now in the rutted dirt street amid the dried welts of carriage and motorcar wheels, a hoofprint next to his own boot as deep and wide as a soup bowl, he suddenly felt like someone else, a boy awakened into a new life. He even had another boy's name: Charles D'Arcy Euphastus Cload. His mother was dead, his father a fugitive. Everything familiar was gone or fading away. His old clothes were folded away into a bottom drawer. He gazed up at the Cload house with its open shutters and closed curtains, a years-old bird nest in the gingerbread under the eaves. He looked up at this new life and saw it for what it was: he was her Lazarus, her great gesture of hope, and now her kindness and regimen were leading him on a guided tour toward adulthood. He stood in as her new family.

But Jack Boulton knew the hard truth of things: he was as parentless as she was childless, and there was no remedy for either of them. This was all just a happy dream she was dreaming, a story she was telling herself, a tale so obviously false it ground him down until, with increasing frequency, he could stand it no longer and must run away from her, run into the trees and bellow out his anger, weep, make plans to affront everyone he encountered, shock the old woman, swear red hell at her until she slapped his face, anything that might wake him, wake him, wake him.

But once he had blown himself out, exhausted his angry heart and laid his head back against a tree, he always returned to the notion that it wasn't wrong to want joy. Someone should be happy. If it couldn't be him, let it be her.

Everyone said she looked younger than she had in years. She woke earlier, laughed more. The boy was resurrecting the woman and they both knew it. Sometimes she held his hand and together they gazed out at the yard and the sparkle of river, and she hummed to herself, happy in her new vocation. For days at a time, it was contagious.

It was the only reason he stayed with her as long as he did.

→ *Thirteen*

EVERY NIGHT THAT WEEK Jack had imagined he heard some-one moving about outside the house, and every night he fought with the knowledge he was hearing nothing. His father was not outside. No one was coming to take him home. He kicked off the covers and put his bare feet on the floor, and sat with his head hanging.

His father used to say, "I have to go exploring," and then he would leave them for weeks.

It was now almost spring, almost Jack's birthday, and the boy had been lying for hours watching the moon rise and the bare arms of the trees outside his window throw a shadowplay against the wall. Dappled light that formed and unformed the silhouette of a man.

The boy thought: *All right, you bastard, you're not the only one.* Resolutely he rose from the narrow bed and walked down the hallway. He stood for a moment and listened to the sleeping house, then entered the library. The room was fusty-smelling, silent, and he stood on his toes and reached for *Brehm's Life of Animals*, which he lay on the glass-topped desk. Quickly, he gathered other, smaller books and placed these on top of it. He found two fine pens, which he decided to leave, but he stole a lump of India rubber for erasing pencil.

In a presentiment of nostalgia he went to the horrible medical shelf and found the notebook heavily inscribed with the nun's lovely handwriting, and he stole that, too. Perhaps someday he could learn to copy the nun's calligraphic script.

He reached deep into the back of a desk drawer where he knew she had hidden his buck knife. When he opened the blade he knew by feel that she had cleaned and oiled the thing, cared for it in a way he seldom had. Holding it in his long palm he digested this information. Odd that among all the trivial things that frightened her this knife did not.

Back in his bedroom he drew open the bottom drawer and flapped out his old trousers and flannel shirt. The doe-hide jacket was pretty thin but it had his mother's expert embroidery on the cuffs and across the chest — ropes and sprigs of greenery and flowers and leaves gathering themselves into *J*'s and *B*'s for his initials. This was nothing to leave behind.

With a naked ass he slipped into his pants and tucked the long shirttails into the waistband, amazed at how soft his real clothes were. He folded his pajamas and lay them on the foot of his made bed. Then he armed his way into the jacket, stuffed as many books into the pockets as he could, and stood with his hands out before him, grinning at his wrists where they jutted white from the cuffs. He had grown.

The great encyclopedia of animals under his arm, he lifted the window sash, stole out onto the porch roof, shimmied down and fell into a one-handed dangle, then dropped soundlessly to the lawn below.

The shadow of the house lay across him and darkened half the roadway. He hopped in glee, heavy pockets flapping at his thighs, before composing himself and sauntering out into the road. Traitor. Jailbreak. He proceeded like any gentleman out for a stroll, walking the length of the main street, resisting the urge to grin in goofy camaraderie with passersby, some of whom turned to watch the tattered young thing pass.

What was her boy doing out at night, dressed like *that*?

LONG BEFORE HE reached the stables at the edge of town, he could smell them. The sign hanging from the tall ranch-style gate said:

TRACKERS GUIDES OUTFITTERS
EXPLORATION PONY-RIDES
WILSON & CO.   Est. 1893

He hauled on the tall stable door and stepped into the consoling fug of horses. Jack stood there for a long time letting his eyes adjust, and sauntered past all the stalls, passing rump after rump. So far, none were his horse. He made a little shrill whistle with his lower teeth, and immediately there was an unholy fuss at the far end of the building, a horse reversing itself in a confined space, and the Morgan's pretty face levered over a gate.

The horse having been located, Jack slipped into the stockroom and gazed up at Pearl. The wall was lined with shelves that went to the ceiling so the boy clambered up them like a monkey and perched atop. He shimmied himself along until he could reach out and grab a fistful of the doeskin fringe and yank the rifle off its pegs, and then he dangled it onto his lap. There he sat near the roof inspecting the scabbard minutely, checking every puckered seam. Everything was intact, but the thing was dusty as hell, untouched since Christmas. And now it was March.

Back down to the floor, where he slid the gun from its sheath. He'd never handled it before, but it was lever action, after all, so he swung the trigger guard forward and back. A live cartridge spat out and danced in a glitter across the floor. The boy scurried after it and then froze, his mind churning, for that bullet and every other one in the breech must have had the impression of his father's thumb on it.

He stood there, gazing round him at the room and its surprising plenty: pack saddles and riding saddles, blankets and pack boxes, cinches and latigos and rings and bits. Ropes of every gauge hung in coils on the wall, snarls of babiche cording, lanterns and boxes of flares. On the desk was an altimeter in shattered condition, four compasses, masses of paper, and tacked to the wall, a food manifest — what Wilson called a grub list. To the south was a rack devoted to tents; everything from pup to eight-man, store-bought tepees, simple rolled canvas, oilskin flies, tarps and bundled faggots of poles. All the gear an outfitter needs. Still, precious little ammunition.

Why hadn't Wilson unloaded this gun? Instead he had mounted the thing on the wall like pink taxidermy and left it there. The boy looked up at the wooden pegs and saw for the first time that they had been spaced perfectly to mount that exact small rifle. Wilson had deliberately made room for Pearl, put it aside for his old friend and employee, William Moreland. How much had his father told Wilson? Come to think of it, he might have told him everything.

The boy remembered Wilson's drunken face hovering over him in the hospital months ago, livid and unshaven, the wet cigar as always in the crook of his lips. "Listen to me, sprout. Your life might be short like your mother's was. Then again,

it might be long. You'd best think about what to do with a
long life. Your dad thought it through. He's working it out
for you. So don't bugger it up, hear me?" An orderly had been
fussing behind Wilson, trying to drag him out of the ward.
This eventually earned him a brutal cuff in the jaw and he
ran out of the room to get reinforcements.

Your dad thought it through.

Jack holstered his rifle and went rooting through the
entire moonlit stockroom, collecting the rest of his belongings, repacking and tidying as he went. One by one he ferried
his goods into the stables, stacking them on the upturned
saddle. It was impossible to tell which of several dozen horse
blankets had been his family's, so, just as his father would
have done, he simply took the best one. At the back of his
desk Wilson had erected a dyke of paper: books and newspapers and calendars and brochures, and these the boy picked
through carefully. In the end, all he pinched was a ranger's
exam booklet. Wilson had written "bollocks" on the front
cover in black pencil, so he likely wouldn't miss it. The boy
also stared long and hard at a fine new saddle that did not
belong to him. It was light and trim, and had hammered
embellishments. He knew that taking it would be stealing,
so he did not take it. But he wanted to. He was his father's
blood, after all, but he was not his father.

When he walked down the stable's aisle to the Morgan
there was no unease in the horses and mules, and he passed
among them as if he owned the place. He unlatched a gate
and the Morgan shuffled forward and nosed out at him. It
scented his shoulder, his hair.

"Me too," he said

Wilson would miss the Morgan. He was a cautious buyer,

verging on finicky, but thanks to the nun's peculiar fears he'd got a calm, healthy horse for free. His best purchases included the big bay gelding, the roan with the long face, several well-mannered mules, and a quarter horse mare. Not one of them was hard-mouthed or unruly, and they were all sweet. His one oversight was that unruly American paint. Wilson had named it Colonel Petch, named, he said, after a former commanding officer in the Australian army who had an identically bad temperament.

The Colonel was a handsome and well-built horse, graceful and responsive when it wanted to be, able to stop on a dime, turn on the point of a pin. But this animal had no manners at all, and it nursed a kind of bored intelligence that occasionally gusted to malevolence. The boy had seen it witch its ears back and walk slowly around the yard, dart out, biting and shouldering the other cayuses, then tear round the paddock in widening circles, kicking every horse, dog, or human too slow-witted to vacate the area. Afterward, it had paced the cleared ground, visibly pleased with itself. This horse was a bastard. Despite endless training it was still useless as a pack horse, would lose its mind if burdened with provisions, and you absolutely didn't dare put a paying client on its back. Therefore the Colonel was Wilson's own horse. They suited each other. You could see them bickering together in the yard, exercising or training, Wilson losing some arguments, the Colonel losing others.

There was a wondrous pattern on its haunches that fascinated the boy, like a map of pale islands spattered across a dark sea. An archipelago where pirates hid. Now Jack approached the stall door. "Hey," he said gently, *"psst."* The paint seemed to think for a second, then answered with a ferocious kick on the stall door that rattled the hinges. The kid hopped back, grinning.

He took the bridle into the Morgan's stall, and drew the Morgan out into the stable aisle. In less than a minute they were saddled up and the boy was lashing bundles behind the cantle more or less correctly. Around the Morgan, other horses stood in silence and watched the familiar sight of a man packing a horse. Outside, he drew the long stable doors shut again, swung up into the saddle, and they trotted out into the dark yard, making their way under the outfitter's sign onto the street.

The animal was as excited as the boy to be out, so Jack had to rein in hard to keep it from bolting down the avenue. Squirming in the saddle he noticed again that he'd grown, and out of habit, he'd made the stirrups too short. They went awkwardly along in feigned composure, past dark shop windows and rows of parked motorcars. Their dark reflection loomed on the drugstore's plate glass, the boy with Pearl slung across his back, the Morgan chewing the bit and hip-hopping in a comical dance of failing self-control. Past the tobacconist's. The church with its bed of dead annuals. They rode under the hotel's garish frontage, the street lit up almost like glaring daylight. Two tourists crapulous with drink leaned on the twinkling balcony and watched them go.

Somehow they made their way to the corner and left the paved street before they both could stand it no longer and the boy let fly. They galloped down a dirt side road, streaked past the last few cabins that remained of town, skidded to a halt, and hooted round in circles. A dog woofed perfunctorily from a distant porch. They trotted toward the river, away from people, away from the lights of town. The rider panting, the horse blowing. Soon no sound reached them save pines sighing in the wind, water sweeping the riverbank. The smell of frying bacon chased them on the wind like a fretful memento, followed later by gasoline. At the farthest edge of town, a whiff of garbage dump. Then nothing but river water and conifers and cold air, as the human world faded out another faded in.

Still awash in the surprise of freedom, the Morgan jerked at the reins, but the boy spoke gently to it and soon they were walking easily. They followed the river's winding spine until it intersected the vacant railway line. They stepped lightly over those tracks and went on following the river.

A herd of elk congregated on the far bank, easily a hundred of them, mostly calves and mothers, the moon silvering their backs. A young male stood dressed to its knees in the river and watched them go by. Then they were alone, rider and horse. The boy ran his hand along the Morgan's neck, closed his eyes, and exhaled into the night.

By the time they reached the Sawback Range, he was Jack Boulton again, and the Morgan was still nameless.

→ *Fourteen*

AT FIRST, WHEN she found his bed empty, she assumed the child had gone downstairs earlier than usual and she might even find him cooking their breakfast. But when she got down to the kitchen he was not there. She huffed when she saw the long-cold fireplace, and then she stamped upstairs to her own bedroom and dressed, for now it was obvious he had snuck out to the river to play. Something he was not allowed to do.

She opened the back door onto a cold blue morning, trotted down the steps, her face set and reproachful, headed for the river. Tresses of vapour floated above the gurgling surface and swam slowly in the chilly air. She could see along the empty banks and through the sparse pines in both directions, but there was no movement, no figure anywhere; the boy was not there. She called and called into that bland vacancy until her voice took on a tone of fury she hadn't known she felt, and then she just froze, hand to her belly, and let the echoes fall away. The sun was coming up, a red glow between the peaks, red sky at morning.

Lips moving in silent self-counsel, she hurried along the riverbank, scanning the water as if she might spot some clue, footprints, a place where he had waded. She fought the image of his body sunk to the rocky bottom like a river fairy or sprite, and she must reach down into that frigid water, seize him, and pull him out. But there was nothing on that floor but pine debris and more rock.

She went back to the house and hollered up the stairs. Nothing. A silent house. As a last resort she opened the long-disused drawing room, stared into the gloom at the sagged divan, breathed in the stale air, and shut the door again. She ran out into the street, stood with shaking hands on the corduroyed roadbed where wheels and rain and hooves had left their mark. Not a soul in sight. She went back inside and clopped up the stairs, heart hammering in her chest, and entered his bedroom.

Finally, in that room, she saw things as they were: the bed had been made one last time, his town clothes were folded and laid neatly on the blanket, the window was open.

As if in a dream, she leaned over and pulled open the bottom drawer of the chest and saw that his old clothes were gone. Nothing in there now but the wood grain at the bottom of the drawer, the squared edges of a dustless box.

She jerked upright, hand to her throat. A pitiful voice in her head whispered: *He left you.*

What followed could only be described as a becrazed interrogation of the entire town. From neighbours to school-teachers, to the bewildered Chinese groceryman, to the hardware store owner, the town warden, the baker women, bank tellers, tourists eating breakfast in the diner, the entire lobby and restaurant of the hotel. She harried them the way a collie harries sheep. By the end of the day she had grilled everyone in town. But she started, of course, with Thom Wilson.

• • •

THE OUTFITTER HAD come in that morning with a hangover
worse than death. He walked with exaggerated dignity past
the horses, who watched him in anticipation of food. He
lowered himself slowly into the hard chair, carefully lifted one
leg after the other, and lay his filthy boot heels on the calendars and food lists and invoices and bills of lading. Leaned
his head back against the chair and closed his eyes, nursing
the idea that something here had changed, something was
wrong. His head began to hum.

He groaned and rose again, went out into the stable and
walked straight to the far end, where he stood open-mouthed
at the Morgan's empty stall. Gate closed. Everything tidy.
He tracked a single set of footprints in the sand and sawdust,
long strides. In the stockroom he stood with arms crossed
and assessed the shelves, determined exactly which items were
missing. He shot a glance at the pegs where he'd mounted that
ridiculous gun William had asked him to keep for the kid.
Gone, too. Wilson took in every sign and pondered the two
shocking possibilities: either Moreland himself had spirited
through the building and collected all these things, or the
boy had finally abandoned the nun and buggered off home —
wherever in hell their home might be. No one in town knew
where that family lived, and anyone who might be capable of
tracking them would never do so, out of common politeness
and fellow feeling. Everyone needs their privacy, some more
than others. In any case, Moreland exercised unusual caution
in that regard, and his wife was even worse. And they weren't
the only hermits in the area Wilson knew about. Over ten
years of friendship and occasional employment Moreland had

never offered a single word about where home might be. So, whether it had been father or son who had been here, their things were now gone. Wilson went back to the office to rest his face on his desk, still vaporous with booze.

He knew exactly who it was when he heard the stable door dragged open and footsteps coming up the nave toward his office door. Soft, quick footfalls. He lifted his cheek from an invoice, raked the hair off his forehead, and braced himself to meet her. It occurred to him as bleakly amusing that she wouldn't be able to stamp her little foot at him thanks to all the sand on the floor. If that woman didn't keep her voice down, if she made his headache any worse than it already was, he'd revenge himself by telling her the savage truth, and he'd rub it in. But when at last he saw that raw, aghast face, all he wanted was to get rid of her.

"Please," she said without overture, "I'm looking for my boy."

It took four seconds to disappoint her. "I have no idea where he is."

Part Two

The Known World

→ *Fifteen*

FROM THE SECOND his boots had hit the nun's lawn, the Ridgerunner had headed for Laggan and then hiked uphill to Lake Louise and the grand chalet that stood by the lake itself. A brief side visit to a place he'd always longed to pilfer. Over a single night he gave the parked cars, outbuildings, and four hotel suites a thorough going-over while everyone was on the hotel's main floor drinking and, from the sounds wafting out of windows, waltzing. He even crept around the log home occupied by the Swiss guides, those exotic experts advertised on every brochure, and it seemed they too were off drinking. He got a little under eight hundred American dollars, a few pound notes and an impressive wad of pesos from the Argentine. How much were pesos worth? From the guides' cabin he took two knives, an excellent pair of boots, and all the chocolate he could find. Standing alone by that icy blue lake, gazing at the chalet lit from within, figures moving in the windows, he wondered why he had spent time in mining towns when tourist spots offered so much. Then again, few tourist spots were this remote, this expensive, and this far away from law enforcement.

• • •

FOUR DAYS LATER the Ridgerunner had walked his way out of the mountains and into the foothills. Once again he was moving ever southward on the lee side of the Rockies, avoiding roads and well-worn walking trails, giving any visible habitation a mile-wide berth. He was aiming for Beaver Mines, at the entrance to the Crowsnest Pass. He hoped the town existed, for it was a such new coal-mining interest that its existence might be hearsay; he might arrive to find nothing more than surveyors living in tents. A little more than ten miles east of Beaver Mines there had long been a rail stop called Pincher Station, a mostly uninhabited crossroads where he intended to catch a train west into the pass. With rolling land to his left and the mountains to his right, he was following the same route as before, following his own footsteps, as bent on crime as he had been during the first trip. But Moreland was a different person than the one who had set out four months ago. Now he was twenty pounds lighter and hardened in every muscle, joyful, buoyed up, almost euphoric.

If the boy had ever been sick, you could no longer tell by looking at him. Despite the nun's inexplicable failure to tell Jack about her pact with Moreland, she had protected the boy just as she had promised she would. Jack was safe; he was displeased, yes, but he was gloriously healthy, pink-cheeked, a little taller, and to his father he'd looked wonderful, even as he wept and fumed. Just like Mary, Jack was pretty when he was riled.

Moreland had expected a certain amount of impatience in the boy, a yearning for the plan to be over and done with. That was to be expected. And as much as he wished to stay with his son, bring him home so they could finally rest together, Moreland knew he had to keep the visit short, keep Jack from hopping out the window and running after him. He must keep moving, follow his plan. The harder he went at it, the sooner it would be over. Walking now, he mouthed the words *work to do*, as if the boy and Mary were there with him, companions striding alongside.

It was still light when he arrived just outside the precincts of Beaver Mines and to his relief, Moreland saw the place was definitely a running mine. At that time of day the men were everywhere, streaming across each other's paths as the night and day shifts changed places. He settled into the trees to await dark. From where he crouched he could see the office clearly, a small log cabin obviously moved from somewhere else, now resting on a raised platform about four feet high. The move had done it no good as a structure. All the windowpanes were cracked and glinting in the sunset, and the whole building had a woozy, trapezoidal appearance, made worse by the perfectly square and level foundation it stood on. Gradually, the workers all disappeared either into their bunkhouses to sleep or into the mine. At about ten p.m., Moreland dashed from shadow to shadow and kneed his way up onto the platform so he was standing at the rear of the office, peering through that cracked glass into the simple room. A few chairs, a long desktop that ran the length of one wall, below which had been built several drawers with rough handles. A typewriter, and a stack of paper surmounted by a cast iron notary stamp set there as a paperweight. No safe, no lockbox bolted to the floor. The money, if it was even being held here, would be in one of those drawers.

He stole round to the front door of the cabin, where he tried the handle and swung the door in. Some large dark form lay on the floor in an untidy pile, and that mass made a moan and rolled over onto its back, resolving into a man woken from his unhappy slumber. In mere seconds Moreland was into the trees and invisible, looking back in dismay at that small building and the confused sleeper who now wandered out onto the platform scratching his scalp, his long coats twisted round him. A clerk working too late? Husband ejected from the marriage bed? A drunk who, like Moreland himself, had aimed to pilfer the place but who passed out instead? No, this was most likely a night watchman, though a distinctly bad one, or someone new to the job, unused to the necessarily nocturnal life. Moreland watched the fellow play with the door, opening and closing it in a way that showed how totally unaware he was of an intruder; to him, the door had blown open on its own.

The Ridgerunner turned his back on the scene and thought for a long time, until he came to the conclusion, a familiar one, that moving on would be the best plan. And so he made his way out onto a road halved by tree shadow. When he looked back, giving Beaver Mines one last resigned glare, the figure was sitting on the platform swinging one boot, bent over his hands in the unmistakable posture of a man rolling a cigarette. Moreland growled and headed off again at a trot.

IN THE TINY station just north of Pincher Creek he slid into a boxcar that seemed headed west into the mountains, for the Crowsnest Pass and the towns of Hillcrest, Frank, Sparwood, Fernie. But this was a mistake, for the train had in fact come from there and was heading east, toward flat land. Tired as he was, he'd failed to notice which end of the train had an engine.

The boxcar was frigid and nearly airtight. After twenty

minutes the Ridgerunner hauled back the door to see the land whizzing by, blond snowy grassland blurring with speed. Holding the doorframe and craning forward he saw nothing but flat land ahead; only when he looked back did he see the mountainscape he'd been aiming for drawing farther away. For a moment he stood stunned, braced like a trick rider on that rocking, icy metal floor. Then he closed the door. His breath bulbed in the air before his face and floated there.

The train slowed but did not stop at Fort MacLeod. Instead it rolled through, howling as if the town were on fire. Moreland lay the knapsack on the cold floor and sat on it, feeling every mile that he must somehow traverse again whizzing away beneath his ass. And the moment he felt the engineer slowing again, he drew the door open and got ready to jump.

A painted rail marker slid past.

"Fuck me," he said. "Lethbridge."

And so, for the first time in his life, William Moreland found himself wandering the streets of a true city, population nine thousand four hundred souls. Late king of the whiskey trade, largest wartime producer of coal for a thousand miles in any direction, a hub for all rail traffic in the area, with streetcars, no less, and water mains and any number of modern improvements, Lethbridge had started off as a tiny fort full of drunks. With a robust history of arson and revolt, innovation and greed, this was a city where ten years earlier the mayor had read the Riot Act, literally, to a mob of angry whites bent on massacring the residents of Chinatown. Back then, the only thing between Lethbridge and the Wild West was a military police service on horseback that was spreading west. Otherwise, mayhem.

The Ridgerunner wandered into the city with his hat down, playing the common traveller, a tired itinerant looking for a room, a little grubby from the rigours of a long journey during wartime, admiring as any traveller might the many signs of prosperity and progress. Here was a currency exchange; there a hotel with a games table; in an alley he saw the glare of electric light in the back room of a closed tavern where, surely, someone was counting the night's money. Normally all of it would be of interest to him, especially during the hour after revellers had gone home to fluff their pillows, incompetent with drink. But Lethbridge was no workable village or small town, no oversize logging or mining interest, where a thief might come and go in the dark without notice; it was a busy, open city, with police and gas lighting and distinct neighbourhoods. Where cranks and night owls might sit by their windows to watch the street, sipping coffee, sipping whiskey, spying on their neighbours. The damned place was awake all night. Entirely unpleasing to a man of Moreland's skills and cautious inclinations.

Even on the outskirts near the train station, there were working light standards illuminating empty intersections, and an endless flit of human figures along the streets and alleyways. A hiss of life everywhere, voices and music.

He lingered by the gates of a racetrack where a poster announced that horses ran twice a month. The grass field in the centre of the track was littered with the cages and tents and bunting, the smoking caravans and collapsible stages of a travelling show. All along the perimeter fence were nailed broadsides depicting their captive Asian tiger, Queenie, a resplendent cat as painted, her muscular body pictured in a murderous leap, white claws extended. More likely she'd be aged beyond her years, depressed, and reclining at that moment in an unheated cage. Moreland tried to imagine a world in which he could let her loose, to run free of that cage, without any peril to others; he imagined a world in which he could outrun a tiger.

On one street he saw a line of almost twenty parked automobiles, more of them gathered together than he had ever seen before. He walked the line and peered through the thin glass windows, and he assessed thereby the basic character of each owner. One was dented all over by minor collisions, leaning on its injured axle, front seats spangled with cigarette ash, a pair of goggles hung rakishly from the steering column. Another car's passenger seat was burdened by a stack of identical schoolbooks, the words LITTLE GRAMMARIANS stuttering down the wall of spines. In another car, the back seat was ornamented with a pair of women's white knickers beside which lay a crumpled pocket handkerchief, both of them opalescent with dried semen.

He passed a little clutch of businesses closed for the night that included a bakery and a shoe repair shop. Even the bakery was padlocked. Stealing food had of course been in Moreland's plan, but he was absurdly insulted by that lock, as if, in securing the place so well, the baker was being rude.

As he wiggled the point of his knife into the padlock, a staggering pisstank made his way up the road, thin as a scarecrow, heading for the closed tavern. He gave the Ridgerunner a glance of complete indifference, and kept going til he hit the tavern's door, whereupon he started tugging at the handle. There they were, the two of them, working on the doors of closed establishments, until finally Moreland broke the lock on the bakery, and the drunk let out a moan, gave up, and wobbled away up the street.

Twice the Ridgerunner encountered the same posse of garbage dogs that swirled round him and snapped and howled. During the second encounter he was forced to clamber up a high wooden fence, using the rails as steps, and sit atop it, enduring their horrible din until they finally lost interest in him and tore away down an alley, gambolling over one another and snarling. He saw them stop halfway down and churn over some shape on the ground, probably something edible, and he thought, *Any child who runs into that pack might be killed*. During his long lifetime Moreland had run up on a lot of wolves. He'd made the best of maybe one-tenth of those encounters: skinned and cured the pelts. But mostly he had demurred on wasting the ammunition. Sometimes there were too many animals to deal with, sometimes whatever gun he happened to be carrying was meant for smaller game and not up to the task. Therefore he had more than once found himself up a tree looking down at a wolf, or several wolves, who were just as intently looking up at him. Those keen, swift animals bore no resemblance whatsoever to this screeching rabble. Moreland wondered what it was about a city that drove animals crazy. Maybe it worked the same way on people. He pictured Jack, not long from now, grown to manhood and entering for the first time a metropolis like this one. Well dressed and tall, a fine hat on his head, those long legs striding the train platform. But Moreland's mind stopped there, at the outskirts, on a train platform, for he had not the slightest idea what might come next.

With the ragged edge of the fencing grinding into his buttocks, he stuck his nose in the air and breathed in the unambiguous stink of a stockyard. He swung his legs the other way so he was facing windward and scanned an open area full of scrub and grass, fluttering garbage and broken furniture, until he saw the many silvery pencil-lines of a wire fence. A small business concern, by the looks of it, but convenient to the rail line, and contiguous with the T intersection of two roads. Here was a place where cattle could be trucked in or brought by rail, where they could be assessed in tight pens or run through the auction arena and sold as they bellowed. Moreland perched for a long moment, listening for any sound of lowing or men's voices or the rattle of automobile engines, but he received only the sour wind. He leapt from the fence's summit, landed with a thump in the scrub, and made his way toward that distant establishment, thinking that perhaps a stockyard would have auction money, and maybe it wasn't so bad that fate had brought him to this city.

Moreland followed the wire fence until he was in the shadow of the largest building, probably the auction arena, where he rested his boot on the lowest wire, which screeked against the staples that held it in place. No spring left in that weathered line, so he stood on it and bounced until it snapped. Stood on the next line, and worked his way up until five of seven lines were broken and dangling, then he ducked under.

The air was so acrid with the piss and shit of terrified cattle it was eye-watering. The ground had stained black over the decades, churned into a hellish mud during auction season, a dry sponge on the off season, the bad news always blowing on the wind. Moreland knew little about this kind of business. He gazed at the honeycomb of holding pens, the narrow chutes and gates, the loading ramp, all of it vacant. He walked through the great front entrance of the arena, as open as an airplane hanger. A flutter of birds in the high metal rafters. He made his way to the only door that could be the office, twisted the handle, and stepped into the room.

It took him a full ten seconds to understand that he was lying face down on the gritty plank floor. Sand was grinding into his cheek, his eyebrow, his lips, and yes, someone was on top of him, knee in the small of his back. A jubilant voice said, "Hooo! I got you."

Moreland stayed perfectly still. He stared along the scuffed floor and into the shadows under what looked like a desk. A wooden door wedge lay on its side under the desk.

"I have been waiting," the voice said. It sounded young, excited. "And here you are. At least, I hope you're him."

Moreland said nothing. He just breathed, felt the man's knee punishing his lower spine, the hand at his shoulder pressing down so hard the bones threatened to dislocate. During the tumble his knapsack had rucked up so high it was almost over his head.

"Are you him?" the voice said.

He gave no reply.

"You can't even believe how long I've been waiting. Eight days."

"Get off," said Moreland.

"'Scuse me?"

"Get off or I'll throw you off."

"Oh, that's rich. I'm about twice your —"

The Ridgerunner braced his palms on the floor, jerked a knee up and bucked the living burden off his back. In a single movement he slid the knapsack off his back and swung it at a mop of brown curls atop a young face whose mouth was open in an O of surprise. The handle of the hatchet inside the bag made contact with the kid's ear, and the O became a rictus, all teeth and agony. The kid yowled like a cat and scrambled away to the side of the desk, where he crouched and put out pleading hands.

Moreland hefted the bag — he'd forgotten the hatchet was in there. "You all right?"

"Don't kill me!"

"Dry up. No one's killing anyone."

They stayed like that for a moment, squared off, the Ridgerunner holding his bag like the weapon it was, until slowly the boy plunked down on his buttocks and let his heels slide out in front of him.

"You've been here for eight days?"

The watchman nodded.

"When was the last auction?"

"How should I know?"

"What did you do with yourself all that time?"

"Waited for you."

"I take it," Moreland said, "that you looked around for money."

After a long moment the boy said, "Yes."

"And?"

"You're welcome to try." He was at best twenty, with green eyes, freckles, legs too short for his body, shoulders too wide, nothing to indicate strength except overworked biceps. A local tough whose meanness was all show. He was breathing fast, but it was excitement, not injury; everything except the bright pink ear said he was just fine.

"How old are you?"

"Fifteen."

"What's your pay?"

"Twenty cents a day," the kid said smugly.

He could have made eight times that on a farm baling hay, but he fancied himself a man of action. A low growl came out of William Moreland. Annoyance with himself, with life, with companies that would hire a night watchman this inadequate, that would expect a dumb kid to handle a bomber.

For a long moment the Ridgerunner stood in the room and his eyes wandered every wall, rafter, desk, bookcase, floorboard. A filing cabinet next to the desk had been shifted so many times it sat on a pale carpet of scratches and sawdust. He strode to it and the kid recoiled, shuffled on his ass to the other side of the desk as Moreland pushed the cabinet to reveal a square hole cut in the floorboards. Inside that hole there had been installed a shallow metal box with a lid. He looked at the kid. "Eight days?"

The boy had gone back to making an O with his mouth. A false look of surprise.

The metal box turned out to be empty except for a single five-cent piece set in the exact centre. A witticism perhaps, in case the Ridgerunner should actually appear. Moreland just stared at it.

"So," the boy said, "Are you him? Because you don't look like it."

"Him who?"

The kid sniggered like he'd been included in a great joke. "I won't tell them what you really look like," he lied, and then slowly withered under Moreland's glare.

Moreland was running his hand through his hair over and over, a man beset by anxious thought. He was struggling to understand why an auction house closed for over a week would take on an inept watchman, regardless of the pitiful pay, to stand guard over an empty safe. It made no sense at all.

"Who hired you? Not these people," he pawed at a pile of papers with letterhead saying ESTHERBROOK AUCTIONS.

"Yessir, they did," the kid said proudly.

"What the hell for? There's no money here."

"Just to be the outfit that caught you." The boy put out his hands as if to indicate the whole office, the yards outside, the whole enterprise, as if all of it was his, and grinned, "Bragging rights."

Moreland sagged. This kid wasn't the only one, there might be others like him all over town. They couldn't have known he would appear in Lethbridge — even he hadn't known he was coming. Therefore the policy of hiring temporary guards was general to the entire area, hundreds of miles, and who knew how many establishments might get the idea. The watchman at Beaver Mines made sense now. Some of the hired men might even be professional guards or police or former servicemen, far more dangerous than this nincompoop. They might only catch local sneak thieves in the meantime, but it was worth an underpaid watchman at any rate. If Moreland had once had the element of surprise, it was gone now.

With a flurry of movement, Moreland armed his way into the knapsack and made for the office door.

"Wait, where are you off to?"

Moreland turned and looked at the kid. "You already found that safe, didn't you? And left nothing but a nickel."

The watchman's face slid into a smile of cunning and satisfaction; this kid's brain moved so slowly you could see him thinking. "Yup. It was me."

"How much?"

"Doesn't matter, 'cause it's all gone."

"You just fucked off every night and drank it up, didn't you?"

"I had myself some times."

"I bet you did." Moreland snatched up the door wedge, exited the office, slammed the door, and savagely kicked the wedge into place until the door was truly jammed shut. He was around the auction house, under the broken wire fence, and across the vacant lot in forty seconds. In another two minutes he was behind the train station, where he leapt up and over the rail line and into moonshadow on the far side.

A mile beyond he slowed to a trot, still keeping his head down, his gait steady, breathing slow, telling himself: *Think later, conjecture later. Run.* Only once did he look back at the sprawl of that true city, the sulphurous glow of it, the sheer size. You could see light reflected on the low clouds. It really was a wonder of progress. But like all wonders, natural or otherwise, it made your own life seem temporary, and it told you things about the passage of time you didn't want to know.

TWO LONG DAYS later Moreland was off the flat and into the rolling foothills, where everything was quiet. He wove his way between hamlets of low scrub, shallow ponds, and long runs of dwarfish trees.

Sometimes he turned and walked backwards, just to gaze at the unaccustomed sight of a flat horizon. He understood changes in elevation, and he could assess grade down to the nearest ten degrees, which was not hard — he'd taught Jack to do it at eight years old, using his hand. But the prairie had puzzled him; the way you could walk for hours and seem not to advance. All around him were roads that ran so long and straight between wintering fields of unknown crops they seemed to vanish over the curve of the earth. He saw a ranching truck in the distance heralded by nothing but a soundless dust plume leaning with the wind. He watched it go, wondering where the driver was headed. Ranches, feed barns, maybe a killing house, where someone was making money on wartime bully beef. To the truck's right, a tiny fist of terrible weather hung over the land, so corralled by the miles it would never make it to where Moreland stood. How beautiful to watch weather work at a distance, without the slightest need to decide what that weather would mean to you. Rain, snow, lightning, it was happening to someone else.

By evening he passed a sign that promised a town named Lundbreck. The name meant nothing to him, but finally, beyond the town, he saw the V-shaped break in the mountains that he knew held a winding road pushing steadily uphill into the Crowsnest Pass, through mining towns, logging camps. He knew where he was now, like a bat in the twilight, flying headlong into the exact crack in a stone wall he knew so well.

At a trot, Moreland scrambled his way up a great soft hill, and at its apex stood panting as the pink western sky closed down on the long palisade of the Rocky Mountains, jagged white summits fading.

He closed his eyes and pictured his boy, days and days to the west-northwest, in the town of Banff. At this hour, the nun's house would already be in shadow, the boy long since home from school. Perhaps they had eaten dinner and gone for a ride together along the river, each talking about their day. The boy would put away the horses as she made herself ready for bed, and then he too would retire to that small, tidy room. Jack would flop down on the bed, just as he always had at home, and lie sprawled like a starfish on top of his blankets, or perhaps there would be a book held over his face, his mind travelling to unknown places, his foot swinging off the bed as a candle flickered on the floor. Moreland imagined that candlelight framed by the window. The boy would read until he could no longer keep his eyes open.

The Ridgerunner trotted down the hill's gentle incline and waded through grass, headed for the Crowsnest Pass.

→ Sixteen

JACK WAS INDEED sprawled on the bed, alone in the family cabin, far from the town of Banff, finally, deeply asleep and dreaming. As night passed and dawn began to ruminate behind the ranges, an enormous dog stepped out of the trees and walked across the clearing. It was pale and lanky, and there was a lot of wolf in its ancestry. There came a short hiss of wind through the upper branches. It went to the paddock where the Morgan stood, and they regarded one another for a long moment and read each other's scent.

Then the dog went silently around the building, nose down, drawing its shadow along the walls. When it found the front door again it sniffed the handle, the front step. Then it reared back on hind legs, placed paws on the door, and shoved it open. It dropped to all fours and eyed the dark room. As if the air within had stunned the animal it stood unmoving for many minutes, brooding on the news. Then it padded into the cabin.

The bed was wide, covered in a tumble of stale wool blankets and quilts and pillows. The dog approached the kid sleeping there and panted hotly in Jack's face until he moaned and pushed the muzzle away. As always it hopped up onto the bed, stepped over Jack's sleeping body, circled twice, trampling the blankets, flopped down at his back, and lay with eyes open. It sighed the way some dogs do, a protracted groan. Icy air poured in through the open door until the boy rose and closed it. He whistled under the blankets again and covered his head. His hand came out and explored the dog's familiar head, the stiff ears. He scratched the filthy chin whiskers. The pallet was large, the cabin silent, and the two of them lay warm and together in the dark.

DAWN FOUND THEM both at work sprucing up the cabin. For its part, the dog nosed around in corners, breakfasting on mice, snapping them up mid-scurry. It sniffed deeply under the kitchen shelves and pawed til something rolled out to its doom. Then the dog trotted outside to make a thorough search of the cabin's perimeter, where it found vole smell under the mulch, and dug madly.

Meanwhile the boy constructed a tinder nest in the stove with gnarled twigs and dry grass that spat and crackled when he put the match to it. Holding half-charred logs at the ready — relics from previous fires, last held by his father. It was still so dark inside the cabin that the stove provided the only light, and when he shut the grill, it glowed and smoked merrily, a black jack-o'-lantern.

He opened the cabin door onto a soft blue morning and stood there shivering and grinning. In the old lady's house he had never risen this early. Refused to, in fact. He'd always closed his eyes against the light, against whatever chores, schooling, and civilizing nonsense the day held. He'd slowly cultivated the ability to ignore even the worst of her halloos, knowing that the long staircase would conspire to buy him time. But here he was now, skinny landlord, standing at his own front door at dawn.

He ferreted among the kitchen shelves to see what food might be left, and almost immediately crowed in triumph, holding up a hinge-stoppered glass jar with a fistful of oatmeal dust left in the bottom. "It's still dry," he laughed to the dog, and joggled the powder within. The animal wagged its long tail, chewing all the while on some small unfortunate creature with its back teeth.

He found a crusted brick of salt his mother had kept in an empty ammunition box; sugar in pretty good shape; some chicory, which he generally refused to drink, but without coffee it would have to do; and at the end of a plank shelf, he discovered a blackened blob of . . . something. He bent to sniff it, immediately staggered back, stood aghast for a moment, and then gagged. It might once have been jerky of some sort but it was now spongy with rot and mined by ants, lying in a shadow of its own grease. He took it between finger and thumb and straight-armed it out the door, side-shuffling across the clearing, past the creek, toward a rock precipice, where he flung it into the air and watched it flutter stiffly into the bristling forest below. Wiped his fingertips on stiff moss. For a moment, he and the dog stared at the tips of the trees where it had vanished, as if the thing might come leaping back up like running salmon. But the world down there was tranquil. The boy sprinted back to the cabin, the dog whining and dancing ahead of him, and together they resumed their work.

By noon, the air had warmed and he had a decent pile of windfall branches stacked near the stove, broken under his heel into foot-long pieces and stacked together almost neatly.

He'd scrubbed out the water trough in the corral, filled it with buckets of creek water, and bent to watch for drips at the corners, but it was still well sealed. And the little windowless shed, where his family stuffed anything they didn't want in the cabin, stood with its door closed. The floor inside the cabin was swept and the blankets were now hanging from branches outside to dry in the sun. Waterproof matches in their little case still hung from a nail on the wall. The bed was a simple, raised wood platform, knee-high, burdened by a heavy tick that was still in pretty good shape. That was where all three of them had once slept together. Sometimes the dog, too.

The big blue water crock in the kitchen was full again, sweating from the cold liquid it held. A small pot of boiled water steamed on the stove. Jack Boulton sat on his own threshold and sipped stale, soupy oatmeal from a tin bowl, and when he was done he let the dog lick it clean. Together they watched the Morgan as it wandered its corral, at work on the long grasses. The scene was almost domestic. The corral was a wide, spindly affair, running somewhat downhill at the outer edge, and more than a few bars in the fence had collapsed. It was habit more than wood that kept the horse from wandering beyond its confines. At the lower end of the corral was a three-sided windbreak Moreland had constructed for the Morgan, unnecessary in most weather but in a bad wind the Morgan would be glad to wander to it and shelter there. For a hairy cold-weather animal, this was a good solution.

Inside the cabin, the family books were still lined up on a shelf. It was set low enough even a small child could peruse spines and reach for them. A scrawny offering compared to the library in that eminent house, but to Jack it felt like plenty.

They were in unchanged order, no hand had touched them in his absence. Some volumes had bloated in the spring damp, their pages fanning so that the endmost volumes had tumbled to the floor. *Moonfleet* was not bad, as was *The Merry Adventures of Robin Hood*. But *Toomai of the Elephants* was badly rotted and unreadable past the halfway point. Of course *Alice's Adventures Under Ground* was pristine. It would be. Mary had loathed the book for its nauseating unreality. The boy disliked it because it was boring and about a girl whose choices seemed to him to be mostly terrible. He had no problem with a talking rabbit, but what idiot would follow one into a hole? But the book had charmed the hell out of Moreland. He found it uproarious. He would read sections to his wife and son as they begged him not to. He would quote the Cheshire Cat often, saying *We're all mad here*, and then beam at Mary.

"Very interesting," she would say. "Especially coming from you."

Above the bookshelf, looming huge and homely, was his father's map. It was not made of paper or canvas; instead it had been hand-carved directly into the wood, etched with knives and chisels, daubed with paint and pencil, with notations everywhere, even across the chinking between logs. From a distance it looked like an amorphous mess, but when you stood close and studied its details the thing was admirable, and it made perfect sense. Like every map-maker, Moreland had put himself at the centre of the world. The cabin was a simple red O carved into the wood at an adult's eye level. The rest described the jagged ranges in which they lived, the lakes and towns, the rivers, the rail lines, and everything beyond.

He had even devised a way of conflating distances. Two areas that in the real world were some distance apart might be placed side by side with notations between them, "2D↑" to denote a trek of two days on foot and a rise in altitude. The mark "5H↓↓" meant five hours of steep downhill travel. You always knew direction by assuming the traveller was going away from home, or failing that, you read directions left to right. The two major towns were Banff and Laggan, the latter having only recently been renamed Lake Louise, but even most folks who lived there still used the old name. Moreland would likely never change it on this map. These had been inscribed in some detail, with larger buildings and notable houses shown, and they looked like squashed candy boxes with a ribbon of road trailing across the box. An arm's length to the right was the great, unimaginable metropolis of Calgary, but since Moreland had a marked aversion to everything a city promised — crowds, noise, police — he had never visited, and its existence was indicated with a simple nailhead and the letter *C*. At the lower margin of the map was a snake-like chiselled indentation meant to indicate the Crowsnest Pass with its daisy chain of mining towns, and below that was nothing but the cabin's floor. Everything south of the Pass, including the American border, was out of frame.

Now Jack lay his stolen books on top of those precious older ones, to press them flat. He riffled through the nun's notebook, the flowing blue-black script blurring and waving at the margins, her drawings and diagrams and charts flashing past too quickly to read. Then he lay it at the apex of his pile of books, and went about scrounging again.

The whetstone was eventually found where it had landed under a collapsed shelf. But there was no longer anything for him to sharpen. The hatchet and the enormous axe, as well as the snowshoes, pots, and frying pan, were gone. From this fact the boy knew someone had been in the cabin and taken whatever was useful. He knew who'd done it, too. Their nearest neighbour, Sampson.

That old man was a little superstitious; he believed in omens and was sometimes worried by his own dreams. It was just him, Sampson's own unique way of seeing the world. In some ways he was like Jack's own mother. The two of them always vigilant, attending to the ebb and flow of fortune and misfortune. Mary had once said, "He's seen bad things and that can wear you down in ways you don't expect it to. You must behave around him, Jack, and for goodness sake, don't argue with him. You're a child. He knows more than you do." So it was a shock to the boy that Sampson had even crossed the threshold of a house so marked by misfortune. But somehow he had managed it, and out of kindness and care removed valuable or delicate things, objects that might rust or attract animals; otherwise he'd left the place untouched. No, it wasn't the old man who had wrecked the place. Time and winter had.

At the back was a ladder and Jack clambered up to a small loft by the eaves. Broken axe handles. Jars full of nails. An empty barrel. The dinged tins that used to hold India tea and tobacco. He pounced on a leather pouch full of old tobacco and little white papers, formerly forbidden to him but now fair game, and he pressed the thing to his nose and assessed the stale perfume. Tucked it into his pants pocket, already feeling like a man. There was the large roughsawn trunk with leather handles. His mother's sewing box with its little black clasp, within which she had carefully arranged fine things: scissors, needle cases, a tuft of steel wool for buffing pins, tambour, embroidery floss, buttons, ribbon. A tailor's measure. He remembered her amusing him with it, before he could even count, slowly unwinding the tape and counting out the numbers — *eight, nine, ten, and what comes next?* — covering the number with her thumb. And when he was older, she laid the tape out before him and asked: *Ten plus three is . . . ? Seven-eighths of an inch minus one-quarter?*

He lifted the box and set it gently on the trunk. He told himself not to open it and look at her handwriting. He could bear looking at the nun's notebooks. But not his own mother . . . to gaze at the indigo lines and see her thoughts and her energy there. Daylight came through a ruined shingle, a shaft in which the boy stood, his movements having stirred up a liquid wash of motes.

He followed the smell of some soured thing until he found old bolts of cloth, now mouldering together in a mass, stratified and hard as shale, gone to weather and rot. So he impelled it toward the brink of the loft with the toe of his boot and watched it drop to the floor below with a mighty thud. The dog skittered outside and swung round to watch from a safer spot.

There was a yellow-and-blue girl's church dress wrapped in paper and folded into a cedar box, all that was left of his mother's tailoring career. He drew it out and held it up by the shoulders, then let it crumple back into the box. The dog wandered back inside and stood at the foot of the ladder, looking up.

Finally, he found what he was looking for: the tin of Dr. Oronsee's snuff with a smiling chow dog on it, in which his family kept all their money. Jack sat at the edge of the loft and counted out $257.43 between his thighs, the sum total of what his parents had saved on this earth. He looked at the bills and coins for a long time. Remembered the old lady cooing to him, "Don't you listen to one word they say about your daddy. That man has no interest in money."

There on the table lay Pearl, a scabbard stuffed with more than fourteen thousand dollars, a burden his father had laid on him; other people's hard-earned cash.

Slowly the boy let the coins fall across his palm into the tin's dark hole, folded the few bills and poked them inside, and fitted the lid back on. This was his family's money, earned fair and square. It would be his bank, this and no more.

LATER THAT AFTERNOON he smoked out the one-hole back-house. He took the door handle and pulled it open, trailing into the air gauzy tatters of web in which were suspended whole civilizations of insects — dozens of last summer's spiders and constellations of their victims, now little grey husks. Deliberately, and with full knowledge of the screaming crawls it would give him, the boy looked closely at each of the small horrors suspended there. Then he paced about the clearing, hunch-shouldered, a delicious tingling all over his scalp, before going back for another wincing look.

His mother had dreaded going to the outhouse. Not for the reasons most people did — night animals, the cold seat, insects. It was something else. She would approach this door and hold the handle for a second before flinging it back with something resembling defiance. As if she hoped to catch some interloper hiding inside. Father and son would watch this show from the bright cabin door, waiting for her inevitable shake of the head. No one in there. Not this time.

The boy now stood at the selfsame door and wondered: What had she expected to see there? Or who? The woman was unafraid of the dark, of spiders or mice or snakes, of cougar, bears, of lightning or dynamite or guns. She was troubled only by strangers, the vulnerability of sleep, and the workings of her own mind. He looked into the simple box. It was quiet and empty and unremarkable. He became aware of a gentle sucking of air from the hole, a natural breeze caused by the open door, tresses of speckled cobweb yearning toward it from the doorframe. What had his mother seen in this empty air that he could not? Was something there, some invisible thing, crouched and looking back at him?

The dog, he noticed, had backed away from the outhouse and was now standing at a distance of ten paces, by the cabin's door, still curious but watchful.

So Jack set to smoking every last thing in there, real or imagined, to extinction. In his zeal he used too much tinder and came close to burning the entire crapper down. There he was, laughing with his boy's cracking voice, shovelling handfuls of soil onto the blaze while the box belched white smoke into the air that plumed and twisted into the trees, a white pillar visible for miles.

Seventeen

THE OLD MAN's hearing was still acute, so he was waiting at
his open door long before his visitor emerged from the trees.
Jack had guided the Morgan laterally down the slope, coming
from the south, because he'd been taught it was polite to come
the long way round to this man's front door, make noise,
approach slowly so his host had time to prepare himself —
which might include pulling up trousers over his long johns,
finding his hat, clearing the usual mass of gun parts off the
table. But that day, the old man stepped trouserless from his
front door, crying, "You came back!"

The boy swung the reins round a convenient branch and
stood grinning.

In a canvas shirt and a union suit that only came to his
knobby knees, the old man crossed the clearing in five enormous strides, seized the child and raised his thin body up as
if he weighed nothing. Jack Boulton couldn't help himself:
he shrieked with laughter, and then just dangled there like
a happy child, beaming down at the old man, who grinned
up at him. Jack put his palm on the salt-and-pepper hair and
said, "I was scared you'd be gone, too."

Sampson Beaver II, who sometimes called himself "the
second," or simply "the other one," put the boy down and

stood back. It was still the boy's face, but already the man-to-be was staring out of it. Sampson took in the taller body, the hollow eyes, the limestone complexion. Too long down there, among the crowds. The old man considered it an unhealthy choice to live in town.

"Ah, little boy," he said, as he always had.

Jack threw his arms around the old man's ribs and began to hop up and down.

"Okay okay," Sampson said, staggering with the assault. "Wonîdîkta heza?"

"Nah," the boy said, "I ate plenty."

At this the old man sobered, for he knew what pitiful scraps of food he himself had left in their cabin. Dust and dregs. He took Jack Boulton by the shoulders and propelled him into the house, which was warm and dark. He slid a pot forward on the stove so it would heat and sat the boy down in the single chair. Bread dough was rising in a bowl under a damp tea towel. Wild onions on the table, and a potato. No gun parts visible today; Sampson was cooking. Neatly stacked wood against the back wall and above that hung an oilskin coat. On the bed lay a tattersall quilt over which was spread-eagled the headless pelt of a very large grizzly, couped forearms dangling to the floor. Sampson stepped into his canvas pants, hiked them up, and tied the rope belt, then he went about taking the blocks away from the glassless windows to let in some light, some air, setting each square of wood on the floor at his feet and blowing evergreen debris out of the corners. Meanwhile he kept up a constant parley with himself in Nakoda, only a smattering of which the boy understood.

He had seen the smoke rising from Moreland's cabin. In fact, Sampson said "your father's house." He would never refer to Mary by name for he was superstitious, about everything, but particularly death. It couldn't be smoke from a stove — far too thick — so what was on fire? He was too far away to ride up there and douse it himself. He'd never arrive in time; he could do nothing but watch. And so he had gazed at the belching white smoke and checked the wind, increasingly worried that it would turn into a serious blaze, catch the nearby trees. But slowly the billows had withered until it was just a rill, a few wisps, then nothing. Danger over, the fire had gone out. He'd wandered back into his cabin, sat at the table, and marvelled at the obvious fact: *someone* was at Moreland's old place controlling the fire. No question about it.

He'd sat there for a long time pondering who exactly had moved in to the cabin. Who was his new neighbour? And why would anyone choose to live there, given that the cabin was undoubtedly haunted? And why were they setting things on fire?

He had made himself some coffee and considered various potential squatters — after all, it was a good cabin. It might be those two Swedes — brothers or best friends or whatever they were — but the Swedes preferred to build their own cabins and lean-tos according to their own foreign specifications. Incredibly well built, well situated, their little refuges were all over these parts, perfect for hunting and trapping. No, as weird as those boys were, they would never need to squat in some old, possessed cabin. Sampson had not guessed it was Jack, for he had assumed the child was forever lost to the miseries of town. And so he had pondered the possibility the fugitive Moreland had come back from wherever he'd been wandering. But that didn't follow, either; why would he set his own cabin on fire?

Sampson stopped talking. He looked at his guest for an answer.

"I smoked out the crapper," the boy explained. "It got away from me."

The old man said nothing but he looked unimpressed. He put a bowl of impossibly thick venison stew down in front of Jack with a wooden spoon stuck upright in it like a shovel in a pile of soil.

The boy began a fevered gobbling. After a few mouthfuls he feigned self-control. "Good," he said. "Thank you." Then he went after the stew.

For a long time, Sampson watched the kid eat, hands in his deep pockets. Jack was a little taller now, growing out of his clothes. His arms beginning to show muscle, the wrist bones thicker than they had been. To Sampson, the boy was looking increasingly like a dark version of William Moreland.

"Boy," he said, "you shouldn't believe what they say about your father."

Jack stopped eating. To him, the unwelcome subject had come out of the blue.

"He didn't do any of that." Sampson said.

The kid said nothing. He could hear the uncertainty in Sampson's voice, the vaguest hint of underlying worry that it was all true. Jack knew the old man was trying to convince himself.

"Why would your father steal money?"

The boy sighed. "I truly don't know."

"It doesn't make sense. It was someone else. Has to be."

Jack Boulton stirred the mess around in his bowl. He could no longer eat. He must not cry or the old man would be appalled. He ventured, "What if it *is* him, Sampson?"

"Your father's not that kind of man. Money's not a good enough reason."

"No, it's not," Jack said. "But people think it is."

Sampson nodded for a long time, and finally sighed, "My youngest son never stops talking about what things cost. I don't know how to stop him."

He said this like his son had visited that morning, but of course he hadn't. No one had. Sampson's wife, Lena, lived seventeen miles away in a little village recently renamed Lake Louise, though Lena and most everyone else still called it Laggan. She and Sampson had three grown sons, the oldest of whom was starting to grey at the temples. But Sampson's family didn't live with him in the Sawback Range. In fact, the government refused Nakoda people the right to live in the park at all, for it had become a kind of game preserve, tourist destination, and spa — the latter thanks to the natural hot springs, the extraordinary beauty of the place, and the two massive luxury hotels. Long before the boy was born, the Rocky Mountains Park had been created, and immediately the Stoney Nakoda people had been forced en masse out of the mountains. They were banned from hunting and fishing inside the park lest paying sport hunters from Europe or America, or any other place where money was abundant, be led to disappointment. Sampson himself didn't leave the Sawback range, and the warden knew enough not to force the issue. Everyone liked Sampson, but he was not the kind of man you argued with.

The old man had sometimes agreed to paid employment with local outfitters like Thom Wilson, leading treks to remote areas, tracking game. He liked Wilson, and he found the man's ceaseless irascibility amusing. Mostly Sampson lived up here alone, but he visited his family frequently and joined sometimes in the kind of town life they preferred. His wife, for one, hated isolation, and she absolutely would not tolerate being a day's ride from the nearest grocer.

So it was his habit to visit her every few weeks. She wasn't afraid of the icy weather in that range, for Lena was used to cold. Mountain weather is changeable, so she had taught him how to predict the weather. She would rise late at night and assess the brightness of the stars; that method offered a fair degree of accuracy, and it worked for Sampson. But there was little you could do besides predict, correctly or not, what was about to hit you.

One week it could be a struggle just to exit the cabin, snow up to his hips. Or maybe the air was so parched and frigid that it caught in his throat, and he had to wear every stitch of leather clothing he owned to keep from freezing, and waddle around, plump as a toddler. But the next day might bring a windless sky and bright sun, and thereafter he might sit bare-chested on a chair outside and sip coffee while melt-water streamed from the cabin's roof and ran in rivulets past his boots, the forest all athump with falling clumps of snow.

It was not a life that appealed to most, but it pleased Sampson.

Now the old man reached out with the toe of his boot and pushed a wooden box full of gun parts out from under the table and away from the kid's feet. He gazed into the box, assessing its contents, then said as an aside, "Where's that ugly thing?"

"What?"

"The stupid gun Wilson put on his wall. Where is it now?"

"You knew it was mine?"

"Wilson told me it was your favourite gun."

"It's not!" Jack barked out. "And I left it at home. Didn't want to carry it."

"Good. I don't want you using it. Not that gun, or any gun."

"Why?"

"You are too young," Sampson said slowly in a tone that forbade argument. "No hunting on your own. Only with me. You understand?"

The kid nodded meekly and said, "Okay." There was something reassuring in the man's authority, in the familiar air of that cabin, and Jack's anxiety abated a little. He spooned up more of the stew and said, "Can we go hunting soon?"

"I'll think about it."

The dog came to the door, unfurled its tongue, and panted at them.

"*You*," said the old man. "I wondered where he'd got to. That dog just comes and goes."

The dog came wagging inside, claws clicking on the floorboards. Sampson thumped its side. A leggy mongrel, all muscle and bone, it might weigh almost as much as the kid did.

"He was with you last night?"

"Yup."

"How did he know you were home?"

The kid looked down at the dog and chewed thoughtfully. "The hell if I know."

Sampson sat heavily on the other chair, more of a stool since the back had fallen off, put his elbows on the table, and fixed Jack with a look. "When your father comes back, you will be glad."

The kid stared him down.

"Until then, it is a good idea if you live here with me. Just until he comes back."

"What? No, no. I'm going home."

"I will make you a bed. It can go near the stove. You'll be warm."

Jack shook his head. "I'm fine on my own."

Sampson looked at the kid's thin spring jacket, ornate with Mary's embroidery: flowers, equilateral crosses, vines curling into letters. "You need a warmer coat," he said.

"This one's perfect."

"It won't do. The cold's coming in."

The boy threw a dubious glance out the door into the bright sunny yard. "Naw," he said with confidence, "looks good to me."

Sampson sighed. He pointed to the west wall, where he'd collected everything he'd taken from the cabin, all stacked and tidy. Pots, the frying pan, snowshoes and saws, tools and the axe. Atop the pile was Mary Boulton's striped blanket coat, and on top of that sat her hat. It was small and grey and well kept. The boy realized that the old man had forgotten these things were hers, or he would never have touched them.

Before he left that afternoon, Jack Boulton shrugged into the heavy coat then took the hat by the crown and levered it onto his head. He looked like exactly what he was: a lanky kid wearing his mother's clothes.

Sampson had told the boy to finish his lunch, and then had given him a few provisions for home, just to start him off: necessaries for baking bread and biscuits, strips of extraordinarily dry and chewy smoked meat, coffee grounds that the old man wrapped in a blue kerchief, currants as dry and hard as

stones, and a scrap of paper folded around a few pebbles of salt.
They had talked about the boy's plans, from which he would
not deviate and which were fairly simple: Go home. Stay home.
Fish if you want, make bread, read books. Do not hunt except
with Sampson. Fix the corral fence. Do something about that
mess of tools and junk in the shed, at least tidy up some of it.

"You'll visit some, then?" the boy said.

"Tomorrow."

Sampson stood in his doorframe and watched Jack loading
the horse with his family's belongings, ready to pack them
home. He was doing it properly. He stood taller now and had
the muscled shoulders of a man, but his dark hair fell to his
nape, and that neck was still impossibly delicate, a child's
neck. He was a chimera, neither grown man nor young boy;
for the moment he was both, or neither. Sampson wasn't sure
how old Jack was, but with parents like those two, he must
surely have a *few* good skills. Then there was the mitigating
calm that was his basic nature. In contrast to Sampson's own
sons, who even his wife admitted had taken turns being wild-
cats, Jack had been a quiet baby, a watchful toddler. He did
possess a startling temper, but it flared so infrequently and
lasted such a short time you forgot it was there. Mostly he was
pensive, and a good student. If you showed him something
once, he never forgot it. Despite this recent idiocy with the
outhouse, he seemed to Sampson a practical kid. But now,
for the first time in his life, Jack Boulton was alone.

Watching Moreland's son begin to lead the loaded horse
away, Sampson tried to keep the words from coming out of
him, but they came anyway. He said, "Don't do anything
else stupid."

"I won't."

Jack started up the windy slope toward that empty cabin, under high cloud and the waving creak of pines. Even the way he walked looked different.

"Be careful," Sampson called.

Jack turned and smiled at him. "You, too."

IT WAS COLD that night when Jack Boulton awoke to angry voices. He sat upright on the bed just as his mother stepped across the threshold. He opened his mouth to speak but nothing would come out. Sunlight, or perhaps torches, some kind of fiery illumination burned through the door behind her, light so intense that tears sprang to the child's eyes and Mary's body appeared a papery silhouette; cool blue, and standing between him and all that fire.

Get up, Jack, get up now. They're coming.

There were many men out in the yard, in the brightness. The boy could hear their angry voices, hear their feet trampling the ground outside, and they brought with them a horrible sound, some instrument or mechanical thing that tolled like a cracked church bell.

The boy tried to scream. And then he jolted awake, really awake. Lying on his back, panting.

"Oh god," he sighed and put a hand to his eyes. He struggled to sit up, to hold himself on thin, trembling arms. Of course there were no men in the yard. But the dog was with him in the bed. He rubbed his cheeks with his hands. Heart still throbbing horribly, the dreadful sense that something was imminent, some inexorable force headed his way, followed by the slow, vertiginous drop out of the dream, where none of it meant a thing. Just a dream. The patina of the awful clanging sound still fading in his ears.

It was full night, a high silver moon, and pure darkness where he lay, the sound of dry aspen leaves clawing the wood floor in gusts, blown across his threshold from the outer dark. He figured the dog had pushed the door open again. It was cold enough that it might have begun to snow. Sampson was right, he'd be glad of his mother's blanket coat.

The dog clambered upright out of sleep and towered over Jack, sniffing the boy's face. It knelt and rubbed its eyes against his chest, and finally nosed under his armpit until the child's eyelids sank, he flopped down again, and they rearranged themselves into sleep. His arm lay round the dog's warm ribcage. They were together again, sleeping where they had always slept, as if time had not passed. The bed alone was unchanged in this utterly transformed cabin—the boy and the dog in their warm capsule, floating on a magic carpet high above someone else's sad tale. Leaves scattered on the floor. Snow riding on the air.

After a moment, Jack scooched down under the covers, extended a naked foot out into the room, and eased the cabin door closed with his toes.

➤ *Eighteen*

WARMTH STILL RADIATED from suntanned bark as William Moreland made his way through the trees and deeper into the Crowsnest Pass, heading west and toward the Great Divide, heading for mining towns and logging camps he remembered from decades ago.

Avoiding now the actual rail line lest he encounter people, Moreland moved necessarily in a meander, uphill and down, into gullies, moving parallel to the tracks, just far enough into the trees to be out of sight. When he saw at a distance what looked like a moonscape he knew exactly where he was, and over the next hour worked his way toward the devastation of the Frank slide. Once he reached the edge of the rubble he was necessarily forced onto the road. There were no trees anyway to give him cover and the ground was so uneven and littered with boulders it was almost impossible to traverse it. And so he trotted along that road, the pale limestone wreckage standing ten feet above his head on either side. Here a strip had been wiped off the green earth leaving nothing but broken rock.

Mining in the town of Frank had caused faults in the mountain, and water had flowed into those fissures, and ice had formed. One night in 1903 the summit had simply detached, and a hundred million tonnes of limestone roared downhill, right over the town. The slide had moved like a hand with fingers spread, so that some houses were obliterated, others were untouched. The deluge of rock flowed across this very road, passed over the rail line, dammed up the river, and in its great unstoppable speed, carried over the valley floor and partway up the other side of the Pass. It was the worst mining disaster Moreland had ever heard of, and somehow Mary Boulton had survived it.

He stood looking up, not breathing, a hand pressed unconsciously to the pang in his chest. She had been nineteen years old and pregnant with Jack, though neither of them yet knew it.

He took off at a sprint and ran until he could no longer do it, walked hard until he was wobbly with the effort, reached the far edge of the debris field and cut uphill, panting and scrambling.

Mary would say, *Look forward not back, and keep moving.*

NIGHT WHEN IT came was tranquil and crisp, constellations blooming above him whenever he crossed open areas, Moreland's black figure rocking its way forward, hunchbacked under the knapsack, under those stars. Just before Blairmore he began to hunt out a sheltered spot to sleep.

An hour later, he was sitting upon his knapsack allowing himself the luxury of a modest fire. Tarp unfurled and ready for him to roll up in it, cover his head, and sleep. His legs were spread wide, and he held a long green branch to stir the edges of the fire, watching a ballet of small flames atop the logs, each pop of light roused by something inside the wood, now wavering, now seeming to slide to another spot, where it roused again. At first the sight was lovely to him. But then some instinct began to nag, an intimation that he was missing something. This was a tale told in light and blackened char, in twirling ribbons of smoke and steam, wordless and indifferent to human understanding, but a story nonetheless. A tree's last breath as it burned, the exhalation of all it had witnessed in its many years alive in this spot.

William Moreland jolted and his eyes raked the trees about him. Indeed, he was missing something.

Half-blinded by firelight, he could still hear furtive footfalls and a man clearing his throat. Five more strides and then silence — he estimated the man to be twenty paces west-northwest. The stranger knew he'd been perceived, since the Ridgerunner was staring directly at him blindly.

Moreland's mind whispered, *Police*. His hearing swung round behind him, trying to sense other men out there, moving or breathing. He listened to the windless dark. No one else there, he was almost certain, just one man.

The stranger came into the firelight, a greyish upright figure sauntering as if he'd been expected. "Goodness," the man said, "I wasn't sure what to do." His voice was so long unused it was soft as fingers through sand.

He was a tall man, cadaverous and wiry, cocooned inside a dressing of many coats and sweaters and shirts, everything so worn and decayed he was mostly gone to thread and seam. The torn collars of two different shirts hung like tongues over his left shoulder. His hat no longer had a brim, nor did it have a top, and he looked like he was wearing a paper party crown. His skin was lacquered with what, to Moreland's practised eye, looked like decades of unaddressed filth, but out of that slate-grey face stared startlingly clear eyes.

Moreland allowed his held breath to ease out of him.

The guest simply plunked himself down cross-legged on the ground. Then, like an actor on stage, he extended his skeletal and bloodless fingertips toward the fire in a pantomime of warming himself, but he was a body-length away from the fire and could not possibly feel heat from where he sat. He tilted his head to one side and regarded his host almost fondly. "Been a while," he said.

Moreland blinked.

"Have you searched for me very long?"

"I haven't been looking for you at all."

The man's mouth cracked open in amused delight, his gums swollen and purple, and his laugh was all air, like a fast-panting dog. "You found me, anyway. Well done."

"Mister, I don't know who you are."

This produced genuine astonishment. "You don't?"

"No."

The man fetched up a pine cone, hopped it in his palm a few times like a Ping-Pong ball then tossed it into the fire to burn. He said, "I understand. It's not your fault. You just lose track of things sometimes."

A mad thought crossed Moreland's mind that this man was a vanguard for the police, some harmless simpleton sent ahead to keep the Ridgerunner occupied and puzzled while they got into position, like dangling a bright object before an animal before you strike it down. He shifted slightly on the knapsack, horribly aware of the money under him, and of the smiling and uninvited guest watching him from across the fire. He forced out, "Perhaps I forgot. I've had a long walk today."

"You look good, in any case. A lot better than I do." The

man opened his arms to show the condition of his clothing. "Compared to me you look like a bridegroom on his wedding day." Again came that panting laugh, and then it stopped as a thought occurred. "Are you a family man, Ronnie?"

Moreland managed to shake his head.

"Now, see? *That's* how a man should live. Don't let 'em get their hooks into you. Don't get dragged down. Would you believe it to look at me that I am a father?"

Moreland's face registered nothing at all. He simply waited for more.

His guest meanwhile slid into disappointment like someone who has botched a joke. "I don't blame you not believing me."

"I didn't say that."

"And I know your name's not Ronnie. I just like the sound of it. Don't you?"

They looked at the fire together for a while and the spectre murmured to himself, his voice too low for Moreland to hear and his eyes unfocussed, staring at his knees. After a while he shuffled his skinny ass closer to the fire, and grinned. "Goodness," he said again, "that's a nice feeling." Clearly, the heat was a surprise to him, as if he'd thought the flames were an illusion. He hunched over his crossed legs, russet fingernails playing in the loam as he reckoned something. Many minutes later he nodded slowly, dreamily, and said, "I think she had four babies." His hand rose to his neck, worked its way like a spider through his layers of collars, and scratched.

Moreland rose abruptly. "I'd best be heading on."

The stranger stopped scratching and goggled up at him, those clear eyes widening. "Why go? I mean, you just got here."

But Moreland was already rolling up his tarp and collecting his things, forcing himself not to look at the poor demon sitting on the ground as the fire failed, the night giving itself over again to cold starlight.

"Did I make you mad? I didn't mean to. Now, you just settle yourself back down here, I'm telling you what you ought to do."

Moreland said, "I'm on my way now."

"The hell you are." The stranger started to scrabble up but saw Moreland's hands working something out of the knapsack, and when he saw what it was, he sat down again.

The hatchet emerged handle-first and the Ridgerunner slid it through a belt loop as casually as if it were a hammer and he a carpenter. He straddled his knapsack ready to heft it, while both hands smoothed the front of his coat, the way a gentleman might do before he went for a stroll. He looked intently at his guest, seeing himself, or a version of himself if life had been different, if he'd never come across Mary Boulton. In his teens Moreland had had skills this poor creature still didn't, but ability only gets you so far. You might survive into middle age, but then months and years of cold, the hunger, the whole, hard world would close in on you, and you'd simply vanish, just as animals vanish when they die, mourned by no one, missed by no one, with no more purpose to your life than the loam that settles over you and breaks you down, brings you into the earth. The whole of you nothing but hide and bones, and very little of those. This man was halfway there. William Moreland sighed and said, "Where are you camped?"

The stranger's hands were claws at his sides. He did not speak.

Moreland drew out two cans of pork and beans and a small can of orange slices and set them on the ground on his side of the fire. "Do you have a can opener?"

The stranger was already fighting tears, his Adam's apple working and his eyes blinking. His *no* was soundless.

A can opener came down with a *click* on top of the cans. Moreland shouldered his knapsack and stood looking down on the stranger, who was now openly weeping. He said, "Eat wild onions, they're good for your gums. Do you hear me?"

The man nodded.

"And you need salt. I'm sorry I don't have any."

The man nodded again.

"Don't follow me."

The spectre slapped the ground and sobbed. He tried to say something but his voice had abandoned him. Moreland left him to the failing fire, and backed away into the trees.

✦ Nineteen

THE NEXT MORNING Jack Boulton opened the door to a cold March day. He boiled coffee, he made unleavened biscuits full of currants following a recipe he'd found handwritten on a card, and then he ate half of them. It seemed to him a leisurely day, a day of rest after his travels. He had to admit Sampson was right, none of his childhood clothes fit well anymore, so he put on one of his father's shirts and rolled up the sleeves. The collar was loose and it had a mild pong of mildew, but it fit well across the shoulders.

Thus dressed, he went outside into the clearing and chopped wood until his shoulders ached. The swing of the axe, the rip of wood parting lengthwise and falling away to the littered ground. Chips everywhere. He swung the axe in slow, careful rhythm, letting its weight do the work as he'd been taught. The chopping block stood lower than he remembered, the axe felt lighter. The warm sun lay on his back like a hand resting there.

With a good pile of split logs that might last two days he swung round and leaned the axe against the house, under the eaves. There, in the dirt just to the left of the door, he saw his mother's footprints, inches from where he now stood. Perfectly clear impressions of her small boots. He'd been just about to step forward and scuff them away forever, but he leapt in a twisting stagger, righted himself, and stared down at those artefacts. She'd been standing there, alive.

Carefully he collected heavy logs and set them round the marks, like an archaeologist blocking out a site. He didn't know what else to do. Then he sat heavily on the front stoop and allowed himself to imagine she was standing next to him. In some small way, it helped.

Of course his father's bootprints were everywhere, as always with their heel marks, an *M* for the left foot, a *B* for the right. But time and weather and the boy's own fresher prints were slowly erasing those.

He looked now at the ground and it was scissoring and trembling as his eyes welled; he could not stop. His home was teeming with absence.

That first night, when he had arrived at the cabin in the pitch dark, he had simply flopped down into the clammy bed, choosing as he always did his own spot and leaving his mother's vacant. It is a hard habit to break for those who sleep together: your side of the bed, my side of the bed. His father never had any side at all, he simply slid in wherever he could, like the dog did, seeking warmth. But now, left alone, Jack was beginning to spread out, to sprawl, to wrangle with the dog for space.

He had realized early in life that his mother was not like other people. He knew somewhere in his heart, too, that she heard things. Maybe even saw things. It didn't happen often, nor did they seem to be awful in nature, but they sometimes took her by surprise. Mostly she seemed to find the episodes tiresome. One day she had asked his father to cut down two dead pines that were rubbing together and making ludicrous haunted-house creaks in the wind.

"I find myself listening to them," she said. "They parley with me. And frankly, I'm sick of it."

She whispered to herself when she thought no one was looking, perhaps to keep those other whispers at bay. Then again, his father sometimes talked to himself too, winning an argument with someone unseen. Two hermits settling into their grand privacy. Of course, she was constantly talking to her child as they played or did chores or as they did their lessons together — the two of them learning from the same books. A little ledger in which they pencilled their calculations. They reproduced entire passages from novels, word for word.

Moreland went into town sometimes and came back with newspapers; with books and pencils and rubbers "donated" by the local schoolhouse, after hours. Mary looked amused, but the kid simply pounced on these great gifts, never questioning their provenance. Moreland read out loud to his family serial stories from last month's newspapers, and Mary tried to teach them both how to commit even long runs of text to memory, for she had a prodigious mind for that. She taught her son to launder and sew and bake, so that, in her words, "You will not be a burden to your wife." Running stitch, back stitch, couching, welted seam, French seam. She taught him to mitre his corners, sift three times, to feel mild temperatures with his wrist. "Hold this bag of flour — that's what a pound feels like." But after he was supposed to be in bed and asleep, she had a way of whispering to herself as she worked, as she sewed or scrubbed pots, always whispering, the words too indistinct for him to make out. The child drowsed and took comfort in the sound of his mother's soft voice, the little tick of a word with a *T* in it, the slide of an *S*. He would lie in the bed and watch her lean into the lamplight, her lips moving, always moving, with barely a sound.

It came to him one night that she was speaking to him, telling him something important, imparting secrets, tales of shipwrecks and lost children, wolves that could speak like men, wondrous caverns in the earth that she alone knew the lay of. Whenever his father was gone on one of his rambles, they could stretch out together in the bed, and the boy followed her breaths, translated the half-words, English to English, alighting on clear landmarks like *cinnamon* or *shooting*, and rushing off into his own imagined stories, adventures that he put in her mouth and let her tell him. It was best when she sewed, for during these hours her whispers came urgently and she gazed at the cloth in her hands as if it mirrored her thoughts. Sometimes she would pause to look at him, deliberately, to calm herself, to gaze at her own good boy, and her restlessness would ease.

He remembered being very young and pressing his cheeks down into her cupped hands and crying because he'd been bad, and knew it. He remembered waking between them, with his fingers in his mother's hair and his foot pressed against his father's belly as if to push the man off the bed. He remembered shouting at them, "You never let me do anything!" He remembered her slim fingers, the smell of woodsmoke in her hair. He remembered her blowing on his face and saying, "The fox, the clever fox, ran so fast through the wind and the grass to catch those mice." She blew again and said, "He ran and ran, so quickly, the clever fox ran, until . . . Oh!" and she pressed her hand over the boy's eyes. "The poor fox fell off the edge of the world. And what did he see then?"

The boy would sing out, "Nothing."

Or he'd say, "The king of the mice."

Or he would conjecture, calmly, as his eyes gazed into the darkness of her warm palm, about the trees and buildings and improbable animals and magical devices and civilizations, about the people living and dead, about everything that was surely there, at the final reach of things, and the fox would find them all.

It was a story they had concocted together about the edge of the world. Beyond which . . . who knew? Of course the earth was round and had no edge, they knew that perfectly well . . . but the *world*?

One time, she had asked him what the fox saw and he said, "Just a big old hand," and Mary had fallen back onto the bed laughing.

Like most children, Jack had an almost total lack of interest in his parents' origins, except as they explained his own. In any case, they rarely spoke of their lives before him. If he cut or scraped himself badly enough, there was no poultice. Instead they would discuss who would "rub salt in the wound." That wasn't what they did, strictly speaking, but it felt like that to Jack. As the boy grew, only Moreland had the strength to pin him down and wash the wound. It was an old woodsman's trick, and it worked. Mary would boil and cool the water and add the salt, and then Moreland caught the boy and washed the cut, pouring and pouring the water over it, rinsing out debris, cleansing the cut without touching it, as Mary offered criticisms as to his technique and Jack winced and whimpered and glared at his father, and when it was over, the kid would tear himself free and run into his mother's arms, as if she'd had no role in it at all.

At home she wore woollen pants, men's shirts, and boots that came up to her knees. She had sewn many dresses for the ladies in town, but didn't own a single one herself. When she rode into town to deliver tailored goods to various women, she dressed "formally," in her doe-hide trousers and a long embroidered riding jacket, her dark hair in a single plait that hung to her waist. And she wore that same wide-brimmed hat. She looked like something grand and strange, a woman out of a Wild West show.

Sometimes she brought the boy with her, lifted him onto the Morgan and hugged him to her almost as a talisman, for his presence always calmed her. He himself thrilled at the outing, a chance to see the wonders of a town teeming with twelve hundred souls, and not least because he always got a treat. But as they neared the outskirts his mother's unease rose perceptibly, rolled off her in cold waves. Jack would crane round in the saddle and look up at her, put his hand on her encircling arm and counsel her to be brave. She would smile and say, "You're right," and sometimes she did look composed, but she cut no less bizarre a figure. Loathing crowds, she avoided the main street. She was so tongue-tied when buying supplies in those stores that eventually the boy, hopping in anticipation, would burst in and act as a kind of translator, helping strangers communicate with the distant planet that was his mother.

To her customers she was Mrs. Moreland. She seemed to trust no one in town, unless it was the nun herself, Sister Beatrice, who alone knew her given name, and with whom Mary had a private business deal: every tapestry, every altar covering, the cassocks and surplices, even the rector's shirts and collars were tailored or embroidered by Mary Boulton, for money. The nun would meet mother and child at the back door, accept the offered package, and say, "Good timing, Mary. Coffee's on." And then she'd go make some.

Sister Beatrice, Emelia Cload, the nun, *she*, affected nonchalance during these visits, but her face suffused with pleasure and her movements became lively, for she too was a kind of hermit, if an unwilling one. On one visit, the boy played a trick on her and hid behind his mother's body. When the nun came to the door he watched as her eyes leapt everywhere, as they raked the Morgan, raked Mary, until finally they locked on him. As he sauntered out into view, the nun had heaved a sigh: "*There* you are."

Mary once said, "She's got no one. I know what that feels like."

His mother refused to enter most houses, but simply waited at the door for payment, or took verbal orders for more tailored goods, committing the collar sizes and waist measurements to memory without use of pencil and paper. But with the nun, she would sit sometimes for an afternoon, and they would talk together as friends. Two quiet and thoughtful women, they still managed to make one another laugh from time to time. To the boy their conversation seemed to go in no particular direction but wandered randomly over the many dull aspects of adult life, or over those points of female existence that seemed important to them but meant nothing whatever to Jack.

He would beg for coffee whenever it arrived but the nun always denied him. "Coffee is for adults," she would say and lay the cup in front of Mary. But there was cake for him, as much as he wanted. She would inquire about his favourite treats; did he like Turkish delight, peppermint stick, rock candy, humbugs? Sometimes, when she bustled off to find her pocketbook, Mary would lean over and let Jack lift the coffee cup to his lips, saying in her quiet voice, "Just a sip." And in this way, they would both go home happier, the pepped-up boy bouncing in the saddle, Mary with money in her pocket and orders for another tailored item. But a block away from the relative safety of the old lady's house Mary's arm went round Jack, and her calm would drain away entirely. She was rigid and watchful, keeping to the side streets, and her eyes when they passed over people carried a feral warning.

You can't stop a very young child from blabbing out whatever they are thinking, but for years, Jack was too young to reliably describe his home, and when he did try to direct a stranger, he would point, often in the wrong compass direction, and opine that it was "Ages and ages that way."

So no one except Sampson and his wife knew the location of their home. Mary wouldn't allow it. Whenever either of his parents ventured into either Banff or Laggan, they deliberately swung round to the far end of town and entered from the opposite side, hoping to misdirect anyone who might be curious enough to take note of their entry or exit. But anyone paying attention would have been quite perplexed by Mary sauntering along on the Morgan, a woman in doehide trousers and overcoat with a long dark plait down her back, as unlikely to be arriving from the blackened village at Bankhead mine as to have come from tea and crumpets in the luxurious dining room in Mount Stephen House at Field. Still, that had been his mother's strict rule for more than a decade: enter town from the wrong direction, leave the same way, do not correct your trajectory until out of sight.

To the boy it seemed an excess of caution, and it added to the trip. Ages and ages. And he never thought to ask why any of it was necessary. To him, it was just the way his parents were. They were unlike other people in so many ways, this was just one of them.

Later, during his illness, as he lay in a long hospital bed, Sister Beatrice had held his hand and spoken to him, already using the name she had given him, saying, "You are a unique creation, Charles, special in God's eyes." He'd replied weakly that he didn't know about God but everyone was unique. Still, perhaps she was right about one thing: he felt as different from his mother and father as any random visitor would be, as if he had walked in from some other world and seated himself between them. At his age, he saw only the differences.

Sitting now in the sun, at the door of his own cabin, Jack Boulton had to admit that he'd abandoned a woman who cared for him, he'd up and left just as abruptly as his father always did. Worse than that, he'd stolen from her. Books she didn't want, surely, but also her nurse's notebook. It was like stealing private diaries, peering into her thoughts. He'd been motivated by a flash of sentimentality at seeing her clean, restrained handwriting, but it was still stealing. He hadn't the right. He'd done a savage thing to her, to leave her without warning. Now they were both alone again. The difference was, he wanted it that way.

In this regard too he was no better than his father, and to Jack that idea was almost unbearable.

At least his father always came back bringing news, curios, treats, and tales from his various rambles. A mountain lake so cold it was filled with ice crystals and when the sun hit the water it glowed an unearthly shade of blue. He described the workings of box cameras to the boy and explained how the glass film worked. He told them how aneroid barometers could predict the weather, and once, he brought back bits of a broken device that, if they could fix it or find new parts, would detect altitude down to the nearest hundred feet. The boy was introduced thereby to the notion of sea level.

He had lived his whole life at eight thousand feet without ever thinking about it, and he had never seen the sea. All those oceans he had floated on in his imagination. The boy in *Treasure Island* marvelling at the grown men around him, "What blood and sorrow, what good ships scuttled on the deep"; the boy in *The Coral Island* thrown terrifyingly free, "Alone, in the midst of the wide Pacific." Those stories no less real than his father's tales; how strange to feel he had really been there, in all of those places, and know he had not.

On the wall map, in the areas describing lakes and mountains, William Moreland had taken a hand drill and augured a hole for every one of the known locations of the Swedes' cabins and lean-tos. To date he'd found fifteen of them, in various sizes.

No one knew too much about the Swedes. But their building acumen was extraordinary, exceeded only by their total lack of interest in the rest of the human race. You might see them at a distance, two blond heads bent together, skinning a kill or cleaning hide or smoking the meat in long, thin strips, and you might wave to them or call out, but they would never look at you or wave back or give any acknowledgement that you, too, were present on the earth. Either they couldn't handle a horse, or horses couldn't tolerate them, so they carried their own goods on a travois, taking turns dragging the long X behind them. Covered in skins and furs, weather-beaten, their pale skin streaked by smoke, they looked like European cavemen. On the rare occasions when necessity forced them into town to sell fur and purchase ammunition, people had no idea how to even speak to them. Sometimes women simply snatched up their children and hurried away. Merchants who normally didn't buy fur sometimes chose to trade or even pay for the goods rather than argue. No one cared as long as the wild blond men went on their way. Moreland had marked their shacks onto his map because these had become handy places to squat during his own hunting trips. Whether the Swedes noted his trespasses no one knew. And anyway, it was much in William Moreland's character to use whatever was at hand, whether or not it was strictly his property to use. Each time he came back from his wanderings, he added to the map, and the known world grew.

Moreland often brought home an entire elk, butchered and strapped expertly to the saddle, and the Morgan walked along with the elk's antlers balanced on its withers like skeletal wings. Elk stew was his favourite dish and he claimed to prefer it to beef. To Mary's delight, he arrived one time bearing fine cast iron pans and cooking utensils pilfered from ranger's cabins owned by the Rocky Mountains Park, and there was burned into the wooden handles the words *Do Not Remove*. He would sit at the table and read to his child, count with him, scrounge through the dictionary with him. He gave Jack his lessons, and as long as the subject was a practical one, the boy didn't mind.

What is nine hundred minus eight?

How many inches in four feet?

Make a bowline knot, make a clove hitch. This book is a pack saddle, draw me a diamond hitch with your finger.

Where is the Big Dipper? Where is the pole star? Now find Orion.

But sooner or later Moreland would begin to rise at night and pace the cabin; he would find reasons to fetch water and an hour later they would find him still standing by the creek at the precipice, watching the stars. He would walk a very long way to find kindling. Mary would see his rising energy. She would nod and say, "It's all right. We'll be fine." And then he would be gone again for weeks.

Of course he took guiding jobs from time to time, but more often he would tell his son, "I have to go exploring." The next morning he would leave them. Sometimes the boy refused to kiss his father goodbye, but Mary always put her arms round her husband's neck and said the same thing: "Come back to us." After that, the boy was alone with his mother and they could stretch out in the bed together and it seemed like there was nothing but room in the cabin.

With so many absences, Jack had become good at studying and remembering his father, the way an animal eats every last scrap and readies itself for lean times. He could call to mind the feel of Moreland's bristled cheeks; the smell of his skin; the fourteen scars on his body, each with a tall story to go with it. The wondrous lines of his weathered face. The man's rough palm passing whole over the boy's face to smooth him to sleep. His canvas pants and suspenders hung upon the door. His homemade boots with their flat heels, the little studs hammered in place with *M* on the left heel and *B* on the right.

When his father arrived home after weeks of wandering or weeks on a guiding job with Wilson, they could hear him coming, whistling. He would drop his packsack, bend down and clap his hands in welcome to his glowering son. The child, angry at him for leaving, jubilant to see him again, suffering an agonized mixture of fury and love, would wait like a sprinter until the moment his father said, "Come on, kiddo, let's have it!" And the boy would spring at him like a cat. There they were, the two of them, wrestling and grunting, the boy trying to deliver haymakers to his unresisting father, until they fell to the ground and rolled together. Mary Boulton would shadow them like a referee, wringing her fingers and saying, "Be gentle. Don't hurt him." Only later did the boy understand that she had not been speaking to him but rather to her husband, despite the fact the kid never held back and Moreland got the worst of every exchange. "Payment," he'd said once, panting, as his son hopped up and down in triumph, "for my various sins and misdemeanours."

"Payment? I see," Mary had said, fighting a smile. "Well, you're both filthy now, and who do you think is going to wash your clothes?"

One night, half-awake in the dark, lying on the pallet and sighing into his sleeping father's arms, as if the man's warmth and muscle were in fact his own, Jack had watched the glowing grate of the stove disappear behind his mother's pantlegs as she paced and stooped and tidied. Those flickering orange squares of light in the black metal looked to him, through half-closed eyes, like a town on fire, seen far away at night, and only his mother stood between him and all that misfortune.

Now, utterly alone and staring out at the clearing, wearing his father's shirt and his mother's hat, Jack was unable to look at those small bootprints, unwilling to conjure an image of the woman who had once stood right there, outside her own door, alive.

He rose with a sigh and went in to heat coffee and eat the rest of the biscuits.

Twenty

SHE SAT WAITING at the kitchen table, her back rigid, veil in her lap. The upstairs clock now stood before her under its glass bell, the little ball-weights spinning in perfect measure first one way and then the other. Nothing to be done but watch them oscillate, since she'd long ago stopped counting minutes. A cellmate at the abbey had taught her to do this, to control the nervous fits she suffered, the night terrors, the spates of fury: *Watch the weights spin forward, Bea — that is your sinful life. Watch them spin back — that is God's clemency. Do you see? He always comes back to you.* Such a good woman. So many good women there, ranged around each other in protection and love, imagining they knew the one they called Beatrice, the sister they so cared for and admired, blind to the terrible flaw in her.

Now her bloodless fingers worked the hem of her veil, picking at the seam. Meditation was fast falling apart into the ragged apprehension of time draining away.

Every electric light in the house was on, every lantern was lit, and the generator in the basement chugged. The stove was at full heat, and there was a roaring fire in the grate, but she could still see her own breath coming out in small, quick puffs because all the doors were wedged open in case the boy should wander home again like a stray cat. In that dark neighbourhood, the old house blazed out like a stranded steamboat, grinding its engines and belching a world of light onto the river.

The boy's bedroom window was propped open with a mason jar and his bedcovers were folded back. It had seemed plausible to her that he might prefer to sneak back home that way, and so she had made it easy for him. But in the morning there would be squirrels in the house and he would still be missing.

For a desolate moment the nun put her face in her hands, then shook herself crossly and sat upright. She would watch the clock. The minute hand trembled, trembled, and then sagged from II to III. She stood and went to the kitchen door for the seventh time that hour and stared out into the trees.

→ *Twenty-One*

SAMPSON BEAVER PAUSED at the elbow of a switchback to wait for scudding cloud to pass overhead and release the moon. The drowsy horse behind him bumbled against his shoulder. The old man was in discussion with himself, and with the horse, and with the unseen trees around them, the subject being how old they all were, and how he was too old to be a father to this boy, or an uncle to him, or whatever he was trying to do here. But what choice did he have if the boy refused to live with him? Preferred instead to stay in that cabin, to live alone with a ghost?

The horse hung its head over his shoulder and Sampson warmed his hands in its breath. Ice shook from the trees above and the crumbs pattered on his hat. Finally the cloud passed and they went on again, moving down the slope in their slow, heavy gait, the horse saddleless and Sampson's capacious backpack stuffed to the flap with food for the boy.

He heard the sound of running water before he saw it. They splashed through a shallow gravelled stream of runoff making its kinked way downhill from the summit and across the switchbacks, the water trickling sometimes under transparent panes of ice and swirling there. When they reached lower ground they both walked more easily, the old man talking away as they entered the first meadow. The whirr of wings above. A young, affronted fox exploded from a thicket and loped away through snow, wheeled round to take their bearing, then turned and slalomed through the trees until it was gone. They waded through snowy grass after the fox. When they got to the second meadow, the old man stopped as usual and turned to face his horse.

"Willow," he said, "it's all right."

And as usual, the horse scanned the area ahead until Sampson felt she was ready, and he took the hackamore and they left the green meadow. What they entered then was an area of burnt timber, lifeless poles all askew, the bark silvery as wasp paper. The horse's gait was tight now, uneven.

Ten years previously, in the waning weeks of a summer of unabated heat and drought, a passing train had thrown a cinder into the parched weeds. Or at least that was the theory everyone had formed after it was all over. Flames crawled along the weeds and moved in smouldering fingers into this very meadow. From there, dead grass began to smoke and burn. When it reached the trees, they too went up. Sampson had awoken, lying on his bed alone, without a wife, and heard the rare and unaccountable sound of Willow losing her mind in the corral. And then he smelled smoke.

He had burst from his sweltering cabin into the sweltering air and seen an enormous red S inscribed on the slope below. It was beautiful and appalling and already too big to do anything about. But it was moving away from him. So he had cornered his maddened horse, bridled it, and dragged it, jerking and dancing, away from his cabin, going the long way round the far side of the mountain to arrive backwise at Moreland's place, until he was standing there in nothing but his boots and long johns and hat, the horse sore in its mouth and tonguing the bit. Mary was already in a frantic effort to pack up everything useful, and the baby was trailing her like a gosling and getting underfoot.

By eight p.m., they were packed up, both horses were loaded and standing more or less calmly together in the visibly smoky air. Mary had paced the ground outside the cabin with Jack asleep in her arms, a kerchief covering his face. Together they watched the fire's progress, delaying that moment when they would necessarily have to abandon their home, Mary unwilling to even close the door of the cabin where her child had been born, saying, "It's all right, it's all right" to the sleeping boy's ear, to herself, to the soil under her black boots.

Far down by the river, the figure of the park warden arrived on an exhausted horse and, like Mary, proceeded to pace in rising anxiety back and forth along the riverbank, his hands on his hips. Ten minutes later four volunteer firemen from town slid up the rail lines on a handcar, trailed on the road by several motorcars full of excited tourists who'd followed the smoke. The warden sent the tourists packing with as much tact as a man kicking dogs off a veranda. Then he and the firemen sped off northwest to start cutting a firebreak.

Sampson remembered the gentle suck of convecting air, live embers floating in it like infernal fairies. Here and there stood a white spruce or lodgepole pine, its canopy hissing with flame, cones popping in the heat and blowing seeds into the smouldering grass. Sometimes there would be a crack like a rifle shot as a tree split, boiling in its own greenness.

But before dusk the wind changed direction subtly, then changed again, and a cool breeze came up in the west, pushing against the fire just enough to woo it back across its own charred path, across barren ground. By dark the fire was mostly extinguished and the wind had died.

Sampson and Moreland had walked the periphery with kerchiefs tied across their faces like outlaws, stamping at stubborn ground flares, their leather bootsoles smoking. They climbed above the burn area and sat all night together watching, what for they knew not, but vigilance seemed to be in order, and anyway, sleep was impossible. So they sat together, and Moreland told jokes Sampson failed to find funny, which in itself amused them both. All that night the ground was spangled with embers. They watched the weird illumination of the forest and looked up at a blank night sky, stars erased by smoke. Now and then came a cracking and a long whoosh as a ruined tree swooned against its neighbours and hit the ground, blowing fireworks into the air.

In the days afterward, they laboured to cut a path from one cabin to the other through the fallen timber, Sampson swinging the axe and Moreland going after smaller limbs with the saw. They looked about them at the devastation, their faces sooted and owlish as coal miners'. Without apparent irony, William Moreland had sighed out, "This is scenic."

They'd both been younger then. Mary was still alive.

First came news of this war. Then, to Sampson's rage and fear, his son had gone to Calgary to enlist. But he was rejected, mostly because he was too delicate of physique and badly short-sighted. Sampson's son had come back fuming and humiliated, unable to abide his parents' relief, and worse was the scorn in his brothers' eyes for even thinking of volunteering. For a time, it divided the family.

They'd all watched the sudden disappearance of young men from the area. Newspaper photographs pasted face-out in shop windows. The uniforms, the black armbands, and soon the almost total lack of men in town. Immigrants from newly enemy countries were rounded up and interned. Sampson had seen prisoners of war at a distance, a gaggle of dun-coloured figures expanding the grand hotel's golf course, or struggling to upgrade the trestle bridge in town. Or here, extending the highway, following the old trail straight through the trackless forest toward the far town of Laggan. The train stopping where no train should, only to disgorge hell onto the railside. Horses clattering down the gangplank, crates of tools, and a wagon, guards, and dozens of prisoners whose job it was to cut an incision through the trees, their work rimmed by smoke and fire and noise. In town there were fewer tourists, fewer guiding jobs for men like Sampson and Moreland, so they took to shooting animals they would never have bothered with before, foxes and mink for the fur, and they set up looms in their yards and cured the pelts and hides, their hands stinging from the lye in the ash mixture, a stink on the wind that even smudge fires could not carry away. And then, last fall, Moreland had ridden his sick child into town, and Mary had died. Sampson pondered the awful possibility she'd been alone when it happened. Moreland had buried her, who knows where, and then he, too, had vanished.

Weeks later, Sampson had stood outside their abandoned cabin, calling through the open door, telling the ghost within that he was there to remove some things for safekeeping. The house was desolate. He could see nearby where a kitchen shelf had fallen to the floor and animals had skirmished over the abandoned food.

"Mîyech," he said. *It's me.*

There was utter silence. A blackened pot lay on the floor.

A scattering of dry leaves wandered the floorboards and faded into the lightless hollow of the cabin. He'd felt something in his throat, a flutter of dread.

It had taken Sampson four tries to step inside. When, finally, he crossed the threshold, he had braced himself for her presence, her anger or sorrow, something that might blow over him and cling, like sand in his hair. Instead, very clearly, he'd felt nothing. Nothing. He'd pondered this for a moment, lifting a pot from the floor and placing it gently on the stovetop. Had she gone somewhere else? Was she there in the room with him, watching? He'd tidied what he could, collected up anything that might rust or attract animals or that needed fixing, and then he'd left the cabin, looking back once into the sad debris of other people's lives, and then he'd closed the door.

To Sampson's mind, it had all seemed like an awful message, a stageplay put on for him to witness, proof that the world was grinding toward its end. He was old, and he often thought about the end.

Sampson realized now that he was standing still, his voice and his progress having faltered. That morning he had woken without the slightest idea what else to do with his life except to visit the boy, check on the boy, feed the boy. And here he found himself passing through this burn area, falling help-lessly again into a remembrance of fire and the smell of fire, remembering that now-shattered family, as he always did when he made the mistake of coming this way. He wondered how long it would be before he could pass through this grey mess and feel nothing. How long before it was just a burnt meadow like any other.

Despite what he'd told the boy about his father, Sampson

himself wondered if any of these awful stories were true. After all, William Moreland had worked in mines and in logging camps, and he knew perfectly well how to use dynamite. There'd been some trouble in his younger days, some fondness for stealing useful things out of ranger stations, which had resulted in a nickname in the papers, and even caused him to spend a short time in jail. But none of this recent news made sense to anyone who knew the man: stealing money, doing harm to other people. He was still out there, spooking into towns and camps at night, his small crimes recounted in local newspapers, his movement relentless. The kid's open, trusting face closed down on any mention of his father.

Sampson took off his hat, turned his face up to the moon, and closed his eyes like a man sunbathing. Perhaps, he thought, we are toughest when we are young and life wears us down; we become increasingly tender with age. Certainly, it felt so to him.

He put on his hat and went on again, the hackamore swinging loose between them, and the old man's face once again in shadow. He was obliged to work his way around the crowds of infant trees that now grew in profusion and came to his shoulder, those blown seeds come to life, an impassable green fuzz in the hollows, and the whole meadow still streaked with fireweed. The old man began to talk again, about the wisdom of going the long way around next time, his voice droning away to the contented horse behind him.

OF COURSE, THE BOY was not up when they arrived. The man's ceaseless rambling had failed even to rouse the dog. Still talking, Sampson put Willow in the corral, where she made her way over to the Morgan. He was telling the horses that Jack had surely got weary down there in town, where everyone was run ragged, but this sleeping-in thing was no good, and a time came in every boy's life to stop lying about and get busy.

He made his way to a chair by the icy fire ring and lowered himself groaning into it. After a moment he rose again and scrounged for dry wood under the eaves. The sound of kindling snapping, the *ching* of his metal lighter — nothing roused the kid. When the fire was crackling merrily and the rocks around it were steaming, he rooted through the rucksack and withdrew smoked venison, oats, coffee and sugar, a loaf of hard bread, and a battered pot to heat water in. The horses smelled dry oats and crowded the fence. They hung their heads over the rungs and blinked at the firelight. It was quiet, and the stars were fading.

→ *Twenty-Two*

WHEN JACK BOULTON woke it was to the smell of braising meat. He opened his eyes and croaked, "I'm up!" It was pitch black in the cabin. The window showed nothing; in fact, he couldn't even see the window. "What time is it?" he called, but the old man's voice outside was an indecipherable rumble.

Bleary and shivering despite the sweater, long johns, and trousers he'd slept in, he pawed blindly over the bedclothes and found the dog. It raised its head, flopped back down, and yawned. He stroked the ribcage and his hand drew static electricity through the pale fur. In that total dark, all he could see were rivulets of blue chasing over the long body, lightning in a cloudy sky. The dog went slack with sleep but he dragged it closer to him by the legs and scrubbed up a storm of static in the thick fur, running his hands back and forth until the sparks were audible and the animal scrabbled off the bed away from him.

The boy laughed; the dog sneezed and sneezed.

"Get over here," said Jack. "Come," and he slapped the blankets, but the crackling dog stood its ground and slowly faded into nothing.

Jack pulled on his boots and, pawing blindly, found his mother's coat and drew it on. It cinched round his narrow waist with the thick leather belt, the buckle connecting exactly where she had always kept it. They were the same size now. Jack closed his eyes. It was dark inside him and out, and he was standing there in the pitch black with her.

"Okay," he whispered.

When he drew back the door he could see a kind of amber spotlight by the corral where Sampson sat cooking over a fire. The kid stepped out and made his way to the old man, feeling like he was joining Sampson on stage.

"Are you hungry?"

"Hell yes. What have you got?"

The dog bounded out of the cabin. It sniffed every part of the old man until it had his reading, then it trotted away and stood three-legged, pissing on a tree for so long that it began to lose balance.

The boy winced up at the black sky in disbelief. His teeth began to chatter. "What time is it?"

"Time you got up."

"Oh fine. I'm going back to bed." But instead Jack leaned under the old man's hat brim and hugged him round the neck. An avuncular thumping on his back in return.

The dog had by now trotted off into the trees, leaving behind a pool of steaming urine.

Sampson seemed thoughtful, a little melancholy. He said, "Dosnâhûchi mage sîch."

"But you just saw me yesterday!" the boy said. And then he figured the meaning properly. "Oh, you mean last time you had breakfast here . . ." He looked for a long time at the soft crown of the man's hat and remembered what they'd eaten that breakfast long ago. "I guess that was more than a year ago." His mother in pants and black boots by the stove.

She'd made pancakes. Sampson had actually been inside the house that day, seated at the table, one leg crossed over the other, using his knee as a hat stand, punishing the chair he leaned back on. Back then he'd been perfectly happy to enter the house. Jack figured that was the last time Sampson had seen Mary.

Now they breakfasted outside, slowly reviving on coffee and strips of salted venison, watching as the oatmeal blubbed in the pot and took forever to soften. The old man nattered in Nakoda mostly to himself, and Jack offered a thought in English whenever he caught the general meaning of the discussion. Jack's Nakoda was rudimentary, he spoke a mostly childish version and mixed up his male and female address. After a year in town his scant vocabulary was almost gone.

The subject now seemed to be town, and specifically, the recent spate of Swiss tourists who were, according to the local newspaper, the *Crag & Canyon*, getting stink-eye on the street because they were speaking German and could not reliably explain the concept of Swiss neutrality.

Sampson said, "When I first arrived I didn't know what a tourist was. My wife had to explain."

"What are you talking about, when you came here?"

"I wasn't born here."

"Okay . . . so . . ." The kid waited.

Sampson thought for a long time, gazing at the fire, before he said, "I came up from Oklahoma. A long way from here, in that direction."

"Oklahoma." Jack mouthed the word. "Do you have people down there? Do you have brothers?"

Sampson sighed. "Yes."

"What are their names? Is Oklahoma on the ocean?"

"I shouldn't have said anything. Stop asking questions."

"Why did you leave?" Jack simply waited with his eyebrows raised.

As if it was an explanation, and to him it was, Sampson said, "I was a kind of police. I found men, brought them in."

The boy's merry curiosity drained away. He looked at the fire ring at his feet. He said, "You chased criminals."

"Yes."

"What did you do with them after you caught them?"

"Took them into Fort Smith and got paid. There'd be a trial, and I'd have to be in court to give evidence. They usually got hanged. One man escaped. For a while, anyway. I got him the second time."

Jack swallowed. He realized he was holding his thumbs inside his fists like a terrified child. The stick man on the scaffold. The voices of young children chanting, *Sing, sang, sung, your daddy's on the run . . .*

Sampson saw the kid's face and understood that he was going into a hole, so he spoke softly: "That was a long time ago. Things are different now."

The kid nodded, but he wasn't listening.

Sampson leaned in and fixed Jack with a look. "No one will find him. Don't worry so much."

"But what if they do?"

"No. He's had lots of practice getting out of things."

"Would you have been able to catch my dad, when you were police?"

"Him?" Jack's question seemed to genuinely interest Sampson, and he pondered for a long moment before saying, "Probably not. Now stop worrying, you're making me worry." And then, like a conjurer, he began to take basic supplies out of his packsack, saying, "We will get you more groceries soon." Jack Boulton gathered food into his arms and ferried it all into the house. His boots thumped on the floorboards.

"Somewhere dry!" Sampson bellowed, and he heard the kid change direction and place the items somewhere else.

✦ Twenty-Three

THAT BRIGHT EARLY morning, after Sampson had left, the boy took Pearl outside and stood in the strong wind. Despite his promise, Jack intended to hunt. He slid the rifle from the scabbard and pinned the pink thing in his armpit.

The rifle itself was basic, with a scarred wooden stock and dull brass mouldings. The barrel had been shortened and the magazine drawn back to fit it. The boy had never seen such a thing done to a gun, and he instantly mistrusted its ability to fire straight. It was uncleaned, uncared for, a time-worn wreck. He tilted the rifle to its side and inspected the breech. Short as the magazine was now, it still held an unusual number of cartridges. What calibre was this? What size animal was it intended to kill? Rabbit, deer, bear . . . buffalo? It did not occur to him that the thing was designed to shoot people rapid-fire. All he saw was an old, unreliable, unclean weapon, worth nothing. It seemed a sour irony to Jack Boulton that he'd been carrying it in a scabbard worth enough to buy Wilson's entire business. After a moment of reflection, his natural prudence kicked in and he took Pearl back indoors.

An hour later he was walking along the eastern ridge with lunch hanging from his belt. A dead shot with a rock,

Jack Boulton had winged four red squirrels to their deaths, and now they were tied together by their tails and dangling at his waist. Tiny, sinewy creatures, they might almost add up to a decent meal if cut into strips, fire roasted, and served with bread. He was a few minutes from home at an easy walk, chewing handfuls of Sampson's smoked jerky.

Down in the valley a great herd of elk loitered over the greener areas with a few shy mule deer sheltering near them. The animals foraged and wandered, calves capered, females lay ruminating in the safeness of numbers. A lonely cloud hung in the middle of an otherwise blue sky, tethered to its shadow. The boy watched that shadow draw across the valley floor, touch the edge of the herd, then slowly move over them. It was like watching spilled coffee seep across a tablecloth.

Closer to the boy's view, at about half a mile, there was a grove of deciduous trees, maybe fifty of them, a bouquet of white sticks standing in a bright pool of their own dead leaves. And there, trotting through the leaves was a man, a single shape weaving his way through the trunks. A hunter perhaps, oddly unaware of the abundance of game behind him.

The boy spat out an unchewable knuckle of jerky, pondering this fool who unaccountably was running away from game.

And then, out of the corner of his eye he saw movement in the elk herd, a swirling rearrangement of its margin as a second figure moved past them, following the first.

It was not entirely out of Jack's experience to see at a distance men in hunting parties. Before the declaration of war, there had also been amateur explorers and outdoor enthusiasts and painters and photographers, always led by one of the local outfitters. Several times a year Jack would spot humans, so unlike any other animal in their movements, dotting a meadow. But at the outbreak of war, the younger outfitters had sold off their goods and horses, and enlisted as officers. Thom Wilson was too old, and he'd volunteered long ago for the war in South Africa and had regretted the choice. By the time news of Gallipoli finally reached the Canadian mountains, he had formed a rigid abhorrence of hierarchy, nationalism, and duty. April was his drunkest month. Tourism had slowed in wartime to a trickle, and so Jack had not seen a sport hunter in almost two years. His mother had been as relieved by the sudden absence of strange men as if, overnight, someone had cured a plague. But here were two of them, running about.

The first figure had now trotted through the grove and was heading for a thick stand of pines that ran uphill. There was no other way to go, for if he wished to make his way toward Jack he would have to scale sheer rock for fifty feet. The second man exited the aspen grove, closing ground between himself and the first man — he was not chasing but following. Jack Boulton could see now that they were both very pale, and the trailing man was lame on his right side, hop-running, as awkward as a marionette, his elbows wheeling at his sides. Like so many hunters they both wore muted, dun-coloured clothing. The man in front was smaller, perhaps even a boy, but he was faster than the other, and when he slowed and swung round to shout encouragement, his voice was lost to distance and wind.

Jack stopped chewing.

He was standing at a cliff where a few tall, ancient pines stood like divers along the crumbling edge. One had keeled over and now hung by its twisted roots, its tip nestled in the rocky scrub below. As if moving a foot or two closer might make the scene clearer to him, Jack stepped out onto its carpet of roots, and felt the great flexible weight bounce under him.

The younger man closed the distance between himself and the trees and was swallowed by them. The lame man jigged and swam his way into the cover of the forest, and with that they were both gone.

Jack started chewing again.

A daylight moon hung above the treetops, what his mother used to call a "child's moon." She would point up and say, "It's come out in the daytime to see you."

His home. His side of the mountain. His moon. He had woken that morning and relished his own total freedom, responsible only to himself now. He reached to the back of his long, slim trouser leg and scratched lustily at an itch. He wondered if it might be time for a bath.

BACK AT HOME Jack lay the squirrels on the table next to Pearl. He straddled his usual chair and considered how many buckets would be necessary for a bath that would come even to his hips. His mother had taught him to sweep the floor first and lay blankets over the zinc tub to keep the heat in. He'd have to haul the water into the cabin, leave it in the tub to come to room temperature, stoke the stove, boil bucket after bucket. It would take hours.

Instead he ran his fingers over the old rifle's rough stock, and began to think about the running men. At that moment he realized neither of them had been carrying a gun. One hunter might conceivably lose his gun, perhaps relieved of it by an enraged bear, but both of them? Unarmed men running as if pursued, heading for the cover of trees. Slowly and unwillingly he decided that what he had just seen was in fact two escaped prisoners of war, and the injured one might have been shot.

Newspapers. They were good for belated news of the world, for reading lessons, for wrapping things, for fires. The boy himself had pored over them page by page and read every last word, even the adverts for men's hats and suspenders, colliery horses, diarrhea powders, and farm machinery. So he'd read more than one editorial on "the Hun in our midst."

One quiet afternoon when Jack was still eleven, he'd been sitting at the table, the wide delicate sheets of a weeks-old newspaper spread out in front of him, his father perusing the righthand sheet, Jack reading the left, when the entire newspaper slid away under Jack's fingers.

He burst out, "I was *reading* that."

William Moreland had walked away, folding and refolding the paper down to a rectangle, and held it out for Mary.

His mother put down her sewing and her expression slid from curiosity into something else, some well-worn anxiety. Once she had read the entire news story, with slow, deliberate attention as was her habit, taking in every word, she looked up at her husband and asked, "Where is Castle Mountain?"

Moreland had gone to his map on the wall and placed a finger on the red dot. "Here's us," he'd said. "Here's Johnston Canyon. And that's Castle Mountain." His finger was touching a blank area of wood.

"That close?" Mary began to wring her hands; any appearance of false calm had vanished.

"Let me see it," said the boy, reaching for the folded newspaper.

But Mary had stood up and said, "It's nothing." She peeled

the news story off in a strip of ragged paper, and fed it into the flames of the stove.

Jack had stared dumbfounded at each parent in turn, and then, with his jaws set, stamped up the ladder to the loft, where he sat with legs dangling over the edge and glowered at them.

Moreland was the first to relent. He'd looked at his wife and said, "He'll find out soon enough."

Mary walked under the loft, reached up and held her son's besocked foot. The warmth of her hand on his instep. "I suppose," she said. "But, oh Jack, why can't you stay a child just a little longer?"

After dinner that night Moreland had hauled Jack up into the saddle behind him and they'd ridden down the canyon and out its mouth, turned northwest toward a spot Jack had never been before, arriving in a pink twilight. There they had paused, out of sight, standing in the lee of that great block-like peak of Castle Mountain, and they had gazed at an internment camp, their new, unwelcome neighbour.

"That's a prison," Moreland said. "It's because of the war."

"Prison!" Jack craned and peered round his father's shoulders to get a better look.

There was an enormous rectangle of cleared brush, a perfect geometric shape. Wooden fencepoles as thick as the boy's chest stood every twenty feet, knitted together with barbed wire, and within that enclosure stood many huge tents, each enough to house two dozen men. All those tents were still alight and Jack saw shadows strafing the canvas walls. There were very few wooden structures to be seen, and those were small and basic, probably sentry boxes, latrines, the biggest might have been an ice house for storing food.

It looked to the boy as if most if not all the men slept in canvas tents. At this elevation it could snow no matter the month, even in summer. And on the coldest winter days, when the temperature dropped to forty below, there would be no way to properly heat those tents; anyone weak or ill would soon be in distress.

Jack had slowly become aware of a sound: the distant murmur of hundreds of men — a sound so alien to him he did not at first recognize it as human. He began to shrink against his father's body. When a pot or something metal fell and spun on the hard, trampled ground with a protracted clatter, Jack's curiosity had snapped off like a light and all that was left was dread.

William Moreland sat in the saddle, vigilant and still. The posture was so familiar to the boy from their hunting trips that it almost calmed him: Moreland motionless, waiting for game, the boy suffering twitches and itches, seeing deer where there were none.

After some time, a lone officer stepped from one of the far tents and made his way to the latrine, loosening his belt as he went. They saw no sentries, though those men were surely about, and they would be armed.

The boy had whispered, "Why don't the prisoners come outside?"

His father said simply, "Curfew."

In the pinkish twilight, the ordered white roofs of the tents presented a nacreous sheen. A bizarre spot of man-made order lost in the wilderness, the prison camp looked like a paper boat floating on a green sea. And that was really the point of this thing. If any poor prisoner managed to escape with just the clothes on his back, where could he go?

In the looming dark, father and son swung round and walked the Morgan back along the path they had come. Jack dozed in his father's arms until he squirmed and fussed, and on that familiar cue, Moreland had dismounted and let Jack reverse himself and flop face down on the Morgan's smooth back, head on the animal's rump, arms and legs swinging with the horse's gait, his cheek against prickling hide. The horse was a cradle, and the boy was lulled to sleep by its motion.

Later that night, he had woken repeatedly as his parents whispered together at the table, everyone unnerved by it all, the whole family wakeful, even as the wind rose and birds began their morning chorus and the trees shook the way they do when the green world worries itself just before dawn.

From then on, they had paid keen attention to the news, to town gossip, to rumour. The prisoners had remained at Castle Mountain only a few more weeks before winter proved too cold and they were shipped to Banff, to a different, more sheltered barracks at the far edge of town.

They were known generally as Austrians, thanks to the ongoing history of European conquest — though in this camp, not a single one of them was actually Austrian. They were from countries to which the empire laid claim. And these men were definitely not German. That much was clear enough. Wilson had said, "If anyone puts a German in with those boys, they'll kill him." They were Ukrainians, Galicians, Ruthenians, all enemy aliens. Some of them were arrested simply because they didn't yet speak English, did not know the hard rules of immigration, and therefore could not explain themselves when they fell foul of them. Austrian or not, citizen or not, one misstep and they were interned in camps and put to work in the interests of national security. Free labour for the government, not least because able-bodied men were hard to find with so many dying in Europe. The more trusty prisoners were sometimes rented out to farming interests and mining companies, exactly as one would loan a horse or an ox. But for the most part these men worked locally, rain or snow or forty-below temperatures, always under guard. It was prisoners who had built the new trestle bridge in town. Prisoners who worked at the rock crusher to produce gravel and stone for any number of municipal and park projects. Prisoners extended the luxury golf course. And after Christmastime, they built an ice maze on the main street of town for the enjoyment of tourists.

Now, sitting alone in his cabin, Jack leaned his elbows on his chairback and began to consult his father's map on the wall, nursing a feeling he couldn't put a name to. Apprehension, the pang of obligation to those two lost men, or just curiosity where they had come from? Only now did he see that of all things in this known world, his father had not inscribed a single mark on his map to show the location of the internment camp, perhaps refusing on principle to allow even an acknowledgement of it in his home.

Jack counselled himself not to leave his own good life again, telling himself there would be no real way to find those escaped men. But in the end, he could not ignore the hum of worry in his chest, so he shot up out of the chair and went to the corral. The Morgan came slowly up to him, bobbing its head. Saddleless they rode out into that lesser-known country, following a route mostly from a childhood memory. Even from a distance he could see the prison camp, a clear area in the brush, pale, squared off, and uncanny in the daylight.

It was deserted, emptied of anything useful. The prisoners therefore were still being held near town. Wherever those running men had come from, it wasn't here.

Jack strolled the horse along the fence, following the perfect lines of wire, past each massive pole in turn, past barbs on which dangled weedballs, windblown debris, fluttering knots of grass, until he found the gates. They were padlocked. Surely not to keep humans out but to stop animals from wandering in.

In the dirt were inscribed two wide semicircles where day after day those gates had been dragged open to let the wagons and work gangs out, and drawn back together at night to shut them in. He saw the large and vacated tents standing in perfect rows, each with its doorflaps tied back to allow airflow, now emptied of cots and stoves. Not a sound, no movement at all except a pair of ground squirrels wrangling at the mouth of the nearest tent, lithe and silly and possibly hoping to mate. One sprang onto the canvas tent wall and made the apex of the roof, the other followed, and then they were both gone. The tent billowed in the wind, and the weathered ties that held the doorflaps swivelled, stiff as flypaper. Out in the yard, the latrine had collapsed into its own pit, leaning drunkenly to one side, the door agape, four seat-holes showing. Outside the camp, at a remove of fifty feet, was a massive patch of scorched ground. It looked like a meteor had struck, or lightning. This turned out to be a firepit wherein were the jumbled remains of broken cots, old clothes, ruined blankets, and the red spangles of rusted cans. They had burned whatever was too far gone to transport. The camp, it seemed to Jack, had been vacant for months. So where had those two men come from?

• • •

BY THE TIME he found his way back home he was gurgling with hunger and wanted lunch, but he paced from cabin to corral to creek water, settling the horse first. He did not notice that the cabin door was ajar until his hand was on it. In his childhood it had often been open and someone was inside, whether father or mother. Jack had rarely needed to worry about doors up here. He made for the table, only to find that Pearl had been nudged about, his mother's hat had tumbled to the floor and been trod upon by tiny feet, and his dinner was gone. The squirrels, when he found them outside near the trees, had been gnawed to the bone by some small-toothed scavenger. He lifted four scraggly little horrors to eye level, untied them, and flung the bodies away into the brush. The twine he fashioned into a tiny coil, stuffed it into his pocket, and headed back inside, deeply annoyed. He particularly liked roasted squirrel.

The cabin was damp and cool and smelled of woodsmoke. He swept the hat off the floor and plonked it onto his head and, in a kind of irritable trance, he straightened books on the shelf, tidied things on the table, started a fire in the stove, ladled water into a pot. Oatmeal for lunch again.

As the water on the stove heated slowly he hefted *Brehm's Life of Animals* from the bookshelf and carried it to the table. The book was organized into species and subspecies, and each animal was presented in its own tableau. Particularly arresting were the great apes. The thoughtful gorilla; the slyly amused chimpanzee; the pinched little tamarin, which, now he thought of it, bore a striking resemblance to the nun when she had her veil off and her froths of hair showing. There was something about their faces, the admixture of human and animal, that struck the boy as diabolical. This male sinking his teeth into the throat of a leopard. That female lazing on the roots of a great tree with twin infants at her feet. Curled tails and clawed hands. Lavish fur covering some of them, but others presented a kind of scrofulous nudity, with their leathery bare arses and wrinkled pates.

The boy gave up on them, seized a handful of pages, and swung away through the animal kingdom. Here were enormous African birds with crowns of thorns. The American buffalo falling to its massive shoulder, bristling with arrows. Terrified peccaries fleeing hunters. He flipped along until he came upon a general discussion of skunks. Rare in this latitude but not unheard of. The boy snorted. Several years previously, the agonized dog had galloped into the cabin, skidded to a halt by the stove and pawed frantically at its weeping eyes. Shortly thereafter he and his parents had galloped out of the cabin, shrieking and covering their own faces. Up close, skunk smell was unbearable.

He read on: *All accounts of American travellers and naturalists agree that no chemical laboratory, no heap of refuse, no foul carcass, in short no stench on earth is as fetid and unbearable as that which the graceful animals of the genus Mephitis give forth. The odour is said to be pestilential, and a person who has had the misfortune to come in close relations with one of these animals is avoided by everyone, as though he had the plague.* With that the boy put the book down and howled with laughter. Of all the books he had stolen, this was the prize.

Slowly he closed the book's cover and found himself staring into the keen eyes of the great, reclining African lion.

Those enormous, knuckled paws in repose, the terrible claws retracted.

His father had once advised against complacency when it came to big cats. "They're shy and smart, Jack," he'd said. "If you see a cougar, you can be sure it saw you half an hour ago. Best ask yourself why it didn't just run away."

Jack Boulton rose and made his oatmeal and when he had finished eating, reclined on the bed and looked at his home.

Food cooked on a stove. Warmth. Books to read. The roof over his head that, Jack knew, had taken his father four months to build, mostly on his own, with occasional help from Sampson when something needed two strong bodies to lift it. His mother had once said, "It was just a frame when you were born, so you spent your first months in a tent." She'd said it like it was all pretty good. Like it was an adventure.

The large bed, the storm lanterns, the remaining chunks of Swiss chocolate, the fresh water, paper and pencils, books, at least ten blankets, pillows, the solid door through which he would go tomorrow, and there he would see the Morgan, and perhaps Sampson might visit. Jack saw it all, and then he pictured it gone. Imagined himself stranded outdoors, frightened, lost in the dark.

Over and over his mind went back to the second man, the one struggling along. But each time, he told himself to let it go. What could he do for them now, hours later, with no idea where they were? Jack opened the door and sat down on his stoop. Cold wind flowed past him and, after a moment, the pages of books on his bed began to flutter. The Morgan was grazing, its long neck bent to the grass and its tail waving.

Twenty-Four

SHE STOOD LOOKING at the folded clothes at the end of the boy's bed, the pajamas set on top of the pile. The room was frigid, the window still open, and there was a star pattern of ice on the glass. She gathered the clothes into her arms and carried them down the long staircase and along the hall into the kitchen. She would launder them, hang them to dry, iron and refold them, ready for his return.

All that night she had managed to stay away from her cupboard of herbs and the calming injection she had concocted for herself. She had decanted it into a green glass bottle and inscribed a Latin word on the paper-and-glue label: PAX. A single dose from a syringe, five milligrams, a drop of liquid so small it could rest on the tip of her finger and not spill over, that was all it would take to erase this feeling and leave her calm and unworried. Two drops worth and she would sleep for an afternoon — a dreamless respite.

But the boy would be home soon, and she mustn't let him see her under its influence, so instead she forced herself to burn off her fury by readying the place for him. Already the second floor had been swept and mopped, the small rug in his room taken out back and beaten. For, surely, he couldn't linger very long out there, wherever he was hiding. What could he do alone out there on foot with nothing but his old clothes, without food? He must come home again. There was no other choice.

Alone at the grocer's store that morning she had looked desolately at the glass cabinet of sweets and chocolates. Two beautiful little boxes of sugar-encrusted fruit jellies. She'd never bought him any such treat. Perhaps she should have.

She had not prayed in years, that comfort was beyond her now, so she had fought the urge to buy a single sweet for him, as a talisman, a gesture of hope . . . no, of confidence that he would return. So she had simply walked away, as she always had, without buying anything.

Do not give him gifts. Set him to work again as if nothing has happened.

Standing at the old yellow stove, watching a pot of water slowly heat, she held the bundle on her hip as any mother might hold a baby. Her breath, she could not control it. Lungs and heart galloping. The house had spent another night alight and heated, and its sole occupant was ablaze, too.

When the water was ready she set his clothes on his breakfast chair and filled the washtub. Soap flakes came out of the box waxy and they clung to her hand, so she plunged her fist into the stinging water and swished them off, staring down into that milky liquid, the unseen hand shrieking until it went numb and the indignation in her chest abated a little. Pain helped. When she drew her hand out again it was no longer shaking, and it seemed to be wearing a red glove.

His shirt came first. She drew it up by the shoulder seams and flapped it out over the water, the practical part of her brain — whatever was still left to her — realizing it would shrink in the hot water. After all, the boy was still growing, so wouldn't that mean buying him another one? If he had been there, she would have pressed those seams to his shoulders with her thumbs and assessed the time remaining before she must take him shopping again. Now she held wrinkled cloth up on empty air.

And then, subtly, through the kitchen smells of wood-smoke and soap and the stale breath of the old house, it came to her, floating out from the shirt itself: the scent of the boy's body.

She sat heavily on her chair and looked across the table at where he had sat all those mornings, stirring his cereal, asking her questions she knew the answers to. She pressed the shirt to her face, imagined that she now rested her cheek against his shoulder.

After a long moment she rose, folded the shirt, placed it atop the pile of other clothes, and carried them all back upstairs to his room.

→ *Twenty-Five*

IN THE LATE AFTERNOON Jack took his gauge of his father's map on the wall, committed to memory the exact location of the nearest of the Swedes' outbuildings, and headed out.

The first one was to the east-northeast and surprisingly close, settled into a tidy clearing just below a box canyon that had a long, clear lake from which the Swedes might draw fresh water. He dismounted and walked up to the shack, which was only a little bigger than his family's shed. He called out, called again as he approached, spoke politely as he stood outside the door, saying, "Sirs? Hello." There was no window, no way to peer in. The building was shaggy with the pine boughs laid on as roofing. But for all that, no one could miss the good handiwork: the logs were cut in a way to make chinking unnecessary, the walls were plumb and level, the door perfectly framed, and the building was nestled into a windless spot that would face the morning sun for warmth, a natural way to heat it after any cold night. Either the shack was empty or the occupants had refused to come out, so Jack took the handle and swung the door open. An exhausted black marten, locked in there for who knew how long, staggered over Jack's boots and loped unevenly away through the underbrush.

Inside, there was one narrow bed, no tick or blankets, no cooking pots, no knives, no food, but there were many bare shelves, and affixed to the wall, a series of little drawers that also turned out to be empty — it seemed the Swedes really did carry everything they owned with them, down to the smallest knife. Such obstinate commitment to itinerancy. Jack saw a beam of sunlight light that came through a hole in the roof and fell on the empty bed. Unable to get into the building through the solidly built door, the marten had worked its way through the roof and dropped into the room like a penny into a piggy bank, whereupon it was trapped. It might scale the walls, it might leap for the hole it had so recently made, but a marten cannot crawl suspended upside down along the ceiling like a squirrel can. So it'd had no way out until Jack Boulton had opened the door. There was dried crap on the floor and the room smelled like vintage piss. Jack backed out and started scouting the area, looking for the fire ring, which had been so long unused it took him a moment to find it. There was nothing here, no sign of the escaped prisoners. So Jack left the door open and headed back to the horse.

The second of the Swedes' buildings was eight miles north and turned out to be little more than a large lean-to nestled under a rock overhang, one side open to the air, the floor space barely big enough for a single bed. But it had similar shelves built into one wall, and a raised floor to keep the occupants dry. This was like looking at a store window: no question the owners weren't at home. This time Jack did not dismount but merely walked the Morgan up to the tiny structure. He'd never seen a lean-to for people before. His father had built one in the corral many years ago, a simple windbreak, but only during the worst gale did the Morgan ever bother to settle in its lee.

On that smooth, sanded floor Jack saw a great many weeks of pine debris and blown leaves. No hint of garbage, no scraps of food. He backed the Morgan away and looked about him. This place was as vacated and empty as the other one had been. In neither camp had Jack seen a single sign of human presence beyond the building itself. It was amazing, the level of organization required for any woodsman, however gifted, to leave nothing behind, not a single spoon or tent peg, not even a bit of twine. He sighed, turned away from the lean-to, checked his direction with the compass in his head, and set out for the next remembered spot on Moreland's map.

By the time he found the third of the Swedes' camps the sun was already bronzing the clouds. What he found turned out to be almost a full cabin. It had a single, glassless, wood-block window like the one at Sampson's place, and a pitched roof, tar-papered and laid over with evergreen shingles. With a roof that high, surely there were rafters upon which the Swedes could store tarps and tent poles and skis. He glanced at the setting sun; it was time to get this over with and hurry home.

"Hello, sirs?" he called, and then his eyes fell on a pile of stones and dirt and logs that had been erected outside the cabin. The mass had been heaped against the door and it almost reached the handle. Someone had tried to block the door from the outside by piling debris against it.

Jack swung down and drew the Morgan away, and he wrapped the reins around a branch. Something told him to keep the horse at a distance. He looked at that pile of debris and saw incompetence. There were simpler ways to keep a door shut, but they required tools, and whoever had done this had shovelled anything to hand into a mound, with no care for how things fell, and he had kept going at it like a madman until the mess stood four feet high, its base collapsing like a riverbank. Whatever was in there, someone wanted it to stay in.

Carefully and with great attention Jack paced the clearing, taking in the news. He was twelve years old and no tracker, but anyone looking at this area could see what he saw. There were fresh bootprints everywhere. The fire ring was unused, but next to those cold stones lay a single flat segment of wood shingle, likely torn from the cabin's roof. Jack went down on his haunches and picked up a long twig the thickness of a pencil that had been lying amongst many tufts of dead grass rolled into tight balls. Someone had been trying to start a fire like a caveman, using friction and tinder, but he had failed because it was a hopeless technique and because everything here was green and moist and would not burn. Then, for some reason, that same person had barred the cabin door.

Once, long ago, Moreland had said, "If you're afraid of doing something, son, you're more or less obligated to do it." The kid had looked up at his father and immediately understood the trick of it. If you are not afraid you'll do it anyway, because why not. If you are afraid, you're obligated to overcome your fear. So there was only one choice: do it.

Jack began tearing away the pile that lay against the door, tossing rocks and logs aside, until the entrance was clear enough to drag the door open. The air wafting out of the cabin was muggy and offensive. Jack leaned in. And there, as he'd feared, lying on one of the beds, was a dead man. It was not one of the Swedes, for those men had hair so blond it was almost colourless, whereas this man's hair was black, greying at the temples and sideburns. Someone had removed the dead man's coat and laid it over him, tucked it under his chin like a blanket. They had placed a flat wool cap over his face as a death pall. His boots were worn and old and they hung open around his thin ankles. The cloth of his right trouser leg had been torn open to expose a blue shin, bloodied and filthy and the wrong colour entirely. Above the boot, the calf muscle gaped with a terrible hole the width and depth of an open mouth.

Jack did not blink, could not swallow. He was too afraid to lift the man's cap, and no folksy wisdom in the world could compel him to do it. He could only whisper, "I'm sorry," and carefully shut the door.

That door, perfectly hung and square, a door that was not his own, now stood between him and the only dead person he'd ever seen. Another unwanted first in the boy's young life. This was the limping man, obviously shot in the leg, now dead of his wound.

Jack went to the fire ring and toed around the little signs of a hopeless bid to make a fire.

For lack of a single match.

There had been two of them running, now there was one. The smaller, faster, running prisoner was likely still alive somewhere out there.

Jack stamped the pitiful tufts of dead grass under his boot, and paced, and wiped his eyes, and there came small, angry, wordless noises from his throat. Finally he stood for a long time looking not at the building but deliberately at the Morgan, his good, tranquil horse. It was the only way he could think to calm himself.

In a quiet voice, as if someone might be listening, he kept saying *okay, okay*, until finally he could bring himself to go back to the cabin. With bare hands he shovelled and scooped and chucked the debris back against the door, anything to secure that charnel house, to keep scavengers away from the poor man for just a little longer. Jack Boulton was weeping, cursing, for it had already occurred to him that these two might be father and son. If so, that boy had watched his father die.

Now there was nothing to do. Jack couldn't follow the lone survivor in the dark with no idea of direction, no trail to follow. The prisoner might be running in circles. Jack knew he couldn't save that fugitive any more than he could have saved the first man, now a frightful homecoming gift for the Swedes, whenever they might arrive. If the younger fugitive had any sense he'd find high ground, scout for a rail line, flag down a train, turn himself in.

Jack blew his nose sideways and made his way to the Morgan. Swung up and felt the warmth of the horse's body, the life in it. He turned them both away and headed for home.

WHEN HE ARRIVED back home it was somewhere near ten, a bright windy night, plenty of moon to see by, and even the horse seemed glad to be home. The dog was lounging before the door, front paws crossed one over the other, waiting. Beside it lay a bent scraggly mess that the boy knew from experience was probably the leg of a small deer. There would be no way in the world to take it away until that dog was done with it, but there was also no way Jack was going to let him drag that carcass into the house. Therefore the dog would sleep outside, like it or not. Jack took off the saddle and tack and lugged them into the shed. He carried dried oats from the kitchen, hauled buckets of water.

The Morgan allowed him to curry its hide for a few minutes, but the air was growing cold, and the animal felt change coming. It blew and shook out its thick coat. Jack watched it wander downhill to the edge of the corral where it walked in circles, looking for a good spot to graze, then turned its back to the wind.

"Hey," Jack called, but it didn't even lift its head.

Twenty-Six

WHEN HE WOKE the next morning it was to the thin whistle of the dog snoring. Somehow it had shouldered the door open and made its way inside.

The boy lay in a foetal ball, blanket over his head and hands over his ears against the snoring. He was god-almighty cold and wretched with the need to piss.

He counted to three and flung back the blanket and immediately felt the tingle of ice flakes settling on his skin. He put his hand to his cheek: wetness on his fingers. Dawn showed through the frosted window in a kind of diamond sparkle.

He shivered his way off the bed, booted the cabin door closed, and huffed into his cupped hands, knuckles red with cold. The dog raised its head but otherwise didn't move from the bed. On the table was a lantern and he struck a match, turned the wick until he heard the hiss of the flame. Lantern light fell across the tabletop and heeled up the cabin's wall. Jack was wincing from foot to foot, laying his right toes over his left like Christ, then reversing.

In times past, one of his parents would have risen in the middle of the night to stoke the stove, that was just part of life in a cabin, but he himself had always slept through that, and now he'd woken to a frigid morning. The stove was icy to the touch. In the vain hope of finding some coals he slid the cover aside and poked at the contents — they simply collapsed and a half-charred log gonged against the metal hull. The dog was wandering the cabin now, pacing over the muddy bootprints Jack had tracked inside the previous night, before the memory of his mother's voice told him, as it had so often, to turn back around please and leave those boots outside by the stoop.

Dressing involved a sweater and another sweater and a coat before he stiff-legged his way outside, heading for the outhouse. The clearing was bathed in cool light and pocked with muddy boot and paw prints, now hardened artefacts. The deer leg was gone.

His chin jabbered, but he'd seen worse cold.

The boots were standing by the stoop and he snatched at them and stood up. The boots were still affixed to the ground. He reached down again and pulled at them, but they stayed where they were. Last night there had been a small lagoon of mud next to the stoop. Now both boots were frozen to the ground. No matter what he did, they would not come loose. He twisted them side to side, hammered at them with his fist, put his feet in and tried to walk them out, laced them up and leaned forward like a ski jumper, but they held fast.

"Goddamn," he said, standing like an idiot in the stocks of his own boots.

So, in socks, he hobbled and winced his way across the jagged yard to the crapper. It was on his way back — shivering and marvelling at how shockingly hot his urine felt on a cold day, and how getting rid of it made him feel less chilled — that his gaze fell upon the Morgan. The horse was entirely white. It stood motionless in the corral, head sagging, eyes half-closed. A ghost horse, furry with frost.

His first thought was to walk it around the wide corral to warm it. But how to do that in socks?

Inside the small utility shed his father had built Jack seized things on the floor one by one and flung them out the door like a fire-brigader chucking buckets. Skeins of wire, shovels and a pick, a roll of roofing tar paper that unfurled and unfurled and ran away downhill until it bumped up against a tree.

Then he brought the Morgan into the shed and impelled it as far inside as it could go. He brought in two oil lanterns which he lit, then dragged the reluctant dog inside, too. When he finally shut the rickety door there were two blankets on the horse and one around Jack. The idea being that three living creatures and two lanterns might warm the small space enough to revive a freezing horse. The dog leapt onto a side shelf and stood regarding the whole enterprise dubiously. There was room for the boy to stand, but the cold dirt was unbearable, so he hopped onto the shelf beside the dog, and thumped its side.

"There," he said with satisfaction. Everyone was inside the shed.

He fished in his jacket pocket and took out a chunk of chocolate the size of a bar of soap and began to gnaw. The cold had whitened it so the surface looked leprous, but it was still a pretty good breakfast. The horse craned round to beg for some but he pushed its snout away. Jack drew his knees up to his chest and smacked as he ate. Next to him the storm lantern churned heat into the room. He cupped his hands over the chimney until they stung then pressed his palms to his face. His cheeks felt like cold steaks. Jack could feel wind coming in at the cracks and chinks at his back, and he saw the colourless glow of the sky through the ratty shingle roof. Grains of snow fell down through it onto his face. He watched hoarfrost refuse to melt on the Morgan's coat.

Eventually the dog shook itself, hopped down, and scratched at the door.

"Get back here," said the boy from his awkward perch on the shelving. "Come on. This'll work."

The dog stood like a statue, waiting.

"Stop it, you dingus," he said.

It gave him one flat glare and went back to staring a hole in the door.

"Get up here." Jack slapped the shelf beside him.

It sat there inside its thick wolf's coat and wouldn't move.

After forty minutes the boy's teeth were chattering, his stockinged feet had stopped screaming and were now numb, and his breath was visible. What was worse, the horse looked dangerously sleepy. At that moment Jack was feeling the absence of his parents keenly, for he didn't really know how much cold a horse could take, and there was no one to ask. Sampson was forty minutes away on horseback, and Jack had no boots. He was alone with the problem.

Perhaps the Morgan was perfectly fine, warm enough and falling again into a drowse. But what if, instead, it was freezing to death? He ran his hand over the furry rump and swept away the granular snow. It ran off like sand. The air wasn't getting any warmer inside the shed, and Jack himself was beginning to suffer. By that time, the dog had already leapt onto the shelving four times to register its grievance by trampling all over the boy before jumping back down to stare at the door. The whole plan was ridiculous.

"All right fine!" said the boy, and he heeled the door open. The dog shot out and was soon a pale blur among the trees. Jack sighed, then hammered his own thighs and shrieked out in fury, "*Fuck, fuck!*"

At that moment the Morgan's head jerked up out of what had been a pleasant dream. For it was a tough, hairy animal and perfectly suited to this weather, and though the boy didn't know it, the Morgan had been sleeping peacefully. Like Jack, the horse had seen worse cold.

INSIDE THE CABIN proper Jack Boulton paced back and forth before the roaring stove and stamped his stinging, thawing feet. The Morgan now stood inside the cabin, by the back wall, its weight punishing the floorboards, halter tied to the ladder that led to the loft. The air was muggy with the smell of damp horsehair.

Jack had removed the blankets from the horse's back and shaken them out in the clearing; he'd blown out the two lanterns and stoked the stove, and now the place was warm and the animal's coat was glistening with melted snow. Jack whistled a little tune to himself and paced the cabin, icy fingers shoved into his armpits. He was rather proud of his solution. He wondered what Sampson would think of it.

The thought arrested him mid-step, mid-whistle, for Sampson almost certainly would not like it.

Jack wasn't sure what he should have done but he had a sickened intuition that this was exactly the wrong thing. He raked his memory in vain for any time he had seen a horse inside this house or any other. The Morgan stood there with its tail draped over a cedar trunk, its filthy hooves on a rag rug. The sight was preposterous.

Oh hell, thought the boy, *what harm can it do?*

As if in answer, the Morgan began to shuffle-step forward and take on the unmistakable posture of a horse about to take a piss.

"Don't," cried the boy. "Don't you dare!" He cast about frantically for something to catch it in, a bucket, a tub, a blanket that might soak up the liquid, anything to keep what he knew would be a river of urine from pouring across his floor. The bathtub was all the way up in the loft . . .

"Wait!" he called to the horse, who was definitely not going to wait. Finally, he fixed on his mother's precious stockpot, which he snatched up and slid under the descending penis just in time. A harsh rattle as urine drilled off the metal side.

The boy sank down onto the blanket box and pressed his knuckles into his mouth and supressed a giggle. Then began the alarming process of watching the pot begin to fill. Already it was several inches deep, the liquid stirring in a gentle circular motion, and the Morgan was showing no signs of letting up. Jack leapt up and began to scrounge around the room again. He remembered Sampson saying *Don't do anything else stupid.*

✦ Twenty-Seven

HOLDING NOW THE GREEN glass bottle in her hand, joggling the liquid within, the nun felt the intolerable drive and hum of her nerves. This was the drug she had named Pax. It was cloudy and smelled like grass, extraordinarily strong and effective. She opened the bottle but immediately forced the cork back in. If the boy did come home today he would see her under its influence, he might be ashamed of her.

Instead she took down a larger bottle of liquid, a concoction so basic and useful in medicine as to not require a name beyond "calming tonic." She had dosed the boy once with this nameless tincture in his sick days, after he had heard some hospital gossip that his mother had died, when he had cried and thrashed in his bed and begun to understand things as they really were. She had dosed him in order to calm his mind, and at the time, it had worked.

Eschscholzia californica, poppy; *Scutellaria lateriflora*, the side-growing skullcap; *Leonurus cardiaca*, motherwort, which always gentled her fast-beating heart. So many other ingredients, but she knew the recipe by heart.

A drop under her tongue. Two drops. She gave in and squeezed the rubber bulb until the glass dropper was dry.

It was already dusk when she went to the front door to

look out onto the vacant street. She told herself to wait for a sign from the world, a tiding: a person walking by, an animal wandering a neighbour's yard, a bird in flight. Any movement, she decided, would be proof he was on his way back, returning to her. But no living being appeared; she was alone at her door, alone in this town. She went to the stairs and clomped up to the boy's room, saw that it was unchanged, turned woodenly and went to her bedroom, where she lay on the bed, composed her limbs, and closed her eyes. And thus it was, thanks to the tincture, that Emelia Cload finally drifted into sleep for the first time since the boy had left her. A mild, dreamless state that, she later determined, lasted only four minutes.

At first she was sinking into something hollow and dark, then something touched her face, began to push her down, and she was in a sickening plummet. The nun scrambled up gasping, her back to the headboard and the calming tincture in her blood at war with the signal distress that ran through her; something like wrath seemed to permeate the air, to cohabit the room with her.

She reached her hand out, into that cold blue air, then drew it back again, fingers tingling. It felt like snowflakes melting on her skin. Something was there. It was absolutely there, standing in the room, but it would not show itself.

"No," she said firmly, "it's nothing." She looked at the nothing that was not there. "You just took too much."

→ *Twenty-Eight*

IN THE DAYS to come the air grew warmer and Jack Boulton's life settled into an almost domestic pattern. There was a great deal of sweeping and he worked a scrubtowel down to shreds. His body accustomed itself to the nightly chore of waking to stoke the stove. One morning he wandered the cabin's roof with a little pot of heated tar, daubing at the cracks and fissures until the roof was mostly waterproof again. He found rope and hung laundry out to dry between the trees. Now that the great cold had eased off, the little creek that ran through the trees was swollen and gurgling. At the hour when his fellow students would be filing through the front door of school, Jack would sit at the precipice behind his cabin and sip his coffee and watch water roll off the cliff, fanning as it fell, watch it hit bottom and boil there and flow toward the river where, far away, animals congregated and drank. There wasn't much laundry to do anymore, now that he was at home, just a few shirts and one pair of canvas pants, so on that first washday he worked naked except for socks and boots. No one ever saw his socks, so they could look after themselves is what he figured. And most mornings Sampson arrived early with breakfast, and they would sit outside in the dawn together by the fire ring and build up a nice blaze and eat. Sampson would again urge the child to come live with him, always without success.

Before leaving, the old man would hand him more supplies for later, carefully bottled or wrapped in cloth, and he would explain what was to be eaten first and what could wait. He always did his best to impress on the kid that the food was not to be gobbled up the second he turned his back. Most days Jack obeyed him. Then Sampson would pack up and go back to his own life, and the boy would have the rest of the day to himself, sometimes the next day, too. He sat for hours in the sun on his front stoop and read books. He fixed a loose hinge on the front door so it no longer dragged along the floor. He ate sparingly, or so it seemed to him, for he was always hungry. He scrounged everywhere to find more tobacco but there was none, and anyway the papers were all gone. He got out the whetstone and sharpened his buck knife and with it he pared down the last pencil nub til it was perfect. He ran to the cliff and winged stones into the void until his elbow ached. He practised hornpipes and jigs, though he'd forgotten most of the moves, so in truth he was just hopping around the clearing, legging himself silly. He climbed the nearest spruce and clung like a mariner in his crow's nest and scanned the enormous vistas looking for bear or herds of elk or deer. Most days he saw eagles floating out there over the river, hunting. Some days were clear and still enough to see smoke from Sampson's cabin, a finger pointing out of the green.

Jack had always been a climber. At first he climbed his parents' bodies, then the ladder to the loft at the back of the cabin, then the trees outside, and finally the cabin itself. His mother was so watchful he had to do it on the sly, chinning up into the branches, freezing twelve feet up like a monkey with hands and feet on different branches, utterly silent while his mother called and called and finally looked up and gasped, "Jack, get down!" His father playing hide-and-seek, tiptoeing along the cabin's outside wall while the boy, perched unseen on the roof, tiptoed the other way. The game would end when Jack winged a pine cone at his father's head and Moreland bellowed, "Get down off there!"

In the branches around him childhood trinkets still dangled, things he'd fastened there himself, little animal bones and homemade toys, bits of coloured cloth he'd begged from his mother and tied into imagined knots of great complexity, all of them strung up as signals and talismans and friends, a hundred years ago when he was still a child. He had believed one or two of them had magical import, and perhaps they did. These things had looked beautiful to him back then; they felt festive now. Jack Boulton, sticky as flypaper with pine resin, sat in his tree and looked about him at his side of the mountain, heir to it all.

And this was how he spotted the crowd, far down by the river, a dark stain of movement that resolved itself into an enormous number of men. It had taken him a single glance to know this was a gang of convicts, prisoners of war. Where the running men had come from.

He clambered down his tree and ran to the Morgan, worried these visitors might leave at any moment and he would lose sight of them. He rode northeast along a high, fine ridge until he was directly above the work, and there they were, congregated at a bend in the river like a tiny, living diorama. They were hard at work on the trees and ditches that ran alongside the old highway. He stood at his safe distance and watched the prisoners as they swarmed the area. There was a heavy wagon, and two horses were straining to tow the heavier logs off the roadway. Jack Boulton longed to see the faces of these men, in fact he wanted to talk to them. But he absolutely didn't want to get any closer. He was an easygoing kid and he liked people generally, but he had to admit that lately, unchecked proximity to other people had been a trial. The Morgan wandered in circles and grazed, always fetching up with its chin over Jack's shoulder, unsure of the boy's point of interest.

It came to him that they were widening the highway, readying it for grading. Another park works project. But how had such a great mess of men arrived here, half a day's walk from town in either direction?

The answer came at dusk when a train howled up the river valley and stopped just below the work area, tolling its bell. Already the prisoners were in the scrub, waiting in rough rows of four, hefting their tools, covering their faces against the noise and coal smoke. The engineer craned out his window to gawk as two drovers set up a ramp and urged the distressed horses into a freight car. The thunder of dancing hooves inside a metal box continued long after the door had closed, and one animal repeatedly kicked the metal wall like a titanic drum until even the guards backed away from the din. In consternation Jack hissed, "Goddamn it, blindfold them first!" In ones and twos the prisoners clambered into other boxcars, younger men giving an arm-down to older, and they sent lanterns hand over hand until the three boxcars glowed like little cabins at night. It looked like most of the men were now seated cross-legged on the floor, some security measure in play, and at each set of doors only two prisoners remained standing ready to help the guards clamber in. Other guards stood ready to fire as the first of their number was helped up into the mass of seated men, then the rest followed, two guards per car, until finally, with a protracted screech, the sliding doors were all hauled closed at once. The train began its phantom drift forward, a clatter of couplings as the thing accordioned, and then off it went into the dusk toward the town of Banff and the unknown barracks. The long workday was over. Only the heavy wagon remained, its tongue resting on the ground and the horses' leather traces flung back onto the flatbed. Jack Boulton watched the train depart and then he walked the Morgan home, uneasy in his heart.

FOR SEVERAL DAYS thereafter Jack rode out to the spot above the new highway where the gangs were working, and this became his place for eating lunch, lingering until daylight began to fade and the train arrived; and only then did he hurry home to settle the Morgan down with food and water, to reheat the cold cabin, to cook for himself. Too often he found himself chopping wood in near darkness, carrying water through the trees almost blind, in silent argument with his mother, or father, or the nun about how this late-evening routine wasn't really his fault.

Each day the inmates ranged from fifteen to thirty in number, and no matter how early Jack arrived they were already at work. Therefore their keepers must have mustered them out of bed and harried them on board a train in the dark so they could arrive just in time for the dawn light. The better to maximize the short working hours of an early spring day.

Jack knew the old highway pretty well. From that distance it was a pale, hand-drawn line, so soft it was fading out in places and poxed with greenery. The road didn't even stretch all the way to Laggan. It ended about halfway and devolved into a footpath. A horse had no trouble on it, but any automobiles travelling between Banff and Laggan had to skirt around saplings and tolerate an ungodly amount of shaking thanks to the corduroyed dirt; and halfway to Laggan they would run out of road, in the middle of nowhere. In contrast, the new highway started abruptly and ended the same way, a hiccup of order, a perfect, hard line of graded dirt at the end of which gathered a litter of human figures and fire and felled trees and smouldering debris. It hardly looked like progress. In fact, it looked more like calamity at the end of an airstrip. The men were clearing rocks from the roadbed, widening ditches, uprooting bushes and small trees and burning them in piles, felling the larger trees and stacking the cut logs on the new shoulder. They all wore the same homely dun-coloured coats and flat caps. Exactly like the two running men. The guards wore dark uniforms and were almost motionless in their rigid attention. At regular intervals a guard would fire into the air and the prisoners were brought together and counted. Jack watched the gun spit grey smoke, and a half second later came the report. From his great height the boy could see, perhaps better than the guards, those few prisoners at the ragged edges of the work area, those men half-concealed in the greenery, dawdling and fussing and taking too long to join the muster. He wondered what conditions might be necessary for a man to decide he'd break from the group and run.

Jack himself had simply made the decision to escape, and there wasn't much else to it, except to duck out his bedroom window and be gone. He had a home to go to, he had a horse, his own gear, his father's map on the wall. He knew where the water was, where the game would be at any given time of year, the best spots to fish, he was armed, more or less, and he'd lived in this place his whole life. What did these men have?

Two bent figures prepared meals off the tailgate of the wagon, and all the convicts ate sitting on the trees they had felled, huddled together sipping coffee, while Jack took out his packed food and ate along with them. The whiff of smoke from the fires would reach him if the wind was right. He watched them lean together and gesture to one another. He noticed that the guards never sat down.

How antic and clotted a group of humans looked, how much less ordered than, say, an equal number of elk. Two convicts seemed to be always together, bent to their work, and if one walked away the other followed, gesturing. Jack decided these men were brothers, an older and a younger, acting in mutual protection, and they too were plotting an escape. Something inside him whispered: *Don't*.

Now Jack rose and collected the Morgan and swung up onto its warm back. He could not do this every day, hovering over the work area, watching men who would forever be prisoners. For this was a war without end, or it felt like that to him. This was life from now on.

In a last look, Jack watched one inmate rise and go back to his labours before the others, the long axe swinging in easy rhythm, and each time the man paused to adjust his grip there followed over that great distance a phantom clap.

⤙ *Twenty-Nine*

WILLIAM MORELAND AWOKE in the process of falling from a tree. His hand shot out to seize the thin branch he had been holding for two days. Dawn wind riffled the high reaches of the tree, a smell of pine resin on his hands and clothes and face, and underneath that smell, the usual stink of animal. His heart was pounding horribly. He pressed his cheek to the trunk ahead of him.

The grizzly was still down there, sitting on its arse, gazing west. It had the posture of an enormous dreadful baby. It seemed to watch the distant rain clouds boil up and evaporate. Moreland stared for a long time at the gun that lay at its feet. He was too far up to tell if it was even functional after being pawed, bitten, and sat on by five hundred pounds of bear. His knapsack and all its contents, including all the money, were strewn everywhere, all over the goddamned place, and bank notes had been blowing around for so long he knew he could never collect them all again.

It was an unbelievably scarred animal. The bear was missing strips of fur from encounters with other, larger bears, and pocked here and there with poorly healed bullet wounds. William Moreland regarded the lavishly long, mud-brown claws. Sooner or later all bears give up and wander away, or in this case, limp, but this bear was unusually persistent. The one scrawny bit of good news was that, while most grizzlies can climb trees perfectly well, it looked like this one was too damaged to even attempt it.

Stay awake, Moreland thought. *Starve him out. Sooner or later he'll wander off.* He shook his head and blew, shifting his position on the branch, for his left leg had fallen asleep. The bear glanced up to see the man moving up there. Its eyes were flat-brown and cold and looking directly into Moreland's own. No question about the intelligence in them. Moreland's heart began to race again and he was filled with loathing for the thing that had kept him awake — terrified and awake — for two days. "Fuck off, you bastard!" he screeched in pure childish fury. "Get lost!"

The bear's expression was one of calm assessment, and Moreland knew what was coming. It lurched up, shook its thick fur, and approached the trunk again. It rose on hind legs to its full height of seven feet and, for the fifth time that day, began rhythmically to shake the tree. Thick as the evergreen was, it groaned and shook like a willow switch. William Moreland clutched his branch and held on.

➤ *Thirty*

THE CABIN WAS EMPTY of food, and Jack had eaten everything Sampson had on hand. He'd cleared them both out of
food, so the old man badgered him onto his horse and they
rode out together to Laggan, some seventeen miles away
in the opposite direction of Banff. The dog tore out of the
cabin and joined them. Sampson knew about the prisoners
doing road work, so he led the boy the long way round and
once they were clear of it the highway degraded into a soft
footpath, and they walked in single file until they saw in
the distance the first building in Laggan. It was the little
train station.

Three years earlier, the long wooden sign that said in
painted white letters LAGGAN had been pried from the side
of this building and set on the ground beneath the new,
even longer sign that read LAKE LOUISE. The lake itself had
always been so named. But a debate had sprung up, and now
the town too had been officially renamed in honour of some
foreign princess whom few people really knew much about.
Jack remembered the hoopla in the newspaper, photos of the
celebrations, portraits of the old gal in question. There had
been more than a few peevish letters to the editor decry-
ing the imposition of a new name when the old one was

perfectly good, and equally peevish responses from the editor, who by necessity got the last word, saying that the town had had several name changes already, and opining, rather randomly, that those who are against progress are unpatriotic and ungrateful to those valiant men fighting in Europe. So this town was now Lake Louise, but locals are often slow to adopt a new name, especially one imposed by the government, and recluses like those riding past that sign were very much inclined to ignore officialdom. To Jack, this had always been Laggan and it still was.

As yet, it was still not a town, not even a village, but rather a congregation of log buildings, barely livable plank houses, a gaggle of tents for itinerant workers, two small uncharming hotels that catered to tourists arriving too late to take the wagon uphill to the famous lake and stay in the grand chalet there. There were grocery stores, a dinky post office, and a stable or two, all of it fetching up in a mess near the rail station and roundhouse. The area had been so cleared of trees for use in the rail business and the forging of a line through Kicking Horse Pass that the town seemed to be nothing more than a desolate sea of tree stumps.

Jack and Sampson arrived at Carr's, the bigger of the two grocers in town, the other being Fines'.

When they entered the establishment the boy cannoned into Wilson, who was roaming the shelves. "Jesus, watch yer step," the man said, placing a controlling hand on the crown of Jack's hat. "Well, look who it is. The little runaway."

"Hi, Mr. Wilson."

"Stop hopping about."

Sampson's figure filled the door. "What are you doing in Laggan?" he said.

The outfitter rolled his eyes and said, "They want Dutch chocolate. Hard to find."

Sampson snorted.

"And tapioca pudding." Wilson held up a stack of small cans. This was clearly a client request and he was assembling food for a hunting party, likely American or Swiss, some still-neutral country, and obviously well paying.

He said, "You all right, Sprout? No troubles?"

"Nope," said Jack.

Wilson looked at Sampson and said, "Is the kid all right?"

"Looks alive to me."

The trackers wandered the aisles together, Wilson bitching about his choice of vocation, about bartenders and clergy, about the war, Sampson amused but giving him nothing in return. Meanwhile the boy did his own shopping. One by one he collected his goods in a pyramid on the counter, and with each addition he stopped to calculate silently the new subtotal. Three bags of flour. Baking powder and baking soda. Ten pounds of oats. Cornmeal, lard. Sugar and salt. Chocolate, dried currants, cans of sweet milk, cans of peaches and navy beans. Smoked wieners, pickled preserves.

Wilson and Sampson stood by the door and conferred quietly, and in their postures the kid saw they were talking about the nun. Jack slid behind a shelf and watched the two men. Sampson nodded slowly, and then Wilson left in a typical pre-employment funk, stamping down the stairs outside Carr's store and making for his beautiful, dreadful horse.

The boy wandered to the window and watched him and the Colonel go, then he returned to his list. Five pounds of onions. Vanilla custard powder, dried apples, triple-smoked bacon, writing paper and a new pencil, eight pounds of coffee. He chose the smaller can of lantern oil. Waterproof matches. Sampson had continually to shoo the boy away from the stick candy. Together they hovered over the glass cabinet that held boxes of gun rations and they debated the probable calibre of the boy's rifle. In a fit of worry and care, Jack had hidden the gun at home, balanced in the rafters for safekeeping. Sampson had not yet laid eyes on Pearl, and the boy could not reliably describe it, so the old man just said, "Next time."

While Jack roamed the shelves, Carr stood with Sampson over the gun cabinet and conferred with him about various repairs he might do, and about the cost. Carr had done business all over the west and up the Pacific coast and he sometimes broke into a Chinook-Nootka-French-English pidgin common to older traders. He called this kind of negotiation "havin' a wawa." From the cabinet he drew out a Webley officer's revolver he felt was too far gone to fix, but he showed it to Sampson anyway, for the gunsmith had done wonders before.

"It's a bust, Sam."

"Well." Sampson weighed the thing in his palm, then hopped it up into firing position like a sideshow shooter. His face became admiring. "Brand new barrel," he said. "Good balance."

Carr's face went sour. "Okay sure, but lookee. The grip is shite. Lanyard ring got wrenched off. And it's worn down here, and also here. He sawed the trigger guard off and then soldered it back on, which I can't understand the meaning of. Why saw it off in the first place? Mamook pilton."

Sampson said, "I know why he took it off."

"Well, it looks ruined to me."

Sampson agreed to take the old Boer War wreck away to see what he could do with it.

"You're an optimist," Carr said, and Sampson seemed genuinely amused by that idea.

The boy ferried his final purchases to the counter, re-arranged everything, and stood back, his lips moving in silent calculation as to the final cost. Then he took from his pocket the little snuff tin with the smiling chow dog on it and removed exactly one bill and four coins, counted the money twice before handing it over, and when he got his seventeen cents in change he counted that, too. The older men exchanged amused glances.

Jack and Sampson went out into the noon sun. Weathered old flags showing the red ensign drooped from ropes strung across the main street, and there was worn-out bunting on the hotel balcony and other reminders of the war. Their horses and a few others stood uneasy next to hulking black motorcars that stank of rubber and gasoline. The dog was pissing on a tire, answering a previous animal's bon mot with his own. While they were packing up the panniers Carr came outside with a fistful of stick candy, maybe twenty of them, each a different flavour, and handed it all to Jack.

"To thank you two gentlemen for your custom, and to thank you for not going to Fines' for your groceries. I know she has some lower prices, but my quality is better."

"Thanks, Mr. Carr!" Jack said, astonished.

In fact, he'd never been inside Fines' Fine Foods because his mother claimed it smelled unwholesome in there, like a vinegar bottle. Mrs. Fines was an amateur taxidermist, and so her place had the usual chemical smell.

For his part, Sampson avoided the place because the

proprietress fancied him and didn't give a damn if he was married. On two occasions she had made detailed suggestions, and after a moment of frozen shock he'd made for the exit.

Carr hesitated there on the plank sidewalk, hands in his pockets. "It's nice to see you again, kid." His smile was kind. "I'm sorry about all your trouble. Wish I could help more."

"Thanks," Jack said again, his eyes sliding away.

Carr jingled things in his pocket and looked like he was going to say more.

Jack waited to be asked where his father was.

In the end, Carr shut his mouth and climbed the three creaking steps into his store. Jack saw the man's pale shirt up there in the dim air, rattan fans unmoving overhead.

In silence they mounted and walked their horses down the main street. It wasn't until they were at the outskirts again that the boy sighed out, "That was nice of him."

Midafternoon they were back on the dilapidated strip of dirt that was the old highway. It was hazy and warm and the horses picked their way around mid-road weeds. Jack felt a gust of warm air from the north. A moment later the warmth came from the east. It was some localized system of air convecting in the river valley, blowing around them in curtains.

When the boy looked up, he saw not sun but a brilliant golden haze in the air, sunlight blazing through mist. He said, "Look at that."

Sampson said, "Marazu."

"You think?" The boy squinted up, looking for rain.

The surface of the river had begun to steam like a pot about to boil. And then there came an audible patter of droplets high in the trees. The boy saw coins of dust hopping in the roadway, heard tapping on the felt of his hat.

Sampson shrugged off his coat and spread it like a tablecloth over the horse's rump, covering the bedroll full of groceries and his rifle, and he hiked up his ass and sat on the coat's collar to secure it. He beckoned and said, "Hûji," but the boy didn't come to him, so he moved Willow off the road and under the canopy of the aspens and composed himself, hands crossed on the saddle horn. The dog was scouting some scent in the hollows by the road.

It was a simple thing, rain coming, unexpected rain. But the boy's face was pure joy as the first sun shower of his life clattered down upon him, heavy as a hail of pebbles.

"*Hooo!*" he crowed, throwing his head back to face the downpour, and letting his hat tip off and hang by its string from his thin neck. His astonished horse began to wheel on the spot.

Less than a minute later the rain stopped as suddenly as if someone had kinked a hose. All that was left was a gurgle in the ditches, and out in the trees an intermittent hiss as water shook from the high boughs. The dog shook itself from jowl to haunch and trotted over to Willow.

Jack's horse was now sleek, its hide gleaming, and the wet leather tack was pungent and sticking to his hands. The boy righted his hat and threw the old man a daft grin.

"You were right," he laughed. Like it was a surprise to him. Like he had ever in his life known Sampson to be wrong, about anything really. He felt the cold cling of his canvas pants on his thighs. He was awake now, vividly, crazily awake. Pink and blue and green sugar water was drooling from the candy in his coat pockets.

Sampson and Willow were completely dry and they chucked forward into a trot down the middle of the road, and the boy heeled and came after them through the mud.

An enormous rainbow formed pale and fractional over the easternmost peak, its feet lost in the forest. Jack remembered his mother saying, as a kind of lowlander's joke, *Mountains are fine but they block the view.* He kept calling out the colours he could see until the rainbow faded entirely and there was nothing but sky. He wouldn't stop telling Sampson it was the prettiest thing he'd ever seen.

LATER, IN THE WHITE distance ahead, they saw dark figures, dozens of them, moving about on the road. Jack glanced anxiously at the old man. Sampson realized he had forgotten to go the long way around. They reined in hard for a moment and considered the trouble ahead. And then they walked their horses gently into the smell of fresh-cut wood.

Here too it had rained, and the mist over the river was so thick it floated through the trees and mingled with the work gangs like helpful ghosts. Some prisoners were sluicing through ditches, clearing brush and felling trees alongside the main enterprise, while guards in dark uniforms looked on. Others were at work on the road itself with shovels and wheelbarrows. Two enormous horses dragged a rough grader over the new roadbed. It was made of logs that had been chained together and studded at regular intervals with sharp metal hooks. The thing was meant to work like a monstrous flea comb on the rocky ground, teasing out rocks and debris. There were wet wool coats and flat caps left everywhere on bushes and on piles of cleared rocks. Some of the men had stripped down to their stained overalls and most were sweating; the guards were calling to them and they were calling back. A rumble and jingle from the chained logs.

"Oh no," Sampson said. "I don't like this."

And it would seem the dog didn't like it either, for it ducked left and bounded uphill, cutting neat little switchbacks and glaring over its shoulder with the cold, steady eyes of a wolf that has been forced out of its way.

The boy swivelled in his saddle. "Sampson?"

The old man pointed off the busy road into the trees.

They cut right to avoid the grader, and the Morgan stepped into the thick of the brush, where a gaggle of prisoners paused in their work and smiled and said things in an unknown tongue. A few reached out and patted the Morgan's shoulder as it walked by, "Hello. Gid day!" The boy smiled back and gave them a wave. Another five men and more hellos. The riders were surrounded now, and Jack, passing freely among convicts like a princeling on a pony, did not know how else to greet so many, so he saluted. A shout ran through the assembly of men and they saluted back, sarcasm at work among them.

Sampson's voice came in a hiss, "Keep moving."

But the kid was fascinated by all this life he had seen from a long, distorting distance. He walked the Morgan past fallen shovels, an axe, a two-man timber saw left in the ditch, a sprung wicker basket filled with tin cups and spoons, and a battered coffee pot the size of a well bucket. And the men. Their faces. He marvelled at how different these prisoners looked up close than they had in his imagination. The old man with a stoop was actually young, too young to be so broken down. He looked sick. The fat one was not fat at all; he had somehow inherited a much bigger man's jacket and it hung on him like a great bell. The pair he had imagined were brave brothers scheming an escape were probably not related; they looked nothing alike. They were bent together, yes, but were bitching at one another in a tired, incessant drone, so locked in argument they were entirely unaware of the riders who passed them just feet away. Jack's imagining of a brotherly confab, it turned out, was more like an irreconcilable feud.

A loud voice beside Jack made the kid jerk in his saddle as one guard bellowed forward to another, "Parker, civvies coming!"

The horses trotted up the gravel slope and back onto the road, where they were obliged to skirt four inmates working to dig boulders out of the roadbed with their bare hands.

This last group was so miserable they barely looked up. The lone guard assigned to them was standing like a statue atop a cairn of debris, watching the horsemen approach. The riders simply glided toward him, peering out from under their hat brims.

"Boy," Sampson said. "Go faster."

Jack was drifting, lost in thought about the strange effects of distance. He was slightly ashamed of the fraudulent tales he had told himself, fantasies he'd concocted simply because he couldn't see things clearly. How terrible to be locked in close proximity with strangers, to be caged and pressed into drudging service. The "brothers" in particular worried him. Never mind that these were not the young heroes he had imagined, the real story was worse than that. How had he not seen the hatred in their postures, in their gestures? Why had he not suspected it? Jack knew perfectly well what hate was. He'd learned it at the hands of other children.

"Duki na?!" Sampson's voice was sharp and stern.

Jack jolted in the saddle. He realized the Morgan had shuffled to a stop near the guard. There were prisoners all over the road, only a narrow path through them.

Sampson heeled Willow forward and kept at her until she almost climbed the Morgan. The kid was forced into a brisk trot, around and between the remaining men, right past the looming guard, and out into empty road, finally breaking into a canter with goods rattling in the panniers. After three hundred paces the new grading came to an abrupt end in a crest of debris. The horses scrambled over it and slid down onto the rutted old roadway, where they kept at a tight trot, the hooves almost soundless now in the soft dirt.

Sampson kept twisting in the saddle, looking behind him at the receding crowd of men. A catalogue of details had formed already in his mind, a police habit formed years ago. He estimated the guard called Parker to be at most twenty-five. There was something wrong with his hips, and though he did not step down off his cairn, nor did he walk, Sampson suspected a back injury or a birth defect, something permanent that would cause him to limp. His hair was dark but he had two spots of white the size of thumbprints, the kind of mark caused by blows to the head in childhood. There was a grey tinge to the skin of his jaw common to hard drinkers. His rifle was slung across his back by a worn chest strap. Like all of the prisoners, and like the other guards, Parker wore a uniform that was tattered and sun-bleached, with frills of disintegrating fabric at the cuffs. Multiple colours of thread held his buttons on, and his boots were in rough shape. But unlike the other glum watchmen, this man looked perfectly accustomed to such privation, equal to it, mostly immune to weather, a local hunter surely, a crippled young man forced by the war into guard work. He looked strong and bored and mean. What worried Sampson was that during that long traverse around him, the guard had stared directly at Jack Boulton, almost as if he knew him.

Sampson sank into unhappy meditation on omens. The sun shower, Jack Boulton out on the road, his hat tipping off his head, the string across his thin neck like a garrotte.

The riders went on, each studying a different problem, each following his separate rut in the road, deaf to the hiss of the river and the calls of jays skirmishing over berries in the underbrush. The dog reappeared, trotting silently alongside, and soon the sounds of work behind them faded, and the clot of figures was lost in the haze.

THE GUARD, FOR his part, left his charges to their work and wandered a short way over the empty road. It was a breach of protocol to show his back to the men, but Parker was frankly fascinated. He watched the shapes of the riders shrink into the distance.

A very old prisoner with withered shoulders and a chest like a plucked chicken glowered at the guard's back with undisguised loathing. He was shirtless and so old he looked like he'd come out of the ark, and in his hands was a rock the size and shape of an adze. He contemplated Parker's exposed nape until another prisoner seized him and drew him away.

Parker had noticed the lack of tent or any gear, and he'd seen the load of provisions the riders carried. Manifestly they were going home after shopping, and home must be close by. The idea perplexed him. What kind of misfits would choose to live out here? The old man made him a little uneasy. Elderly yes, thinning hair and the cloudy eyes of the aging, but with all that, this man was still strong, he was armed, and he radiated hostility. But it was the kid who really interested Parker.

He remembered the boy. Recognized his face. Knew the exact weight of his thin body, for Parker had been one of the men to rush in from the roadway to stop him from hammering at another student in a schoolyard. That had been an impressive fit of rage. He remembered that, as slim as the kid was, he'd been difficult to hold, let alone subdue.

But that had happened a long way from here. Somehow the kid had traded in his schoolboy breeches for serviceable canvas pants and a blanket coat.

He wondered what this boy was doing, running around with that old man. Or rather, as it seemed, in some kind of domestic situation with him. Parker turned and looked down the road to Laggan, where the riders had come from, then turned to face the open wilderness again. He assessed the ranges and the time of day, calculated the distance to Laggan and the average area a horse could cover in an hour at a walk, then at a trot. The horses hadn't looked bad, so they were probably just walking them. He knew the area, and he began to triangulate where these two might live. He came up with the Sawback Range, a large area to be sure, but it had water, shelter from the wind, proximity to the road and the rail line. Parker scratched his neck, as if he felt the gaze of others burning there. Maybe, when the war ended, he too would build himself something up there. He turned now and went back to his vigilance. The prisoners nearby almost winced when he looked at them.

→ Thirty-One

A FEW HOURS after dawn the bear shambled off. The Ridgerunner watched it go with weary elation, straining to keep the brown, shaggy rump in his sight for as long as he could, tracking its trajectory through the trees. There was a knot in his chest: a painful mix of jubilation and unbearable dread that the animal might circle round and come back.

In an area rotten with bears, black and grizzly, males and females, most of them shy and with a marked aversion to humans, most of them keeping to the upper reaches of the mountains — of *all* these animals, in this grand and wide landscape, why did he have to run up on such a disagreeable beast?

For perhaps an hour Moreland stood on his branch and spied through the swaying trees for movement. He climbed higher and then lower again. Nothing.

He stretched and shook his stiff and cramped limbs, testing them. The news wasn't good. His cold knees were terrible; inflexible and unreliable. His fingers were worse. If he climbed down to solid ground just as the animal returned, there was no guarantee he'd have enough strength left to claw his way back up. No guarantee that the bear wasn't — as grizzlies do — simply circling the site like a watchman doing his rounds, checking for intruders. There was also little hope the rifle would still be in working order. If Moreland slid down this trunk. If the animal came back. If the gun was buggered. If his old body would not obey his brain's panicked demands as he scrabbled at the tree's trunk . . .

Moreland removed his belt and fashioned a loose tourniquet between his ankle and the branch, a kind of tether to keep him from falling, and then he closed his eyes. He settled back with a withered heart and an empty belly. Surely, this was retribution. Pick the sin to punish, there were so many to choose from. The nun's words came back to him: *You have been a curse to them both.* Yes. He'd had this coming.

BY ABOUT TEN O'CLOCK the bear had not returned and the Ridgerunner was still hobbled to his tree branch. Far to the northwest, a snow squall was cresting the mountain ranges and heading his way.

No wind yet, but the air itself seemed to dim, as if the bad weather was bringing with it an eclipse.

Moreland loosed himself from the belt that bound him to the branch and he stood in his tree, shook his legs and huffed like a man about to dive into icy water. He watched that weather roar in and understood that he no longer had any time: his body was giving out. His hands and feet were almost numb. He had no choice but to climb down now and take his chances.

It was more like tumbling down a staircase with his face slapping the stairs. Nothing worked, his limbs were feeble and bloodless, and when he landed it was in a heap atop his own rifle. His bony buttocks hit the stock and with that last insult, the gun broke in half. He sat where the bear had been sitting for so long, leaves and paper money skittering along the ground in the rising wind.

He rose and stared through the pines, spun wildly and stared again, imagining brown shadows moving everywhere. He was hyperventilating, running here and there to claw at drifts of banknotes, stuffing them by the handful into his bag. And then Moreland was running with the bag against his belly, bouncing along as high-legged and wooden as a puppet, sinews standing out on his neck. The direction was obvious: upwind, into the weather, because if the grizzly was downwind it might still smell him but have no idea he had started to run, and if that bear did get the news, Moreland might get enough distance to outrun him. The bear was in rough shape, but any grizzly can outrun a man. If the animal was upwind it wouldn't smell him immediately, and in fact, given the animal's fetid condition, Moreland would likely smell it first. So off he went, half-swooning, heading for the cloud-shrouded mountains, through a smattering of trees and into a vast field of grass at the far side of which ran the long, raised, pale dyke of a rail line. Moreland made for that line. His face in a mad grin as he ran, telling the boy, telling him in his head: *Three days in a tree . . . three days in a goddamn tree.* His dry, cracking laugh as he ran.

⇒ Thirty-Two

THE TERRIFIC BANG that woke Sampson wasn't real. By the time the old man came to himself he was already four strides across the floor and his fists were up. He found himself standing by the stove, swaying, breath frozen in his lungs and the hair on his skull standing up in horripilating waves. He squeezed his eyes shut and sighed. It was nothing, nothing; just his mind barking out old worries. The cabin was warm and quiet. His ear became attuned to Willow and he heard her nicker; he took a block from the front window-hole and saw her there, chin over the fence, looking right back at him. Had he shouted in his sleep?

Anxious mothers wake in the night imagining they hear children crying for help, businessmen at the end of their rope wake to phantom pounding on the front door, alcoholics cowering under bridges hear the paddy wagon rolling overhead, and men like Sampson hear gunfire.

A ladle of water from the bucket, which he held to his lips and drank, and dipped again, but it just hovered there and he did not drink. He wandered out the door into the cold stony clearing and walked until he could spot the moon through the still tips of the pines, and there he assessed the sky, holding his ladle, the silvered surface trembling, and he reckoned the time. No later than midnight. As his wife had taught him to, he took his gauge of the stars' brightness, and from that deduced the upcoming weather.

Sampson had been born in the Indian Territory, in what was now called Oklahoma, but he left his family when he was very young. He'd never known his father as anything but a young man, but he did remember his grandfather, a napping old man who murmured to himself. Sampson's father had been Mvskoke and his mother an Englishwoman, and he had emerged from the womb looking nothing whatever like the woman who had given birth to him. That fact had always troubled his mother and spawned some private amusement among his father's siblings. He figured his own age to be over sixty, which made him a little older than Pucá was when he died. To be older than one's own grandfather, it was absurd. Perhaps someday he too would start napping.

The idea pleased him and he chuckled, but his voice rang hollow and false in that clearing, so he stopped. He saw himself standing there, playing the nice old man, laughing modestly at himself. An elderly husband. A father to three, grandfather to seven. A kindly uncle to William Moreland's boy. It was all wrong.

The first man he ever shot collapsed mid-run, dead before his knee hit the ground.

That particular quarry had cut the throat of a city official, so when the murderer came in dead and therefore beyond the reach of outraged justice, payment was cut in half. After that he gave more careful attention to his work.

At only eighteen he'd been deputized into the U.S. Marshals, and at first, his police work was wild and undisciplined. He never started a fight but yearned for one to begin and would wade into a fracas swinging a woman's bonnet loaded with iron bolts. He broke knuckles, collected belts and suspenders from captured men so they had to shuffle along holding up their pants with blue and swollen fingers. In those days he had adopted the name Wówaśté, and his friends called him Wash. In Sioux it roughly translated into something like *goodness*, the irony of which was not lost on his boss, an older, resourceful Black tracker and former slave who spoke at least three languages. More than once Mr. Reeves had said in English, "Son, I despair of you."

New inductees avoided him because he was frightening, but the rest trusted him because he was smart and always the first one to act. He was the man you stood behind — let Wash open the door.

The bullets had gone into other men this way: kneecap, above the left nipple, cheekbone, through the eye and out the opposite ear, heart, upper lung, heart again, buttocks. The knives did this: through a wooden door and into a man's spine; slashed across a girth strap so the horse screamed and threw the rider to the ground; across the left cheek, opening a white seam of bone; point-deep under the jaw into a great wash of blood; meat of hand; meat of forearm; in the gut above the gun belt. In all of this there had been little noise, no clamour at all, or so it seemed to him. He remembered only quiet and the sound of other men breathing.

By the time he left the U.S. Marshals Service he was nineteen and utterly unstable. He had brought in twenty warrants in one year: twelve alive but in rough shape, and eight dead.

For a while it was the most satisfying existence he could imagine. To do what he enjoyed and was good at, to be paid for it, to have a purpose.

He'd spent his childhood in a kind of irritable haste, avoiding adults, sleeping wherever he wished, running in packs with other boys and wallowing with them in petty crime, to the burning shame and disbelief of his parents, especially his mother, whose alien ancestry was assumed to be the source of his madness. In vain people tried to talk the boy home, in vain his family tried to explain to him that he was unwell and in need of care. But by then he was lost to them.

The truth was, he was simply and undeniably himself: as soon as he was old enough to crawl he'd been heading for the door, away from family and domesticity, furiously heading for the world outside.

When someone offered him the violent and righteous life of a deputy U.S. Marshal, it appealed to him as a man, a very young man, and he accepted the job almost on a whim. He was sworn in by a glaring white judge he'd never met. He was given gear, guns, a badge, money. They offered to supply him with a horse, but he said no. He already rode a stolen Sioux pony he'd renamed Hóta because it was grey. Like the rest of the inductees, Cherokee, Mvskoke, Seminole, Chickasaw, he could shoot straight, could speak multiple languages. And unlike any white marshal he could pass through the Territory mostly unnoticed. Almost all of the warrants were white men, and they were not small game. Murderers, rapists, train robbers, they fled into the vast Indian Territory and used it as a place to rest, to victimize people, to ignore the local police forces, like the Chocktaw Light Horse, whose right to arrest did not extend to whites, or Blacks, or anyone else but the Chocktaw. Jurisdictional limits created opportunity for wanted criminals, until two hundred new deputies rode into the Territory, and Wash was one of them.

For the first time in his young life, he knew what it felt like to matter, to be single-minded, to follow one quarry after another, to plan and wait and ambush. And for almost a year he'd been unaware of the cost of it to his already small, mean heart.

By the time he quit he was no longer angry, but he hadn't felt young in a long time. He was deaf in one ear from gunfire. A scar on his hand marked the time he had dragged a bystander forty feet to safety and cut himself on the man's shattered ribs. He had no recollection of being shot but had three imperfectly healed wounds to prove it, dotted across his torso like knots in pinewood. Sleep eluded him. A palsy played along his fingers. His tongue dried up. And one day, walking up the busy courthouse steps, heading as usual to the judge's quarters to make his report, he began to suspect that he was no longer moving. His legs swung, but in those drawling seconds his own progress over the earth felt like an illusion. Crowds exiting the gallery passed around him, the world flowed ceaselessly toward him then away, the courthouse doors opening and closing like flapping jaws: it was all a dream from which the sleeper was now waking, sickened and confused. The hallway he knew so well began to spin.

He sat heavily on a bench, where his knife and two pistols argued with the hardwood. The courtroom had recently been cleared, the doors were shimmed open and all seats were empty, the hallway was silent. He clawed the Stetson from his head and took in, as if for the first time, his green oilskin coat. It was pocked with stains and holes, corroded by his own blood and the blood of other men. He saw the condition he was in, saw the thin metal star pinned over his lung.

Next to him on the long bench sat a tiny unattended child

who stared up at him in frozen terror. She was clutching her mother's purse and had a clown ring of blue candy round her mouth. A sticklike creature waiting for her mother to emerge from the toilet. He regarded this child with equal dread: those enormous, welling eyes and the fearful blue mouth beginning to open in a shriek of alarm, all the fragile bones in those fingers, in that neck.

He stood abruptly and staggered away, heading for the building's back entrance where all would be quiet. No people. No people. His one thought was to leave his life somehow, stop everything, to get away. He barrelled toward the back door and stood there, hand on the wall, not breathing, staring at a map of the United States mounted on the wall in a gilt frame, a standard thing for a courthouse and something he'd passed innumerable times without much notice. He sucked in a single breath and saw the vast country in which he had always lived without being part of it, and above that, Canada, left by the cartographer entirely blank and unnamed. He looked at that great vacancy for a long time, the way one looks out to sea, and it calmed him. In some irrational way he imagined he would leave this town, this state, leave America, leave himself behind, head north where surely it was quiet and uninhabited, and he'd just . . . cease to be. Wink out and be gone.

Weeks later he rode Hóta across the invisible border between Montana and Alberta and did not wink out, did not cease to be. He was slow-eyed and speechless, and passersby said not a word to him. He carried useful things in his saddlebags, and he had four good rifles and a pistol which he kept wrapped inside a blanket and tarp. This was how he slept, too, lying on the ground, tarped up beside his guns.

Everything was loaded, it was a hard habit to break. He shot game birds. He ate apples off trees and grubbed his breakfast from farmers' fields. As the landscape changed and farms came and went, he wondered what else was edible. He ate the few plants he recognized and left the ones he didn't.

One day he realized the soft blue clouds on the western horizon were in fact the silhouettes of some massive range of mountains. He kept going north, the horse scrub-thin and wading through grass and mud, skirting round little crofts of trees. And one evening in perfect fall warmth he made camp at an abandoned farmhouse where the pump still drew fresh water. Three times he filled the bowl of his hat and let the horse drink, then he bedded down on the sprung front porch among weeds and dust and watched a storm boiling over the mountains. Even at that great distance he could see weather moving in sheets, and it was flashing. It looked like the end of the world. So in the morning he headed that way.

It is remarkable the effect one person can have on your life. The day he rode into the town of Laggan, passing slowly along the busy street, he looked exactly like what he was: a frightening stranger on a gaunt horse, dragging his shadow with him. Without dismounting he let the horse suck at a water trough outside the bank and he considered his own grey image reflected in the windows. The other side of the street was reflected there too in the slanting sunlight. A sign in a window said POTS.

He craned round to look at it straight on and saw:

STOP

SPECIAL ON BOVRIL

Next to that sign stood a tall unbelievably beautiful woman. That day in 1876 Lena was in her early twenties, she had a gaggle of small children round her, and she was staring at him. He dismounted and ventured stiffly into the street to study her, hands on his hips. She didn't move. Her face was set, and he saw warning in her eyes. One by one the children began to hide behind her legs. They held toys, and a few still had uneaten treats.

The stranger swayed a little. In Mvskoke he asked her name — "Naket cehocefkvte?" — though no one for eighteen hundred miles spoke his language. And then his knees gave out in the middle of the main street, and he collapsed spraddle-legged in the dust and began to laugh. Women peered from windows. Townspeople strayed out to look; white people, Chinese people. A wagon veered around him. Three very worried men stood in the street to block traffic and protect him; they spoke to him in Nakoda, in Siksika, in French, but he didn't understand. He gazed up at them, witless in his exhaustion. Meanwhile his horse wandered the boardwalk like a gentleman after dinner, peering into shop windows and eating flowers off the hanging baskets.

Eventually the tall woman herself came close and bent over him. Her eyes were green. Lena put her hand on his shoulder and spoke gently to him, and thus the madman was convinced to come inside, get out of the sun, and lie down.

He'd been nineteen that day. Younger than Lena. Sampson stood in the clearing, looking up.

His name wasn't even Sampson Beaver. Not really. He'd assumed the name of another man, a man who was truly good, who was currently alive and living in the lowlands near Morley. He'd simply wanted out of his own skin, out of his life and his history, and because he'd admired that other Sampson Beaver, he'd taken his name. After a while his wife forgave him for that and accepted it. His children never knew anything different. He'd become Sampson Beaver II, the second, the other one. He held the ladle to his lips and drank, then flung the remains into the whispering grass. He listened to the world breathe.

Thirty-Three

THE TOBACCONIST'S SHOP in Banff was empty save for Thom Wilson, who was in earnest regard of a single cigar. This was always his final, ceremonial preparation before setting out on a guiding job, all the other preparations having been made, gear assembled, the animals ready to load. He put his finger on the glass case and said, "Who would pay that much for one damn cigar?" The proprietor replied that in fact most people would pay that much and more, it was just the Australian himself who had low tastes and took frugality too far. Which was true. Wilson could afford to buy the cigar, he just wouldn't.

The door tinkled and the nun entered. She went straight to Wilson and without preamble said, "Where is he?"

He kept looking into the case. "I have no idea."

"You are a liar. He's been seen in Laggan, and you were there."

"Who the hell told you that?"

She spat out, "Carr's wife told everybody. She was shocked her husband had let him go on his way. Women, at least, care whether the boy lives or dies."

"Dies," Wilson snorted. "He's doomed unless he's living with you, is that it?"

By this time the proprietor had begun to realize who they were talking about.

The nun simply waited until Wilson turned to face her and said in a flat tone, "I saw him in passing, for one minute, all right? But he's gone home now, and I don't know where that is. If he doesn't want to be found then just leave him be."

"You . . ." she said, less a word than an exhalation.

Wilson put his finger in her face. "He wasn't yours. Not your property. You kept him like a lapdog, and you got what you deserved."

Later that afternoon, the tobacconist would relate the scene to any local who entered his store. "I tell you, that woman went off her wick. A voice that would etch glass. She called him a swine and whatnot, just went at him. When she's finished he calls her something I won't repeat. I was going to step in, you know? It's bad for business, people in here fighting like cats, using language."

In the silence thereafter the combatants stood face to face, so close and intent on one another they might be mistaken for two middle-aged people in love. Finally, she stepped back and a look of genuine calm came over her features. She said, "I don't need you," and left the shop.

Wilson stood for a long moment staring into the air, slowly cooling off. Then he cleared his throat and returned to the purchase of three of the cheapest cigars in the cabinet. He thumbed a quarter onto the counter and walked out the door.

For the rest of that day the tobacconist repeated the story to anyone who came in whether or not they wanted to hear it. And weeks later he leaned on his counter and told one of his regular customers, "Of course, *now* I know what she meant: who needs one man when you can get a hundred? A reward of two thousand dollars will bring in decent trackers, sure. But also, every rat and lunatic will come crawling out of his hole. She doesn't know the cut of some of these gentlemen. But, in the end, the rich get what they want. It's the nature of things."

✦ Thirty-Four

IN THE HOUR AFTER dawn Jack rose from dreams through which his mother had roamed, alive and her usual self. Even as he sat up and felt amongst the bedclothes for his shirt, he half-believed she was in the room with him. She was present and not present, dead and not yet dead, and it was all true in the way of dreams. The coffee took a long time to boil, and he stared at the water's oily surface and felt reality seep in again. He had decided that Sampson, with his old man's dreams and omens, was wrong: you couldn't take such things to heart. The mind fusses in sleep, pretends, weaves tales. A dream is just your life mixed with the absurd, the impossible, the subtly wrong; the mind ruminates, chews its cud like a deer. But when we wake, we cannot stop trying to sieve out the truth, to guess at the dream's message, for we are sure there is one. But there are no messages, any more than there are messages in the daytime. His mother saying to him once: *What I see is not always real, especially when I close my eyes.*

The boy rubbed his cheeks angrily. Do not imagine she is here, watching over you, cajoling you. Do not converse with her. What you got from her is all you'll ever get.

He flopped onto the bed and sipped his coffee. He scooted *Moonfleet* off the bookshelf and flipped to the page he wanted, but then he simply sat there, blinking his burning eyes.

After coffee with pan-toasted bread, Jack ate plum jam directly out of the jar with a spoon, then packed a lunch, which he wrapped in a cloth and rammed into his coat pocket. He grabbed the fishing rod and exited the cabin. He lay the rod across Sampson's chair by the fire ring and took up the hackamore where it hung on the fence at the corral and stood there, boot on a fence rung, looking at the motionless horse. The small corral had been left fallow for a year, and previous to that it had been well fertilized with horseshit, so by now it was like a potted plant, bristling with young grass, a fertile mass of feed in the otherwise bare clearing outside the cabin. A withered moon overhead, clouds washing away into a day that promised to be all sun and wind. The animal's rump was facing west. His father used to say: *If you want to know which way the wind is blowing, look at your horse's ass.* Sampson put it more succinctly: *Buffalo face the wind. Horses don't.*

The horse stood slack-mouthed in the knee-high grass. The boy clicked to it but it did not stir. He slung a boot over the bottom fence rung and bent under the upper rung and advanced upon the Morgan. In fact, the horse had been genuinely asleep and it jerked its head up and blinked at him, clomping its jaws.

"Wake up, lazy-ass." He worked the hackamore on. Gentle with the stiff ears. He picked grass florets out of the fur, smoothed the breast, the neck. He pressed his ear to the animal's warm barrel, heard the breath go in and out, eavesdropped on the heart.

He fished a lump of sugar out of his pocket and the animal roused noticeably. It ate the sugar then explored his palm for wayward grains. Together they walked to the far side of the pen, the horse sniffing at his coat pockets and nickering. He reversed direction and the horse turned with him, scissoring its ears. "Stay," he ordered, and the horse stopped. It was an old trick they had studied together for years, ever since the boy was little. It was their only trick, and not an especially accomplished one. The good news was that he no longer had to look at the animal or gesture at all. The word "stay" was enough. Then he said, "Ho," and the horse followed him. "Stay," he said again, and the horse shuffled to a stop. On they went, walking and pausing, and every few times, the boy produced another lump of sugar.

Jack walked the Morgan out of its enclosure, seized the withers, and swung his thin leg over its bare back. He kick-kicked the animal's ribs and the Morgan shuffled sideways, and Jack reached down and took up the fishing rod, where-upon they left home and went along the ridge. From there, the river was visible. So was the rail line and the road in its various stages of repair and decay. In the middle distance, he could see the prisoners.

The highway had rolled far enough north now that the men were congregated exactly where the boy liked to fish. He could always make his way farther upriver, but the trout were best right there.

It was hours too early to eat but the kid could never wait so he took out his lunch and ate it. The horse wandered meanwhile and cropped grasses, going in slow circles, always fetching up next to Jack where it hung its head near his and looked down at the spectacle.

Finally, he folded his bit of cloth and tucked it away, and together they cut uphill, heading for a rock-bound lake and an area of talus where they used to go sometimes as a family to eat a picnic and fish and dip their toes in the water, and where Jack knew his father used to keep traps.

DOWN IN THE VALLEY, the prisoners worked until teatime, whereupon they dropped tools and wandered toward the cooks' wagon, where they all gathered and gabbled and annoyed the two cooks, as they did every day. One of the cooks spoke in a constant stream of invective and blame, for it is impossible to provide for so many when all the best stuff gets pilfered and he knew goddamn well who took the shit, too, and he'd give that man a frying pan across his head one of these days. But this kind of harangue was the norm, no one took it seriously, and it was otherwise a quiet and weary kind of day. The men collected their steaming tin bowls and bricks of bread and sat in a line on a felled pine, grumbling like sparrows on a wire. A few closed their eyes and slept sitting upright, chins inside their coat collars.

Sergeant Buck was doing another head count, the fourth of many today, when the gunshot came. There was a unified jolt throughout the group, and every soul looked up in dread. The guards all raised their rifles in unison as the report racketed down the river valley and crawled the hills. All eyes fell on Parker. He was still in firing posture, aiming at a pale shape in the trees that lay still kicking, once, twice, then not again.

Sergeant Buck put his hand over his eyes. It was not an escapee, thank god, not a man, but a mule deer. A young doe, breeding age, now dead in the brush on the riverbank.

They should all have been used to gunfire by then, but clearly, the horses were not. One began rearing in its traces, dragging the other mare with it, impelling the whole heavy wagon sideways in a rhythmic shudder that jangled the tin cups and bowls and threatened to lever the wheels right off. The affronted cooks were screeching. The drovers struggled to get them settled and even a few prisoners hurried to help. Everyone was yammering.

It was only in the calm afterward that Sergeant Buck approached the shooter and bitched at him in a lowered voice. Parker regarded him with red eyes but made no move and did not offer an apology. Talk stopped entirely and the prisoners watched the hushed reprimand with undisguised pleasure, for Parker was a hated guard. His amusement lately had been to provoke an inmate until he swore or spat, and then to beat him into the ground.

"Come!" called Parker. "You two." The nearest prisoners trotted over to collect the deer, hoist it by the legs. They slung it up onto the wagon, destined to be dinner for the prison warden and his officers. They went back to work with pounding hearts.

Parker approached the sleigh and stood looking at his handiwork. The doe's mouth was still open on its last breath, tongue lolling. He adjusted one thin leg, warm and sinewy in his closed fist. The body was pliant and nearly bloodless, just a little leaking hole at the shoulder. He placed his palm on the motionless ribcage.

JACK BOULTON WALKED the horse to the edge of the lake, but it turned away to find grass. He clambered uphill and, after some scouting, succeeded in finding a few old snares, but as he pulled them up, one by one, they turned out to be almost totally ruined by the elements. The last one held a dead pika, weightless and mummified by cold, which he held up by its garrotte like a horrid doll before flinging it away, wire and all, into a crag.

All around him on the scree slope live specimens *eep*ed in furious censure. He *eep*ed back at them and they replied, the chorus continuing in moronic repetition until he roared and charged through the boulders at them with his arms aloft and they flashed away into cracks and hollows. Then he stood there laughing into the silence. The chorus was over. He trotted back down to level ground with his blanketcoat flapping at his thighs. There was nothing left of his father's work here, and given his memory of how those little rock rabbits tasted, and how much work was necessary to clean even one animal, let alone enough of them to fill a stew pot, he decided that trapping was over.

Jack winged pebbles over the lake's surface and cooee'd into the air, and the rock walls returned his voice to him muted and alien. Fishing produced nothing whatsoever but the calming sound of the line riffling out. He tried different lures, finally resorting to a sardine from a can. He chopped other sardines into bits and flung them into the water as an enticement. He drew the tobacco pouch from his pants and fashioned a cigarette, then patted everywhere on his person searching in vain for matches until he tucked it all back into his pocket.

The time of day was less than ideal for fishing — he saw nothing moving in the water, no sign of life at all, so after an hour he lay in the sun on the shoreline with his back to a mound of rocks and with a warm rock for a pillow, removed the U.S. Ranger's exam booklet from his pocket, and read until noon.

How and for what purposes are national forests created?

The boy had no concept of federal land, no clear idea what governments did, so he wondered if this was a trick question. The word *creation* worried him. Why was the forest created? Perhaps this question was about God. He wasn't sure.

Some problems were as easy to answer as if they were asking his name:

Question 6. (b) How many pounds can the average horse pack for six consecutive days, making 15 miles per day? How many pounds can the average man pack under the same conditions?

Others left him yearning for a book of answers to confirm his guesses:

Question 4. Set up a compass and allowing for the variation given by the examining officer, indicate north 25 degrees of west, then indicate from that, south 50 degrees of east.

Jack imagined himself facing north, then turning. There are ninety degrees in each quarter, so . . . He flipped the pages to see if Wilson had added any notations, but of course he hadn't. Writing "bollocks" on the cover had been his sole contribution.

The sun burned in the cloudless sky, brilliant and tingling his skin; too bright now to read. He half-closed his eyes and let wet scissoring lines of light dance across his vision, his lids trembling, then he lay the book over his face and sighed into the consoling tent of warm paper. His ears followed the wanderings of the horse over that rocky landscape. The hiss of wind through the low junipers. He lay like that for an hour and dozed. He turned on his side amongst the rocks and groaned in discomfort, then flopped back to gaze up at the sky, the vast expanse of clear blue. Finally he rose, uncricked his neck, and shook sand off his coatback. As usual the horse was not hard to catch, it did not try to evade him but stood still and watched him come. He took up the reins and collected his debris from the shoreline and they started walking toward the path back to home.

The mound of stones he had been lying against was, he now saw, an unnatural thing. It stood alone on a slight rise, and nothing else looked like it. Not glacial, nor the result of spring runoff rolling stones into a mound, it was set in a sheltered spot, above the highwater mark of the lake. And these rocks were heavy, but each seemed perfectly angled to fit the exact spot it was in, as if some hand had placed it there. The kid saw intelligence here. The site had been carefully chosen. So he approached the perfect oval of stones again and finally saw what he should have seen right away: a large flat plate of sedimentary rock was laid at its head, and on the surface were chiselled with great care two initials.

Jack Boulton's mind shrieked once and then went blank. For many minutes he saw nothing, felt nothing, heard no sound but his own enormous heartbeat. He simply stared blindly at the spot where he had lain in the sun all that long, lazy afternoon, reading and drowsing, with his head at his mother's shoulder.

Thirty-Five

THERE WAS NO evening sunset that day, no light in the sky. The day he found her. At least it seemed that way to the boy as he sat at the kitchen table. He must have fed, curried, and watered the horse. He must have lit lanterns, stoked the stove, and then simply ground to a halt; he had no recollection of any of it. Now he just sat at the table, his face and chest illuminated by a lantern and the rest of his body sunk in shadow. He lay his hand flat on the table as if to rise but did not move.

Once every long while he looked through the open door into the clearing, where the night wind had begun to suck and gust, and somehow, in those moments between glances, full hours passed. Small creatures scurried in the eaves, but he didn't hear them. Twigs and cones shook from the upper reaches of the pines and peppered the roof of the cabin or blew across the clearing in merry hops and leaps, but the boy was too hard at work within himself to even raise his eyes. His mother was dead. But now he knew exactly where her body was. There was no consolation in that. His last shred of imagining, his last twinkle of hope and childish pretence, born of not knowing, had winked out. He was floating on a dark sea, fathoming the bottom of it, finding none.

He gazed at his own hand on the table, the long, smooth

fingers. The hand was his and yet also, by its shape, hers. It was a hybrid, elongated and barely formed, still forming, characterless and flat; he saw it through angry, welling eyes.

The old lady had said once: *I never grieved for my father, never cried. I can't think why, because it is sad when a person dies.* She said it like a nurse would. Grief as a natural thing.

Now Jack looked around at what was left. His tidy kitchen table, his walls, his roof, his shelf of books, his wall map, his horse, his gun, his window, his uncomfortable boots, his many overlapping blankets, his bed. All of it, this grand solitude, was his inheritance. It belonged to no one but him, no one else was here.

The door was open and he smelled rain, the wind rising to carry it in from the northwest. He could hear the horse pacing the corral, shaking itself out, preparing for the weather. The boy put palms on his knees and levered himself up, looking more like Sampson than himself, and headed outside. He still had to secure the loose rungs on the corral and shim the door to the shed so it would not bang in the wind. He needed to drag the bucket under the eaves to collect water.

On his way back inside Jack snatched his shirts off the laundry line and took them into the cabin. He closed the door just as the first curtains of rain blew across his side of the mountain.

❧ Thirty-Six

HALFWAY UP THE LONG staircase she found herself pausing
on trembling legs, the breath rushing in and out of her thin
chest, washing her heart. The Pax was finally working and
she paused to mark its effect. A grateful numbing that spread
like a hand across her nape and tingled the back of her scalp.

Damp air rivered down from the second floor, flowing
in from the open windows. It fell over her shoes, eddied in
the hallway below, chilling the Persian runners, and cork-
screwed down the servant's passage into the stony basement.
She continued on, rocking her depleted and hopeless self
up each stair until she was outside the boy's bedroom again.
Fourteenth check that day. The mason jar holding up the
sash had not moved. The bedclothes were still folded back,
the pillow plumped and beckoning. She bent to scrutinize
the jar again, one tiny ink mark on the cotton doily, one on
the wood sash; it was a trick to tell her if he'd snuck back in
and run away again. But the two marks were still aligned as
two compass needles, exactly unchanged.

She stood again and looked at the bed, blinking her burning eyes. In that moment she saw the empty joke of it, the
failed artifice, the room like a closed museum exhibit from
which the mannequin has been removed. She saw herself as

she was, or as she thought herself to be: a woman cozened and deluded, tricked by her own mind and by the boy himself. She bent and took away the jar, let the sash sink into its slot, brought the bedsheet up and tucked it under the pillow, then sat on his narrow bed. With palms on the knobs of her knees, she said to no one, "I just don't know anymore."

She gazed out his window, her arms gathered into a thoughtful pose, one palm supporting the other elbow, but she was not thinking. She was weak with fury and, for weeks now, almost totally sleepless. As the minutes and then hours ticked by, people happened along the street, horses and wagons and motorcars. At dusk there came a gaggle of prisoners in loose marching formation coming back from some work project on the main street, heading to their barracks just outside of town. She sat on his bed and saw the sun down, and in that vigil she felt an agonizing camaraderie with the boy, the boy as he had been, when he was still hers. Her great love, her only confidante.

"I suffer," she had told him, "because I left the Order. Because I left the company of good women."

The first time she had told the boy her story was right here, at this very bed, and he had still been a little delirious. He drowsed and hallucinated and babbled to people who were not there, but she felt he could hear her perfectly well, so she had held his hand and, in a confessional whisper, told him everything.

She told him she was slowly forgiving her father, putting behind her the familial duty, the illness and drudgery and dread that had hung over the house like quarantine. Emelia Cload, only child of a banking dynasty, she had greeted adulthood by wantonly throwing herself into service to God. The choice had disgusted her father. Service to others — he understood this only as something mercantile. And if she would never have an advantageous marriage, what was her purpose? He wouldn't speak to her for years, not until he was dying. And then his voice came to her in broken lines by night telegram, and only to order her home. She had known what would be written on the telegram before she read it. From nun to nurse in less than a week. She'd been an apothecary at the abbey, so there was scant difference, really. The train trip back home, the first step through the front door, the staff all gone, the kitchen in appalling disarray, her former bedroom now used as a dressing room, filled with the second wife's frocks.

In her own way, the plump wife had tried to nurse him, but when Emelia had arrived like a travelling nurse, that woman had retreated in obvious relief to her bedroom, where she played cards with herself all day, always winning, or always losing, it made little difference. He wanted only his daughter, and from the look in his eyes she understood this was punishment. *You want to know about service to others? Well, here it is.*

So she had bathed her father, fed him medicine with a spoon, brushed the thin hair from his brow. The young doctor who came and went was a local boy and had known the family since he was small. He never dropped the kindly smile, even when the patient raged at him, ordered him out of the house, begged him to come back, called him a filthy dogan, or an ignorant quack. He leaned close and listened to the spongy heart and the occluded lungs, he said calming things to the patient. But with Emelia Cload the doctor was blunt.

"That man has lived his entire adult life with a cigar in his mouth and a drink in his hand. Everything has been on his terms. Until now he has refused to pay for medical advice.

His decline is unusually steep, and I don't know why. He can't even stand. But, as they say, you should call the fire brigade *before* the house has burned to the ground."

Such had been her own assessment as well, but to hear it from another made it real. So it was hopeless after all. Emelia Cload followed the dull routine, and the hours were marked by her father's circadian rhythm: consciousness, a bald head hung over a bowl of unwanted broth, hooded eyes following her as she went about the room, rasping breath, weakness, sleep. When he was asleep she would accomplish certain tasks; when he was awake, she must accomplish others. The endless laundry. The day he had called her by her mother's name. The night he had said, *I loved you, but you left me.* The surprise of it. A bottle of medication had dropped from her hand and smashed across the lawyer's fine shoes. Had he been talking to her, his daughter, or to the long-dead wife? Who could know?

She couldn't remember the exact day she had spotted her thick black notebook lying on a table in the young wife's bedroom, nor did she recall entering the room, taking up the book and scanning through it, seeing handwriting that was not her own. But with perfect clarity she recalled the minutes she spent riding the shockwave of realization, once she had seen what was recorded there in a childish hand: *Rub thal ointment along spine every night. But how much?*

Thallium salts. Odourless, tasteless, and the central ingredient in rat poison. A rather effective scheme to hurry an old husband to his death. She had flipped through the book and seen where the woman had underlined some of Emelia's own notes, where she had sought out a dictionary and scrawled into the margins the definitions of words like "isotope" and

"soluble." She soon recognized a slow but motivated pupil.
How long had the scheme been going on?

What was less clear in her memory was the moment she
took up a pen and blotter and wrote: *If you wish to murder him,
do it properly*, and then, in nursing shorthand, she marked
the way to do it.

20mg TI, q8h, in water, po, administer ꝫ doctor.

Thallium salts, every eight hours, circumvent the doctor.
She had then shut the notebook and returned it to the little
twit's bedside table.

Was this a collaboration? No. She had meant the notation
to mortify the other woman into stopping. And indeed, the
wifely visits at night with hot chocolate and a warm compress
for his back ceased abruptly.

So Emelia had turned to study, just as any doctor would
have done. She had raked the library for anything useful.
There was nothing about appropriate antidotes in her old
medical journals; nothing in the dictionary, the encyclopedia,
or any of her own books. There was no medical library for
a hundred miles and she could not leave her father, especially now, even for an afternoon. So she had written to a
former workmate at the abbey, a woman who knew everything, cloaking the question about thallium in many others
of related scientific interest. The letter read as chitchat from
an intelligent woman forced into servitude, trying to keep
herself from boredom. The reply came quickly. Yes, there was
a debate among apothecaries and laypeople as to the anti-
dotal properties of Prussian Blue, a pigment used in painting,
which absorbs the poison and carries it out of the body via
excretion. Some anecdotal evidence, but not much beyond
that. That venerable woman at the abbey promised to send

her a sample of the blue powder, saying at the end of a letter sodden with fondness: *Did you notice, Bea? The Virgin Mary is always dressed in blue.*

She had read the letter, then put it into the stove and let it burn.

A week passed, then two, the package did not come, but it mattered little because the poison had already done its work.

On his last day she sat with her father as he withered in the bed. She clasped his thin hand in hers, and as his breath began to labour, pressed her free hand to her mouth to silence herself, felt his pulse race and then slow, watched the colour of his skin adopt a hue she'd never forget, the person long gone but the lungs still trying to work a teaspoon of air in and out, the awful gasping tenacity of his ruined body, and in the end, she sat in stunned silence staring at the still form, while downstairs, his widow, his social retinue, the hangers-on and sycophants and toadies, sipped tea and murmured. After a while she put her father's hand down and left the thin grey doll lying in the bed with its mouth open.

The lawyer had never seen a death before and was clearly terrified, but he had sat on a chair next to the door and watched. He was required by the will to confirm a natural death. No one thought to ask why, and Emelia never said a thing.

Two days later, she saw the new widow reading the newspaper at the funeral home and humming to herself, unable to even pretend she wasn't thrilled now that the will had kicked in. The girl had expressed no interest in which urn, which flowers, which music. "It doesn't matter one bit to me," she trilled. "I have my memories." The smile distinctly sarcastic.

But at the funeral, in front of such a crush of audience, the merry widow had put on a surprise dramatic show, draped her arms over the coffin, boo-hooed dryly into a handkerchief, pressed a hand to her bosom and affected a brave look.

"Those were the best years of my life," she said. She repeated it to each mourner.

The phrase had the ring of a famous quote, heard or read somewhere. Best years or not, the bank account was drained, the widow was on board a train to New York by midnight, and the old house was finally empty.

Emelia Cload, last of her line, remembered standing in the dining room holding an engraved silver serving spoon with her father's initials entwined with those of his second wife, the woman who had, in the end, killed him. She remembered scouring floors in the great house and tidying and laundering everything twice. The long hours and days afterward. The weird nights lying in her childhood bed, fighting the feeling that she had never really grown up, never left. The afternoon she had dragged all the wife's discarded frocks down the stairs, hove them into a heap in the backyard, and set them alight. The day the postman had placed a wrapped package in her hand, brown paper and butcher's string, and she had gazed down at the antidote. Deep blue powder within a little tin box, and a tiny measuring spoon. A little card with approximate measures per ten pounds of body weight. She put it in the high cupboards of the kitchen with the rest of her herbs and minerals.

All this she told the boy. "But now I have forgotten it all," she whispered, "because you are here. Everything is better. It feels like life again." And then she started over, told him again about all the hurts she had forgotten. She spoke of her heart, her hopes, she told him everything she feared.

He had been here in this bed, while she, holding his hand, had confessed to him. And confession it was, as she related to him her seven murders by poison, without excuse and without pride; she said it once as clearly as she could. The boy had been so sick and his mind so distant, he was incapable of judgement, almost a listening angel.

When she had entered the abbey her life had been entwined with those of nearly a hundred women, including a kind but, in Emelia's view, simple-minded roommate, and a Mother Superior so ancient and formidable everyone was too frightened to even look at her. Emelia was given her name in religion, Sister Beatrice, and was seated during mealtimes only four chairs down from the Mother, who often entertained herself by asking the new girls to explain those points of biblical study that would have stumped the most seasoned old nuns at the table. During some meals the girls were so nervous they had trouble swallowing their food.

The abbey was situated in Colorado Springs and associated with a sanitarium specializing in the treatment of tuberculosis, venous disorders, nervous complaints, and "afflictions of the brothel," so there was plenty of nursing practice to be had and the opportunity to learn. The sisters nurtured a garden for medicinal herbs; they had a proper, well-equipped chemistry room; and they themselves provided much of the hospital's chemical and herbal treatments. Sometimes it was a nursing sister who actually administered the drugs.

Like the other women, Emelia had been drawn to the abbey, or perhaps driven to it, by a need to stop being an anomaly in her own world. Some of the sisters struggled with genuine belief, but were there because they loathed being wooed by men, manoeuvred into the squeaking bedsprings and endless toil of matrimonial life. Some had taken orders because they longed to study, there being no alternative way for a girl to receive any education worth having. Others were dropped on the abbey's doorstep like stray kittens because there was not enough food at home, and because a son is employable and cannot get pregnant. In her own case, Emelia Cload had wished to understand and perhaps be closer to a mother she had no memory of. She also wished to flee her father, to renounce him entirely. She understood him well enough to know that her decision had hurt him, and she had spent too many years at the abbey relishing that fact.

All the nursing sisters were given free run of the sanitarium's facilities, including the medical library, where Sister Beatrice spent most of her free time. And they all had keys to the poison cupboard. Which was how a dose of digitalis, also known as foxglove, found its way into the Mother Superior's evening soup. She liked her food spicy, so she didn't taste a thing. The old lady was found dead the next morning, assumed to have succumbed to extreme old age. Thereafter, mealtimes were happier for everyone.

How simple, clean, surprisingly easy.

Later that year a man with tertiary syphilis, one of the worst conceivable ways to die, was found in peaceful repose by a nurse on morning shift.

The exhausted consumptive panting her last, the groundskeeper bitten by a rabid dog — she sat in the library and studied each patient's fatal condition with ferocious focus, and then, with careful attention to dose and detail, foreshortened their agonies.

That was also about the time Sister Beatrice stopped praying.

The second year of her residency was spent in a kind of mourning for her own soul. She would kneel at prayer with the rest of them in chapel but could not close her eyes. She bowed her head at mealtime grace but only stared at the table-cloth. She entwined her hands on her bedspread, pressed her forehead to her knuckles, and said . . . nothing. It seemed to her that praying was like sleeping, like dreaming of a better world, but she had startled herself awake. She knew quite clearly that she had let go of God's hand, there was no going back.

She had recorded everything in her black notebook. Dates, dose, ailment, findings afterward, most of it in nursing code.

Now, in the boy's empty bedroom, she realized that her lips were moving and her hand gesturing, and she subsided. She saw the chest of drawers in which lay all the clothes she had bought him. The bottom drawer was closed, but she knew it was empty. He'd taken whatever he wanted, left what he didn't. Outside, tree limbs raked the shingles and there was a promise of imminent rain.

She rose and went awkwardly down the creaking hall. Her legs were jouncing beneath her, and she realized she had given herself too much tincture. The door to the library creaked open. On a whim she went to the desk drawer where she had hidden the boy's knife months ago. A vicious contrap-tion that folded into its own handle, the kind of thing that would fascinate a boy. She did not bother opening the drawer. Of course he had taken it. Instead she began to make an inspection of the room, wandering from shelf to bookcase to cabinet, finding gaps between books, clear spots in the dust, inventorying the things he had pilfered from her. Finally, she approached the medical shelf and saw that her notebook, that very notebook, was gone. Her heart cramped with the surprise.

She stood for a long time, her breath uneven, her drugged mind working as a worm works through soil. He'd taken it. He would read it. He would know. He might tell someone. Then, as the first drops of rain began to *ting* off the eaves-troughs outside, she put her face in her hands and screamed.

➹ Thirty-Seven

SAMPSON WAS TRYING to understand how Jack needed yet another trip to Laggan for supplies. Somehow the kid had eaten every last scrap on hand, and now he was speaking yearningly about raisins. And chocolate; he admired chocolate. Oatmeal was good. Too bad there was no milk; he'd enjoyed milk when he was in town. Sampson listened in disbelief. He'd forgotten how much boys could eat. He was keenly missing William Moreland.

The dog was nosing around the cabin, following some random animal scent. It lifted its head and thought for a moment, then trotted away through the trees, already hunting, a pale shape weaving through the trunks til it was gone.

"Have you found your father's traps?"

The question was a broadside, though Sampson couldn't know that. It had been four days since Jack had been up there. He went silent for a moment, then said, "Yup. All six. I should have brought them down, but I left them up there."

"You found six?"

"Shit," the kid's shoulders dropped. "Dad had more than that."

"It doesn't matter."

"I don't mind going up again. I'll go and look for the others."

"No," Sampson said gently. "If you don't know where they are, no one does."

Sampson wasn't much in favour of traps and snares, and he was critical of some people who carried around a vial of strychnine just to lace the traps and finish the job. To his mind it ruined the pelts, though he had no proof to support this notion. Moreland had no use for the stuff because he ate the meat he caught and was terrified poison might somehow stray into his meal. The man had a taste for those little rock rabbits; who knew why. A gun was no good because they would drop, dead or alive, into a fissure between boulders and never be seen again; thus the need for snares.

The boy held his hands before the fire and inspected their outlines, shadow-puppet hands ringed with light. The red of his blood glowed in the webbing. "It's my birthday," he said. "I'm thirteen."

Sampson shifted on his chair and stared at him.

Jack Boulton grinned, the fire illuminating his smooth cheek. It was amazing how different he felt already. Despite what he had told the nun, he'd always known the exact day and hour of his birth. He had kept it from her because the date was his alone now, one of the few true things left to him.

Thirteen.

There was no clock in the cabin, so last night he'd risen repeatedly and stepped outside to look up at the moon and guessed at the time, only to go back inside and flop down to wait for the next hour, and the next, listening to the wind rising in the trees outside. But by the time his birthday actually arrived, he was drooling into a pillow. He'd woken only once during the night and remembered his father had promised to return by now, but he had not.

Sampson nodded. "You are still young. But, yes. I will get you a job."

The boy's reaction was a vaudeville of dismay. "What *for*?"

"You need money."

"I really don't."

The old man's finger pointed at Jack's nose. "You sleep too much. And you do nothing around here."

"That's not true."

"No? Tell me what you did yesterday."

The boy's face, at first defiant, went sullen.

In fact, after Sampson had fed him breakfast and left, the boy had lit a hand-rolled cigarette that smouldered and hissed. He'd coughed until he gagged. After eating a whole can of peaches in syrup with a spoon, he'd practised handstands. He could walk from palm to palm for several minutes, wandering like a circus performer into the trees before he toppled into the moss and panted, looking up at the lances of the tall pines as they swayed in the wind. At noon he had opened the door to the shed, hoping to find some turpentine to remove the pine resin, which was now a pox all over him, but he'd stared at the mess in there with a grudging sense of duty and shut the door without tidying a thing. His solution was to rub dirt into the spots so they stopped sticking to everything.

He'd done no evening chores, and had read *Treasure Island* again by lamplight. He hadn't made bread or washed his clothes. He hadn't even cut wood for the stove. The horse was in good shape but Jack himself was pungent. *By this time he stinketh.* So perhaps Sampson was right.

"You need money because you eat so much."

The kid glowered. "Fine."

"We'll go to Laggan today and see my wife," said Sampson, "and the next day we'll go over to Pipestone. Wilson has some Americans up there hunting. You can help him."

"Can we do it next week instead?"

Sampson ignored this.

"Hîn, Tada?" the boy wheedled.

Sampson's face darkened at the term *grandfather*, but otherwise he refused to speak.

Jack Boulton settled down and glared at the fire, thinking, *How can you accuse anyone of sleeping too much when you turn up before dawn?*

It was then that the dog arrived out of the trees. They hadn't heard it coming, because it was moving fast and quiet. It shot across the clearing and strafed round to the fire's lee, its snout focussed like a compass arrow back into the trees it had just fled. It was radiating fear. They looked at the dog. Looked into the blackness of the trees.

Sampson said, "Do you see anything?"

"Nope."

There was no sound at all but the crackling of the fire.

Sampson said, "Me neither. That dog is always coming and going."

And with that, the dog went; it jerked in alarm at a sound only it could hear, whirled, and loped into the forest behind them.

"Oh shit," said the boy.

Sampson's hand came out and floated before Jack's face in a gesture that said stay down, and he rose stiffly from his chair, the bones in his knees ratcheting. He stayed like that for a long time, standing like a bear, breath pumping visibly into the firelight. "Okay," he said, "I didn't bring my gun. Go get yours."

Without another word, Jack Boulton slipped away, as silent and graceful as the dog. Soon, it became obvious from the raspings and pauses inside the cabin that the boy was having trouble locating his own rifle. It seemed then to Sampson Beaver that any child who had not been taught to put the damn gun back in its regular spot had missed a critical lesson. Then again, here he was with no gun at all. He removed his hat and held it by the crown to block the fire's glare, and he scanned the night trees.

Far from being afraid, Sampson was suffering the hunter's peculiar avarice, and in his mind he ran through the catalogue of possibilities. Wolf, deer, cougar, bear. Each offered something useful or saleable or good to eat: hide, antlers, meat. There were no elk at this particular altitude, nor would those animals wander very deeply into thick forest. He weighed the different species against the dog's terrified reaction. Unfortunately, this particular dog was unpredictable, almost fickle, possibly a result of its mixed parentage — half wolf. The old man had seen it dash a respectful berth around a little marten. He'd also seen it bristle into a snarling nightmare, stand its ground, and rage at a black bear until finally the tormented thing had climbed a tree to get out of harm's way. And once, when Sampson was hunting sheep, he had been almost certain the dog had deliberately circled the herd, the way a wolf would, and flushed them all toward the waiting gun. He hadn't got a single ram that day for fear of shooting the dog.

So who knew what would scare such an animal? The wolf part of it refused to be trained. It seemed to consider each request you made of it, weigh the benefits and costs, and then make up its own mind. Therefore the object of fear could be anything, a two-hundred-pound cougar or a wandering baby skunk. The old man sank slowly down into the chair and crossed one stiff knee over the other.

Finally the boy appeared at his elbow and handed him Pearl. Sampson looked at the bloated pink scabbard in bewilderment, and he shook it off the rifle's end into the dirt, then held the weapon near the firelight to inspect it. He couldn't believe what he was holding. It was an old lever-action repeater, side-loading. There was nothing to identify it as a Henry, but he knew that it was. As manufactured, they had a very long barrel to increase accuracy, but this one had been sawed off to a more modest length and the magazine resized to fit. He'd owned one, back in his youth. He'd used it on people. It held sixteen rounds, rimfire, and was so easy to load you could do it in the dark.

"Your father left this for you?"

The boy nodded.

"And Wilson actually kept it?"

The boy nodded again.

"Unbelievable."

Sampson knuckled the trigger guard forward and back, which automatically spat out the first shell and levered a new one into place. The workings sounded all right.

"Now we see if it fires," he said.

"Don't shoot into the trees," whispered the boy, thinking of the prisoner, thinking of the dog.

Sampson shooed the boy behind him, held the gun at arm's length, winced in case pieces should fly off, and discharged it into the sky. The report was loud. Willow was just surprised but the Morgan squealed, and echoes banged and syncopated down the black distance.

"Jesus Christ!" shouted the boy, hands over his ears. "It fires, all right."

Sampson levered and fired a second and third time, each bang a warning to every animal within a half-mile radius that said: *go away.*

Scorched dust curled in wisps along the barrel's length. There was silence in the trees about. No movement except the two uneasy horses.

The boy was waiting for Sampson to say what animal was out there, whether the noise would frighten it away, or whether, in fact, there had been any animal at all. But what he saw instead was the slow bloom of dismay on the old man's face. Those hooded eyes were unblinking; that kind, weathered face now grey and ghastly.

"What is it?" said the boy.

Sampson said nothing.

"Tada?"

Like the horses, the old man was in a kind of shock — the jolt of recognition, of gun memory. Of being sixteen and lying at night with other young men by a fire like this one, after all the shooting was over, his hands bruised from the kickback and still shaking, staring into the blue night clouds, the rattle of gunfire still riding his nerves for hours. He saw his life burning forward to this moment: his old, hardened palm wet against the familiar gunstock.

So he didn't hear Jack Boulton's repeated questions. He didn't take notice when the kid took the scabbard up from where it lay too close to the fire, dusted it off gently, and held it behind his back. He didn't feel the boy's light hand on his shoulder.

✦ Thirty-Eight

THEY GOT READY that morning to ride toward the town of Laggan, planning to start directly after breakfast. As if it could read minds the dog came running up the slope of the corral, leapt between fence rungs, and was already pacing the clearing, ready to go. Whatever had frightened it, the dog no longer gave a damn.

Jack put on his mother's coat and hat, and then he shut the cabin door behind him, carrying Pearl to the Morgan where he saddled up and strapped the ridiculous old gun under the saddle's fender, copying carefully the way Sampson had secured his own Winchester. Then he walked out of the open corral gate and swung up.

The horses chose a walking order and followed the path away from the cabin. Jack bounced his calf against the horse's side, feeling there, for the first time in his life, a rifle under his leg. It wasn't entirely comfortable for Jack, but it seemed not to bother the Morgan at all.

Above them stretched a sky of uncanny blue, ludicrously beautiful, but so common to this latitude that neither of them noticed. After an hour, they had crested a rise and were traversing a long, rocky fin that ran between two low peaks. Sunrise shone red through the trees and the riders trailed their own shadows along the ground like outriggers. Jack yawned and shivered, and his shadow yawned, too, with its ridiculous puppet mouth.

The dog trotted alongside with the effortless gait of a wolf, always a little faster than the riders. It drifted ahead of them. Sometimes it angled suddenly away into the trees after something unseen. It would be gone for a few minutes only to swing in again at their flank and trot alongside for a while before lapping them once more.

Sampson was talking again, and the subject was his recent dreams. These he recounted in detail, but Jack could make no sense of them except to understand that, to the old man, they were disquieting and portentous. Bad omens. Jack began to contemplate the black horse ahead of him, Sampson's wide, still-strong back, the Winchester rifle strapped behind his saddle, the barrel of which was pointing right at the old man's shadow.

Jack ran a hand over his face. He was not paying a lot of attention. And no matter how restless the old man might get, his enormous horse sidled along contentedly, soothed by the drone of its rider's voice.

Sampson was talking about a dream in which a sudden cold wind blew a door closed in his face. The unseen room beyond. The boom of it slamming. The puff of foul air, like carrion, hitting his face. It was the fact he had smelled death in a dream that had alarmed him. "You ever have a smell in your dream?" he said.

"No," Jack said. "I see really bright colours sometimes, though."

"Okay," said Sampson. "Colours. That's not my point."

The kid squinted through the trees at the rising sun. "It's

not real. You just had a bad dream. You have a lot of those."

"Not like this one."

"What about the poisoned water dream?"

"Well . . ."

"And you had one about snakes."

Sampson said nothing.

"It's just bad dreams," he said. "It's not real life."

Jack's mother had been a stranger to sleep, so she rarely dreamed. But one night she had sat up laughing, put a hand to her forehead, and said, *you were crossing a river, and you were on a horse*, which made no sense to either of them. He had sighed *okay*, wrapped his warmth around her, and driven them both back into sleep.

Heading downhill, Jack and Sampson leaned back in their saddles, palming low branches away from their hats. Once they had gained flat ground and were on the open road the horses walked side by side. It was getting warmer. The dog smelled something fascinating to the west and loped away through a meadow to the spot, where it inspected some object the riders couldn't see, tipped over, and rolled in it, legs kicking the air. Then it rose, shook its thick fur in satisfaction, and loped back to them, bringing the news with it.

Jack's stomach was growling audibly and no matter how often Sampson told him to stop, he chattered endlessly about food. He loved jams, apple butter, lemon curd, cinnamon cakes. The nun, he said, used to put up a clear apple jelly that was beautiful on biscuits. She made bowls of hot chocolate, and sometimes a kind of ice cream flavoured with purple liquor.

"Purple?" Sampson sounded disgusted. "What kind of liquor is purple?"

"It's made of black cherries. Or black currants maybe."

"Sounds awful."

They had reached the spot where the coach road started to disintegrate and fade into bush. In fact, from here on to Laggan there was nothing more than a well-worn trail, and anyone wishing to visit Lake Louise itself was obliged to either ride a horse or take the train, which was clearly the reason for all the road work. Sampson made his way round a young juniper bush and the boy followed.

"It always bothered me," he said.

"What did?"

"Her."

"Who her?"

"She walked into the hospital and told them to hand you over."

"Where else could I go?" But as soon as the boy said it, his mind answered, *home*. And in the end, that's where he'd gone. Jack shuffled his butt in the saddle, tried to think of a defence of the nun that would mean anything right now.

Sampson said, "There's something wrong with her."

"Aw, she's okay."

"No. She's afraid of everything; who is afraid of horses?"

"I was sick and she looked after me. It's not her fault I lit out."

Sampson thumbed his hat back and said, "Mnâ zan."

The grin on the boy's face fractured. He had to think for a long time before he remembered the exact word, and when he got it, he rode in stunned silence. *Wolverine.*

Jack drifted the horse forward and tried discreetly to read Sampson's profile, but the old man just looked peeved, exactly as he had all morning.

•   •   •

THEY CUT DOWN TO the river and walked over the gravel banks to the water's edge. Here they let the horses suck at the icy shallows, and they too sipped from their cupped hands and squeezed the cold from their fingers, scanning for fish or moving debris or anything of interest that floated by in the river. The boy hove stones as far as he could and watched them all fall short of the other bank.

Sampson gestured at Mount Temple. "Why does your father call that the Onion?"

"He never told me."

"It doesn't look like an onion."

Jack cocked his head to the side and considered. "Looks like a train engine," he said.

"No, it doesn't."

"Maybe mountains are like clouds. Everyone sees something different."

Sampson fixed him with a scowl. "And how come you never gave that horse a name?"

Jack looked at the Morgan. "What for? He knows when I'm talking to him."

This was so true it stumped the old man. The closest he came to admitting it was a good answer was to hitch up his trousers.

Jack said, "Mr. Wilson calls him Buttercup if you like that any better."

Wilson too was funny about names, and he called his animals things like Two Bites, Barrelhead, Cricket, and I Said So. If he couldn't remember a man's name he would resort to belittlements like "Lord Pisspot" or "What's-his-nuts."

But Sampson did not like it any better. He glared at the river, and said, "The dog has no name. The horse has no name. And *that* thing's called the Onion." He was radiating displeasure, and the boy suspected he'd been brooding about William Moreland. Jack wondered for the first time what it must be like for Sampson to be doing this, mopping up after a tragedy he'd had no hand in, watching over someone else's kid, visiting a cabin miles from his own home. And now here he was, like some truant officer, carting the boy off to Wilson, handing the burden over to another man.

Jack Boulton fiddled with the reins. "I'm sorry," he said. "I try to do things right. I keep things tidy at home."

Sampson settled on him a look of shredded patience.

Jack tried to defend himself and his voice ran feebly over the sound of the water. "I look after this horse at least. The gun is always on the table now, like you said. I keep the stove running all night, most nights. And I'd make bread more often if . . . okay, I *will* make bread more often."

Sampson was ignoring the litany, watching the river's nap as it flowed sleek over submerged stones and boulders. "You are young," he said, "but you could be good with horses." It was the closest thing to praise the old man had ever uttered. Jack remembered his howling error of bringing the Morgan into the house, and let the compliment slide.

Sampson said, "Your father never liked that part of guiding. Especially mules. He never got used to mules."

The kid grinned at him, "And you never got used to the clients."

Sampson snorted, then seemed to relax.

Jack stared across the river at a rill of mist that had begun to flow out of the trees, coiling like a girl's hair. "What was it like down there?"

"Where?"

"Oklahoma."

Sampson thought about that for a long time. He seemed to be trying to find a way to sum up something too big to condense. "Awful. For me it was awful."

"Does it look like here?"

"Nothing looks like here."

"I can't believe it," the boy shook his head. "You were police."

"Neither can my wife. When we get to her house, I'll show you my old deputy's hat with three bullet holes in it."

"Someone shot at you?"

"They all did."

"Were you hurt?"

"Yes," Sampson said. Then he chuckled. "But this time, a man named Reeves took my hat off my head, put it on the ground, and shot it three times."

The boy burst out laughing, his voice rising to an involuntary squeak. "Why would anyone shoot a hat?"

Sampson said, "I will get you a better gun. This one is ridiculous."

It was exactly the sudden switch of subjects that was common with Sampson, and over the years, the kid had become used to it. But Jack knew he must not relinquish Pearl, so he sobered instantly and shook his head.

"Little boy." Sampson strode to the Morgan and went for Pearl. Despite the kid's attempts to stop him he muscled the repeater out, unloaded its many shells, and dropped them into his capacious coat pocket. Then he fished out a single cartridge and held it up like a specimen. "Forty-four. Too much for you. Can you clean an elk all by yourself?"

The boy just faced him down, a determined gaze that reminded him of Mary.

"Okay, look." Sampson thumbed the lone cartridge into the breech, and swung the trigger guard forward and back to load it. He held the workings up for the boy to see, finger pointing at the little hammer. "With this gun, the bolt is always touching the cartridge. If you drop it, it might fire." He walked over to the nearest aspen and struck the butt against the trunk. The gun went off and both horses tap-danced on the spot.

Smoke drooling from the downturned barrel. "We used to say *leave it fired*. Do you understand that?"

"I think so."

"Leave the dead shell in there. Don't lever a new one until you are ready to fire."

"Okay," said the boy. He already had his hand out for the rest of the bullets.

Then Sampson did an incredible thing, at least it seemed so to Jack. He swing-cocked the rifle. He held the trigger guard, dropped the rifle, swung it behind him, *clack-clack*, and jerked it back up again into firing position. The spent cartridge spun off into the grass, and the magazine was empty. It was a completely unconscious move, muscle memory from decades back, so fluid and graceful it stunned the boy.

Sampson looked down at the rifle in his hand. He looked at Jack's admiring face. "Don't ever do that," he said.

"Amazing."

"No."

"It was amazing."

"If I catch you doing it . . ."

"You won't."

Sampson stared at him for a long, cold moment, not at all pleased with the mendacity of the child. "Little boy, I am not joking."

Jack put his hand out for the remaining cartridges. "They're my bullets."

Sampson shook his head.

"Oh, come on!"

"No. You'll shoot your foot off." The old man slid the rifle back where it had come from. Then he wandered away down the pebbled shore, turned his back on Jack, and pissed into the river for a long time.

Jack glowered in disbelief. "What am I supposed to do with this damn gun now?" He got nothing in return. Behind him the fond horses bent their heads together and rubbed cheeks, scratching an itch. The kid stood holding his useless gun and two sets of reins. He was like the boy tricked by a genie into making the wrong wish.

→ Thirty-Nine

LAGGAN ANNOUNCED ITSELF by the distant sound of a train getting ready to depart the station. A tattoo on the engine's bell, a merry sound for the tourists, so different from the Morse-like howls meant to communicate with railway personnel. Jack and Sampson were still a mile away, and there was a pulsing headwind. Jack's soft hat brim was folding over his face or else flapping up against the crown to let the sun zing into his eyes. Finally he pinched the brim and held it level as he rode, a gentleman forever tipping his hat to the trees. The enormous dog trotted by and looked at him with its pale eyes so he blew it a kiss and simpered, "How you doing down there, honey?" The dog sneezed with pleasure, made a feint at the Morgan's hooves, and loped ahead.

The kid laughed, his voice surging into a piping soprano. He swallowed. This was happening more often, the hopeless squeaks, and very occasionally a toad-like croak, so that he could no longer trust his own throat.

At some distance a man was standing square in the middle of the road with his rifle pointed at the sky. The riders edged forward, perplexed. And then a dozen ducks crested the tops of the pines, crossed the road, and made for the river. The flower of gunsmoke appeared before the sound. One duck seemed to totter a little but kept flying, and a second later pellets rattled down through the trees around Sampson and Jack. The old man growled in disgust at the idiot hunter, who now trotted away, trailing his quarry to the river.

Just at the outskirts, they were obliged to slow their horses on the road to allow a small black bear and two cubs to wander across their path. The tiny cubs padded along behind their mother. Horses and bears regarded one another with distrust and stayed their courses, but the dog couldn't tolerate it, and he shot out after them. Seeing what appeared to be a wolf coming straight for them, the bears seesawed into a run. In a few strides even the cubs were making surprising progress. The dog spotted the tree they were making for and tried to cut them off, but one by one they all sprang up the trunk to safety, making the midway point as easily as if they had been hopping up stairs.

"Oh thank god," said the boy. "He would have got the worst of that."

The dog skirmished the trunk, whining, and one of the infant bears urinated in terror. Droplets caught on the wind and pattered the dry leaves.

Sampson said, "That dog does not like bears."

"He has opinions."

Later, the riders passed a little wooden hut, a signal station for the CP Railway. In the yard of that building was a recent delivery of lumber, with a tarp tied down over the pile that was billowing wildly in that gusting wind. As the riders watched, the guy ropes snapped one by one until only a single rope was still attached. The fabric wheeled and flapped in the wind and within seconds most of it was hopelessly entangled in a tree. The lone rope sang and buzzed under the pressure.

An unbelievably petite tow-headed woman of middle age exited the hut, marching along, a barrage of invective pouring from her mouth. She gave the two riders a scornful glance and made for the buffeting tarp, her skirts plastered to her thin legs. Presumably this was the station mistress. She hopped up and snatched at the tarp, pulled and yanked at the cloth until it gave a little. She got two "fuckin'" handfuls down, pinning the excess under her arm before she reached up for more.

"Not that you fine gentlemen are doing a goddamn thing," she said.

Sampson's hand came off the reins and he waved as if to shoo her away from the enterprise. "Stop, Lydia," he said. "Just let it go."

"Never mind me, Sam," she said. "Go on about your business."

The wind quieted for a moment and the tarp began to slither down out of the bare tree into her gathering arms. She had most of it in her hands before a gust came and the canvas whizzed out of her arms again and snapped hard as a mainsail. The station mistress was jerked off her feet and dragged along the ground, her heels in the air. She got out a pinched little yelp before Sampson was off his horse and halfway across the yard to her. Her body swivelled west, then spun south, still clinging by one hand to the tarp. The final guy line broke with a *zing*, and thus freed like a parachute, the tarp and the station mistress scudded toward the station. She was screeching "Help me!" while the old man tramped after her, shouting, "Let go of the damn thing!"

The boy sat in disbelief. How could anyone get beaten up by a piece of cloth? He swung his boot over the Morgan's withers and hit the ground in a run.

Together they got the woman untangled and the flapping tarp folded and packed away under the eaves of the station. The woman was now dusty-faced, standing in filthy skirts, a haircomb dangling from the lopsided nest that was once her bun. She was the kind of person who would blame you for seeing her like this.

Sampson patted her arm. "I told you to let go," he said.

She stood rigidly. The words *thank you* did not come out of her mouth, but she invited them in for "a cuppa tea."

"No," Sampson said. "We have to go."

The woman seemed to notice Jack Boulton for the first time.

"Oh!" she said. "You're that boy." A smile spread across her face. She said to Jack, "Come in for tea. Sit with me."

Sampson shook his head. "We're on our way, Lydia."

"Well, that's natural," she said. "Off to see your wife. That's just fine. But why not let the boy sit with me for a bit. You go on by yourself."

Sampson turned and went back to the horses. Despite all the flapping and screaming, they were almost exactly where he'd left them, reins dangling.

"Let Sam go on his way," she whispered to Jack. "Stay here with me."

"Thanks anyway . . ." Jack turned to go, and then he remembered to say "ma'am."

When they left her yard Lydia was standing by the station door looking like she was about to cry.

• • •

ON THE FRONT PORCH of Lena's house, in the shade, an elderly dog with the size and colouring of a raccoon lay on its side as if dead. At the sound of their approach it struggled to its feet and limped woodenly down the steps and out into the damp yard, where it stood barking. Or rather it made the furious motions of barking but no sound came out.

Sampson and Jack Boulton dismounted and tied their horses to the hitch while the little dog wandered amiably amongst the new arrivals, getting jumbled up in all the long legs. The bigger dog sniffed the smaller one and bowled it over. Sampson scooped it out of harm's way and tucked it under his arm, where it hung in a stiff C shape and licked his wrist. He looked at his wife's door and waited. She was home. They could see her moving around in there. After about four minutes, nothing had happened. She wasn't coming out. Perhaps she hadn't heard them, perhaps she was just refusing to acknowledge them. The expression on the old man's face said he didn't know which it was.

"Why don't we just go in?" the boy said.

"She was a little put out with me a couple of weeks ago."

"Oh crap."

"It's probably fine. Probably."

The little dog began to kick and grunt and wanted to get down.

"Is he blind, too?" asked Jack.

Sampson held the dog up in the air where it wagged and shrimped at him, and they were face to face. "I don't think so. He's looking at me."

"Can I have him?" Jack took the dog and cooed to it. It certainly looked blind to him.

At that moment Lena emerged from the house wearing

a dark green dress over trousers, her hair in a kerchief. She was even older than Sampson and she was in the process of flapping out a small rug when she saw them. She cried "Sam!" and dropped the rug, hurried down the steps, and folded herself into her husband's arms. Sampson was trying to affect a neutral expression but he was unmistakably relieved. She looked at the kid.

"Ne duwe?" she said to her husband.

Sampson grinned. "Don't you recognize him?"

She cocked her head and gazed at the lanky boy. Years ago, she had put Jack on her knee and fed him with a spoon, wiped his face and put him to sleep in her own bed. She'd sat with Mary and they had nattered together in hushed tones and occasionally one woman would nod and touch the other's hand. Jack had crawled from lap to lap. At six he had run endlessly in her house with other children until he grew tired and wept. At eight, he had run in and out of the house, as free as a dog, and had spent most of his mother's visit outside, up a tree. But what she saw now was a man, or almost a man, with a sagging hat and her little dog in his arms.

For his part, Jack remembered Lena as a sort of distant aunt. Her voice, her amazing height when she lifted him up, her floral tablecloths. He remembered crawling into the lower cupboards in her kitchen and spinning the flour sifter like it was a marvellous device. He remembered a previous dog, a huge animal that had knocked him over and trod on him with its enormous weight and made him cry. He remembered that dog's awful paws, rough as pumice.

"Nîhû ze duwe?" she asked the boy. He knew the question, *who are you*, knew the polite answer, so he said his mother's name.

She laughed aloud and put her hand to her mouth. But then something crept into her eyes, some sobering apprehension. Straight away, she took the dog from his arms and put it on the ground, where it wobbled a little and started to peg-leg its way back to the house. She put her arm round Jack's shoulder and hustled him into the house, and to his surprise, closed the door behind them. There she led him into the main room and sat him at the table, then went off to prepare food.

The boy sat alone at the long table, empty chairs all around him. He turned and glanced at the closed front door. Sampson was on the wrong side of it, left in the yard with the dogs. He heard her in the kitchen, closing the curtains, pumping water into a pot. He could hear a clock ticking somewhere.

Presently the door opened and the husband of the house entered and stood uncertainly in the main room. He closed the door and went to the table, where he chose one of the ten chairs and sat down.

"I told you," he said lamely, "she never stops talking."

The boy gave him a worried sidelong look but stayed silent.

The room was large and simply furnished. There was the long table at which they sat, a kind of steamer trunk in the corner, a good number of hardwood chairs lined up against one wall, a fireplace with a raw log mantelpiece, and a little daybed under the window that once was meant for several children and babies to sleep together and perhaps was still used so, of an evening, when people came to visit. It looked like this woman was eternally ready for a local meeting or a family dinner or a gaggle of neighbours to descend upon her.

Sampson sat at the far end, taking the patriarch's seat, and the two of them waited together in the quiet room and listened to each other's stomachs growl. The husband put his palms on the table and ran his fingers along the wood grain. It was a gesture simultaneously proprietorial and exploratory: absent husband returns home. This was his house, and yet not his house. Lena was his wife, and yet they didn't live together.

Finally she emerged with a metal cup full of sweet black tea and a single china plate heaped with buttered bread and roast chicken and gravy, a rare treat for men who live in the woods. She lay the plate before Jack and gave him a fork. He said, "Thanks," around the first mouthful. And then again, "Îsnîyesh."

Lena lifted the hat from his head and smoothed his hair, then went to the pegs by the door and hung the hat there. The familiar feeling of a woman's hand on the back of his head.

Sampson, meanwhile, was looking in disbelief at the empty spot where his plate should be, looking at his wife, looking at the kitchen, then back at his nonexistent dinner. But Lena was clearly in a state of high agitation and she opened the front door and stared pointedly at her husband. Her eyes bored into his. He sat immobile for only a second before he rose and followed her mutely out the door.

Jack Boulton watched them go, his jaws working on the chicken. When the food was gone, he sauntered into the kitchen to look for more meat but there was none. He snuck a crust-end of bread from the cutting board, folded the whole thing into his cheek like a rodent and chewed until it was gone. He took two carrots from the crockery bowl on the floor, put one in his pocket and ate the other unpeeled, and then he amused himself by spooking around the house, spying into these few familiar rooms. She had left a pair of her boots by the door, and next to these stood a pair of simple lace-up shoes. There was a screened porch with nothing on it but several beds with clean, bare ticking. He found her bedroom with its old iron bedstead. At the end of the bed was a trunk on which lay a few woven grass bowls with lids, a hairbrush, and folded scarves. The floor of her bedroom was a multi-coloured jumble of many overlapping rugs. There was no cupboard in which to keep clothes, no dresser, no books. The few clothes she owned were all dark-coloured. Dresses were hung on the back of the bedroom door by hangers, and two pairs of her slim trousers hung by their waistbands from a hook, one pair atop the other. By the bed, a man's nightshirt, clean and ironed and folded, and atop that, a ball of handknit socks: Sampson's sleeping getup. The boy couldn't imagine Sampson standing there in a nightshirt with his bare shins sticking out, but clearly this was how he dressed for bed at Lena's house.

In the main room above the fireplace mantel hung an old hat with three holes in the crown, positioned where people tended to hang taxidermy, antlers, a favoured weapon. He approached the hat and saw tucked into the band a small metal star, maybe three inches wide. The star had been turned inward so the etched name was against the hat, invisible, a star-shaped concavity. The bullet holes were soft and weathered in the old felt, ovals now. He touched one with a finger.

Everything was tidy and simple. It wasn't until Jack wandered back to the kitchen to see if perhaps she had crackers or chocolate or milk that he discovered the mess. Beyond the sink and tidy counter stood a narrow doorway that led to a tiny anteroom mostly filled with a black metal sewing machine. Spools of thread in many colours hung from the ceiling on butcher's string like garlands. A man's white dress shirt lay disassembled on a wooden table, the starched collar pinned to the cuffs. The floor was a chaos of little snippets of thread and stray bits of fabric. There were bolts of cloth and folded squares and a basket stuffed with scraps and strips of many colours. He had a visceral childhood memory of pulling these strips out like tickertape and festooning his own head with them while the women laughed and scolded. He found jam jars full of beads, and a box filled with tattered rags of hide. He leaned farther into the room and peered behind the door. Hanging from the bare wood wall was a woman's beaded vest and headband in mid-construction. A bright, complex white-and-blue design. He reached out and ran a finger over the smooth, perfect lines of colour. Was this for Lena herself? Would she sell it? Did she make them for Nakoda people to wear, or for tourists? Or both?

The multi-coloured garland of thread spools hung before his face; yellow, white, blue, brown. His mother always kept hers wrapped in paper and inside a drawer. Women and their methods for everything, their bits of cloth, their threads, pins, and scissors, the heavy pots and frying pans, the knives, and their tired, ruined hands, which were always more or less clean.

The last time he saw his mother she was lying beside him in the bed, burning with fever, half-conscious. All the work in her life was finally over, though neither of them knew it yet. His father was gone, as usual, but even once the boy realized how truly sick she was, he could do nothing because he himself had begun to succumb. She had told him what she was seeing; she had admitted to naming him after someone named John. "As an apology. A life for a life. What else could I do but that?" None of it made sense, and her ravings upset him. She expressed no interest in water but when he gave her some she drank hugely. He had tried shaking her. He had tried leaving the cabin to get the horse but had immediately retched and was driven back inside by the racking chills. With no other option he had retreated into her arms and sighed, and dreamt of dying.

The complete cessation of pain. That's what dying promised him. He felt it coming, floating just ahead of them both. He followed it down a long, winding path until he woke screaming, held in his father's arms as they galloped. He was wrapped in a blanket and facing his father's body, his long legs exposed and his calves stinging with cold, the horse's lungs pumping. He remembered the Morgan's agonized breath.

The boy staggered back into the kitchen and closed his eyes. He fought a rising image of this house abandoned, Sampson's kind old wife dead, her kitchen cold, front door left open, rain and snow coming in, fallen leaves in drifts across the floor.

He was still standing there when he heard boots coming fast up the porch steps and the door swung open and the couple was there, their faces set and sober. As if he'd been caught at some mischief, Jack held the carrot out in witless apology. "I didn't touch anything."

Sampson pointed west, right through the wall. His voice was sharp and loud. "There's a poster in the telegraph office," he said, "and it's got your face on it."

"My face?" The statement struck Jack as bizarre. Like saying: *There's a bird out there with your nose on it.*

"Two thousand dollars." The old man's cheeks were ashen. "That's what she's done."

"What are you talking about?"

Sampson shook his head. "I wondered what was wrong with Lydia. She looked at you and saw a kid whose mother wanted him back. And there was money in it."

At first Jack Boulton didn't understand. And then, in a rush, he did. The photograph taken at Leeton's, the smell of chemicals, the wobbling backdrop. His hand on the nun's shoulder. Now his face was on a poster in a telegraph office. Not a pencil drawing or a poor likeness done in paint, but a photograph, as clear and undeniable as Jack's own face. An unpleasant clockwork ticked away in his head until he knew exactly what she had done, why she'd done it, and he understood what it meant.

"She's put up a reward," Jack said. "She wants me back."

"Yes."

"And that woman at the station knew."

"Everyone will," said Sampson. "Everyone in town. More, if it's in the papers."

He stomped into the bedroom and emerged with a simple green dress. He held it up by the elbows like a drowned thing. "Put this on."

The kid stared at him.

"My wife says it's the best way. You can't just walk out there."

"No."

"Boy, I can't get you out of here in daylight unless —"

"I'm not wearing that."

"Yes, you are. Put it on."

Sampson's wife moved quickly between them and went to peer out the window. Then she turned and shook her head: no one in the street outside the house. Not yet. Just the horses and dogs. She came back and took the dress from her husband's hands, carried it away into the bedroom.

Sampson and Jack stood together by the long table in stunned silence.

The old man let out a long breath. He said, "Let's go."

Part Three

Cross the River

⇾ *Forty*

ALL THE WINDING WAY up toward Pipestone, Jack had not dared say a word. The old man was frantic to get out of Laggan and out of sight. He'd forced the horses into a tight trot, no galloping, nothing to attract attention. The dog loped along behind, its jaws open. Once they were clear of people, Sampson eased off a bit, but he kept them at an efficient trot. Riding into the cold vapour of the old man's fury and bewilderment, Jack had ventured finally, "What did it look like? The photograph?"

"It looked like you."

"But, was she there, too? Are we both on that poster?" To Jack Boulton, the answer was important. Had she gone to a photographer and asked for the image to be altered? Had she removed herself? Was it an image of mother and son, hopefully to be reunited, or was it a target?

Sampson said, "Just you."

Fully half an hour later the man turned in his saddle and snapped, "Why did you let her change your name?"

The boy shot back, "I didn't." But then he realized that he had in fact answered to that other name, Charles.

After three hours at a hard trot, the horses began to blow foam, and white tidemarks of sweat on their hides gleamed in the moonlight. Jack made the mistake of whining, "Why are we in a hurry? Who in the world could find me up here?"

Sampson reined in Willow and waited until Jack was alongside him.

Seeing the look in his eyes Jack blurted out, "I know, I'm sorry."

"Little boy." Sampson reached out with two fingers and hooked the Morgan's reins. "You know nothing."

The kid knew to keep his mouth shut.

"I would have found you. For one-tenth the money. It's not that hard." Sampson released the reins and the puffing Morgan drifted to the right. He held up an index finger. "One week, I would have found you," he said. "You're lucky she doesn't want you shot dead."

Sampson didn't relax even when he'd spotted the haze from a campfire in the evening air, not even when forty minutes later he located Wilson's hunting party.

The Australian was sitting on a folding camp chair before the fire, wearing his usual expression of bored annoyance, but when he recognized Sampson he rose. The riders stopped short of the camp and remained mounted. Jack couldn't help but give a surreptitious finger-wave.

"Sprout, that you? Jesus, you get around."

Already the dog was winding itself round Wilson's legs, sniffing the ground, snapping up fallen bits of dinner.

Wilson's hat brim was always clipped up on the right side, and the firelight blazed on his face. For Sampson, he wore a rare, wide grin. "Hope you brought food. We've been lost for weeks and we're starving."

Far from starving, the clients were, as usual, well fed, well looked after, and already in their tents. The trophy animals they had managed to shoot so far were wrapped in tarps and roped tight. It was cold enough that nothing would stink yet.

One client peered out the V of his tent fly and began to monkeywalk outside in his long johns to greet the unknown visitors, but when the cold air hit him he crawled right back inside. Jack saw movement at the far side of the clearing. There were the trek horses and one mule, lined up like students at school, each hobbled on a front leg, and their thin rope halters affixed to a highline that ran taut between two trees.

"Come on up," said Wilson, but Sampson did not dismount, did not walk his horse any closer to the campfire, he simply waited.

Wilson's smile dwindled and a look of alarm came into his eyes. He took a deep breath and blew out — as a man who is filled with dread might do before opening a telegram — then he approached the riders, his body a blank shadow against the firelight. He let the two horses smell his hands, ran a palm over Willow's nose. "Go ahead, tell me," he said. "Is he still alive?"

"I think so," said Sampson.

"Well, what's he done now?"

It occurred suddenly to Jack that the outfitter's poignant anxiety was not for himself but for William Moreland. Wilson feared they'd come up here to deliver bad news.

"It's not him." Sampson jerked his thumb at Jack. "It's this one."

"What, the kid?"

"Yes."

"*Him?*"

"I'm telling you, yes."

"What in the world could he have done?"

Sampson handed his reins to Jack, swung down from the saddle, and walked off, Wilson following. The two men moved away from the pup tents and hunting gear and the fire, withdrawing into the trees, where they stood together for a hushed confab in the deepening gloom of evening. Once or twice, Wilson's eyes darted to the boy, and then his voice barked, "Jesus Christ."

At the sound, Jack shrank into his coat. After a moment he slid from the saddle and dropped to the ground between the horses, still holding two sets of reins. There he cowered, between the two warm walls of their bodies, and from time to time he peered around Willow's throat to watch the men. Sampson kept running his hand over his salt-and-pepper crown, and in the gesture Jack saw vexation and deep fatigue.

Wilson shook his head at the ground, then he seemed to rouse himself. He clapped Sampson once on the shoulder, turned and started back to the fire, calling to Jack, "This man needs to eat, so you get those horses settled on your own. Feed's in the brown box. You can see where the picket is."

That night, after he'd finally been given a proper dinner, Sampson took his leave. He gave Jack one backward glance and led Willow away into the night trees, heading back down to Laggan and his wife. The dog stood deciding for a moment, then it trotted after him.

Jack wandered after them for a short way down the rocky trail, until the three moving shapes were no longer visible, and finally he went back to the fire.

⇜ Forty-One

THE AMERICAN CLIENTS seemed delighted at the sudden appearance of a boy in the middle of nowhere. Dressed as he was in oversized hat and blanket coat, Jack Boulton looked like something on a postcard that said: *Visit the Rockies.* They crowded round him and asked his name, thumped his shoulder, and almost bowled him over with their warmth. One man said, "So, does this kid know anything about hunting?"

Wilson looked at the boy. "Do you know anything about hunting?"

"Yup."

"There you go."

The men roared and jostled him some more. One of them said, "No lack of confidence," and then they wandered away.

It took Jack four days of solid work before he stopped thinking about Emelia Cload, or Sister Beatrice, or *she.* The bewildering problem of her. The unanswerable question of what she wanted from him. He was alive and well, she knew that by now. He was no longer sick, so he didn't need her help anymore. Her nursing had done its work, so all she could offer him was church and schoolyard bullies and gossiping neighbours and Bible lessons. No, he had stayed as long as he could stand it. Surely she understood that if he were dragged back to her by the scruff, sooner or later he would leave her again. The reward would be, after all, money spent on nothing.

By the end of the fourth day, the clients were sitting together on folding stools in the tent, playing euchre in the quiet of evening, partway up the trek to Wilson's favourite hunting spot near an area known to locals as Pipestone. They were all big, wealthy, cheerful Minnesotans in middle age and they'd spent most of the day arsing around and getting themselves into jackpots.

One had dropped his loaded rifle butt-down and blown a hole in the brim of his own hat. Another had got off his horse and waddled into the trees to have "a moment alone," but because he hadn't secured the animal, and because the horse disliked him, it had turned toward the pack and trotted away without him, stirrups swinging. It was twenty minutes before anyone noticed the horse was riderless. Meanwhile the wealthy client was wandering alone through bear coun-try. Luckily for him a pack train of horses and mules leaves a trail even a child could follow. When he finally caught up, panting and spiteful, his companions roared with laugh-ter. For the rest of the trip they never stopped asking if he wanted another break.

Jack grew to like these men, and the distraction of work kept him from brooding, but Wilson had become taciturn over the course of the trek and clearly regretted taking on these clients. Truth was, he regretted all his clients, eventu-ally. And clearly, he was grinding away inside himself about the nun. Tonight he had refused to join the after-dinner card game and instead settled his ass and long legs on a tiny folding chair, and vented his temper on the various bits of damaged or weathered gear. Currently he was splicing rope, weaving the strands together like plaiting a girl's hair, his lips moving in a constant stream of inner argument.

Jack Boulton sat at some remove from the men, avoiding Wilson by working on the tack. He had finished sewing up a frayed halter with waxed brown thread. He looped the halter under his boot and tested the seam with a fierce upward pull — for a horse can bring a massive weight to bear on its tack — but the sewing held. The dry old leather would give before the seam did.

Jack hunched his shoulders and realized that his muscles ached, unused to working eighteen hours a day. He still had to hobble the horses, build up the fire, grind a little coffee for the morning and get the kindling ready for Wilson to make breakfast. He didn't want to do any of it yet, he just wanted to watch as the last of the sun washed the ranges toward night. The nearest peak was waning into a blank of itself, and the enormous sky boiled away until nothing was visible but a burning filament laid along the brink of the southwestern range, flaming for mere seconds then fading and cooling into night. The kid held his empty halter and watched it all.

Someone lit a lantern and turned the wick down. The big tent glowed and subsided. Wilson was standing there, his hat turned in the boy's direction, and Jack knew his work ethic was being assessed. He made as if busy, took the needle from his mouth and began to collect the leftover thread, ignoring the *thwap* of cards behind him. He'd expected these rich men to gamble for serious money but they played for cigarettes, extra dessert, or the right to call each other "miss" and "darling." None of it made much sense to Jack. They had even invited him to play a few rounds with them, and they'd let him name his price, but Jack Boulton had won every hand until, flabbergasted, they'd evicted him from the tent. Poker, euchre, whist, bridge. There wasn't a card game the boy didn't know how to play, and he was good at most of them.

This had been an unpleasant surprise for Wilson. His opinion was that an employee who is lucky at cards is humiliating to the clients and bad for business. William Moreland had worked for Thom Wilson off and on for nearly a decade, he'd been good company and expert at his job. He'd also been a fortuitously dreadful card player and usually gave back half his wages to the clients, always in good humour. He simply didn't care if he won or lost, his mind was always somewhere else. The boy, by contrast, did not particularly enjoy cards, but once he sat down to play he became deadly serious and tried to wipe the floor with his opponents. One affronted Minnesotan had stood up and bellowed, "Thom, where did you find this little shit?" After that the boy went back to his regular work, but not before the losers had handed over eighteen dollars and a brass pocket lighter from New York. Thinking about it now, the boy regretted that he hadn't wagered for more.

At that moment there came a commotion from the cayuses out in the trees, a milling and shuffling of hooves. Jack listened for a moment. These were mostly reliable animals, but now and then all horses get ideas, usually about snakes. A screaming horror of snakes is in their genetic makeup. Even a little colt that has never seen a snake might leap away from a suspicious stick lying in the road as if basking. In the mountains, where snakes were nearly unknown, a tin cup rattling inside a pack might alarm the animal carrying it and sow havoc throughout a pack team. Therefore, left alone in the dark with their poor eyesight, they might hear things, smell things, get spooked.

"What's the problem with those animals?" Wilson barked. "Find out, and cork it."

The boy spat out the thread in his mouth, and fussed with where to put the needle.

"Get going."

"Yes sir."

Jack headed out into the dark, and then he slammed to a halt. He put his nose in the air like a dog, and fear washed over him. There was something on the wind, a rich funk even he could smell. It wasn't the salted steaks and wild onion they had fried for dinner. Corn biscuits and jam. Coffee with sugar and canned milk. Swiss chocolate in heavy foil. Expensive tastes these men had, expensive guns and dubbined boots, and they themselves were tall and bulky and talkative as children. The sheer exuberant weight of their expedition was so great that Wilson had been forced to put on two extra pack horses to carry it all.

By now Jack was certain what animal was out there in the dark. The fact that he could smell it meant it was upwind and very close. Please god let it stay away.

He called over his shoulder, "Mr. Wilson?"

There was silence for a moment. But those horses out there were smelling exactly what Jack was, and inevitably, one of them started hopping. He heard the picket rope start to creak under pressure and horses were stamping. The entire pack train was starting to boil up.

"Thom!" he screeched. "We've got a —"

His voice was lost in a series of squeals as panic blew through the pack, and with a rumble all eight horses broke picket and launched. In three strides, they were at a full gallop, thundering through the trees toward camp. Jack Boulton shouldered the nearest trunk and the animals flew past him, the soft earth under his feet jouncing like a mattress as they passed. He could not stop himself, but peered with dread into the dusk to see the horrible great thing that might be loping after them. In his hand he held only a two-inch sewing needle. But there was no predator coming, and meanwhile the entire pack train bore down on camp like greyhounds on a rabbit. Jack took off after them.

Illuminated inside the tent, cards frozen mid-air, the Minnesotans had turned to see what was coming. One man actually threw his forearms across his face in an X.

Thinking about it later, Jack Boulton had no idea why the horses had not simply stampeded right over the tent, trampled the clients to death, and thundered away into the trees. Instead, following some primitive sense of safety, all eight of them fetched up in a swirling choreography around Wilson. They were squealing, leaning back on their haunches and shouldering each other, tripping on tent guy lines and rucksacks, tripping over stacks of upturned saddles, clanging amongst the pots and pans. One of them kicked a Carnation tin and it went wheeling away, trailing a scarf of airborne milk. Eyes rolling. Ears laid back against their skulls like wet cats.

The boy skidded to a stop where he could see the clients in their tent, four bloodless faces staring through a blur of dancing legs and dust. Everyone, human and animal, seemed to be shrieking. The lone mule was see-sawing in mindless terror, kicking at the empty air until the boy raised the halter still in his hand and swatted its neck. The poor dumb animal came to a halt and stood shaking like a confused sleepwalker.

Already removing his coat, Wilson slalomed through the

churn of bodies and put himself directly against the shoulder of the worst horse, which of course was Colonel Petch. He snatched at the hackamore and gently drew his coat over the Colonel's face to blind and calm it. It kicked, danced, but finally subsided. The boy ran to the Morgan and did the same. Thus began the slow process of gentling the mad assemblage. They blindfolded some, paired others likely to calm one another, separated the ones that were still hoppy.

By the time it was over, camp was a mess, all the men were in shirtsleeves, and two horses were missing. Those animals would be found the next day unharmed and grazing together in a wide sunny valley full of boulders, and when Wilson whistled to them, they would pick their way back to the waiting pack train like domesticated dogs.

Now one of the Americans came out with his hands balled up at his sides. He looked as if he couldn't decide if he wanted to punch someone or burst into tears.

"Oh my god," he said through his teeth. "What happened?"

"Well," said Wilson lightly, "probably a wolf."

Both Wilson and the boy knew it wasn't a wolf. But the answer pleased the clients, and for the rest of the evening they discussed the prospect of hunting and skinning timber wolves, for they felt that the rifles they'd brought for the mountain goats and bighorns would surely do.

When he had Wilson alone the boy whispered, "Did you bring it?"

It, in this case, was an enormous and elderly gun they referred to as "Esther." Wilson had been in the habit of leaving it at home, thanks to its weight. It could be broken down, the stock removed, the barrel unscrewed, and that was the way it was stored until a client came along who wanted really big game: buffalo, grizzly. That was the way it travelled, too, packed away like tent poles, because who needs a gun like that always at the ready? Hunters generally expect to go after the game, not the other way around.

"Yes I brought it," Wilson said sourly. "Thank you for asking."

"What?"

"I forgot the cartridges."

"Are you joking?"

"Don't start."

The boy didn't even look for Pearl, what was the point? At least the clients were loading everything they had. For a moment Jack gazed at the weathered face before him. The impossibly blue eyes.

"Which one was it?" he said.

"Who knows?" Wilson glanced back at the men in the tent and lowered his voice. "Probably the female. She's been around here."

"What happens if we run into the other one? What if it's the young one, Rudy?"

"We won't," Wilson gave him a false smile. "Now, bring your bedroll into my tent for the night, sprout. I don't want you sleeping outside like you do. Move your ass."

That night the boy was sleepless, sitting cross-legged on the ground like a bodyguard by Wilson's cot while the man's snores rose and subsided and shredded his nerves. In the morning Jack ventured out, and he found what they both expected him to find: bear tracks across the far meadow, pressed deep into the wet earth, the crushed grass. Enormous paw prints for a female, skirting the camp and heading away from it. A massive animal, and obviously shy. So it was the female, the one Wilson had hoped for. That bear had been spotted as far north as Golden and as far south as Kananaskis, and she always kept moving.

The other one, the adolescent male everyone in the area had started calling Rudy, lacked any caution or tact. Small for a grizzly, and with a distinct taste for horseflesh, he was as a result dangerously attracted to people, and was eternally hungry. Completely fearless of men and towns, even automobiles, Rudy wandered between Banff and Laggan, and had recently disembowelled and eaten a riding horse on the lawn of the luxurious Banff Springs hotel while stablehands fled like geese in all directions, a leisured horror for the breakfasting tourists who watched from the hotel windows. Rudy was young and healthy, but he wouldn't last long. By contrast, the female was wary and sensible. She had raised multiple litters of equally sensible cubs, and despite her age and great size — or perhaps because of it — she was well fed. She had no need to mess with a hunting expedition that stank of men and fire and guns.

The boy stepped forward and placed his slim boot into one of her paw prints. He stood there a long time with his eyes closed, pacing in his mind the canyon meadow under the stars, the long, wet grasses touching his belly, the river's glitter from which he drank, and all around him the bright yellow flowers, these flowers here, breathing perfume into the air.

✤ *Forty-Two*

THE SUN WAS SETTING over the town of Banff when Sampson Beaver trotted Willow up the river road, followed by a skittish audience of local dogs. He was talking aloud to himself and to the animals, trying to recall where in this town Jack had lived all those months with the nun. Was it on this side of the main street or the other, closer to the bridge or farther away, and why couldn't he remember something he'd learned only a few months ago?

With the whispering water to his right, the old man looked up a side street where a line of buildings stood with their backs to him, businesses that ran along the main street, now aglow in the sunset. It had taken him two days' travel to get here. He'd left his wife's house in Laggan just after lunch and ridden through the night, following the pale line of the empty highway, continuing straight through the rest of the next day without even a stopover at home.

Sampson realized he was at the bottom of Caribou Street. He was a dozen yards from the tall gates of Wilson & Co. The outfitter was still out on trek, so those stables would be empty. Sampson would have his pick of stalls for Willow, and there'd be feed for her. He would leave a few coins on Wilson's desk and spend an uncomfortable night sleeping on the ground. He'd done just such a thing many times before.

He chucked the horse past Caribou, and Willow's surge of movement and her great power startled the dogs and they flared away from her for a moment, only to settle round her again, drawn like mayflies.

He remembered white painted columns, a roofed porch with a balustrade. There'd been peeling gingerbread on the eaves; a dry, mostly dead lawn hopping with sparrows and magpies; and somewhere back there, just barely visible from the road, an unused four-horse stable with closed doors.

He was stiff and sore, but Willow was in good shape, so they trotted to the end of the river road and briskly up Buffalo Street until they stood at the busy main street, where tourists were emerging from late dinners or lingering on the stone bridge under ornamental lanterns, watching the river flow under their feet. A local boy of ten ran under Willow's chin, then turned and back-skipped on his heels, grinning the way a kid grins when he's late for dinner. He called, "Hi, Mr. Sampson! How's the hunting?" and without waiting for an answer he took off again. The mutts ran after the boy, swirling and getting underfoot, yipping like puppies.

The old man took Willow across the main street and continued up Buffalo, a winding residential road, looking for the nun's house, until the houses became cottages. Then cottages and shacks petered out and there was nothing but river overlook. He doubled back and followed Otter Street until that ran out, too.

The horse halted of her own choice at the joint of a residential street and an alley, and whinnied. Ten properties away, something whinnied back; a horse or mule calling from a backyard in equine greeting, or question, or just curiosity.

Sampson took off his hat and looked up at the red-washed clouds. He told himself he'd never wandered aimlessly like this before, through streets and alleys, past houses and shacks and sheds and churches and empty lots and a small cemetery, looking for nothing more precise than a familiar bit of ginger-bread on a front porch. He put his hat back on and worked his way methodically back and forth, up and down the grid-like streets, following a whiff of memory. And all the time the light was failing.

Not until he went back to Buffalo Street to start the search all over again from the beginning did he see that familiar white-painted gingerbread, still visible in the gloom. Not the biggest residence in town, but pretty close. Somehow, despite a lifetime of tracking, despite the benefit of warm evening light, he had walked right past her house without seeing it, so worried was he by the mess and closeness of town, by tourists and running children.

Sampson dismounted and stepped up onto the nun's wide, dark porch and hammered on the oak door, knowing perfectly well the rules of polite society and the preferences of rich people: that salesmen, cleaning women, poor folks, teachers, and strangers like him were expected to come to the kitchen door. He had no patience for that. It took a lot of knocking before the front door opened and a small face appeared in the crack by the jamb. No veil to hide her hair, and she said nothing, just looked at him.

Whether she recognized Sampson from his forays into Banff over the decades, or from his association with Wilson, he couldn't yet tell, but the distrust in her gaze was palpable. The hall behind her was dark, and no light shone from any of the downstairs windows.

Long ago, when Sampson had been an eighteen-year-old marshal, the newly deputized had been ordered to follow older marshals in order to be shown how to interrogate, notably how to get information from witnesses and bystanders. So he'd learned how to get through a door. Three ways: offer something they want; threaten something they don't want; and if that doesn't work, kick it in.

Now he found himself falling back on the artificial diction of a marshal, a style of address dating from the 1860s. It was a script, one that he often dropped when people panicked, or fell into a terrified silence, or even started shooting. But just now, on this night, it popped out of him, as easily as if forty years had not passed. He said, "I would speak with you, ma'am."

She was shifting from foot to foot behind that door, and her eyes began to dart about. She looked at his boots, gazed past his arm out onto the lawn where Willow stood. He knew she could see the Winchester in its leather boot by his saddle. She seemed to become resigned to the impending bother of speaking to this man, and sighed out, "What is it about?"

"Will you open the door?"

"I will not," she said. And indeed she did not, but neither did she shut the door.

For a moment they simply looked at one another.

Sampson said, "It's about Jack Boulton."

The effect was so immediate it was almost comic. She said, "Oh," as if she'd been struck, swung the door wide and stepped forward so quickly she nearly touched Sampson's coat front. The words came out in a rush: "Where is he? Do you have him? Have you found him?"

Everything in the old man wanted to step back, he did

not like those trembling hands. But he stood his ground, and said, "Invite me in."

She remained there for only a few seconds more, lips open and the breath going in and out of her, the picture of desperation, before she regained herself and said, "Come in, please."

More from physical habit than respect, Sampson removed his hat and stepped inside.

She was in bare feet, a fact that worried him more than anything else so far. It was not only intimate but entirely wrong for the temperature, outside or in. Her toes looked blue. He followed her as she padded down a long, unlit hall that smelled of old wood polish, past chairs piled up with books, fallen volumes at their feet, past a man's hairbrush lying on the floor, and a convex, gilt-framed mirror in which her reflection hurried along followed by the dark bulk of his own.

And then he spotted the photograph — the original unaltered image. As it swam past his eyes he saw that she too had been in the shot, reclining in a chaise, and the boy's hand was on her shoulder. While she was radiating contentment and pride, Jack's gaze held a poignant distress. That unhappy boy looked out from her hallway, just as he now looked out from the walls of post offices, telegraph offices, hotel lobbies, and the notice boards in small and rustic train stations. The missing child — and only Sampson knew exactly where he was.

The kitchen was very poorly heated by the glowing grill and door seams of an old, yellow enamelled stove. In one wall was an old-fashioned kitchen fireplace, cleaned of ashes, and so large that Sampson himself could have crouched in it. It didn't look like it had been used in a long time. Every wall was lined with counters, above which hung glass-doored cupboards. The counters were littered with boxes and vials and odd devices Sampson recognized vaguely from pharmacies. In the middle of the room was a table that could seat ten people, and this he surmised was where the boy had eaten his breakfast every morning. An icebox bigger than any he'd ever seen, big enough to chill an entire butchered sheep, stood by a doorway, and through that door were visible the shelves of a great pantry, now empty. Like the house itself, this outsized kitchen spoke of an affluent life long gone; it spoke of staff. She was alone now, last survivor aboard a drifting ship.

She whirled on him and said, "Do you know where he is? Can you find him?"

Sampson settled himself on a chair without being asked, crossed one leg over the other, and rested his hat on his knee. "I'm not here for that."

After a moment of indecision, she sat across from him.

He said, "I want you to withdraw the reward."

She looked incredulous. "I will do no such thing."

He reached to his knee, rested his hand on the crown of his hat and tapped a finger thoughtfully, his head slightly to one side. She hadn't asked him his name yet, which was curious. "I'm going to tell you why you will withdraw it."

She waited, her face sunken and hard, her hands clenched together in her lap.

"First," he said, "it's too much money. Competition is dangerous."

"It's just money, for goodness sake. The first person to find him gets it."

"You don't understand the world. Being out of it for so long."

"I understand it perfectly well."

"If that's true, then you know not everyone has the money you do. Most people's lives were hard even before the war.

There are rough men living around here, and some of them aren't very smart. They know how to hunt, but that's about it."

"Yes, yes," she said. "I know all this."

"And there's the war. I know a man in Laggan. He's smart, funny. He taught my son to speak Italian, they used to go hunting together sometimes. He came back from the front, and now he's broken and sick, not right in his head. His wife is afraid of him."

"Why are you telling me this?" she said, more to make him stop than because she wanted to know.

Sampson shifted in his chair and in that quiet kitchen the *screek* of the old chair back sounded loud. He said, "Killing is a hard habit to break." He could see the notion beginning to work its way into her mind, and saw her fighting to dismiss it. "You sent a pack of dogs after a little boy without thinking he might get hurt."

"Oh, stop it, I don't believe a word of it. I'm not a woman you can frighten."

Despite her bluster, Sampson knew doubt had begun to simmer in her.

"Second reason. If you get him back, Jack will run away again."

"He will not," she said, and there was certainty in her tone. "He will decide on his own that staying with me is the only way. He'll see it for himself."

As if the woman was hard of hearing, Sampson repeated, "That kid will leave you the second you get him through your door."

"Then I will put up another reward," she said. "And another, and another, until he sees the light."

This surprised him so much his hat almost tipped off his

knee. He could say nothing at first, and then he sighed out, "What the hell . . ."

The nun placed her hand on the table and leaned forward to make her point. "Boys need training if they have any hope of growing up to be decent, trustworthy men. If you let a boy do whatever he wants, then yes, he will become one of those worthless, brutal creatures you just described to me. I won't let that happen to him. I will not allow it."

"There is something wrong with you," Sampson said.

"Further," she said, with no more notice of the insult than if Sampson hadn't spoken at all, "that boy stole something from me. I want it back."

She appeared to be serious, and yet to the old man the idea was preposterous. Jack Boulton was like his father in many ways, but not that one.

"What exactly did he steal?"

"That is my affair, not yours."

"Was it valuable?"

"It certainly is to me." She tried to affect a smile, but it was oily and false. It slid off her face leaving clear proof that she was about to weep.

Sampson had been hoping for just such a change in her, a collapse of her rigid defences. Four decades earlier, he had watched as older marshals had worked on witnesses, wheedling information out of wives, charming children until they giggled out the hiding place of their fugitive fathers, convincing neighbours too terrified to gossip that their lives were about to get significantly worse if they didn't. Mostly, the marshals used threats. But his boss had once said, *Go in hard, scare them. Then turn around and be sweet. It knocks them off the rails.*

So Sampson said, "The boy shouldn't have done that to you."

"No, indeed." Her voice was plaintive, a near whisper. "But he did." She looked down at her lap, and the tears fell into the dark cloth of her skirts. "I did nothing more terrible than care for him. I loved him, I truly did. It was I who saved his life. Without my care, he would be dead right now. Me, not those doctors. But he is, at heart, no better than his father. That boy took a great deal away from me. You can see, I'm sure," she faltered, "the state I'm in."

"I see it." He waited until her eyes rose from her lap and she could face him down once again with what brittle courage she had left, and then he asked what he'd come here to know: "But if he hurt you and stole from you, why do you want him back?"

The reply was immediate, and it had the rhythmic quality of an incantation. "He owes it to me. He must return to this house. He owes me an apology. He must pay his debt."

There, finally, was the honest answer, what Sampson had been pondering and worrying about for days: What did she want from the kid? Without much prodding at all, she had admitted it, and the answer was worse than he'd thought. Revenge. She was wounded, and she wished to wound the boy right back, to force him to return and look upon his work. And to accomplish this she would use her money and the rest of the world as a weapon.

Sampson ran a hand over his weathered face and sighed. He had already spent too long in this house, communing with a troubled person whose illness, he now felt, was so acute it might be contagious. From the moment he'd come close enough to read her expression, his chest had been humming like a hornet nest. The marshal in him had carried him this far, but now his only wish was to get away from her. He put on the hat, braced his hands on his knees, and levered himself up. Without a word of goodbye he left the kitchen and went down the long hall toward the front door.

Just like Jack Boulton had, the old man avoided those mirrors and the gloomy photograph, and like the boy, he escaped that house, stepping into the shade of the veranda, down the steps, into the blaze of full moonlight and the free world outside, his heavy boots crunching the gravel of the front walk, his hand reaching out to Willow's halter as a swimmer reaches for a dock. He didn't even waste the time it would take to mount, but drew the horse away from the grand old house, walking over that dry lawn onto the dry road, caring not where, nor which street, nor what direction, as long as it was away.

SHE DID NOT EVEN watch the man go, but rose and made her way upstairs toward her own bedroom and the syringe in her side table. The tears had come far too easily. A sudden onslaught of uncontrollable sorrow and, with it, the apprehension that if she didn't stop immediately, she might never be able to stop. Weeping might be her permanent state.

At the door to her room, she was arrested by a creak from the first floor. A foot on the bottom stair. Her eyes slid to the bannister and the dark hollow of the stairwell. But she knew her own house and all its sounds. This was nothing. The man had not come back. There was no one down there.

She sat on her bed and gazed out at the empty hallway. Sometimes she woke and heard creaking on the stairs, but it was just an echo of herself hours earlier walking upstairs, the house cooling, the floorboards shrinking, readjusting one after another in eerie sequence, so it sounded exactly like halting footsteps.

As a little girl she had stamped up those stairs into her bedroom, or pattered along the hallway into her young nanny's room. And long afterward, they had heard the floor *squeak-squeak* on nothing, and the nanny had said, in her lovely Scottish accent, "Here you come again," and they had both laughed.

Whenever her father was away Emelia had loafed in her nanny's room, and slept with her nanny because she was seven and the nanny only fourteen and tender with children. There was no one else for either of them.

Like most houses, this one had enjoyed a heyday. Before Emelia's birth there had been cocktail parties, loud and exclusive balls at winter solstice that often left the premises in need of repair, business dinners for unsmiling bankers who argued points of finance and fouled the air with their cigars. But the birth had been difficult and the mother had fallen ill, and as the woman slowly sank toward death she had turned back to her old religion, much to her husband's revulsion. There were howling arguments about God. And when Emelia's mother died she was replaced by a succession of women paid to do the job in her stead. There were few of the common celebrations of childhood, for those are mostly religious in their provenance and her father wouldn't allow that.

At Christmas her nanny had put a finger to her lips and presented Emelia with a little package that held a knitted cowl with ribbons woven through it, a lovely thing that fit her slim neck perfectly. With no money of her own and therefore nothing to give in return, Emelia had slipped downstairs and come back up holding a ripe apple folded into a doily. The nanny had looked at it with great emotion and said she'd been yearning for just such a treat. They were both children, really, full of ardour and sentiment, and they loved each other. But that had lasted only until Emelia's tenth birthday, when she was shipped off to a private boarding school for girls, and the nanny, who had been the only mother Emelia had ever known, was fired.

This house had seen no children since, until the boy.

Now Emelia Cload slid open the drawer of her bedside table. The syringe lay in a slim case with a lacquered lid, and inside was a silk-lined indentation in the exact shape of the capped syringe. Something coffin-like about the interior of this case. The green bottle of Pax was next to it. Inject the tiny amount of five milligrams into her blood and a gorgeous lassitude would flood through her, release from this constant hum and anxiety and grief. Twice that and she would sleep all day. She closed the drawer and thought: *Stay awake.*

→ Forty-Three

THAT NIGHT THE AMERICAN clients camped by the water within view of a lake and a sheer wall of rock. They ate dinner and lay in their tents calling to one another and soon fell asleep with the lanterns still lit. Wilson too lay slumbering on his narrow cot, mouth hanging open corpselike.

The Minnesotans had been out a total of two weeks and the boy had been with them for one of those weeks. They had made their leisured way up into the high country, where the air was thin and where small, icy lakes lay like cauldrons in the rockbound hollows. It was on the shores of one of these lakes that Wilson had promised his clients they would find plentiful mountain goats, and indeed they had found them clambering up the almost sheer canyon wall, perched white and exposed and hopping slowly from ledge to ledge. They were gorgeous. Impossibly thick, white coats; black hooves; sharp black horns. The hunters had skirmished round the lake on foot, shot the animals as they fled and watched them fall. In ten minutes they had eight dead goats. One had tumbled and bounced into the frigid lake, rolled leisurely down the incline to the deep bottom, and vanished from sight. Only a few miserable stragglers made their way to safety at the top. These goats had picked a decent spot to avoid cougar, but it was no help against guns.

The men had skinned the bodies where they lay, the boy doing most of the work, his arms slaked in blood to the elbow like a midwife's. He knew how to roll the hides so that the fleece would not stain too much. Now all the heads were facing the same direction, stacked up next to the tents cheek to cheek, with a scraggle of hooves piled up before them. But the rest, the raw red bodies, were left to rot in the juniper scrub.

The boy had no experience with such behaviour. To leave all that good meat and take away only the head, and of all things, the hooves. To him it seemed like pouring out molasses and keeping the tin can. He'd looked at Wilson in disbelief, but the man's face was unreadable.

And now, as they all slumbered, Jack Boulton went among them quietly and drew down their lanterns one by one. He stood in the dark, in the cold, with nothing but embers in the fire ring and a blanket round his thin body. Above him the peaks rose blue-white with old snow, gleaming under the moon. He decided the highest one was Pipestone, but he didn't know for sure. In fact, he wasn't sure at all where he was. Maybe Pipestone was just an area. Maybe it described a geographical shape, or a system of canyons. For all he knew it was so named because someone had found an old caveman's pipe here.

Holding the blanket round him he wandered the shore of that alpine lake, toed a few egg-sized pebbles around, and listened to the hollow sound of rock scraping rock in that empty amphitheatre. He thought of the Vikings and their frost giants. His stolen book said they came out at night or in the fog, and they hid from people, travelling inside a cloak of blizzard or low cloud. If touched by sunlight they turned to stone. Jack took the measure of a high ledge on the canyon wall and imagined a creature that tall, standing there, camouflaged in rock and darkness. It was unnerving to think of a sentient creature of such immense size looking down at him. He decided it would have a wrinkled pate and a long, terrible face, and when it was angry it would open its cavernous yellow mouth and roar. This idea gave Jack the gleeful willies. He wrenched the blanket tight round himself and felt his breath pumping. He imagined the earth shaking under its footfalls. Did giants run? The book suggested they did: *He comes — he comes, on the rushing wind, and the trees bow as his fearful breath goes past.* It was the ice giants who were said to have built the mountains, like colossal stone-masons working toward a purpose unknown, and when they grew old they did not die but only faltered, fell motionless, and became mountains themselves. Every avalanche was the result of an old giant waking up, shaking snow and rock from his brow. A race hated by the gods, and hating them right back. The boy admired these stories very much. The Vikings surely came from a place just like this, and he figured they were never bored.

Jack sincerely hoped the Vikings really had existed once, that it wasn't just a fib someone made up, like leprechauns and fairies. But he had no evidence except the book. He didn't believe in fairies, of course, but the nun had assured him many people did; some even claimed to have seen them flitting in their gardens. When he asked what fairies looked like, she'd said they were naked women the size of a dime, and they had wings. He had burst out laughing at the idea, and she had too. Then again, she believed firmly in angels, and in ghosts. He asked if she'd ever seen either, but her reply was, "I don't ask for proof when I believe in something. That's what faith is."

Which meant no.

Jack thought about proof. The old dying pirate in one of his books, waving off an easy belief in God, saying, *'Tis easy for a man to point to a rope and say, "I believe that will hold my weight." It is another thing for that man to swing himself by it over a precipice.*

Trust. We are born without the slightest concept of betrayal but, as sure as the turning of the earth, the idea dawns on us sooner or later. What to make of that fact?

Jack hugged his thin shoulders and stared into the cold black water where, somewhere down there, was a dead goat. Who knew what else might be submerged in the total dark of that alpine lake, mummified by cold. He could imagine tree trunks, dead animals, maybe even people, lost woodsmen, prehistoric burials. But he would never know for certain. If you can't see something, if you will never see it, if there's no evidence for it at all beyond what your own heart tells you . . . is that knowing?

And what if you see something at night, actually see it, reach out and touch it, but nonetheless cannot bring yourself in the light of day to believe that it was real? He had been feverish three times in his short life and each time he had become delirious, his hands rising over the bedsheets working a toy that was not there. Apparitions and scenes projected themselves wantonly, inside his skull, through the walls and ceiling of the cabin. They followed him into the darkness under the blankets, where he sweated and wept and grumbled. Sometimes he was aware of his mother, felt her hands plying him with camphor, fresh clothes, sugar water as he lay under his blankets suffering. At night he struggled upright, unable to stand the rise of heat within his body, and he let the blankets fall and felt droplets of sweat crawl down his chest and spine. He hung his damp head and, in the relief of coolness, he half-slept sitting up, his mother's hand on his brow. He imagined that he had called to her and spoken in measured tones of the need for them all to evacuate. The fire was coming. He imagined the walls were crumbling, the books, the pantry shelves collapsing into ash. But when he awoke again he was dry and dressed in a fresh shirt and drawers, lying under many blankets, and his mother was sitting cross-legged beside him, her hand on his chest. Her terrified gaze never left him, she seemed not even to blink. Meanwhile, his father waited out there in the cold clearing, huddled in his coat, holding the saddled horse, ready for a ride into town. In case, just in case.

And months ago, alone in the hospital, dying of the same illness that had killed his mother, he'd seen the roof simply lift off the entire ward where he lay on the icy sheets, and he watched helplessly as spears fell from that black sky, riding the distant rumble of the clouds, and he raised his hands against them and screamed. The next night, it was the white shape that had materialized before his eyes like milk suffusing the fabric of the air, wandering the floor as if lost, and he saw lassoes of blue fire wheeling about its head, flame in which, unconsumed, it was burning. He believed it was his mother all alight, and that she was trying to find him. Because by that time he'd been told she was dead.

Jack had known, in the way a hallucinating person knows, that she was frantic to reach him, but she could not find her way, was lost on the wrong side of things. He had called to her, cried into the vast gulf between them, and the figure had seemed to turn. He beckoned her in a voice increasingly shrill until finally a nurse had rushed in and tried to quiet him. But he thrashed and struggled with her, pointed at the figure, swore like a demon until the nurse had finally drawn back her hand and slapped his face, driven him down into the thin pillow, into the awful empty reality again. It was the first time in his life an adult had struck him.

He'd turned his head and seen his fellow prisoners in the ward, all those aghast faces woken in the night. The woman in the next bed reached out a hand to comfort him as if he were her own boy, her thin arm reaching for him between the beds. He'd closed his eyes on it all.

Dream or not, you know what you have seen.

Mary had often warned him: *What I see is not always real, Jack. The world is tricky for me. Just be careful what you believe.*

Standing now in the utter silence, Jack Boulton was abruptly aware of his own body, his fingers pressing through the blanket into the meat of his shoulders. He let out his held breath. *Stop it*, he thought, *stop imagining. You're not a little kid anymore.* The thought soothed him; the safe harbour of his own advanced age, thirteen years.

A noise, a kind of snarl from somewhere behind him. Jack whirled and looked into the dark. For a moment he saw nothing, then, at some distance, he discerned a hunched form in the scrub, ripping into one of the carcasses. The thing was big and it stood between him and the camp. Nowhere to go but into that cold water, which was no choice at all. He bent and took up a rock and whipped it at the shape, heard a good *thunk* as it struck ribcage. The creature yipped and scrambled sideways, then stood there, head down, regarding the boy.

It was the dog, and it came wagging toward him through the brush, licking its bloodied muzzle. Jack Boulton bent at the waist and pressed a hand to his exploding heart. The dog ambled up and leaned against his knees. "Jesus Christ." He thumped its filthy side. "Where'd you come from, dingus?"

And that was Wilson's first question the next morning. "Where the hell did he come from?"

"No idea."

"He went off with Sampson last week. You saw him go." Wilson considered the enormous dog. He scratched deep into the thick ruff and watched a back foot kicking at empty air. "Has this animal been shadowing us the whole time?"

"Who knows," the boy laughed. He remembered Sampson saying: *That dog just comes and goes.*

THE HUNTING PARTY left Pipestone in single file. Wilson rode in front, the four clients behind him, the pack horses behind them, and Jack Boulton brought up the rear. The dog trotted alongside as usual, moving ahead, dropping back. The clients were charmed by the idea of a dog that had appeared out of nowhere; first a kid and now a dog. They whistled and slapped their thighs, *here boy*. It ignored them completely. They asked about a name, they asked about breed. They proffered small treats from their pockets, but the dog would not even look at them, so they put the treats away.

One man said sadly, "That's one good-looking dog. Where'd you get him?"

Jack called forward, "Nowhere. He just walked up to the house one morning."

They were two easy days away from Laggan so it would be no more than that before the boy could sleep in his own bed again. The Minnesotans were calm now, quieter, more comfortable in the saddle. To Wilson's shock, a couple of them had formed the habit of helping with dinner, and with the cleanup after. They had eaten through most of their heavy food supplies, but two of the horses were now burdened by the remains of the hunt, and the displaced boxes of gear were distributed over the mule and the other horses. Wilson had warned the boy that if they managed to bag even one more ram before home, he'd have to give up his horse and run alongside. He assumed Wilson was joking, but then again, maybe not.

Jack looked up the long line of horses at the severed heads and rolled-up hides, expertly roped onto the pack saddles, and he tried to picture these clients as Vikings after a raid. Men travelling together through the wilderness, heading home with great spoils. Then he saw the man ahead of him riding Cricket, so named for her awkward scuttling gait, saw the man's head bobble weakly from side to side like a girl's doll. And he remembered all that good meat left behind, mutton being far less appealing to these guys than the canned stuff on hand, and he amended his view. They particularly favoured tapioca. Not Vikings, then. But raiders of a kind.

They stopped early that night, for the clients were exhausted, and the boy, unused to work, was tired too. Against Wilson's advice they made camp in an unsatisfactory spot that was plagued by wind. They all sat together facing a fire that sucked and hissed in the ring of stones. The boy always carried a book in his pocket, and one of the men asked about it. Wilson had already read *Moonfleet* and he shooed it away as if it were liverwurst, but the clients were amused and asked Jack his assessment of the story. He decided it was "about smuggling, and a girl." They passed the book around and took turns reading passages with suitable histrionics, as if on stage, to the amusement of everyone but the boy. The men were learning to be useful, so they sat shoulder to shoulder in windbreak formation to protect the fire from the wind, and they even took turns venturing out into the dark to scrounge the rocky ground for dry wood. By dark it was Jack's turn and he stepped soundlessly out into the night. He was gone long enough that they began to crane round and ask after him. Wilson called, "*Coo-ee!*" and received a distant cooee in return.

"Where's he gone?" laughed one man.

They didn't see the boy at first but rather heard him approaching. He had his back to them and was dragging something.

"Jesus, he's found a dead body."

"What have you got there, sprout?" said Wilson.

"You're going to love it, Mr. Wilson."

Something in the boy's tone, some hint of William Moreland, produced in Wilson the first half smile of the trip. "That'll be the day," he said.

Jack dropped what he was dragging. Eight feet of desiccated conifer and what was left of the root system. The line of unshaven faces stared at the thing. Jack Boulton now straddled the tree frontwise, heaved up, and forced it right into the fire, clawing sparks as he went, and dropped it with a *whoosh* into the flames. Men leapt from their seats, driven back by fireworks and smoke, and they coughed and laughed and the boy beamed at them. The tree just perched there like a monstrous spider, held off the ground by its gnarled roots.

"Superb," growled Wilson. "You've buggered the fire."

But the Minnesotans were tired and punchy and they began to laugh. When the flames banked and guttered, as Wilson had predicted, they found that funny too. But when the fire recovered and the rootball ignited with a whoosh, they began to howl and wipe their eyes. The boy hopped around in triumph and pointed at the flames. He gazed round at his companions, happy in his work. They all looked like hobgoblins, their faces lit by wild dancing light, infernal bees floating about them.

Wilson got up and went over to the pile of saddles and panniers and pack boxes. He scrounged for a while and finally returned with something rolled up in a pair of old long johns. He took the ankle cuffs in his fist and slowly unrolled a full bottle of Bratty's Special Old onto his palm. He held it out ceremoniously to the firelight for the clients to see.

"Boys," said one, "he's trying to kill us." But he looked exultant.

"I'll drink it!" said another.

The boy bent to scrutinize the label as if he were a connoisseur. "Can I have some?"

The men all said no at once.

They brought out the tin cups and wiped them clean on their shirts, and each man poured his own idea of a dram into his cup. The boy sat there, his eyes moving from face to unshaven face as they drank.

"Horrible," said one, swallowing hard.

"Oh my god."

They all took a second wincing glug, which seemed in its anaesthetic way to be less painful.

"It has something," said one man, nodding. "I'll give you that."

"A hundred proof is what it's got," said Wilson.

The men were tired and filthy and happy and grinning. They raised a toast to Minnesota, and then to good health, then to the dog, to women with long legs, to Wilson, to bloody good times, to the dog again, and finally to the sons of whores who had lately invented the income tax, may they die and rot in hell. They laughed and sucked droplets of booze from their moustaches, and the boy, unconscious of himself, mimed the action.

IT WAS THE MIDDLE of the night when the outfitter shook Jack awake and told him to break camp on his own. He told Jack why it was necessary, and then, as the clients snored, Wilson extracted the Colonel from the picketline, and rode toward Laggan.

As instructed, the kid woke the men at dawn. The Minnesotans rose bleary and sat by the fire. Jack handed them plates of bacon and tinned meat, pan-fried bread with jam, and bars of chocolate. He got them and the horses properly fed, and then he washed and cleaned the camp kitchen.

Finally, one man looked about and said, "Where's our man Wilson?"

Jack confabulated as best he could. "He's just gone ahead to make sure your train is ready, and also, that it doesn't leave town early. It does that sometimes."

"Well that's decent of him. Wilson's all right," said another man. "And you're all right too, kid."

After breakfast they sipped coffee, took turns "going for a stroll," which was code for a toilet break, rolled their own tents, and did a creditable job of packing their private gear.

A couple of them tried to help Jack load the pack horses but he shooed them away. They had no concept of a proper knot, and an unbalanced load could easily lame a horse by evening. He gave the men more coffee, and did it all himself, a process taking over an hour.

Riding in front of the pack for the first time that trip, Jack Boulton guided them only as far as the outskirts of Laggan. The Americans clapped him on the back and wished him well. Two of them tried to buy the dog. They all stood there on the road bidding a sweetheart's farewell to their horses, *goodbye Barrelhead, goodbye Cricket,* all the clients looking filthy, barbarous, and happy. When they heard the howl of the train, which signalled their ride in luxury back to Banff, they hooted with joy and took off running, leaving the boy alone with all the gear, all the animals, whether dead or alive, everything they had shot in more than two weeks.

As they ran, one of the Minnesotans hollered back, "Goodbye, you little card sharp!"

The pack train were heavily loaded and tied halter to tail, and for an hour the boy fussed over their comfort, packing and repacking, balancing loads until Wilson arrived.

The outfitter had ridden into Laggan before the sleeping clients had stirred in their tents. Once there, he'd pounded on Carr's door and bitched him out of a dead sleep, then harried him into the store, where he'd purchased supplies from the kid's pay. By the end of which the Colonel hated him, Carr hated him, the clients woke to his absence, and only Jack knew what in the hell was going on. But at least the fugitive kid now had enough food for a month. Indeed, Jack understood the purpose of it all: thanks to Wilson, he could vanish into the hills before the clients could talk to anyone about him, or name him, or even worse, spot the poster themselves and get ideas.

"That's as much as I could get for the money," said Wilson.

"Is there any change?"

Wilson rolled his wet cigar from one side of his mouth to the other. After a long interval he produced two quarters and a nickel. And then, since the boy kept staring at him, he retrieved another quarter. "Aren't you the little accountant," he said.

"No. It's my money. I earned it."

"Your money?" Wilson grinned round the cigar. "You didn't get that notion from your dad."

Jack's eyes skittered away and he shook his head.

"Money fell through his hands, sprout. But to me, he seemed like a happy man. Then one day I guess he looked at you and started caring." Wilson sighed and said, "And, here we bloody are."

They sat there on their separate horses, the Morgan in silent abhorrence of the Colonel. The dog meanwhile sloshed through ditch water and wandered the bank, then it trotted straight back into town. The boy tracked its path and saw it was headed for Lena's house. Maybe the old man was still there, maybe he wasn't.

The outfitter and his weary animals had five hours' walk ahead of them along the highway back to Banff. After weeks of work and the constant presence of other men, Wilson looked like he was going to enjoy the quiet. He mounted and said, "You stay off that road."

"I will."

"And don't eat it all at once, you little pig."

"Thank you," Jack said, "for everything."

"Get moving."

"Wait, I . . . I stole from you."

"What are you talking about?"

"That ranger's exam. I took it off your desk."

Wilson looked blank.

"It's a booklet? It was on your desk."

"Oh, that thing." Wilson scratched his filthy beard. "Did you take anything else?"

"A horse blanket."

"Fine."

"And I took things from her. The nun. Mostly books, and things she wrote in."

"Why would you bother with things like that?"

Jack opened his mouth, but all his reasons for taking those books, for admiring her handwriting, seemed flimsy and pointless.

Wilson ran his hand down the Colonel's neck. "What are you going to do about this, sprout? About this woman. Do you have a plan?"

Jack thought for a moment. "Isn't hiding a plan?"

"Not much of one. You can stay up there, wherever you people live. But you're just like your father now. You can't work, go shopping, can't show your face in town. Food costs money. So, what are you going to do in a month? In a year?"

"I don't know."

"Well, I'm done. You have to see that."

"I do."

"They'll be all over me, asking where you are. I'll be covered in human fleas. No chance I can come near you anymore." Wilson wiped his forehead with his sleeve, readjusted his bush hat. He looked exhausted. "So what are you going to do for money?"

The kid went silent. He had fourteen thousand dollars in the rafters of his cabin. He was trying to gauge what Wilson knew, but the man's expression seemed to be saying the same thing right back. Jack said, "Don't tell me to go back to her."

Wilson looked aghast. "Christ, no. She's mad as a hornet. Hates me to death. And it wasn't *me* who defected, you did." Wilson nodded. "You got her attention, all right."

The boy bent and unbent the reins in his hands, thinking *you're just like your father now*. He felt the miserable welling of tears and kept his hat down as he said, "I didn't mean to make a mess. I just had to light out, couldn't stand it anymore."

"You did nothing wrong. Your mother died, is all. And your father looks to have lost his wits. I like him, but I can't understand him."

"Neither can I," said the boy.

"Well, don't be an ingrate, he's doing it for you."

"For me." Jack rubbed hard at his face. "He never asked me a goddamn thing about it."

Wilson said, "No one ever did any such thing for me. And he's your father. So cross yer bloody fingers for him."

Jack said, "Oh hell," gave up, and wiped his eyes. Then, speaking to the saddle horn, he said, "You could have turned me in. It's a lot of money."

There was silence for so long that Jack forced his gaze back up to the outfitter's stony face. Wilson said, "You don't know me very well."

"Yes sir. I mean no. But if things were different. If I was a stranger —"

"You don't put a *price* on a human being. Get that through your wooden head. Ask Sampson. No, she can tell herself pretty lies, but wrong is wrong."

"What about stealing? What about blowing up buildings?"

The man's face softened. "Forgive your father, sprout. Sooner or later, you have to."

"Sure."

"You don't think so."

"No."

Wilson was red-eyed and weary and he looked along the range where Jack must go alone, walking the horse uphill through the last of the night's shadows toward light at the peaks, the mountains furred with pines and sweating mist. He turned and began to walk the entire pack train along the footpath that followed the river, calling over his shoulder, "Go home and stick with Sampson. Try to help the old man, at least until your dad gets home. Just fucking do it."

The boy wheeled his horse and started uphill.

Wilson's voice came roaring after him, "And stay off the bloody road!"

Forty-Four

THE KID WENT CAUTIOUSLY in the poor light, and indeed he stayed off the road. Once the sun had fully risen he came upon a little stream and a very slanted meadow full of spring grass, where he sat for an hour and let the horse graze, opening food packages wrapped in newsprint one by one and reading stories about his own father.

William Moreland had been all over the northwest, first below the border in the U.S. and then above it in Canada. He'd spent months in Montana and Idaho pecking mine owners to pieces, burgling some of them for the second time. Far too often, reporters invoked the bosses at St. Croy, who had thwarted the criminal through the use of a modern safe. A brief pause in his activities that caused some to speculate the Ridgerunner had died — Jack alone knew that he had been in Banff bringing the spoils to his son — then he had appeared in Lethbridge, where he'd cleaned out a stockyard.

The most recent incident, at least on the pages the boy scrutinized, the date being not much more than a week previously, was in New Michel, a booming mining town in the Crowsnest Pass. There he'd stolen the week's take at the movie theatre, "a cautionary tale for those entrepreneurs with too much trust in their own lockboxes and too little trust in banks." That was two weeks ago. Jack wasn't sure where Michel was, but he'd seen it on the map on the cabin wall. An eyewitness described Moreland as "no common ruffian, but tallish and having a handsome countenance." The kid's face went dark with anger as he read. He wrapped his goods back up tightly, mounted the horse, and went on. For an hour he fumed. How awful it was to have a father willingly destroy his own life, and in doing so ruin yours, following a plan you disagreed with.

Jack blew out a sigh to calm himself, closed his eyes. "Stay," he said, and the horse stopped.

He felt the animal shift its weight, felt it swing its head round to look at him and chomp the bit. The sound of wind in the trees above.

"Ho," he said and the Morgan started on. He opened his eyes and smiled, ran his hand down the muscled neck. It was something, this communion, some modicum of control in Jack's life. Not much, but something.

Now a friendly relay of crows floated low and paced him as he rode, calling into the echoing valley. Jack pressed his hat to his head and looked up at their black breasts, their angled heads spying him. He reached his hand into the air and one of them floated there above his fingertips like a kite, wingtips riffling in the wind. A bald eagle appeared from nowhere and the crows burst into loud reproach as they banked and sailed away, and soon the eagle grew wary of Jack and it too banked and shrank into the distance. A tired old hunter, worn and lustreless.

Below the eagle, in the narrow valley, a thin rill of smoke rose toward the sky, broke apart, and made the air milky. The boy drew the horse to a stop and looked. Down there, in the rocky valley, at a distance of two miles, the Swedes were bent over a small dark form on the ground, likely a deer carcass. They were pacing between the kill and what looked like a stone oven or a simple smoker, setting the meat inside, walking back. Their familiar, bulky, fur-lined coats had been discarded thanks to the sun. Even at this distance the boy could see how lean these men were, how agile, startlingly pale and half-naked, hard at work down there. What singular focus they had. Jack watched as one of them went to the fire, then that man turned and called something to the other two men.

Jack said, "Jesus."

Where once there were two Swedes, now there were three. It was like a trick of the eye.

He swung his boot front-wise over the Morgan's withers, hopped to the ground, and stood with hands on hips, grinning.

FORTY MINUTES LATER, and a steady climb downhill along the gentlest route he could navigate with the horse, Jack Boulton found himself traversing the meadow and fetching up by that same stand of pines. Of course, they had seen him coming a long way off, and they held together as a group near the smoker. All three wore the same leather leggings and homemade mukluks. Just as Mary Boulton had done with Jack, the Swedes were standing in front of the escaped prisoner, shielding him with their bodies. Jack stood next to the Morgan at a polite distance, letting them size him up.

The men approached, leaving the prisoner where he was. Jack saw tension in their gait. They stood no more than ten feet from him now, their pale eyes startling in the sunburned faces. He realized they were really quite young, and clearly related, brothers or cousins, for something familial echoed between them, a strong set of the jaw, the upturn of the eyes, the high foreheads. They were like variations on an original theme.

Jack raised his free hand in a wave and said, "Hello."

He didn't expect a reply, and he didn't get one. They stood for a long time in silence, with nothing between them but the wind. The Morgan was less than pleased with these men, and it raised its head high, drew in, and snorted. A great rattle of a sound. One of the Swedes was eyeing it as if it might be dangerous.

"Okay," Jack said, and drew the horse to a tree twenty paces west and wrapped the reins around a branch, but the men seemed no less put out than they had been before.

Jack put his hand to his chest — *me*. Then he pointed to the smoking oven — *I will go there.*

The two men glanced at each other and seemed to confer silently. He saw agreement pass between them, and so, without entreaty, he walked briskly to where the prisoner stood squeezing his hands together in obvious anxiety, standing as close to the warm oven's mouth as he could. At his feet, laid out on oilcloth, was what appeared to be at least a week's worth of good smoked venison. The prisoner was not much older than Jack was himself, perhaps sixteen. He was thin and grey and his eyes were hollow.

"Did you escape from the camp?" Jack looked around at the three staring faces, but if any of them understood him, he sensed that they weren't going to let it show. Here, there was no common language. The Swedes were well known to not give a shit about communicating with others, let alone allowing anyone to come near them physically, which made the prisoner's apparent domesticity here with them truly amazing. He walked right up to the fugitive. As he did, one Swede reached to intercept him, but the other held his brother's arm and let Jack pass by.

Clearly, one of them was fearful of the interaction, the other was merely curious.

"Were you a prisoner?" Jack said. He looked into those dark eyes and saw a charge go through them. If nothing else, this boy knew the word *prisoner*. He was tall, six feet at least, thin as a sapling, his black hair had been cut roughly with shears. His lips were parched and cracked, and he looked badly undernourished.

"Are you okay?" Jack said, and he began to pat at himself, pretending to inspect his belly, his legs, a pantomime of searching for injuries. The boy's eyes cleared of suspicion, and he shook his head — no, he had no injuries, he was okay.

"Was that your father?" Jack said.

The boy just looked at him, but both Swedes shifted nervously from foot to foot. Either they knew the word or they had guessed the subject at hand.

Jack tried, "Daddy?" which produced no reaction in the boy. Then he turned to the Swedes and said "Papa?" The word meant nothing to the prisoner, but one of the Swedes nodded sadly. He said, "Ja. Det var hans pappa," and pointed in the exact compass direction of the dead man, who had once been and might still be lying alone in one of their cabins, with a pile of debris against the door. Did they find the father and, just as Jack had done, go in search of the son? There was no way to ask such a complex question in gestures, and language was nearly useless here.

How cheerless they looked now, all three of them. Young fatherless men. The Swedes were capable, that much was clear, and they seemed to be thriving, despite the lack of horse. Jack yearned to know how they had got here in the first place, to the Rocky Mountains, to such a remote spot. Who had taught them to live in such a way?

"Well," he said. "I'm glad to know he's all right. You'll look after him, I guess." He went to the Morgan and scrounged out some chocolate, a small package of dry oats, and a handful of salt, which he carried to the fire and handed to the men. The salt he poured from his fist into the prisoner's cupped hands, carefully so as not to lose any, the grains falling like hourglass sand.

Jack said, "You'll want to get him across the border. He's not illegal in Montana, or Idaho, or any of those. The Americans aren't at war. You understand?" But none of it was making sense to the Swedes — Jack's voice was like a yammering bird to them. The names of those states produced nothing like recognition in their eyes. These men never spoke to anyone. He wondered whether they even knew there was a war on. Even if they could read a little English or French, they didn't collect newspapers, they had no interest in what their fellow man was up to. Perhaps that would change, now they had found an escaped prisoner dead in one of their cabins and had somehow run down his son before the boy managed to starve to death.

These were men living outside of time, standing in a landscape unchanged since prehistory, all three of them now wearing pelts and hides, nursing a fire, the spindly, elongate X of their travois resting on the ground. This could be a museum diorama, if not for the two hunting rifles standing side by side, barrel up, leaning against an aspen.

Jack didn't say goodbye, but once the Morgan had crested the hill and was back on the route to home, he glanced back. All three were likewise looking up at him.

BY THE TIME he reached home the sun had set, so Jack ferried his supplies under the eaves and settled the horse in its paddock by twilight. He curried it and brought water, he cleaned the hooves, brushed the sweat from its back, combed the mane.

The Morgan seemed to be gazing intently at the cabin. There was a bag of oats standing by the cabin door, so he brought it some, only as much as he could scoop with two hands. He'd already eased the animal off its high town diet and back to normal scrub and grass. But oats were always good. He lay the treat at the Morgan's feet — it did not move or eat but rather kept watching the front door.

"Lookee," he coaxed, "down here." The Morgan would only lip at the pile of oats before it went back to looking at the cabin.

"Fine," the boy said, and tucking the rifle under his arm, he took up the panniers of food and went inside.

The moment he entered the cabin he smelled it. The same thing the horse had been smelling: immediately close by, something alive, the unfamiliar funky scent of ditch water and rotted grasses and dirt and sweat. The first thing his mind barked out was *bear*.

A predator outside the house was a horrible idea, but a bear trapped inside was worse. Nimble as a monkey, he dropped the food, clutched the gun, and was up the ladder and onto the loft by the roof. The desire to hold the rifle was habit by now, but he knew it was goddamn empty. Crouched on hands and knees, he was straining to see down into the room below, and he was calculating: cougar and bears can climb perfectly well, damn fast, too, but he didn't really know what one of them might make of a ladder. So he was gauging a safe place to leap, should the animal come after him. Absurdly, the question came to his mind: Why haven't I ever leapt onto the bed before?

It was dark inside the place, but he could still see that tins had been moved about on the kitchen shelves. The half loaf of bread he'd made over a week ago was gone. Something had eaten it. Jack Boulton rose and stamped his feet on the loft and hammered his fists on the rafters and bellowed, "Get out of here, you goddamn lazy bear!"

He waited on his perch with Pearl at his knee, and listened. There was no sound in the cabin, no movement. Any normal animal, whether dog, wolf, bear, or rodent, would have been dashing about down there in a panic. So whatever it was, it had already come and gone.

Had his father come home? No. Even if a man comes home and immediately leaves again, he makes a different kind of mess. He might sleep or change his clothes, he might inspect and thereby alter some of the little home improvements the boy had accomplished in his absence. He might leave something on the floor, a packsack, some weight he no longer wanted to carry. A man coming home leaves a familiar clutter of coats and bags and gear. But here, here Jack saw no other sign of disturbance than a few scraps of missing food.

All this went through the boy's mind at a rush. He paused at the top of the ladder and looked with annoyance at the breadcrumbs. Okay, maybe it was just squirrels, or a marten.

He came down the ladder and made a careful inspection of the cabin, kicked around in every corner and hidey-hole. He found nothing more. So he set his mind then to putting away all the food, wiping things down, generally getting the place back in shape after his trip. He forgot that when he had first entered the house, he'd smelled sweat.

Forty-Five

WHEN THE CLOCK on his desk had ground its way past midnight, Wilson wandered out to the empty paddock and stood in the sand with hands on hips. Far away, a little blue storm was brooding somewhere over the Sawback Range. All the tents, drooping blankets, and an infinite amount of rope in various gauges hung on the fence along Caribou Street, left to flutter in the wind and dry out. The animal remains of the Minnesotans' hunt were sitting now in the back room of the local taxidermist, and the hunters themselves had long ago hopped off the train, washed and shaved and dressed themselves to the nines, and got plastered in one of the bars in Banff. By now they'd all be out like a light in whichever luxury hotel they'd descended upon to celebrate the end of their trip.

The outfitter went back inside and sat on an upturned salt box with his elbows on his knees. The trek was over and he wouldn't have another for two weeks. The animals were washed and fed and resting in their stalls, a process that had taken him hours, during which time Wilson was missing Jack's help. He was a clever boy, almost as capable as William Moreland, but he wasn't quite strong enough yet, and there was this sticky feeling of responsibility that comes with any kid, in fact with any young, vulnerable creature in your charge. The fact they haven't lived very long makes you wonder if they will. And they can be disastrously impulsive.

Ten years earlier, Wilson's former business partner Sean Macklin had gone out with two British landscape painters on an easy trip to Johnston Canyon, where there was a meadow full of scenic flora, as well as deep, spring-fed pools called inkpots that attracted wildlife. Macklin was tall and fair and had a Belfast lilt, and he was more than a little pleasing to women. The paying client on this trip was that most unusual of things, a university-educated woman, and she had with her a niece. The girl was a leggy, sidling, resentful, tow-headed eighteen-year-old who had been ordered to visit the Rockies by parents who felt she was callow and lacked a sense of adventure. When Macklin, a genuinely organized trek leader, was an entire day late bringing them home, Wilson had ridden up to the canyon himself. It was warm, almost hot despite the altitude, a fragrant breeze in the meadows. Around dinnertime he found their empty camp. The horses were safely picketed but stamping with hunger, and as the light failed Wilson followed a distressing trail of human debris: clothing, a fallen lantern, a broken box of paints that spewed gaudy colours onto the moss. Finally, half a mile from the campsite, he spotted the two adults, Macklin with a missing tooth and a welt across his cheek and the aunt pale with terror and weeping. The two of them were still searching for the niece. They were holding hands, and they looked for all the world like terrified parents.

Wilson saw the situation for what it was, and his fear that someone had been killed by an animal snapped off like a light. Both women had taken a shine to their guide but the niece had lost the competition. Sexually rejected, and bested by an older woman, the girl had thrown everything at them including, as Wilson heard later, the iron frying pan, which had hit Macklin in the face, and then she had run away, screaming that she wanted to kill herself. She had been missing for most of the day.

Within the hour Wilson found her in perfect health and not overly chilled thanks to the warm weather. Any other night and she'd have been forced to return to her aunt and end her tantrum. She had been cleverly avoiding her two searchers, but had not expected a third, so Wilson had come upon her so quickly she'd had no choice but to crouch, froglike, her body half into one of the frigid pools, and hope that he would pass by and not see her. He'd rushed the girl, pulled her out of the water by one clammy arm and said, "There you are." After only moments in the water, her lips were blue with cold, so he draped her in his own coat.

It had been a miserable group that rode home the next day, both outfitters fully aware of how much worse the outcome could have been. By the time they got back to town, Macklin had accepted the obvious: his partnership with Wilson was dissolved and he was out of business. He hadn't even asked for his own horse back.

Wilson rose now and went out to stand by the Colonel's stall. He rested his arms on the gate. The variegated rump shifted gently and the horse swung round to look at him.

"How you going, you old bastard?" he said.

Those weird blue eyes considered him. He reached out and lay his hand on the animal's haunch and patted it. The Colonel nickered to him and looked away, calm and waiting.

It was then that she arrived, melting out of the blackness

beyond the stable doors. He saw movement in the corner of his eye and there she was, the nun, walking up the nave toward him.

"Christ," he said. "What is it now?"

She threw sidelong glances at the stalls. Some were empty, some held enormous and, to her, fearsome animals. "May I speak to you in your office?" She was in full nun's regalia and clutching a cloth purse with a drawstring that she was working in ringlets round her index finger.

Wilson thought for a long, cold moment. His mouth began to form the first word of a brutal dismissal, but then it closed again. He pushed off the gate and went without gesture or welcome into his office where he took up the only chair. A second later she trailed in, her boots soundless on the sawdust floor. Her pupils were enormous and dark and she radiated a kind of dread, like a student expected to make a speech on stage. She looked around the room for a place to sit and, seeing that he had given her none, faltered and held the cloth bag to her belly.

"Go on," he said.

She stood in her voluminous skirts and veil, the white apron cinched to her shrunken waist, and seemed about to cry. "I don't know. I'm unclear on what to do. You see, I have come to a conclusion."

Wilson expelled a long, theatrical sigh. "If you don't make it fast I will throw you outside on your arse."

She froze. She squeezed closed those wet, terrified eyes and smiled. "You are right," she said. "I must get it over with."

"Good," said Wilson, increasingly uneasy with what he was seeing in her ragged face. He wondered if she might be drunk. He waved his hands as if to shoo pigeons. "Get on with it."

"You had him with you, for a week they say. Indeed he was with you until today. Is that true? He was working for you?"

Wilson's smile was bitter, "Doesn't news travel fast when money is involved."

"Yes. Money speeds things up."

"I don't know where he is now, so don't ask me."

"Of course you don't know," she said. "And if you did, you wouldn't say."

She fussed with her cloth bag and, to his astonishment, withdrew a quart of whiskey and a heavy cut-crystal glass, which she placed carefully on his desk. Then she poured a slug into the tumbler, somewhat expertly as he saw it, and pushed it across the desk to him.

He stared at the bottle. It was an almost full bottle of thirty-five-year-old Charles Hyndman's whiskey, something only the owner of a bank could afford. A stout, chiselled bottle usually seen only in advertisements, made of a glass so dark it appeared black and admitted no light. The grandiosity of her gesture amused him.

She saw his review of the bottle. "Is the brand all right? I'm not an expert."

"It's very fine." Wilson said, and he threw it back. She reached over the tumbler and poured him another one, and he scrounged on his desk until he found a tin coffee cup behind a pile of papers. He set it down next to the tumbler. "Is this a peace offering? Will you have one too?"

"No."

"Well then, not a peace offering. What do you have in mind?" He swirled the liquid. It coated the glass like oil and ran in tears down the sides. Not a drink to throw down your neck — but he did it anyway.

Somewhere out there a mule had woken tired and confused and was calling out in its loneliness to anything human or animal for comfort. There was a shuffling among the other animals. He would have to leave this woman pretty soon and attend to it.

She began what was obviously a rehearsed preamble, "I am tired of the animosity between us and I want to put it to rest. I have never done anything to you, I have not impeded you in any way, and yet you continue —"

"Madam, I have no interest in this."

"You see? You are illustrating the problem."

"I have no problem."

"None that you are aware of."

Wilson eyed the bottle still standing on his desk, and wondered rather hopelessly whether she would leave it for him. It wasn't as if she herself drank, nor was it likely she'd miss the stuff. And while these thoughts crossed his mind he looked up and saw her watching him, as intently as if she were trying to read his thoughts.

One by one he crossed his boot heels on the desk beside the bottle and leaned back in his chair. "Well, this has been a fine party."

"That's all you have to offer?" she said. "Sarcasm and ugliness? A horrible show of pride?"

His gesture was one of curatorial welcome: *The horrible show is now open for your edification.*

She snapped, "You are *impossible*," and she upended the bottle over the tin cup until it was overflowing and sitting in a pool of whiskey.

His feet came off the desk. "Stop!" he barked. "Do you have any idea how much that's worth, you stupid woman?"

She squeaked the stopper back in place with the heel of her hand, as final as a bartender, and forced the bottle back into her string bag, followed by the cut crystal glass. Then her face came down level with his, she was inches away, like a teacher fixing a student's attention on her eyes to make a point.

"He looks up to you. Admires you. The life you lead appeals to a boy. But what you don't realize is that you *have* something. You have this." She stood and gestured to the building over their heads, to the bills of lading and invoices and letters from abroad, the stable full of healthy animals. "What does he have?"

Wilson's toe began to tap the floor. "He made up his own mind."

"A boy that age barely has a mind."

"Where did you get that bloody notion?"

She ignored him and forged on. "By disparaging me in front of him you lessened my influence. You impeded me, aggrandized yourself, and led him to believe a lie: that he was better off out there, living like a monkey. Well, now he has nothing, and I don't have him. You are to blame for that."

"The kid is fine. I don't know what you think *out there* is, but to him it's home. Let him be."

"No. I will get him back."

"Look," Wilson blew out a breath. "Will you let it drop? Jack is not wandering the woods like a lost kitten. He has a home, there is a roof over his head, he has food, and he's not alone. There's been someone with him the whole time."

Her eyes remained on his face but she was not seeing him.

This news had dumbfounded her. Only after a long pause did she say, "His father?'

"No, of course it's not his bloody father."

She reached out to brace herself on the wood surface of his desk. He watched her expression of righteous determination begin to waver and curdle, first into confusion, and then into a bright-eyed anguish. "A woman?" she said.

The meniscus of whiskey in the tin cup trembled in sympathy with her shaking arm, and several dollars of Charles Hyndman's slopped off the edge of the outfitter's desk into the sand and straw at his feet.

"I have no intention of talking about this any further. I've told you everything you deserve to hear." Wilson made a gesture again of shooing pigeons, and to his relief, this time it seemed to repel her. She turned abruptly and went out into the stable.

Wilson lifted the tin cup of whiskey from his desk and followed her out the office door, stood in the aisle to witness the queer way she went, veering this way and that to avoid occupied stalls until she reached the exit and slipped out again into the night.

After she was gone, he stared at the rectangle of darkness between the tall stable doors, and those squirrel-like footprints leading to it. He waited many minutes to see if she might return, but she did not. His shoulders relaxed. Unsettling, that's what she was. Increasingly unhinged. The notion of that poor kid, collared and imprisoned again, in close proximity to that mind, to that astonishing will — it was an awful idea.

He went to the mule, which had fallen asleep again, and he hung over the gate and considered the large tin cup cradled in his hands. Every quart of Hyndman's was worth more than a new saddle, and she didn't even know that. The bloody rich. The quality. They worried about everything, unaware of the soft life they enjoyed. They looked down on everyone, including other rich people, and not a single one of them, in his experience, was ever happy. They lacked respect for life.

Wilson turned and flung the finest whiskey he had tasted in his life across the stable's dirt floor.

⇢ Forty-Six

HURRYING AWAY THROUGH the dark, carrying with her the blinding hurt, the nun finally slipped into the moonshade of a grove of trees, where she froze like a rabbit. Somehow she had made her way behind the schoolyard, so that now the great brightness of the main street stood between her and her house, and she did not know how she could bear to cross it, to open herself to public scrutiny. She pressed a shaking hand to her mouth. How deeply that man distressed her, confounded her, for in her agitation she had almost left the tumbler behind. That would have been a bad mistake, for people might ask what cut-glass crystal was doing in an outfitter's stable.

By now, according to her careful calculations of dose, a gauge of his weight and alcohol tolerance, Thom Wilson would be feeling what he thought was a great sense of relief washing over him. But it was not relief, it was something else entirely. To the whiskey she had added a potent sedative, the better to slow him down should he attempt to seek help, and she'd mixed in enough thallium salts to kill him. Four times the amount she had given to Mary Boulton.

In a liquor as clear as whiskey, the poison would sink visibly to the bottom like lees in vinegar, but the bottle glass was almost opaque, and she was sure she had swirled the bottle before upending it. Almost sure.

She waited in that soothing darkness and quiet for a long time. *The guilty flee where none pursueth, so do not flee.* She whispered entreaties to herself until finally she was composed enough to raise her chin and walk steadily toward the bright street, stroll the board sidewalks of downtown, nodding in cold civility to neighbours as she went. Heading for home, devising already in her mind the concoction that would be powerful enough to calm her leaping heart, silence the whine of her conscience, stave off repentance.

Once across her own dear threshold she shut the door on the whole world, dropped the bag on the floor, where its contents smashed, hiked up her skirts and hurried toward salvation in her kitchen cupboards, while the tainted liquor blubbed out of the bag's drawstring mouth and infused the Persian runner.

HOURS LATER, SHE lay on her bed, looking up. The herbs had failed to help her sleep but had instead driven her down into a low, idling anxiety that would not lift, so she spent hours motionless on top of her eiderdown, mesmerized by the ceiling above her. Not like a sky, and not like a ceiling either, but rather like a hole. A great, black laundry chute out of which would come . . . what?

She said to the ceiling, "Did I give him enough?"

How long was it? Minutes, hours, before she found herself standing in the hall outside the boy's bedroom, drawn to it by the sensation, almost a changing pressure in the air, that he had come back to her. She was in her nightdress and felt cold air flowing out of that room and over her bare feet. What day was it? Had she only imagined she had shut that window?

Her eyes rose from the floor to see William Moreland standing by the breached bedroom window. He was gaunt, begrimed, burned by the sun. Her mouth shot open.

"Not to worry, Sister," his hand flapped the air. "Don't make a fuss. It's only me."

She felt her feet congeal into the floorboards like melted wax. The father of her child, come back to claim him. It was the most unwelcome sight of her life.

"*You*," she said. The word an accusation.

"As per our agreement."

"Oh no," she huffed. "There was no agreement."

"Don't you remember? You promised to —"

"I promised nothing. You just thought I did."

For a baffled moment Moreland looked back and forth between her and the window he'd come through, as if perhaps he'd entered the wrong house, found the wrong woman. Gone was the nun's habit, the veil, the boots. She was pale, naked of foot and head, standing in her shift. But it was her, no mistaking that.

He said, "Stop playing."

"Why in the world would I ever live with a contract like that? Rescue a child from the likes of you, give him a good life. And now that you are a criminal, a filthy, unrepentant" — she searched for the word — "*highwayman*, what should I do? Hand him back?"

Moreland looked about the unoccupied room. There was no longer anything to indicate anyone slept here, except for the folded schoolboy clothes on the bed. For one mad second, he felt as if his son had died, and that this woman had simply tidied up after the fact. He pointed at the clothes and said, "What happened?"

"Why don't you tell me, since you know everything?"

"Sister, where is Jack?"

"His name is *not* Jack."

Moreland dropped the knapsack with a thump and came across the floor toward her, moving fast. She tried to step back but he was on her in a second. "Listen to me," he said. "I don't know anything."

"Very true," she said.

"So . . ." Moreland cast about for the right thing to say. "You have to tell me what's going on. Sister, please . . ."

"He's gone," she said. "Like everything else. Gone away." She trilled it, as if it were somehow amusing, but she could not maintain the ruse, and something in her chest, some hot, hard thing began to crumble. A cascade of grief and wrath showered down inside and she raged at him: "Look at you. What you've done to yourself. Oh . . . *men!*" she said. "You ruin everything. You destroy the world, destroy even your-selves, and you have —"

Her tirade snapped off like a radio when Moreland's hand settled on her forearm and the fingers closed. She tried to jerk away from him but he was surprisingly strong.

"You're ill," he said, and those clear eyes were assessing her.

"No." She enunciated the next words: "I am perfectly fine."

"Well something's wrong, goddamn it."

"Oh yes, something is wrong. How intelligent you are." She was swaying on her feet and for one shameful moment only Moreland's icy grip on her arm kept her vertical. She righted herself and said with authority, "You will release me."

Moreland did as she said. There they stood in the darkened doorway of the boy's bedroom, two confused and abandoned parents inches apart. She was watching the white finger-marks on her arm fade, where slowly the blood suffused the skin like an augury.

"I've been foolish again," she said. "Believing in things that aren't true."

Moreland was afraid to move. "I see," he ventured.

She seemed calm, but what she said next made even less sense: "What exactly do *you* ever see? You're completely blind. All of you. Every last one of you is as simple as an idiot."

He shut his mouth and blinked.

"The truth is," she said, "you can't bring boys back once they're too far gone. Doing whatever they want, living wher-ever they like. Thieving." She glared at him. "Sooner or later, they become brutes like you. They wrong decent people. They lose their souls forever. Even the best of them. Even him." She shook her head as a schoolmistress might before a caning. "Some of you can't be saved. I wanted to save that child. You understand me?"

"You did. You saved his life."

"But I no longer understand myself. In truth, I should have put him down like a sick dog."

For the briefest of moments Moreland was unable to move, and then he recoiled from her as if a furnace door had been flung open in his face.

He flew past her and ran down the hall, bursting into empty rooms, calling his son's name, then he slipped down the stairwell, taking the steps three at a time, and the sound of his boots went along the hallway, into the drawing room, the dining room, the kitchen. Even in her distressed state

Emelia Cload noted how adroitly he moved through an unlighted house he did not know the lay of.

She returned to her bedroom and sat on the edge of the bed, closed her eyes as this trespasser roamed her main floor, listened as he came back up her stairs two at a time, as he went through drawers in her son's bedroom, pulled back sheets, and finally as, in vexed silence, he stood alone in that vacated bedroom.

She called out, "He didn't wait for you," and heard the sour triumph in her voice. "He left you too."

Then William Moreland fled out the same window the boy had. Went across the same roof, dropped to the same front lawn, disappeared into that same half-light. Father shadowing son, ridgerunners both.

MORELAND MOVED FAST through the sparse trees with the knapsack high on his back and knuckles white on the straps, his hunchbacked shadow legging it beside him as he made for a dark footpath that ran alongside the riverbank. In four minutes he was almost at the main street, so he scrambled down to the pebbled shore, where he startled an elk and her baby out of the water and up onto the lawn outside a closed banquet hall, their two heads high with alarm, their long legs loping. He trotted to a confused stop as he realized where he was, illuminated by the many gaslights of the ornamental bridge over the Bow River. A single female voice in the hall was singing "Ever Thine," as Moreland tumbled under the bridge into the shadows of the abutment, perfectly hidden in the little V of darkness that lay between the fans of light that fell either side of the bridge. He heard hooting from the cheap hotel far down the main street. The smell of cigar smoke from somewhere. A young laughing couple sprinted hand in hand on the same footpath he had run down, and they were pelting along as if outrunning a chaperone. The girl heard the singing voice and pulled on the boy's arm to slow him, saying, "Oh listen, it's beautiful!" Then they both came to a halt by the abutment, mouths open in angelic grins as they took in the sight of Moreland, hunched and spectral in the shadows. The boy shouted "Boo!" and they scampered up the incline and onto the main street, their laughter floating away as they crossed the bridge and moved away to the north.

Somehow he had fled to the centre of all foot traffic in Banff, and was now hiding under the only streetlamps alight in a town supposedly mourning war, a town economizing and rationing and dimming its lights in a fruitless show of solidarity with those other destroyed towns in Europe. Tonight the two urges of mourning and merriment were in a concerted war of wills, and for the moment light was winning.

The distant, beautiful voice was repeating a chorus of "you and me and we," and it rose above the gurgle of the river. A young woman's voice. It was likely, at this hour, to be a cleaner. She was alone in the building, enjoying the acoustics.

The elk and her calf walked back down to the shore and waded into the river up to the baby's knees and they sipped at the frigid water. For a moment they both lifted their heads, seeming to ponder the song, though of course they were not, for what was that sound to them? Moreland did listen to that voice. A pretty song late on a Friday night. When it came to its end, the voice paused, repeated a random line twice, as if practising, stopped mid-thought, and that was the end of it.

William Moreland was already bent over, and tears ran along the weathered contour of his nose, drip-dripping into the gravel. He'd met Mary Boulton when she was nineteen. The way she looked at him when she thought he couldn't see. The way she had once run straight at him and leapt onto his body in joy.

Suddenly, inexplicably, he couldn't reckon what day it was, what month. After so long following his plan, he didn't know what to do next.

He had entered town tonight with a grin on his face, a runner crossing a finish line. Ready to collect his son and finally rest. But Jack was missing and the nun was an utterly changed woman. He had detected no smell of alcohol on her, but there was no question that the once bright, determined woman, that fierce creature who had hovered over the boy in almost maternal defence, had somehow disintegrated. She knew where Jack was, but she would not tell him. William Moreland, who had lit four dynamite fuses this month without much concern as to the outcome, had had no idea how to negotiate those few moments of conversation with her, because Jack, the only thing in the world left to him, was on the other side of that exchange. He stood upright again and wiped away the tears, leaving a clean spot along his cheek. He took his bearings and started running again.

THE TALL DOORS OF Wilson's stable were already open and a lantern was alight in the office, unusual for this time of night. Moreland slipped inside and soft as an owl he called, "Thom?" He heard nothing at all.

By the end of his third check of the entire stable, Moreland was finally satisfied the Morgan was gone, so he ventured into the stockroom, where he looked up at the spot he and Wilson had mounted the little gun in its pink scabbard.

It was gone.

A great rush of joy flew up inside him then, for it meant Jack had left town on his own steam; he had retrieved his horse, collected his Christmas present, and made his way home. Thirteen or not, the boy knew exactly where home was. Moreland's begrimed face was all smile as he swiped the best tack in the place and trotted along the row of stalls until he found what he was looking for.

Kub was a powerful, hairy Welsh pony with a placid disposition. He slipped into her stall. The bridle was set for a full-size horse, so Moreland was obliged to fiddle with the straps, all the while glancing anxiously over the rough wall of the stall, watching the front doors. It was unlike Wilson to leave those doors open at night, and Moreland began to fear that perhaps someone was expected, a client, a drinking friend.

Anyone entering the establishment would wonder why a man in Moreland's condition — manifestly a vagrant — was saddling up a good horse while the proprietor was nowhere to be seen. Worse, a local might recognize Moreland and run to police saying they had spotted the Ridgerunner.

With that alarming thought, he urged himself on, trying to get the damned halter over Kub's ears while she bobbed her head and nosed out at him and just generally made the job harder. When finally done, he drew her out of the stall and trotted them both into the band of light falling from the office door. A lamp was lit but Wilson's chair was empty.

Absurdly, it struck him that the chair, it looked new. A new barometer had been mounted on the wall, held in place with a horseshoe nail. The old Hudson's Bay calendar had been replaced with a fresh one showing the right year and month. With a kind of dull surprise William Moreland took in the simple changes that had happened since he had last stood in this spot.

He faltered by Wilson's office door and was about to call out again when he heard the harsh rasp of someone vomiting out back, and a moment later Wilson came though the rear door looking angry and ghastly pale. Moreland made a little dry whistle with his bottom teeth and the outfitter froze.

What followed was a series of silent gestures from Wilson, pointing at his own head, flapping his arms, translating into

What is wrong with you, coming here?

No, you're not taking that horse . . . all right fine, take the horse.

Are you out of your mind, close the stable doors.

Moreland left the pony and sprinted over the sand and straw, shouldered one of the tall barn doors and slid it along its rail until it was closed. Wilson meanwhile stepped into his office and drew the lantern down until the flame was no brighter than a match.

Left to her own devices, Kub began to wander in the gloom, and together the two men gathered her to a stop, looking across the saddle at one another, each surprised at the ruinous state the other was in, but each unaware of his own. The outfitter was weak and strangely depressed, as if the two swallows of rich whiskey, so recently evacuated from his body, had told him something about life he didn't want to know. And Moreland was so dirty, desiccated, and worn, he looked like a primitive creature thawed out of the ice.

"Tell me you got it done," Wilson said, "Are you finished?"

Moreland nodded.

"Thank god."

"I got everything I planned to —"

"Don't tell me about it. I don't want to know."

"Jack was here?"

"Your kid lit out of town about three weeks ago. He's fine. You'll find him at home. Sampson's been playing nursemaid. You'd better thank the old man when you see him."

Slowly, the Ridgerunner's head lowered in profound relief and rested on the saddle.

Wilson said, "You are a crazy bastard, you know that? Tell me you're good and done with this stuff."

"I'm done," said Moreland, and he patted Kub's shoulder. "Can I borrow her?"

Wilson's nod was resigned. In an unconscious gesture of ownership, he cinched up the girth strap a little and ran his hand gently over the pony's muzzle. "You'll bring her back?"

"If I can. You know I will."

Wilson shook his head, cheeks green in the dim light. He said, "Middle of the night and everyone's visiting me. The Ridgerunner makes his grand appearance. And before you it was that nun, babbling about god knows what and plying me with whiskey."

Moreland's eyes narrowed. "What did she want?"

Wilson chuckled, truly enjoying the reply, "To convince me that I am a son of a bitch."

"I saw her, Thom, just now. I was looking for Jack. She wasn't herself."

Wilson's smile faded. "She's different."

"What's wrong with her?"

"I don't know what. But the kid made it worse. He dropped her hard and went off without a word of goodbye."

"But why? He was in a good spot, safe with her."

Wilson started to reply, but his voice dropped away as the sound of a heavy wagon approached outside on Caribou Street, the driver *gee-gee*ing at the horses, and the harsh squeak of the wheels. They waited to hear if the wagon would turn in to the outfitter's dirt yard, Moreland's mind working as usual to identify the quickest route out of the building. But the wagon slowly trundled past and made its way across the main street and kept going. Even Kub's ears followed the sound until it was gone.

Wilson stroked his chin. "William, you've been gone a while. She paraded around town telling everyone he was her son. Even changed his name. Everything you left for him, she dumped it on me like it was worthless, including the horse. She acted like you were dead."

Moreland said nothing, but at the news, his exhausted body quaked once as a massive shiver went up his spine.

"I did my best for the kid," Wilson sighed, "but she hates me, she was done with you, she had Jack, and that was that. He put up with it for as long as he could, I suppose."

The two men looked at one another across the saddle, and Moreland said, "I'm sorry. I didn't mean any of this to land on you."

Far away down Caribou they heard dogs barking from their porches. It sounded perfunctory, the kind of fanfare accorded to a neighbour walking past those front yards, at worst an elk, or a deer. Not the relentless, frantic howls you might hear when domestic dogs smell wolf on the air, or grizzly.

"Thom, you look sick."

"And you look like four sticks tied together."

They stood in the stable in the dark with nothing else to say.

Moreland saw that Wilson was wondering if he'd ever see either his old friend or his horse again; he was trying to camouflage his sadness. Moreland drew Kub away and headed for the back paddock.

"Hang on. There's something else. She's put up a reward. Two thousand dollars."

The Ridgerunner pondered this for a moment, and the news seemed to amuse him. "Good luck to them," he said and gathered up the reins. He walked the pony toward the back entrance. He said, "Good luck finding me."

"William?" Wilson said, and Moreland turned. "The money's not on you. It's on Jack."

→ Forty-Seven

WHEN JACK BOULTON woke it was to the smell of cigarette smoke. He was bleary and still in his clothes, and he felt like he'd been in the bed mere minutes. He hauled the boots onto his feet, and with that he was dressed. He opened the cabin door and stepped out into a kind of grey moonlight. There was no fire. A weird slant to the moonlight told him it was still long before midnight.

Sitting on Sampson's usual chair by the cold fire ring was a figure. It said, "Are you alone?"

The boy froze mid-step. A cigarette came up and a red spot flared by the man's mouth. Jack's eyes drifted to the other hand where a black service revolver hung, heavy and pointing down like a long finger, as if the metal was part of him.

"You don't live here all by yourself. That much I know. So where's the old man?"

Jack felt a ripple of shock go through him, and he knew in an instant the situation he was in. This was not Sampson, not his father finally come home. It was his own photo on a poster, come to call. It was two thousand dollars. This stranger was the real reason the Morgan had stared so long at the cabin, the reason the place had smelled of sweat, the reason the dry bread was missing. This man had found the cabin, seen in its interior signs of the presence of multiple people, and withdrawn until he could be sure Jack was alone. He'd probably watched Jack come home, watched as he had settled the horse, entered the cabin alone, and he'd waited while Jack slept, until he was sure no one else was coming.

The red cigarette ember flared long and then bounced as it was hard-flicked into the fire ring.

With his unslept mind Jack Boulton began to make hopeless calculations. He could just hop backward and shut the door. But how then to keep the door closed? Would he even have time to do such a thing before this stranger could sprint the distance between them? There was no lock, so he would have to bar it with his own body. Could he withstand the man's weight? How then to defend himself once the man got through the door. And there was the Morgan, standing in its corral, gazing at the stranger with its large, pretty face. Jack had a vulnerable horse out there in the corral, no way to protect it, or himself. He might hold out for a while. But if this man wanted in, sooner or later, he was coming in.

"How old are you?" said the man. "I can't even tell." And then he stood up.

Jack Boulton just watched him come.

The man seized him by the back of his collar and heaved him right off the ground. "Anyone home?" he shouted at the open door, then waited and listened for a moment as the kid hung by the neck and twisted in midair. Then he went through it, holding his hostage like a cat by its scruff. Jack was dancing along the floorboards on tiptoes now, wincing, trying to claw the shirtcollar off his windpipe. He felt himself hurled onto the bed, where he rolled and scrambled and righted himself in the mess of blankets.

The man kicked the door closed and there was a long silence during which Jack didn't even breathe. He was alone in the dark with this stranger, his senses following the man's movements. The room was black air with something blacker moving through it.

He had a limp, and Jack followed those uneven steps, the strange wet breathing. The sound of a chair being moved and sat upon. There was a *clink* that sounded like the handle of the storm lantern. A sweet alcoholic reek on the air; this man smelled like an old fruit barrel. The sound of Pearl sliding softly across the table, then nothing but a dull rustling sound as of someone rooting around in his pockets.

Jack glanced at the door. He looked at the shape sitting at the table and wondered if he could sprint to it before the man could reach him. Then there came the flare of a match and the guard named Parker hung there in its light.

Other trackers were looking for him, surely, but Jack himself had given the guard an unexpected advantage when he and Sampson had ridden right under his eyes that day out on the road. Parker bent now over the wick on the lantern and lit it and cranked the wick up to bring more light, and then shut the glass. The boy saw the revolver lying on the table, a dull thing next to Pearl's soft felt. Parker watched the match burn down and then blew it out.

"Do you know why I'm here?"

"No."

"He says no. Want to try again? Why am I here?"

Jack said nothing

"Your mother wants you back."

"My *mother*?" In that moment, Jack thought the man was insane.

"She misses you."

"I have no idea what you are talking —"

"Who is that in the bed with you?"

The boy just blinked.

"You," said Parker. "What's your name?"

Jack's voice rose to an impotent squeak, "There's no one else here!" and immediately regretted those words, for they were horribly true and saying them felt like bad luck.

The guard's long sigh slid into a laugh as he passed a hand over his face. "You know what? I am drunker than shit." With a nod, he lifted a pint bottle from the depths of his coat pocket and pushed it to the far side of the table, away from himself. "Okay, string bean, let's take a look at you."

Parker lifted the lantern and swung it toward the bed. Jack Boulton's miserable face blew into view. He was fully clothed, with a livid streak round his throat, and there was a look of furious insolence in his eyes. He tried to maintain a staring match with the older man, but it was difficult, given the blare of the gas flame.

"You don't look like much," Parker said. He put the lantern on the table.

"Don't take me back," said Jack.

"Like it or not."

"I'll just run away again."

"That's her problem. As soon as your little ass goes through her door, I get paid."

"I can pay you!" Jack said. "I'll pay you."

"Sure."

"Same money as she promised. Two thousand dollars."

"That so?"

"Yes. Yes, goddamn it! I have the money."

"Well, fancy that." Parker's voice was level, but a wild, almost half-witted grin had spread across his face. The boy was too young to know what was coming, he couldn't read such a change in a man, but this was the crooked smile of the barroom drunk about to start a brawl. There was a kind of cracked joy in it.

Without preamble the guard stood and swung a hard right at Jack's face and poleaxed him into the mattress. He stood over the half-conscious kid and watched him wallow on his back, the long limbs slewing in the blankets, like a lazy swimmer. "You lying little shit," he said, and lifted a boot and began to stamp at his victim's belly and groin until Jack rolled screaming into a ball. Parker stopped stamping only when his balance began to fail. He bent over with hands on his knees, panting.

For a long moment they stayed like that, the boy weeping so hard it was almost noiseless, the man's fermented breath going in and out. No other sound, no movement except the hiss of flame in the lantern's chimney. Jack Boulton pressed his hands to his pouring eyes. Everything hurt so much his limbs felt numb and icy. But still, he was raging inside himself, willing his body to spring up, to push the guard over, to somehow get past him, make for the door, run for the trees.

Parker sniffed once, then he seized the child by the hair and held him up so they were face to face. He was awful up close. Those black, pupil-less eyes. But when he spoke it was in a measured tone. "I'm taking you home," he said. "I'm getting my money. You are not to trouble me. Understand?"

A thin, wordless whine came out of the boy. The hair was tearing out of his scalp and he was obliged to clasp himself against the guard's fist.

Parker slapped him so hard that a thin rill of blood trickled from his nostril. "I'm speaking to you," he said.

Jack heard his own feeble voice say, "Go fuck yourself."

The man just snorted, dropped his victim onto the bed.

Jack Boulton tucked his chin down to hide his tear-streaked face. He gathered the blankets into a ball against his belly and breathed into them. After a moment his teeth began to chatter.

Parker went back to the table, where he reached for the booze and wiggled out the stopper with his thumb. He held the bottle on his knee for a long moment, considering the boy with that flat gaze, and then he raised the bottle in a toast to nothing in particular, and drank.

→ Forty-Eight

AT MIDNIGHT A STORM moved silently to the north. Jack lay curled on his side and stared through the cabin's only window, watching the lightning flash and fade on the aspen trunks outside. Each square of frantic light blanked his vision, then the image of a window full of trees degraded slowly so they looked at first like sticks, then straw, then grass, then threads. As darkness suffused his vision again he imagined whorls and lassoes of blue light pacing the world out there. To his addled mind this was his mother coming to find him, and it seemed sad to Jack that her brightness would travel such great distances only to flash and disappear. Time measured out in stabs of light and hope. He remembered that lightning brought thunder, but it never seemed to come . . . or perhaps there was something wrong with his hearing. Jack opened and closed his jaws. He heard a grinding sound, like brick on brick. His tongue explored his loose teeth.

The houseguest was pacing. Sometimes, when Jack opened his eyes, Parker's long coat was just swinging by. Against that dun material he saw the man's loose fist. Somewhere in the boy's knowing, far down a tunnel full of cotton wadding, there came the barks of a man cursing, slurred self-pity and self-comfort. Parker was in conversation with himself or with some invisible other, deep into a confused interrogation of his own cowardice and greed and martyrdom. *You*, the word kept coming, *you*, but it was himself he was talking to. The guard's footfalls reverberated through the floor, and each time he approached the bed, Jack Boulton's breath stopped and his heart winced in his chest. Parker was talking now about his own father it seemed, a churchgoing liar, a lecher who ruined his good wife's health and broke his children's bones, groaning at what a unique torture it was for any son to be lashed to such a man. As helpless as livestock, children have no choice in the cut of their keepers.

For a brief, crazed moment the boy understood Parker fully and he felt a galling wad of pity ball up in his throat, as if he were about to weep for this bastard, his new keeper. But soon the guard shut up and simply paced the cabin, and in the slowing rhythm of his steps, Jack realized he was walking to keep himself awake.

Jack Boulton stared into the murk that had once been his own home, that was now something else entirely, and he waited, counting each time the mud-coloured coat swung by. An hour passed like this, and it took almost another before the guard wore down like a failing metronome.

FOUR HOURS LATER PARKER was sitting on the floor with his back against the door, legs crossed and his head hanging. He had positioned himself there to keep the door shut and bar the only exit, and then he'd drifted into sleep. The man looked for all the world like a monk in prayer.

On the floor by the guard's hip lay both guns on their sides, so close at hand that his knee touched the rifle. Jack's mind leapt into a frightful, hammering awareness of the service revolver, only inches away from the man's thigh. It was the only loaded gun in the room.

If Jack could somehow make his way there and crouch over the guard . . . reach out and take the revolver.

But if the guard woke before he got to the gun? Parker had administered a grown man's beating to a slim thirteen-year-old boy, and with every blow, Jack's lesson had become increasingly clear: this man could kill him so easily he might even do it by mistake.

Jack peeled his cheek from a pillow crusted with blood and raised his head enough to look about the room. He gritted his loose teeth and rolled onto his back. It was a vain attempt to lie flat and then maybe sit up, but fiery ropes of damaged muscle burned down his belly and into his balls, so he curled up again like a squirrel. *Do not pant. Do not make a sound.* There he lay, gazing at the sleeper, the man's soft hair fallen over his forehead, the hands open in the bowl of his legs. Jack pressed a palm into the bedclothes and slowly levered himself up onto his knees, his mind assessing the muscles that worked and those that didn't.

It took him many long minutes to get to his feet. It took another two to make his way to the sleeping guard, bent almost double and holding his breath. When he was finally within the man's reach Jack's mind ceased to be his own and he cringed like a cat, watching that face, those closed eyes, unaware of anything except the opponent before him, until the cold weight of metal in his palm told him that somehow he had reached out and taken the revolver. It was in his hand, the gun was his. Now in retreat, he placed his boots with deliberation on each floorboard that he knew would not creak, like a boy stepping on riverstones to cross a stream.

As he made his way to the ladder that led to the loft, Jack felt a twinkle of ice go up his back. This was a test, the guard was toying with him, playing a trick, and when he whirled round, the man would be grinning, rising from the floor. But no, Parker was still resting against the door, slack and placid and dreaming. Jack Boulton made his way to the ladder leading to the loft. He tucked his shirt into the waistband of his pants and dropped the cold pistol into the gunnysack of his clothes, and thus, two-handed, he climbed into the loft where he legged his way painfully over a trunk and sighed into the shadows behind it. Careful to retrieve the gun from his clothing without knocking it against wood or making the least sound in the still cabin. Even in that feeble light he could see the dull yellow crescents of live rounds in the cylinder.

He trained the barrel on the top of the ladder, right between the rails, right where a man's face would appear. He was a boy at a shooting gallery; one where they use live ammunition, the one at the edge of the world.

✦ Forty-Nine

JACK'S HEAD SNAPPED up. It had been only a few seconds, surely. It could only have been for a moment that his head had sunk to his chest and his smarting eyes had closed, a fraction of a moment, until he had heard his mother calling him, waking him for breakfast.

But now a feeble blue sunrise was working the edges of the windowframe. In that deep and quiet place through which he had been sinking — a fishing lure drawn by its own tiny weight, down, down, to float just above the pebbled bottom only to be yanked back up—in that peaceful space — he had felt a thud through the floor of the loft.

As quietly as possible, with great attention to the hard soles of his boots against the wood, he inclined himself forward and up and peered over the trunk, down to the cabin below. Parker was exactly as Jack had left him, in repose. And then it came again, the sensation of a thud that he felt in his feet and legs, and clearly, the guard's body rocked a little, rocked again.

Parker's eyes opened.

In the first moment of real fear in his life, Jack thought: *He'll kill me. He'll beat me to death.* Jack was bloodless with terror; his icy finger was actually on the trigger, stiff and hooked, and every muscle in his body was shaking. His mind whispered: *If he climbs up here to the loft I should shoot him, if he even starts up the ladder I must shoot him, if he rises from the floor I will shoot him, if he stands up, if he looks at me, shoot him,* and his mind went on, narrowing down to a hard point, until there was no option except to kill Parker.

But the guard was not rising. He did not look at the bed or otherwise seem to know where Jack was, he seemed instead to be looking at his own legs and wondering how he had arrived where he was. This was just the dumb calm of a man still mostly asleep. The eyelids blinked themselves back down and he was gone again.

Jack eased the cold fishhook of his index finger out of the trigger guard and placed it in his own mouth to warm it. Slowly the tendons unsprung like cold wires.

Through the cotton stuffing of his hearing there came the sound of a voice. Definitely he had heard a voice. Then came three thunderous thuds on the door. The first rocked Parker; the second pushed him forward over his legs; and the final one flung him, Pearl, and what little was left of the pint bottle of booze across the floor and deep into the room.

William Moreland stepped into his home for the first time in many months. Thin of body, sunken of cheek, and recognizable only to his son under the beard and hair. He wore a silly grin on his face, his mouth working on homecoming greetings, a lame jest about being away only a day or so, words that froze in his mouth as he gazed down at what had barred his way. Not his son or some oddment of junk, but a stranger. A man in uniform, a man now rising from the floor with an expression of white-lipped outrage, pawing at Pearl where the rifle lay at his feet.

Jack was now clambering over the trunk shrieking, and

both men looked up in surprise. Moreland saw his son there, looming above them with a revolver in his hand. He saw the mottling of bruises already beginning to variegate the kid's face, lips swollen and split.

"Oh no you don't," said Parker. "I got here first." He was taking the rifle out of the scabbard.

Moreland said, "Son, what happened to you?"

"Run," said Jack.

Parker grinned. "Go on now, do as you're told."

Instead Moreland removed the knapsack and laid it gently on the ground. His palms forward in a gesture that said *wait*, he started to insinuate himself to the guard's right, hoping to pass him and make it as far as the ladder at the back of the room.

"Stop," Parker said.

"All right, yes, but I just have to —"

"I've already had it with you," Parker said. "Now get your ass back out that door."

"Look," said Moreland, "I want to check on the boy. Will you let me?"

Parker was woozy and red-eyed, but there was no question of his resolve. He said, "Get *out*."

"There's no need for any of this," said Moreland, still moving. "I won't give you any trouble."

"You're right about that," said the guard, and he pushed the twin barrels into the Ridgerunner's belly and pulled the trigger.

A tidy *click*, nothing more. Parker looked down at the gun in his hands in consternation until he realized it was lever action; but as often as he levered, the hammer came down on air.

The two men stood there, each staring at the other. Parker was merely angry, but Moreland had just watched a man decide to kill him. In his long career as a petty thief, a gun had been pointed at him in earnest only four times, by guards or police or detectives, and while there was always the notion that they might have shot him if he'd tried to run, he never had. The weapons were mostly an inducement to obey a request, to go back into his cell, to stay still while someone handcuffed him to a non-portable object. A gun was a polite communication between the law and the lawbreaker. So this was no policeman. This man had tried to discharge a sawn-off rifle directly into Moreland's guts.

For his part, Parker was trying to figure if the rifle had always been unloaded or if the kid had somehow managed to do that quietly while he slept. Further, he began to understand that the boy had stood over him holding his own loaded revolver, and yet, with every opportunity to kill him, the kid had done nothing but crawl away and hide. Parker swung around now and glared up at the loft. "Drop it down here," he said.

"No."

"Toss that gun or I'll come get it."

Moreland nodded vaguely, as if he understood, but indeed he did not. He was still in the humming, unreal space that comes after a shock. He could only look at the face of the stranger who had killed him, for in his mind he was in two places, here and already gone.

Moreland reached out as if to test that this man was real, this shadow in uniform. He said, "Who are you?"

Parker seized the short barrel of the rifle and swung the wooden stock at Moreland's head. It made contact with a dull thud even Jack could hear.

Jack shrieked.

Moreland staggered back several steps until he was tottering on the threshold, his knees quaking visibly under him and a look on his face that said the lights were already going out. Parker waded across the floor toward him and swung again. But his victim was now badly off balance and stumbling outside, so the butt of the rifle swept past his face. Jack watched as Parker filled the doorway and brought the gunstock down like an axe. Like a man chopping wood.

Something inside Jack broke open, a void into which he fell, and kept falling, and so he fired at Parker's back. The gun was loud. It bucked and pounded every bone in his arm up to the shoulder, but still his thumbs worked the stiff hammer, and he pulled the trigger again. He kept firing through half-closed eyes, with no accuracy, fired through his own gunsmoke, aiming at what now seemed only a brownish man-shaped blur framed by the door. One bullet panged off the stove, another blew into the wall above the bed and spat out a great splinter the size of a man's thumb. Jack heard a sound like a dog whining, but it was his own voice; he was keening. In seconds the bullets were gone, and with nothing left to protect his father, Jack wound up and pitched the gun at Parker's back, but by then the doorway was empty and the guard was no longer visible. The empty revolver whumped the floorboards and skittered out the door into the dirt.

It was a protracted and painful climb down the ladder and a slow hobble across the floor, but when Jack Boulton finally stepped out into the clearing he saw two men reclining near the chopping block. They were about two feet apart, as if they had lain down together to sleep in the dirt and pine needles and wood chips, Parker face down, Moreland face up. Both were spattered with blood, and neither was moving.

With infinite care Jack knelt beside his father and lay his damaged ear against his shirtfront. He heard no sound, nothing at all, not even when he had clawed open the shirt and pressed his ear to his father's warm skin. No sound, no heartbeat, nothing. And finally Jack became aware that the chest on which his head rested was rising and subsiding.

The regular breath of a sleeping man.

Even in that dim light he could see a gentle throb in Moreland's throat, the heart at work. With difficulty Jack Boulton slid onto his side and lay beside his father in the dirt. He rested his head on the man's shoulder. With no other notion of what to do, Jack could think only of this: to lie next to his father and hold him, speak into his ear, call him back to his life.

There they lay entwined together on the cold ground as they had so many times before, when Moreland had come home from a long ramble, and the boy had flown at him in a perfect mix of adoration and resentment, joy and hurt, and they had wrestled while Mary hovered and told them to stop it, until finally the father did what he always did: pretended to be overcome by the child's superior strength and let Jack topple him into the dirt, the winner.

→ *Fifty*

THE RIDGERUNNER LAY THERE, eyes open, pondering a sensation in his jaw that told him there might be a knife embedded in it, or a heavy nail hammered into the bone just below his canine tooth. Something very wrong with the jaw. For a moment he considered lifting his hand to touch it, but then let that idea float away inside him.

One thing was certain: if he sat up, it would hurt even worse, and that mustn't happen. Leave the knife where it is. Obedient to this inner imperative he lay perfectly still, attending to the rhythmic ache in his jaw, the ringing in his ears, and somewhere close by, the sound of sobbing.

Pines, lots of them, crowding the periphery of his vision, lodgepole mostly, a single black spruce at ten o'clock. They seemed to lean over him, a bristle of soft green tips in an almost perfect circle, the way an iris surrounds a pupil. Something familiar in the exact arrangement of those trees, something that spoke of home. He'd seen this place before. And then Jack's battered face floated into view, hovering over him.

Moreland tried to rise but with that movement came the pain, the imagined knife twisting, just as he knew it would. Gently, he settled back and lay still.

The jaw was broken, no question.

Had he fallen?

Unwilling to get up, or roll over, or even to smile, Moreland simply lay still, looking up at his weeping son. All he could do was draw Jack's head down until it rested on his chest. All those times previous when he had conjured this moment in his imagination in order to calm himself, to focus, the scene hadn't been real. But now he felt Jack's warm breath on his throat, felt the child's fingers cradling the back of his neck, sensed cold seeping into his spine from the ground. Those friendly pines above; he was outside his own cabin. But when he slid his eyes to the right he saw a figure beside him lying face down.

The boy was kneeling over him now, saying, "Get up. We have to go."

Moreland's fingers touched his son's face. "Wha-happen?"

"The bastard hit you is what happened. And he kept on hitting you . . ." Jack's face crumpled as he sobbed. "So I shot him."

Moreland made a bark of alarm and his limbs began to thrash. With thunder rolling inside his skull, he struggled until, at length, he was standing approximately upright, his boots braced wide, his reedy son trying to hold him vertical, the earth seeming to heave under him.

There on the ground lay a man in uniform. A stranger at his home was bad news, but a stranger in uniform was an emergency.

After more than a decade in this safe place, Mary's crippling terror of strangers had lessened, but it never fully disappeared. It had taken Moreland years of work and planning to create a place where she felt incrementally safer. This scene would have sent her flying.

In the pine needles by the stranger's right boot lay that ugly rifle Moreland himself had picked up in Whitefish, Montana, and alongside that lay a powerful handgun. It looked like a standard-issue officer's revolver. Moreland had no memory of this man hitting him, nor of gunshots, nothing after that moment of confusion as he had tried to get through his own front door. He could not account for any of this.

Jack was trying gently to push his father toward the corral and the horses. "We have to get away from him."

"Wait," said Moreland, for he wasn't even sure his legs would work, and Jack waited, arms around his father's thin waist.

Above them, the blue light of early morning reached across a sky now cloudless and high; a day of unearthly calm was breaking over their disaster. Parker lay as if he were in bed, cheek resting on his hand. A lock of hair waved gently in the breeze, his eyes were open a crack, and he was still breathing. But he was grey-faced. He wore puttees that went from mid-calf down over the tops of his worn-out boots. The faded coat was long and heavy, the seam down the middle of the coatback was split, and the padding showed through. There was a small hole to the left of that seam, a tidy, unremarkable round puncture the diameter of a man's thumb, just left of the spine.

"Oh god, oh god," Jack whispered. "What if he wakes up?"

But this man would never wake again. Like any miner and logger his age, Moreland had seen plenty of dead and dying men, thanks to unstable dynamite, mismanaged treefalls, whipping chains and metal ropes, skidding mine carts loaded with rock; a roll of barbed wire that sprang loose and writhed like a scalded snake, raking the faces and chests and throats of anyone standing nearby; rearing horses using their hooves as weapons; and spooked herds of cattle two hundred strong bearing down on men afoot. And one mine elevator full of workers that broke its chains and plunged into the black. The long metal screech of its fall, and later, the rhythmic creak of the rope as men hauled the cage back up, dripping and swinging gently in the shaft, until finally its horrifying contents rose into the light.

In all of that, men were often left to nurse each other with few supplies and little wisdom except superstition and misremembered motherly advice. So the Ridgerunner had seen men like this one, lingering on the verge of life, not yet gone, but going. The lungs still working, eyes open a crack, seeing nothing.

The guard was on his way out and Moreland knew it. His son must not see it happen.

In Jack's mind, however, the guard was still fully viable, a potent threat, a man who could shake off the shock at any moment and get to his feet. Jack was desperate to bring Moreland to the corral, to somehow get his unsteady father mounted, and ride him away to safety. They must at all costs flee the guard who had beaten them both so badly — for to be struck by a man as strong as Parker also offered a world of information.

Moreland worked his jaw and felt a miserable grinding, but most of it worked. He'd sustained plenty of injuries in his life, and he knew approximately what a broken jaw meant. Things could be worse. The earth had stopped rolling in waves under his feet, and he felt almost stable. He took Jack by the shoulders and staggered with him up the front steps and inside, away from the only trespasser the cabin had ever seen, through the acrid stink of gunsmoke and the lingering whiff of booze, into a home now alien to them both. Moreland looked about the room and saw the marks of bullets almost everywhere. The kid had shot at everything in the room; it was a miracle he'd hit the guard and not Moreland himself.

"All right," he said, "who is that man?"

"I don't know. A prison guard."

"Is there anyone else here?"

"No. It was just him and me."

"Oh Jack, look what he did to you."

"I'm fine."

"The hell you are. How in the world did he find you?"

"I went right past him. Me and Sampson, on the road one day. Prisoners were doing road work. You know where we fish trout?"

Moreland nodded.

The boy could not take his eyes away from the sleeping man outside. He said, "I guess he saw the posters, and figured it out."

"Were there other guards?"

Jack swung on him in a panic. "Yes, Dad! Yes! There were lots of guards. We have to go now."

"Settle down, there's no need," Moreland sighed. "He won't wake up."

The boy seemed to drift sideways a bit, and he put a hand on the wall to steady himself, his palm next to a bullet hole, a deep welt in the wood above the family bed. Jack sat on the side of the bed, put his swollen face in his hands, and whispered, "Have I killed him?"

"You didn't kill anyone. That bullet went off the stove first and then into him."

"It's the same thing."

"Oh hell," Moreland said gently, "if it's the same thing then the stove is a murderer," and he reached out and shut the door on Parker. Then, for the first time in many months, he sat on the bed beside his son, put his arm around the boy, and felt the difference in that familiar body. The shuddering shoulder he held was wider than expected, the muscle firm and round, like a baseball in his grip.

Mary saying, *Oh Jack, why can't you stay a child just a little longer?*

There Moreland sat, in quiet self-counsel, in silent planning, for even in his woozy state, he knew they would have to decamp, and soon. The boy was right. There was no choice but to leave.

He looked around him at a home he had built himself, log by log, joint by joint. Mary had cleaned some of the logs herself, huge of belly, working gamely with a hammer and wedge, peeling the summer bark away. At night they would sigh into the little tent together and curl up, and he would snore and she would elbow him.

Jack straightened and wiped his nose. He looked at his father with alarm, for the man's fingers were beginning to dig into his shoulder. "What?" he said.

Moreland said something the boy couldn't hear.

With the bellow of the temporarily deaf, Jack said, "What are you —"

Moreland's hand slid across his mouth, and he leaned into Jack's ear and whispered, "Someone's coming."

➤ Fifty-One

THE PREVIOUS EVENING, Sampson Beaver had retired to bed and, for the first time in months, slept until the sun was already over the peaks and Willow was pacing around in her corral, unsettled by the late start. He had sat up, unsure what day it was, and swung his legs off the bed, hair standing up in cowlicks all over his head. The grizzly blanket slid off him to the floor and lay there like a rug, ready to warm his feet. The old man blinked and yawned and scratched himself, trying to recollect his dreams, but he could not recall a single one. It seemed the world had no warnings for him at present.

In long johns, boots, and a hat he walked out to the corral with cabin-temperature water and a plate of dried oats, and at the sight of him the horse relaxed considerably, slid her nose into the zinc bucket and sucked water. Then he offered her the pan of oats and listened to the leisured grinding of that long horse jaw. He let her eat a little more of the treat than usual, leaning on the fence rungs as she chewed, his eyes raised to the clear blue sky.

BY THE TIME he was within shouting distance of the boy's cabin, carrying breakfast in his panniers as usual, he was merry and well-slept, and relating to the horse an overlong tale of his first failed attempt to woo a woman. But the horse began to show signs of tension. She bobbed her head and sidled sideways as they approached the cabin, and Sampson's voice trailed away as he spotted a figure lying face down in the dirt directly outside the boy's door.

Now vividly awake, Sampson slid his long Winchester out, lay it across his thighs, and assessed what he was seeing. The man was white, he did not seem aware of Sampson, and he was not moving. He wore a long khaki coat and puttees, had light hair, an ashen face, and looked dead. With a start, Sampson recognized the guard they had passed on the road that day weeks ago. Parker.

The old man's eyes slid to the cabin door, but it was firmly closed. He saw the boy's little rifle lying in the dirt, and another dark shape by the man's side that he adjudged to be a service revolver. Sampson lay his hand over his own rifle's workings to muffle it as he thumbed back the hammer, then he slid off the horse, ducked under her chin, and waited. For three long minutes he stood motionless, holding Willow's reins with his left hand, the rifle with his right. Dead leaves danced across the wide clearing and fetched up against the guard's face. In the corral, the Morgan was grazing and apparently unconcerned. At some distance behind it another horse was wandering up the slope. Either the guard had ridden up here on that other horse, or someone else was here too.

Inside the cabin, there was a scuffle and hushed voices, an argument was happening in there, and from this fact Sampson understood that his presence was known. Without time to lead the horse out of harm's way, he swatted her with the reins until she hopped in surprise and trotted back down the path they had just come up. He didn't even watch her go; his eyes were on the cabin door because it was opening.

Jack Boulton ran out calling Sampson's name. He was gesticulating at the guard, and he was weeping. He'd been beaten and his face was blue and purple.

The old man called, "Hûji," gesturing to the boy to run and stand behind him.

Jack seemed not to hear, but instead gazed at the man lying on the ground, and meanwhile, someone else was coming to the door.

Sampson roared, "Hûji ya îjas!"

Jack's hand came to his throat and he looked up at Sampson in a kind of dumb shock, but couldn't move.

And so it was that when William Moreland staggered woozily from the cabin's door, filthy and bearded and reaching for the boy, Sampson almost shot him.

→ *Fifty-Two*

SHE ROSE FROM THE BED on which she had simply lain, above the coverlet, waiting for another night to end, another day to start. With sore back and burning eyes she stood by the window and watched the bland comings and goings of neighbours, doors opening then closing on the cold morning, children pretending not to hear their mothers calling them in for breakfast. A wash of light in the sky, deep shadows in the lee of each house. She could see clear to the main street with its wall of low buildings, and the mountains all peaked with snow. The pharmacist hustling along the sidewalk; she did not know or care what the time was, but something in his gait suggested he was late opening his shop. A single black automobile was parked poorly and too close to the intersection, its windscreen a glaring rectangle of reflected sunrise. And there, beyond that car, standing on the street outside the tobacconist's door, hands on hips, waiting for the establishment to open, was Thom Wilson. Her mouth fell open.

She had not miscalculated the dose, of that she was certain. And he was not some charmed immortal, immune to poison. And yet there he was, impatiently waiting to buy cigars.

Saved.

The single word came to her, and it was of herself she was thinking. If the police were not already at her door, then he had no idea what she'd done to him. Somehow Thom Wilson had survived, and she had been reprieved of that murder.

But there was a stain on her soul. She knew that. She had a conscience in working order, and it was labouring under the burden of her own history. She'd poisoned two suitors who had lost interest in her despite her father's great wealth; her own Mother Superior; three very ill patients at the sanitarium whose prolonged death agonies had begun to grate on everyone until Sister Beatrice had quietly made it stop; and, but for a twist of fate, Thom Wilson. All of these had come as a result of sober thought, planning, a consideration of the aftermath, and the proper dispensing of an appropriate drug. But in one case, she had simply struck out in pain, without planning or thought.

Mary Boulton had been alive and sitting downstairs in the kitchen as usual. The child beside her, eating from a dessert bowl. Mary, in a rare moment of self-exposure, saying, "I used to feel swept along by life. Powerless. But of course we are powerless, all of us."

Emelia Cload, who never felt swept along, had looked at her guest and ventured, "I suppose."

"Women feel it, especially. Perhaps men do, too. I sometimes think we are just the same as them."

"*That* is debatable."

Mary had been sitting upright in the chair with that admirable posture of hers, wearing her doeskin trousers and the long jacket. She was saying, "I would have loved a baby girl, but I know what a woman's life can be. Even if she has money, as soon as she marries it isn't hers anymore, or won't stay being hers for long. The wrong man can ruin you utterly, impoverish you, humiliate —" her voice snapped off, and the nun had seen a brief flash of ferocity cross the woman's face. Mary had swallowed and continued, "And there isn't a single thing you can do about it. I'm sure you understand what I mean."

"Perfectly."

Oh yes, she understood. Emelia Cload, only child of James Cload, banker, millionaire, serial adulterer, ruthless and dissipated old sinner, who had died at the hands of his second wife. To his wilful daughter he had left a bequest, eight thousand dollars, an insult, a crumb fallen from the great bank that bore his name. Very deliberately he had also left her this old house, the home she had abandoned, far too large to sell during wartime and a burden to maintain. It was a clear and final statement of his contempt. To his wife he had left ownership of a bank with ten million in holdings. Stewardship of the company was resting on the shoulders of a woman who knew nothing whatever about finance. Various managers would support her, surely, to protect their own skins, but the truth was the entire enterprise had been secretly on the verge of insolvency and could only last until that fact was forced to light by the directors. Sooner or later the wife would be ruined, back where she had started. Indeed, Mary was right. The money wouldn't be hers for long.

In life, money is just money — a tool you use to solve problems, and few problems don't go away if you throw enough money at them. But in death it is a message, the last word, it tells you exactly where you stood, whether you were held dear, and sometimes the message is: *This is how much I hated you*. These had been her thoughts, dark, old, resentful, while she watched the boy clink his spoon in the bowl of apple crisp and sip at the cream. And then a question had come to her, "Mary, are you referring to your husband, whoever he is? Has he mistreated you?"

"No," she said quietly. "Another one. No longer alive."

The reference to a past husband was so veiled the boy took no notice, but kept hard at his dessert. And it was a common enough story, during wartime or in peace. People died of violence, they died at work, they succumbed to TB, apoplexy, cancer, old age, accident, they died in childbirth, or of a simple infected cut. And now with this war, there were young widows everywhere. "It is not easy," Emelia had sighed. "Any of it."

Mary had looked at her for a long time. "No, it isn't. But it's not impossible, either. I used to believe all I could do was struggle along. I felt as if terrible things just happened — to me, to everyone."

The nun nodded vacantly.

"I don't feel that way anymore." Mary reached out and stroked the boy's forelock as he ate his treat. "I feel better about everything." And then, smiling, she said, "Which is very strange. I really should feel worse."

"Goodness, Mary, why should you?"

"Because now I have something worth worrying about. All these things I used to care about seem like nothing now."

They both looked at Jack then in silence, their separate minds running parallel to each other, the mother and the childless woman, both in earnest regard of the same beautiful boy, imagining the unimaginable, that he might someday vanish from their lives.

"Well," said Mary, "thank goodness you'll never have that worry, never be a mother."

"Oh, you never know," said the nun. The words had simply popped out of her. It was ludicrous at her age, fifty-eight, but in that moment, looking at the boy, she had imagined him as her own.

"What a funny idea. You're a sister of the cloth." Mary's eyes settled briefly on the nun's pale, ashamed face and then drifted away. "No," she said soberly, "motherhood is not for you."

Mary Boulton missed the spasm of pain that ran across the nun's features. She did not see those eyes fall to the clean wood of the kitchen table and stare unblinking into its grain. The rest of that visit Mary failed to note the change in her benefactor's demeanour. And in any case, what happened next would have been so far from her expectations of that kindly, godly woman, that even in her most vigilant state she would not have seen it coming. This had always been Emelia Cload's greatest camouflage: no one knew her heart.

So the nun had risen from her seat, taken up Mary's empty coffee cup, and carried it to the counter. The boy leaned his long forearms on the table, elbows out, in the full knowledge this was bad table manners, and grinned at his mother, who shot him a gentle warning look: *Not in front of her, please.* The nun watched them, already tinkling a spoon round in Mary's cup, stirring in the tasteless poison. It had been almost involuntary on her part, a reversion to some deep instinct, the way one slaps and kills the stinging wasp. She set the cup down at Mary's elbow, the black and now slightly muddy liquid in a slowly spinning vortex within the cup. She could have taken it back, snatched it up and hurried it to the sink, poured it out. But she did not. Instead she watched as Mary lifted it to her lips and drank, and Emelia Cload had felt a stab of grief.

"Can I have some?" said the boy, and he was already reaching for the cup.

But the nun's hand came down over the rim. "Coffee is not for children." She had managed to give both of her guests, each in turn, what she hoped was a stern look before she hurried away to hide her face, saying as she went that she needed to find her handbag to pay Mary for the new tailored goods.

She remembered huddling in that cupboard, already holding the money and yet, needing to calm herself, she had pretended to keep rooting amongst the coats. And slowly, unbidden, there came a presage of loneliness. Solitude that would be permanent and without remedy.

She had only left the boy unattended for a minute, perhaps less, but somehow, during that time, Mary had allowed him a sip or two of coffee, before she drank the rest.

Looking now at those empty chairs in the silent kitchen, she saw the boy's hands reaching out for the cup, saw Mary whispering to her son — what would she have said? *Do it quickly* or *Don't let her see*? Emelia saw herself being disobeyed and misled.

Was that Mary's fault, Mary's doing? It had been Mary who disobeyed the house rule, Mary who had set things in motion.

I felt as if terrible things just happened — to me, to everyone.

No, it was not Mary's fault. Emelia Cload was not so far gone as to believe that. No tincture, powder, or emetic could blot out that truth. Emelia could sit all day in pious mediation of the spinning torsion pendulum of a clock and thereby contemplate the nauseating repetition of her own sins and God's assumed forgiveness of them, but it didn't change the plain fact she'd murdered a friend. Through strength of will, Emelia Cload had somehow fought her way through the wretched aftermath, and got exactly what she'd long wanted. That boy. Not just any child, but him.

It came back to her then. The words *motherhood is not for you*. Words she'd taken at first as shocking insult, a hurt so deep it could only be answered with another hurt. But at this moment, she heard Mary again, that soft voice and the firmness of her tone, and she knew it now to be a prophesy. The feast will be ash and dust in your mouth.

She rose now from her seat at a table that surely would never see another family breakfast. She and the house were nearing the end of things.

Emelia walked to the kitchen window now to look out at the sparkle of the river under the moon, and in that moment she remembered the exact feeling of the boy's wide hand in hers. It was as if he had indeed died. As if, for all Emelia's efforts to save him, she had lost him anyway.

She went upstairs, entered her bedroom, removed the syringe that was now full of her concoction Pax and stood there, weighing it in her hand, calculations running as usual in her head: the syringe holds seven doses of five milligrams, enough to feel peace; if she took ten milligrams she would sleep for an afternoon. But, of course, she would wake again to this life, in this cold house, like Lazarus dragged endlessly from his cave. The frightful miracle of being alive.

→ Fifty-Three

SAMPSON LAY THE WINCHESTER on the ground and stepped away from it. He was light-headed and feared he would stumble over it and still manage to shoot someone today. With uneven steps, he stormed across the clearing, heading straight for the revolver. No matter the state a man is in, do not leave a gun within reach of his hand. Sampson was mere feet away when Jack cannoned into him and hugged the old man's belly.

"Wait, wait," Sampson said. "Let go."

"My god," said Moreland. "I didn't know who was out here."

"I knew who it was," said Jack, his angry voice muffled by the old man's jacket, "but you never *listen* to me!"

Sampson peeled the kid off him and bent quickly to collect the revolver and the ugly little repeater, and he carried them inside, intending to lay them on the table and check them for cartridges. He was eight steps into the cabin before he realized where he was.

The air smelled of sweat and gunsmoke, cigarettes, and something else, some sweet stink he couldn't identify until he spotted an empty pint bottle lying on its side on the floorboards. He wiggled the cork out and sniffed. Something homemade and harsh, nothing left within the bottle but a teaspoon of cloudy liquid. He confirmed that both guns were empty of cartridges and then just stood there, staring at the wall. His chest was humming again, the unbearable buzz of energy that was, he felt sure, beyond his body's ability to contain. He felt on the verge of fainting.

Then Moreland was standing beside him, voice low, saying, "That man is dead."

"Yes, he is."

They stood there for a long time, both looking out the door to where Jack sat on the front steps, gazing at Parker's back.

Sampson said, "I recognize him. He's a prison guard."

"Should we expect more of them?"

"I have no idea. What happened here?"

"He beat the crap out of Jack is what."

Sampson drew the hat off his head and just held it. "Then what?"

Moreland said, "I'm unclear on that."

"Goddamn it," the old man hissed, "I mean why did you kill him? You shot him in the back."

At first William Moreland was stunned. It seemed unbelievable that Sampson, who knew him so well, would assume such an act on his part, but then he remembered the condition of his son's face, the way the boy was forced to hobble, and suddenly it seemed a pretty reasonable conclusion. But now, having taken the blame on himself, and thereby having shielded his son, he was undecided on how to proceed without actually lying. He tapped a finger on the table, a gesture meant to look thoughtful, but in fact he was buying time, choosing his words, "I guess that's a long story."

"I'd never believe it of you, except I'm looking right at it."

Moreland said, "Neither would I."

Sampson sat heavily on a chair and rubbed his knees, mostly to still the tremors in his fingers. "What happened to your face? Did he hit you too?"

"I can't remember, and maybe that's the reason I can't. Jack says he put my lights out. I only remember waking up." Then he too sat down, leaned a bony elbow on the table, and touched the point of his chin gingerly with two fingers. The meat felt pulpy. "Feels like he cracked my jaw. What's it look like?" He jutted his face forward.

"Hard to tell, with all that beard." Sampson's face began to clear, and the shadow of a smile spread across it. "You look a hundred years old."

Moreland nodded slowly and sighed out, "I've let myself go."

The boy trailed in, his eyes enormous. He took the seat his father indicated, hands pressed between his knees as if he had a chill. "We should give him some water," Jack said.

The men exchanged a look and Sampson said, "We'll look after him."

There they sat, three silent figures at the table, while outside the day drew fingers of light through the trees that lay across the dead man's coatback, as if to hold him there, pressing him to earth. Birds at their dawn chorus gusted into a barrage of sound, ancient behaviour, purpose unknown, hundreds of them calling the day into being, just as they had done a thousand years ago and would do a thousand years from now.

Jack said, almost to himself, "I've never seen such an awful thing. He used the rifle butt, like this," and he made a batter's swing. He put his face in his hands and said, "Oh god," and wept silently.

Sampson regarded the boy closely. Jack was grieving, he was in shock, but there was something in his bent posture that spoke of shame. The old man stood and went to the door to look down at the bullet hole in that coatback. He saw chunks of wood missing from the wall, saw the blackened metal of the stove where a bullet had chiselled out a pale divot. He read the room and its brutalized occupants and began to see things as they truly were. Someone had shot up the room, and clearly, it wasn't Parker. Sampson had read the guard correctly: here was a man vicious enough to swing a rifle butt at another man's face. So, somehow, the guard had lost his revolver or surely he would have used it. Sampson's eyes slid to the table where the stout little bottle stood, all but empty. He looked at his old friend Moreland's face. Knocked down and likely unconscious, Moreland could not possibly rise, muddled in his mind, and somehow shoot Parker in the back. Therefore the boy must have got hold of that revolver, he must have been standing behind Parker, firing wildly, until he'd emptied the gun, trying to protect his father.

Sampson ran a hand over his face, then went back to the table and put that same hand on Jack's shuddering shoulder. "Little boy," he said, "you should have lived with me."

Jack's head shook slowly from side to side and his voice, when it came, was barely audible. "I wouldn't have stayed."

IT TOOK THE MEN working together on the boy before they understood the facts: the guard was not there in his official capacity but was a fortune seeker; he'd been alone, without a partner or any expectation of others; he'd invaded the cabin only the night before, drunk and terrifying, and he'd raged until he passed out. The story came out of Jack in half sentences, hiccups, the chain of events related in no logical order, a fractured tale told in the manner of a child relating a dream. He told them about Parker's eyes opening, his body rocking as Moreland had pushed against the door. Sampson watched Moreland's blank face as he heard what his life had been like mere minutes ago, realizing only now the situation he'd walked into.

"How did you get the gun away from him?" said Sampson.

Before Moreland could intervene, the kid said, "He was asleep, so I snuck up and took it."

The men looked at each other in disbelief, and Moreland finally managed, "That took guts."

Far from being proud, Jack's voice was despairing as he said, "I had to. I was afraid he'd wake up and beat me again. I thought he might kill me by mistake."

It was already daylight but Sampson reached for the matchbox on a shelf, drew up the wick in the lantern and lit a penny of bright flame. In that meagre light he saw finally the red line on the boy's throat, as of a garrotte, and realized the guard had exacted a penalty for some unknown sin. The same boy in a sun shower, his head thrown back and his hat hanging from his slim neck by a string.

Sampson watched the spent match smoke its last and crackle into a black delicate thing. He dropped it into the stove, then he went out the door without even looking at the body in the clearing, and headed down the path to collect Willow, who by now had wandered, stirrups and reins dangling, a half mile away, following a seam of good grass.

Inside the cabin, Moreland's hand reached for his son's face, gently, as he swept back the dark hair and said, "Where do you hurt?"

Jack's thoughts went inward for a moment as he surveyed the territory. He touched his scalp where the guard had held him up. Then his hand drifted down to his belly, a furtive caress of the groin. He said, "Everywhere."

And so began the father's careful checking of his son's body, lifting his sweater, a glacially slow peeling up of the flannel shirt where abrasions had glued fabric to skin, where the flat belly was covered in raspberry stains that were already swelling. Moreland probed gently each developing bruise with his thumb. The worst of it was on the lower belly. The guard had aimed low. Once, long ago, an old lady cook had showed him the test for a bad appendix — just above the hipbone, press slowly, release quickly, and the patient will scream — but luckily this trick produced no particular pain in the boy.

"How's your back?"

Jack turned and rucked up his clothes to expose the flawless skin of that long body, the spine like marbles running in a perfect line upward where they disappeared into the worn wool of his sweater. His voice came muffled: "What's it look like?"

To the father, what it looked like was perfection, the beauty of youth. He lay a hardened palm on his son's warm back and patted. "Have you still got all your teeth?"

The boy turned, and ran his tongue over every tooth before nodding.

"Good. Drop your pants, son."

"No." The boy shook his head and glared, the livid stains on his face flamed.

"I need to know your privates are all right."

"They're fine." Something in the demand to strip had caused Jack Boulton to go mulish. The assumption that he had no rights and would willingly expose every last inch of his body any time an adult asked. It was too much like bath time at the nun's house, and he'd had enough of that.

So instead the kid reached out and inspected his father's grimy face, the cheek already ballooning, the thick beard spangled with bits of vegetation. For the briefest of moments, Moreland pulled back his own lower lip to expose a line of blood-pinked teeth with a dark hole where a bicuspid used to be. Still unclear on the chain of events, he said, "I guess he did that?"

Jack nodded. Again, the boy assumed the posture of a baseball hitter at the plate.

The Ridgerunner tried to hook the memory of that impact, to bring it into the light, but he could not, and this was not the time, so he shrugged off the problem as he shrugged off his coat and draped it over his son's shoulders. Almost unbearable, the rhythmic throbbing of everything from chin to eye socket, but he leaned forward on the old chair, where he had always sat at the family table, and put his open hand on top of the boy's clenched one. He felt the heat of his child's skin, felt his own breath going in and out; both of them were still gloriously alive. Something to be grateful for.

Moreland rose and went to his knapsack. It seemed a long way down there on the floor and he knew that when he bent, his face would pound. He toed the bag with his boot. "I've got food, if you are hungry, son."

"Dad? Stop." Jack pointed to the shelves by the stove and several canvas bags on the floor. The larder was full. "I'm not hungry. Are you?"

"Not sure I can chew anyway." Moreland could see Parker's boot framed by the doorway, and beyond that, Sampson walked his horse to the corral and stood her beside Kub, the two horses' reins wrapped around the top rail. The old man loosened Willow's cinch and slung the panniers onto the fence, and he stood there as if inspecting the bags he'd brought, breakfast as usual for the boy. But he was not doing that. Instead, Sampson was thinking.

Moreland was thinking the same thing: if this guard could find the cabin, others might as well. Anyone who made their way here would find a kid worth two thousand dollars. They'd also find a fugitive wanted by police, $31,000 in stolen money, and a murdered prison guard.

Sampson crossed his arms on a fencepost and rested his chin there. He was looking at Parker, calmly, pensively, as one regards a river and ponders the best way to cross it. Moreland saw his old friend's eyes leave Parker and look straight at him. Sampson jerked his head west — *let's get him out of here* — and Moreland nodded. Sooner or later they had to lift that dead man onto a horse, carry him away, and leave him somewhere no one would find him.

Sampson reached for Kub's reins and drew her out of the corral, and on cue Moreland rose, lay his hands on his son's shoulders, and said, "I'll be gone a few hours. That's all."

"No, no, no." Jack felt panic begin to rise, but Moreland pushed him back down and kissed the top of his head. "Eat something. You've been through the ringer, son. You're cold."

Jack just looked up and, out of habit, memorized his father's face, before Moreland left the cabin and pulled the door closed. There were muffled words in the yard, an interchange between the men. Jack approached the door and saw, through a sliver of air between door and frame, two men standing over a third, hands on hips, looking down. At the same moment they bent, one reaching for an ankle the other for a wrist, and the slack body began to roll from front to back; easier to carry that way.

Jack staggered back into the room, hand over his mouth.

There were muffled voices, the sound of the pony's aggrieved squeal as they flung Parker onto her back. The boy walked to the back of the cabin and waited. Long after they had left he opened the door. Everything was gone except the Morgan. Where Parker had been lying they had scuffed the ground with their boots, leaving semicircles and erasing whatever evidence had been there.

JACK MANAGED TO stay upright in the saddle, but his belly was so damaged and he rode so awkwardly it was like he had never fully learned the skill. The Morgan's movements felt iron-hard and jolting. He had collected all the nun's books, packed them into Sampson's panniers, struggled into the saddle, and was now on level ground and following the old highway toward Banff. In his addled state, he had come to the conclusion that this was all his fault; he himself had set in motion a clockwork of death and damage. Without the slightest notion of how to fix it, he had decided that there was indeed one small thing he could do: return what he'd stolen.

The horse was puzzled by his ungainliness and kept swinging round to give him an eye, so they often drifted to the side, and in those moments they wandered the road as aimless as ghosts. Jack was unslept, dumb with horror, and for two hours he let the road take him in a straight line.

He began to see and smell signs of town long before he got there. Scraps of newspaper and tin cans in the ditches.

The pong of a garbage dump. A dinged Oregon licence plate that said ORE 976, half-submerged in moss.

By the time he stopped at the foot of Buffalo Street it was noon and a warm wind pulsed into his face. The Morgan's nostrils grew wide on the familiar air of town and it seemed eager. From where he was, Jack could see three motorcars trundling over the Bow River bridge and a small clot of tourists strolling the sidewalk. Children just released from school were hurrying home for lunch, their voices birdlike and overlapping. Six girls marched arm in arm, howling out a romantic song from the radio, their madrigal harmony perfect for all their practice. Kids were running, clustered in groups, and for a moment it felt as if Jack too was on his way home to the nun's house for lunch.

A lone mutt stood on the riverside path, gazing up at him, tail waving vaguely at this newcomer. It had a curly coat and a beard that made it look friendly. Jack knew this spot near the river was favoured by local dogs. It was a kind of meeting area where they found space to roam; they could convene and watch elk on the far shore, pester automobiles, fight and mate, do whatever they wished. Boy and dog regarded one another for a moment until the dog turned its head and, without rancour, barked at four boys coming toward them. Then, like a forgetful host, the dog returned its attention to Jack.

Jack too had been inattentive, for he knew these boys from school, and his heart sank. Tough boys, walking four abreast, passing a cigarette hand to hand. They were already so close he had no time even to pull down his hat. Their names came to him in a flash, three of them from the same family, and he knew the street they all lived on. Everyone dreaded them, for their noise and abuse and sarcasm, but Jack Boulton had no choice except to wait as they came on, looking him right in the eye.

Of course, there was little they could do to him now, no trouble they could make that he was not already in. No one would gain from the reward today because he was already on his way to the nun's house. But as the boys passed, they showed not the slightest recognition of Jack Boulton, and in fact, they seemed a little afraid of him. One boy nodded in polite greeting, as one might nod to a mounted policeman, and he reached out shyly to pat the Morgan's shoulder. Then they turned onto the street where they all lived, and were gone. More than any mirror could have done, these boys had told Jack how much he had changed. In his blanket coat and hat, camouflaged by the marks of a fistfight, he looked blandly local, a lean rustic on horseback. To them he had been of no interest at all. He hunched into his coat, realizing that the cold was inside his body, not outside in the warm air.

The bearded dog was gone now and the pulsing wind threatened to nudge the hat off Jack's head. He wrapped the reins tight around his fist to hold the Morgan to a walk, and moved painfully up Buffalo Street. Wilson's yard was empty, so the animals were indoors at the moment, perhaps at their noon feeding. Jack was obliged to wait many minutes for the main street to clear sufficiently of traffic. He glanced up at the heavy hanging sign that said DOMINION CAFÉ ROOMS FOR RENT — a sign everyone knew was so poorly hung no local would stand under it. Jack remembered riding into town in his mother's arms, and she too avoided passing under that sign. They'd been heading for the nun's house, just as he was doing now.

Jack went in a slow walk across the main street, past three neighbours' houses, over the nun's parched lawn, and straight up to her wide front porch. The oak front door was closed as always.

It took far too long for him to dismount and unstrap the pannier full of stolen books. Then he stood looking up at the house, trying to read its mood. The window of his bedroom was shut, curtain drawn. All the curtains in the house were closed, though it was noon. He was unconscious of his hands bending and unbending the reins, his mouth forming silent words, practising what he would say if he encountered her in that house: *I took these things from you and I am sorry. I didn't need them but I took them anyway, and I am sorry.*

Somewhere near, a bloodhound bayed from a backyard, the unearthly howl cutting the air, and Jack shuddered in alarm.

"Goddamn it," he said, shaking off his stupor.

He drew the Morgan around to the back of the house where the empty stable stood. Some instinct like his father's was at work in him, the sense to keep the horse out of sight, especially not visible to neighbours who might glance out and remark on a horse on that property for the first time in decades. So he walked the Morgan inside until it was deep in the building's murk, and whipped the reins round a stall post. There was no feed and no water, the horse would have to wait for that.

Outside, bright sun beamed on the clean brick walls of the nun's house. Jack knew with certainty that he alone had any hope of reasoning with her, about anything, and even then, that hope was slim. In their everyday life together she had been inclined, by what he suspected was a kind of love for him, to at least listen to what he said. It was an attention she gave to no one else, except perhaps Mary Boulton. But having lived in close proximity with her, Jack also knew her well enough to be certain of the outcome of such a talk. It would be a doomed confab; it would get out of hand and burst like a pillow full of feathers the moment she understood that he would not return to her.

No, he refused to submit to it. To hell with talking. What was there really to say?

Worse, there was no way to know when his father would return to the cabin, but if that happened soon, Moreland would see that boy, horse, and books were missing. He'd understand the situation immediately. The notion of his son walking right into the nun's house would be stark nightmare, and Moreland might even ride into town himself and try to stop it from happening. Therefore Jack had to move. Now. Get it over with.

He strode out of the stable and made for the back of the house. His boots tromped up the kitchen steps and he opened the door just as boldly as if he were still a member of the household. Inside the air was stale and cold. There by the wall was the old yellow stove, and he didn't even have to check the hopeless thing to know it was cold. By the door stood her boots, lace-up affairs with innumerable hooks for the laces. She also owned silk house slippers, and a pair of sponge slippers for the bathroom, but these were her only outdoor boots, proof that she was at home.

He went to the counter by the sink and gazed at the mess of bottles and sachets, the little Bunsen burner, on top of which sat a glass beaker, its bowl scorched outside, and inside at the bottom was a brownish crust. Some concoction she'd made herself. He sniffed it, but it smelled like nothing more interesting than fireplace ash. Books lay in rough piles on the counters, the table, the floor. She had used spoons and napkins as bookmarks. A steady drip from the water pump over the sink. Out of habit, his hand reached out to wiggle the handle and silence it.

In the hallway he saw a chair overturned on the long Persian runner. He knew well enough how easily that chair tipped over, so perhaps she had stumbled against it. But he could not fathom why she had not righted it. More books lay open on the floor. The boy approached a pale object on the runner and stood over it. One of her father's hairbrushes — the one Jack had used every day of his life here. Painfully, he leaned down over his sore belly, picked it up and saw, tangled in its bristles, strands of his own hair. What was it doing downstairs, let alone lying on the floor? He placed the brush exactly where he had found it.

At the bottom of the staircase he listened for movement. As always, he felt the gentle flow of cool air from the second floor. Something inside him whispered that Emelia Cload, Sister, *she*, had never napped, had never allowed him to do so, and she would never be lying down at this hour. He could not account for the disorder of the place, or its silence.

She too had changed, and given the evidence he'd seen so far, Jack feared to see her in her new form. Not until now, when he found himself again in her house, breathing her air, standing in the pitiful mess of her life, did he realize fully what he had done to her.

Wilson's voice came to him then: *She hates me to death. But it wasn't me who defected. You did.*

Heart hammering in his throat, Jack backed away from the

staircase and hurried back to the kitchen, his hands already pawing the smaller books out of his pannier. At the table he arranged the books in a stack in front of his own chair, the large encyclopedia of animals on the bottom, smaller books on top. Last, he went to the other side of the table and lay her notebook in front of her place, like breakfast. And then he fled to the door.

He was there, with his hand on the knob, when the realization arrived: if he walked through this door and left what had once been almost a home to him, he would be rootless and adrift. No home anymore. Nothing to return to. This was the natural outcome of everything that had gone before, and he knew it. Like a man standing at the edge of a fast-flowing river, Jack Boulton had only to step outside the door and let the current of life pull him away forever. He was scared, and sick of that feeling. Obligated, his father would say, to do something about it.

Slowly, his hand drifted away from the doorknob. He lay the panniers on the floor and, for the second time in as many minutes, made for the foot of the staircase.

During their entire association, he had gently but firmly refused to call her Mother. Instead, in the way strangers do when living intimately with one another, he often just called her "you." After all, when he spoke, she knew he was addressing her. Who else?

Now, rather formally, he called out, "Hello? Sister?" Without waiting for a response, and without attempting to be quiet, he trudged up those stairs, the familiar bannister sliding coolly under his hand.

The upstairs hall was the same as it had always been. No sign here that anyone was present, nor that anything in particular was wrong. He walked to her bedroom, but it was empty. The coverlet was slightly rumpled, as if recently she had sat on the made bed. He turned and went down the hall to the library, but it too was empty.

Jack stood on the carpet and looked about the library, seeing the spaces he'd left on the shelves, where those stolen books would soon return, the nun sliding them into their slots with her own hand. As she did it, she would be melancholy, perhaps, or furious at him, or accepting. His shoulders dropped as he sighed into the room, this wonderful repository, an actual library holding hundreds of books. Jack might never again wish for the noise and activity of town, but he knew he would never stop missing this room. He wandered to the small cabinet by the desk and bent to read the row of spines, his finger touching those volumes he himself had read, tales of spies, the machines of war, sex and intrigue. He went to the window-well, where he had curled up all those nights reading by moonlight while she snored in her room. He'd never been in here during the day. The seat was now bathed in bright noon sun, and the tree beyond the glass was budding. He hadn't even lived here long enough to see leaves on that tree.

He peered down into the road, where he must ride the Morgan back to the main street and out of town, but there was little activity at this hour. Most people, tourists and locals, were drifting indoors for their lunch. No children ran about, since even if they had finished eating, all but the smallest of them would be doing chores before it was time to go back to school. This was a good time to leave. So, in a final step, he went to the desk and lay on the blotter the small lump of India rubber he'd stolen. It was unused, and no smaller than it had been when he'd taken it, for without any adult to push him into his lessons, Jack Boulton had engaged in little study beyond reading a ranger's exam booklet.

Then he went out into the hall, and at the top of the stairs he gave his former bedroom one last look. And there he saw her. Or rather, he saw her feet. She was lying on his bed and she was not moving.

LATER, HE WOULD remember only parts of it, small details that he seined from a frightening blankness that would stay with him for the rest of his life. Mostly he remembered her eyes. Lids open a crack, a crescent of iris showing against the white. Her hands, folded across her belly, did not look like real hands anymore, but artificial, the colour of pinewood. She was still holding the syringe that had killed her. He would remember that his town clothes were folded and stacked on the bed beside her bare feet. He would remember the gurgle of his stomach, life still vibrantly at work inside him. Closed curtain. Swept floor. A clock ticked meanly in the hallway.

Then, he saw sunlight, a dry lawn, his feet moving under him, heading toward the police station at the end of town. A flurry of painful sound to his left, like the screaming of birds that went on and on until it resolved into the sound of someone trying in vain to start a motorcar. He found himself standing across the street from the schoolyard, unsure of his purpose — at that moment or ever — and he discovered that he was weeping. Whether anyone saw him or remarked on his conduct, he would never know. He turned away down a narrow alley and stood alone, until an instinct deeper than any other told him he was without a horse, and that this was wrong. Drawn now by nothing more than a short lifetime's habit, he turned back toward the Morgan.

By the time he was halfway there, Jack had already come back to himself in some small way, for he had finally comprehended that he must not under any circumstances approach a policeman, must not admit his name, must not linger in town any longer than was necessary to alert someone to the disaster, to get her some help. Dead or not, she was still in this world, trapped among the living, vulnerable and alone, and no one but he knew the terrible thing that had happened. He must tell someone, and then he must disappear again.

THE ON-DUTY NURSE rose from her desk in the hospital lobby and saw a young man coming through the front doors on unsteady legs, his face mottled by bruises, lips scabbed, and the left eye half-closed. He was holding something out to her, some black book, and he looked very much like he was about to faint.

The nurse rushed to him and guided him to a bench by the window where she bent over him and spoke in a low voice.

Her hands were trying to touch him, pull at the collar of his coat, to see that red line at his throat, check his pupils, but with each attempt his icy fingers came up and gently pushed her hands away. She asked him his name, she asked who had done this to him. Her questions seemed to have no effect except to make him shake his head and repeat the same thing over and over, "She must have made a mistake. She never makes mistakes."

"Who are you talking about?"

"The nun."

"Her? What in goodness name is she up to now?"

Jack turned his eyes to the nurse. He said, "I think she's dead."

Far from looking shocked, the nurse's demeanour said that, in fact, she would be the judge of that. "Stay here," she said, in the calm, firm tone of all nurses. "I'll find the doctor."

But when she returned, a white-coated man trotting in her wake, Jack Boulton was gone. On the bench where he had been sitting was a black book. Emelia Cload's private diary and study book, in which she had recorded her thoughts, plans, actions, history. It was the journal of a poisoner. Written mostly in nursing code, it was indecipherable to almost anyone else in this town except the young woman who picked it up and opened it.

• • •

MORELAND WAS ONLY ten minutes outside of town and moving fast, so that when he saw Jack, the little pony was frothing and blowing hard against the girth strap. They fetched up together, and like two old men they dismounted carefully and limped round their horse's chests to one another and Jack, finally, let himself be embraced, rested his head on his father's shoulder. He heard no words, only the sound of Moreland's rumbling voice.

→ Fifty-Four

EIGHTEEN MONTHS LATER, Sampson was sitting outside on his single chair, shirt off and the sleeves of his long johns rolled up, face bent over the magazine of a Lee–Enfield rifle. After the close of the war Carr had picked up guns and parts of guns and given them all to Sampson to fix, to fashion a few useful guns from the parts of many. The bolt action of this rifle had been fused somehow, Sampson figured from the heat and concussion of a mortar, and he was carefully sanding it smooth again. Men, weapons, munitions, overdue mail, and even animals — ambulance and cavalry horses — had returned from Europe aboard ship, but most everything, whether alive or not, was in rough shape.

Willow was in the corral, her face hung over the fence, watching the woods. She kept nickering, and slowly Sampson realized it was not him she was speaking to. Then there was a scrambling sound inside the cabin and the dog shot out of the door into the clearing, where it paced circles and wagged its tail in welcome. The old man had forgotten it was there, and he put a hand to his chest to calm himself.

He rose and walked to the side of the cabin to see his wife on horseback, sauntering from the trees. The fact that Lena had borrowed a neighbour's horse and had actually ridden the animal all the way to his door for the first time in perhaps twenty years was so unusual his first words were, "Did someone die?"

She snorted in genuine amusement, dismounted, and wrapped her arms around his waist. Then she began to ferry things into the cabin as he trailed behind her. She had brought stores of food, a few spices, and enough in the way of her own comforts and cooking tools that she clearly intended to stay for a week. She had on her best jacket. It was now clear to Sampson why Lena was there: she had worried about him up here, alone for the first time in over a decade. Not long ago there had been a family living nearby, two capable adults. But now Moreland and the child were gone, Mary dead, the nun dead, the war over. Everything had changed, quickly and forever. And one day back in December, when he had been visiting her in Laggan, she had held his arm and said, almost as an accusation, "You have started taking naps." For Sampson, that had always been a sign that someone was finally elderly. He'd been prideful about it: an old man napping, what a sign of age. But she was right: every few days he drifted to the bed as if to sit for a moment and collect his thoughts, only to wake twenty minutes later with his hair in a mess and pillow marks on his face. Life, it often seemed to him, was a long lesson in humility.

Clearly, Lena had decided to do for him what he had so often done for her, and for the little boy: visit. That night they shimmied together into his uncomfortably narrow bed and tried to sleep. The heavy grizzly pelt slithered to the floor; they wrangled over the tattersall quilt. She woke near dawn to see her husband sitting on the only chair in the cabin, right beside the bed, looking at her. She propped herself up on one elbow.

"I have something to tell you." He could see so clearly that she feared this was an impending rejection, that he would tell her flatly he wished to continue to live alone. Her beautiful old face said, *I have pushed him too far, I have embarrassed us both*. She sighed and sat up on the bed. She composed herself.

Sampson said, "The little boy killed someone."

She blinked. It took her a long time before she managed to speak. "Who did he kill?"

Sampson explained it all, starting from his first sight of Parker on the road and ending with a description of the guard's final resting place, a dry alpine gully far higher than any game trails likely to be followed by hunters. A spot carefully chosen. Moreland and he had conferred on it, and for many months now, the body had been exposed only to sun and wind and scavengers on the wing.

He watched his wife sift through the information. Finally, she said, "How old was that man?"

The question was unexpected. Sampson pictured again that grey face. "Young. Twenty-five."

"Will anyone miss him?"

"War's over, they don't need guards."

"I mean, does he have a wife or children?"

Sampson might have gone the rest of his life and never wondered such a thing about Parker. He looked at the woman he loved but did not live with, knowing that some relationships are inexplicable from the outside, and anything you assume about other people will likely be wrong. He said, "I hope not."

"Why did you tell me?" She shifted and patted the mattress with her palm.

"I tell you everything," Sampson said, "sooner or later."

Epilogue

✦ 1928, Terlingua, Texas

JACK WOKE FROM the day's great heat, naked above the waist, sprawled across the decrepit sofa he'd fallen asleep on. He swung his boots to the floor, forearms on his knees, and ran a calloused hand over his stubble. His skin was as dry and hard as sandpaper. A noise had woken him, and he tried to call it to mind, identify its source.

A brilliant shimmer on the tile floor, blue moonlight unimpeded by cloud or tree that shone through the glassless adobe window and gave the room a marine feeling. Some nights that blue light crept along the floor and touched his face, beaming through his closed eyelids, waking him to the night.

He thought about putting on his shirt, but left it where it was on the sofa's armrest. The roof above was made of planks, ocotillo, brush, clay, so it was cool most of the year, but the brick wall at his back still radiated heat like a griddle. Books in a tidy stack on the coffee table, a new atlas at its centre that was closed upon the world. Book cabinets all around the room. This was his office. There was a narrow desk against the far wall, covered in papers. No glass in any of the windows, they were open to the air, and the doors were more like shutters. All to let the heat out.

Outside, the stud began to cut up rough in its pen. This was the sound that had woken him, the voice of an irate horse. A new purchase, it was still unaccustomed to this place and making its opinion clear. The other two stallions were silent, standing in their own separate pens, sniffing the air, but giving it nothing in return. Jack went out the double doors into the bright night, dust and heat on his bare chest, jeans hanging off his hips.

The rhythmic *bung bung* of the water windmill rocking against its lock. A grove of springtime ocotillos on the hillside that crackled together as they swayed, tufts of windblown grass tangled in the spines, and bright flames of bloom at their tips. Beyond that, nothing but the black heavens and the glory of the Milky Way. No mountains blocked this particular view. He walked to the stud and stood at the fence. He clicked to it, but it only paced its pen like a tiger in a zoo, searching endlessly for a way out, so he spoke to it gently for a long time until the pacing slowed and the horse began to bob its head. It stood sideways and listened to his voice. He held out his palm, on which lay a broken twig of stick candy. The animal knew it was there, could smell sugar on the wind, but finally it turned its back on Jack Boulton, showed its ass to its new owner and to the wind, and just stood there, tail swishing. Calmer now, but no less ill-humoured.

There would be no more sleep tonight for Jack. After more than a decade in Texas he was still unused to the heat. So he walked to the main paddock, ducked between the fence rails, found his way among the many bodies of horses, some reclining, some standing up. He passed the new foal, which trotted shyly around its mother's body and peered at him from under her belly, and finally Jack found himself standing next to the Morgan. It was dozing. He held the stick candy under its nose and when it roused, he let the old horse follow him out of the paddock into the yard, then he closed the gate. The Morgan's jaws worked and its breath smelled of peppermint. Jack swiped one of the many hackamores from the fencepost where they always hung. It was a rule he had formed, one halter for every adult horse. Useful to have these handy in case of a kerfuffle among the herd, especially if a run to the barn would take too long — it was something he'd learned the hard way. He swung up bareback and turned the horse toward the wide, dry wash of Terlingua Creek.

In his first months in this place, as a kid of only fourteen, he had treated washes like this one as if they were natural roads, smooth, cleared of scrub, a good way to get somewhere. It wasn't that he didn't know about runoff, he'd just never seen the desert kind before. It hadn't taken him long to discover these dry washes were in fact aimless and organic, they looked different going down than they did going up, they forked, broke apart, ended in the middle of nowhere. And he'd learned to respect them the first time he'd witnessed a desert rainstorm, runoff surging through this very wash, powerful enough to take cattle off their feet, roll a car onto its roof, batter a man to death. A sudden cataclysm of water — a good way to drown in the desert. The next day, the world would be dry again, baking in the heat, a few more blooms on cactuses, and but for a trickle in the deepest vein of the wash, there was no clear sign that rain had touched the hard ground in months.

But the dry Terlingua Creek was Jack's best route to the canyon, there was no rain in sight, and he knew exactly where he was going: due south.

Walking the Morgan now slowly down the creekbed, cactus and pinion brush ten feet above him on either side, and the crumbling banks offering few opportunities to clamber up onto the desert floor, Jack thought, as he often did now, about rain.

The Morgan at seventeen was just past middle age. It had seen forty-below, blizzards, sleet, and killing cold wind. In Texas it had seen such heat as to kill anything less adaptable than a horse. Jack ran his hand down the smooth neck, all that winter fur long gone.

A half hour later they were standing side by side, horse and man, up to their knees in a bend of the river where it flowed through the deep Y of the Santa Elena Canyon. They stood in Texas, and the far side of the river was Mexico. The sheer black walls of the limestone mesa were bathed in brilliant moonlight.

A sparkle on the water, and they both drank from it. Jack used his hat as a bucket and poured water over the Morgan's body until the hide glistened. The animal shook itself in satisfaction. Then he upended a hatful of the Rio Grande over himself and stood dripping. His boots filled with water.

Jack looked at those dark mesas. The ride from his ranch to this spot, if done at a gallop, took only eight minutes. Jack had timed it. Every few months he walked the Terlingua Creek to check his route, make sure nothing much had changed, there were no new obstacles a galloping horse couldn't handle. Any rider who reached this bend in the river could make the far shore in another eight minutes. If necessary, Jack could get his father into Mexico in less time than it takes to cook oatmeal, make a pot of coffee.

He'd decided he would ride the Morgan and put his father on a strong mare named Julieta. If he could, he'd bring all of his horses, for the sheer value of them, run them down the wash and herd them into the stream. He knew exactly which mare to choose to lead them, since they usually followed her. But if they didn't, if there was confusion or they scattered, he'd leave everything behind. All but his father. Jack was unsure if his father could swim; but it didn't matter, because any horse can. You slip off the saddle, relieve the animal of your weight, hold on to the saddle horn or the animal's mane, and float alongside. In spring, the strong current would carry them about two hundred yards downstream, but in the dry months, sandbars appeared, and you might find a backbone crossing where the water only reached the stirrups. In winter you could wade into Mexico.

There was nothing on the far side except high canyon walls and scrub and sand, caves created by wind erosion, footings of talus and scree. A long way to the east, there was a tiny town named Boquillas with a cantina in which Jack liked to drink and practise his Spanish pleasantries on a particular young waitress, he and his horse arriving soaked from the river, staying long enough to dry, and for those evening hours he pretended to have no other purpose in this life than to nurse a single beer. The girl seemed to find Jack amusing; her mother did not. The first evening he'd come here, he'd stood still dripping outside the cantina, looking at the river from this, the far side, as dogs waded in the shallows, and behind him was the murmur of voices speaking a language as yet unknown to him.

The clever fox ran off the edge of the world, and what did he find?

Jack turned now and drew the Morgan back to the creek-bed, looking back once at the black walls of ancient rock in that other country, the river an imaginary boundary that no one here paid very much attention to.

When he arrived home again, trotting the Morgan under the high ranch gate with BOULTON spelled out in planks of wood, it was still night, still bright and hot, and by now his clothes were mostly dry. Only the seat of his pants kissed the horse's wet hide as he rode, and his boots were sloshing.

The two young boys who worked for him would wake in their bunkhouse sometime soon and he'd have to get them fed by dawn. Breakfast was eggs and smoked pork and thick bread with butter and sliced onions and, if there was any left, smoked fish. Coffee. They would work for him for two weeks then go home to be replaced by brothers or sisters, older or younger it didn't matter — there were a lot of kids in that family. The girls could do anything the boys did, even, to Jack's satisfaction, trimming hooves, a rare skill.

Jack Boulton, founder and proprietor, not much older than his employees, half-naked and unshaven, rode past the paddock wherein stood twenty-five animals, all of them bred, raised, trained, and sold by him for cattle work in southwest Texan ranches. He trotted the Morgan right up to the house, into the pretty little adobe courtyard, ducked his head under the arched gate, dismounted, and let the horse loose on the dry lawn like an old house pet. As always it followed him to the kitchen and hung its head through the open window as Jack sat at the table and tried to pry off his soaking boots. First one then the other came off with a rude sucking sound. He flung them out the door, where they tumbled into the yard. They'd dry in minutes once the sun hit them. Jack curled his toes against the always sandy tiles. In the desert, sand was in his bed, in his boots, his scalp, the occasional grit between his teeth as he ate.

Footsteps came up the long hallway and his father

appeared at the kitchen door, blinking. Moreland, who was known in the area as Jack Boulton Sr., scratched his sideburns and said, "I couldn't find you."

"I was around."

"But I looked everywhere."

Jack saw his father had done no such thing. Moreland was still bleary and stiff-legged from sleep, he had obviously just woken with a start. He did this sometimes, jolting out of a dream in which he was searching frantically for Mary, but sometimes for his young son, and too often these days the dream was entirely real to him. He woke thinking it was all true. Somewhere in Moreland's sleeping mind, time had ceased to have meaning, everything was happening at once.

"You shouldn't worry so much, Dad."

"I know."

"Do you want eggs with your breakfast?"

Moreland did not reply, instead he leaned against the doorjamb and regarded his son for a while, his head to one side. "Where do you go," he said, "when you disappear like that?"

Jack Boulton gazed at a single damp footprint on the tile floor. Then he stood, hitched up his jeans, and smiled.

➤ Acknowledgements

I AM VERY GRATEFUL to Senator Patti LaBoucane-Benson for agreeing to be an early reader of the manuscript and for giving this book her attention and time. Many thanks to the wonderful Buddy Wesley, Cultural Advisor and Tribal Historian, Stoney/Nakoda Nation, Morley, Alberta, for his translations, corrections, and amazing generosity.

Ridgerunner owes its existence to a book club reading I did one spring day from my first novel, *The Outlander*. After the event was over and people were leaving, a lone book clubber was sitting next to me, wondering almost to herself what Mary Boulton and William Moreland would be like as parents. She seemed a bit worried, which I understand. That offhand question got me thinking, mostly about what their child would be like as a person. So, that's where Jack Boulton came from. To that unknown book clubber: Thank you. I've had a happy time writing.

At the time this book was set, Banff National Park was still named Rocky Mountains Park. The town of Laggan had been renamed Lake Louise three years before the action in this book, but I reason that locals might resist such a government-imposed change. The burnt meadow is not the Sawback Burn, which was a series of recent prescribed burns.

There would be no literature without influence; books are made of other books. *Ridgerunner* is full of allusions to other works like: *The Night of the Hunter, Adventures of Huckleberry Finn, Treasure Island, True Grit, The Assassination of Jesse James by the Coward Robert Ford,* as well as Western and noir movies, songs, and fairy tales. There is no need whatsoever for readers to even notice this element of the book. I did it to entertain myself.

Thanks to Gary R. Allan of the Tundra Speaks Society for information on wolfdog behaviour. Much detail about the Castle Mountain internment camp came from *In the Shadow of the Rockies* by Bohdan S. Kordan and Peter Melnycky; with special thanks to Dr. Kordan for answering questions about the POWs' work on the coach road to Laggan. Any errors are mine. Thanks to the Library and Archives Canada; and to Lena Goon, former head archivist at the Archives and Library, Whyte Museum of the Canadian Rockies. Thanks to Carol Holmes for so much, and to Kevin Van Tighem, former superintendent at Banff National Park.

The author is indebted to the Ontario Arts Council and the Canada Council for the Arts for their support.

To Marina for the coffee grounds; Elyse for the sheep; Helm for mentioning stiff ears on a wolfdog. Apologies to Kate Boothman, whose story about a horse indoors appears here in altered form. And much love to Kelly Hawkins; sorry I didn't use your name in the end.

To my agent, Ellen Levine, for her intelligence honesty and acumen. To my editor, Janie Yoon, for her strength of will and her great big heart. To Sarah MacLachlan, whose friendship and support literally changed my life as a writer.

Enormous gratitude to the wonder that is Maria Golikova. Thanks to Alysia Shewchuk for a truly gorgeous text and cover design. And thanks to Andrew for always being there, and for repeatedly scraping his sister off the ceiling. Finally, thanks to Kevin Connolly for his love, his grace of language, and his endless edits, and for answering immediately when I shout down the stairs, "Give me a good name for a horse!"

AN EXCERPT FROM this book was published in *Taddle Creek* magazine.

GIL ADAMSON is the critically acclaimed author of *Ridgerunner*, which won the Writers' Trust Fiction Prize and was a finalist for the Scotiabank Giller Prize. Her first novel, *The Outlander*, won the Dashiell Hammett Prize for Literary Excellence in Crime Writing, the Amazon.ca First Novel Award, the ReLit Award, and the Drummer General's Award. It was a finalist for the Commonwealth Writers' Prize, CBC Canada Reads, and the Prix Femina in France; longlisted for the International IMPAC Dublin Literary Award; and chosen as a *Globe and Mail* and *Washington Post* Top 100 Book. She is also the author of a collection of linked stories, *Help Me, Jacques Cousteau*, and two poetry collections, *Primitive* and *Ashland*. She lives in Toronto.